Thanks

C000040156

Liz

Hiraeth

a burden – baich

≈

Liz Riley Jones

Matador
9 Priory Business Park
Kibworth Beauchamp
Leicestershire LE8 0RX, UK
Tel: (+44) 116 279 2299
Fax: (+44) 116 279 2277
Email: books@troubador.co.uk
Web: www.troubador.co.uk/matador

ISBN 978 1784624 392

British Library Cataloguing in Publication Data.
A catalogue record for this book is available from the British Library.

Printed and bound by CPI Group (UK) Ltd, Croydon, CR0 4YY
Typeset in 11pt Minion Pro by Troubador Publishing Ltd, Leicester, UK

Matador is an imprint of Troubador Publishing Ltd

I holl Bobl
Teyrnasoedd y Môr

For all the People
of the
Sea Kingdoms

Mae Hiraeth yn y Môr

Mae hiraeth yn y môr a'r mynydd maith
Mae hiraeth mewn distawrwydd ac mewn cân
Mewn murmur dyfroedd ar dragywydd daith
Yn oriau'r machlud ac yn fflamau'r tân
Ond mwynaf yn y gwynt y dwed ei gwyn
A thristaf yn yr hesg y cwyna'r gwynt
Gan ddeffro adlais adlais yn y brwyn
Ac yn y galon, atgof atgof gynt

Fel pan wrandawer yn y cyfddydd hir
Ar gân y ceiliog yn y glwyd gerllaw
Yn deffro caniad ar ôl caniad clir
O'r gerddi agos, nes o'r llechwedd draw
Y cwyd yn olaf ei leferydd ef
A mwynder trist y pellter yn ei lef

There is Longing in the Sea

There's longing in the sea and mountains grey
There's longing too in silence and in song
In murm'-ring waters on their endless way
At sunset hours and firelight's flames among
But fondest in the wind it makes its moan
And saddest in the sedge the wind replies
Awaking echo's echo with its tone
And mem'ry's mem'ry in the heart's deep sighs

As when one hearkens to the chanticleer
At hand with eager song at break of day
Evoking answer upon answer clear
From nearby gardens, till from far away
A last lone songster lifts his voice on high
With distance's sad longing in its cry

Anglesey
Ynys Môn

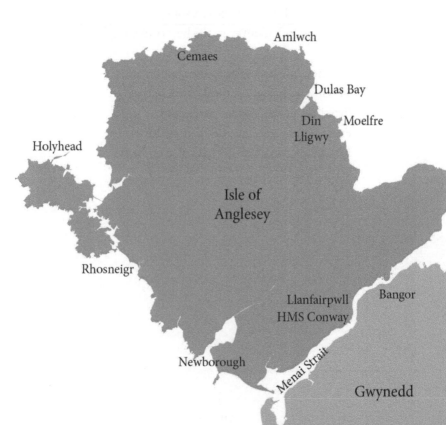

Irish Sea

Amlwch

Cemaes

Dulas Bay

Din Lligwy   Moelfre

Holyhead

Isle of
Anglesey

Rhosneigr

Llanfairpwll   Bangor
HMS Conway

Newborough

Menai Strait

Gwynedd

Sea Kingdoms

Alba

Eire

Ellan Vannin

Cymru

Kernow

Breizh

Galicia

Celtic Britain

Pagan Year

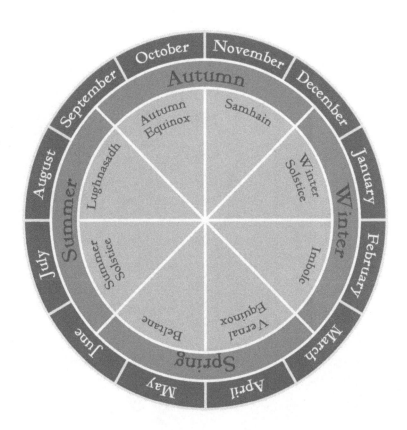

Slighe Roads

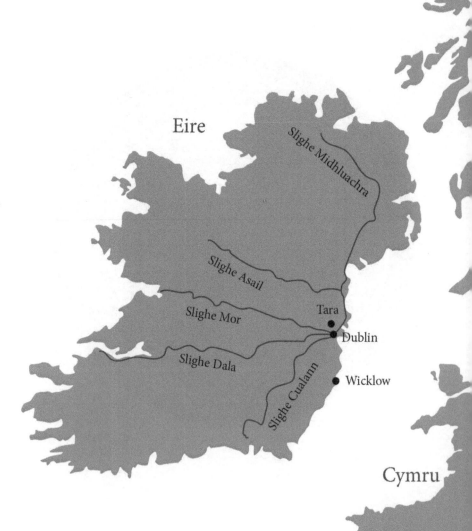

Eire

Slighe Midhluachra

Slighe Asail

Slighe Mor

Tara

Slighe Dala

Dublin

Slighe Cualann

Wicklow

Cymru

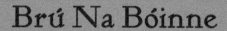

Brú Na Bóinne

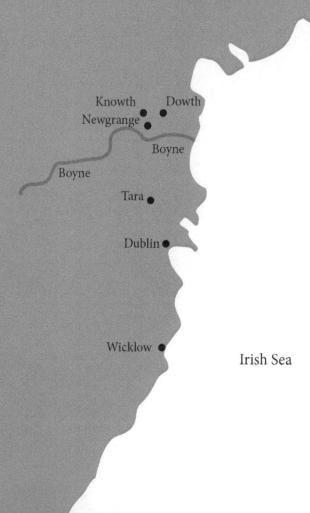

Eire

Knowth   Dowth
Newgrange
Boyne

Boyne

Tara

Dublin

Wicklow

Irish Sea

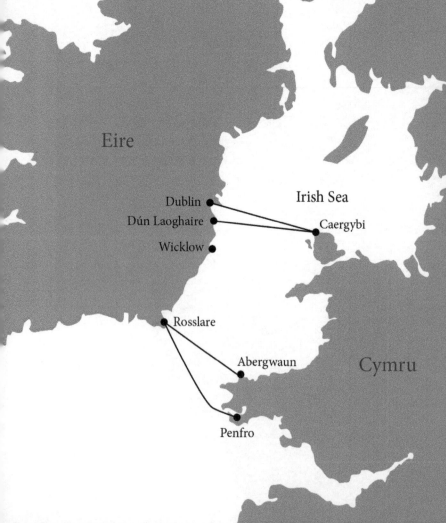

Sea Crossings

List of Places and Pronunciations

Cymru (Cum-ree)	Wales
Gwynedd (Gwin-eth)	North Wales
Ynys Môn (Unis Maughn)	Anglesey
Moelfre (Moil-vre)	Village on Ynys Môn
Swnt (Soont)	Area of Moelfre, on the sea
Traeth Llugwy (Traith Ligwi)	Lligwy beach, Moelfre

List of Characters and Pronunciations

Mona Jones (Moh-nah)	
Idwal Jones (Eed-wal)	Mona's brother
Tom Jones	Mona's father
Molly Kelly	Mona's mother
Brendan Kelly	Mona's uncle

Principal Welsh Druids

Cai Owens (Kai)	
Sioned Owens (Shon-ed)	Cai's sister
Rhiannon Owens (Rhi-an-on)	Cai's mother
Gwilym Owens (Gwil-im)	Cai's father
Ifan (Eev-ahn)	Archdruid
Hywel (Ha-wel)	Cai's grandfather

Emlyn (Em-lin)	Ifan's eldest son
Dafydd (Dah-vith)	Ifan's younger son
Nansi (Nan-si)	Dafydd's wife
Siân (Sharn)	Ifan's daughter
Nesta	
Rhona (Rho-na)	Nesta's granddaughter
Nia (Nee-A)	Siân's daughter
Arwel (Arr-wel)	Emlyn's son
Ieuan (Yey-an)	
Geraint (Ger-eyent)	
Dai (Die)	
Cerys (Keris)	
Bryn (Brin)	

Irish Druids (Wicklow)

Seamus (Shay-mus)	Archdruid
Caitlín (Kate-leen)	Archdruid's wife
Diarmuid (Derm-ot)	Eldest son of Seamus
Cormac	Son of Seamus & Caitlín
Fintan	Son of Seamus & Caitlín
Cian (Key-an)	Son of Seamus
Colm (Col-um)	Brother of Seamus
Cormac	
Kieran	
Declan	

Irish Druids (Newgrange)

Niall (Ni -al)	Archdruid
Aislinn (Ash-ling)	Niall's eldest daughter
Kathleen	Niall's youngest daughter

Others

Rob	A Cumbrian Druid
Cadan	A Cornish Druid
Peder	A Cornish Druid
Carmen	A Galician Druid
Maria	A Galician Druid
John and Liz	An English couple on Eigg

Language

Language, not race, has always been a unifying element of the Celts: Welsh, Irish Gaelic, Scots Gaelic, Breton, Manx and Cornish. Though all derived from the ancient Brythonic language of Celtic Britain, they are now so distinct from each other as to be mutually exclusive. Yet they are still here.

In *Hiraeth*, Druids from the different Celtic regions use English to communicate with each other, though they all have a smattering of each other's mother tongue.

The Welsh, Irish and Cornish used in some of the dialogue in this book aren't textbook. A few words in the local dialects have been used to indicate when these languages are being spoken between characters.

The story so far

Mona Jones has never been told of her Druidic ancestry. After her parents' murder she is destined to spend a month in the Welsh-speaking community of Moelfre, Ynys Môn. Mona has an absolute inability to learn the Welsh language but can also become easily overwhelmed by its poetry. Mona is attacked by an enemy Druid and branded with a Celtic iron symbol – the *mark*. A destructive magic blooms in her and Mona incinerates her attacker. Seized by the Welsh Druids, she is taken to their headquarters in a former naval training college, the HMS *Conway*. There, Mona discovers that not only is she a Druid, but suspected of being on the wrong side of a civil war. Over the past twenty-five years, a split has occurred between Welsh and Irish Druids, leading to bloody conflict – and her family has been the catalyst for this war.

The Welsh Druids are part of a wider ancient community that survive, in secret, over what remains of the Celtic nations. With the waning of magic across these lands, Mona's explosive arrival sends out ripples of distrust and fear amongst the established community. Despite this, a relationship blossoms with Cai, a serial philanderer and warrior. On the eve of Mona's departure, the Welsh Druids learn of an intended attack from Ireland, and a fleet of warriors is sent out to meet them.

Though accomplished in combat, Mona is not trusted enough to fight alongside Cai and stays behind to defend the community. Their destinies now divide as the Irish Druids split the defence of the *Conway*. The small fleet is shepherded away from Ynys Môn, forcing them to circumnavigate Britain in order to return home. It also becomes apparent that there is a spy amongst the Welsh Druids.

The fleet fails to return for many months, but Mona forms strong friendships within the *Conway*: Nia, an academic; Rob, a Cumbric Druid; and Arwel, a talented young tactician. However, during this time, Mona is overpowered and attacked by a newcomer, who seduces her with Welsh, using it as a weapon against her. The devastating power within her burns him to death but she remains unable to understand or control her magic. When Mona discovers she is pregnant, the Archdruid, Ifan, advises her to claim that Cai is the father in order to protect the child.

Meanwhile, Cai is suspected of treason by the fleet and seeks refuge on the tiny Hebridean Island of Eigg where he is taken in by an eccentric English couple who run the renewable energy plant there. The *Conway* is attacked when Mona is heavily pregnant, but they survive the onslaught through guile and fortitude. She gives birth to a little boy in April and calls him Tom, after her father.

Cai is reunited with his countrymen, but the remaining journey around the coast of Britain is still fraught with delay until they land in Falmouth. Once safely among the Cornish Druid community, Cai meets Idwal, Mona's long-lost brother. He and several other Cornish Druids join the Welsh fleet on the short journey home. Tom is three months old when the fleet is spotted passing Caernarfon, after having been absent for a year and a day.

Contents

Bile rose in Diarmuid's throat. His head boiled and his fingers froze. Fear wasn't exactly the right word for the emotion he felt at this moment. That concept was far too clean. Dread swirled in his belly, cowardice sang in his veins and hate formed in the droplets of sweat that ran down Diarmuid's back. In many ways he considered his current state to be a side-effect of his power, a downside of the Sight. Though it was hard to think of any upsides to this ability. Seeing the true colour of people's souls hadn't turned out to be a gift for Diarmuid – especially when you were surrounded by monsters.

He'd been summoned to his father's 'Command Centre', and Diarmuid hated the room almost as much as the man inside it. The myriad screens and beeping needled his head and eyes. There was too much technology in that unnatural place and it fought against his ability to See.

In his heart Diarmuid fretted this might mean another *garnering* trip, as Seamus liked to call them. The last visit to Newgrange had devastated the gentle Irishman, and though he'd tried his best to care for the girls since their capture, he feared for Aislinn's health. The young woman had been 'bred', and having the twins had taken an immense toll on her young body. He should have helped her more, but that would have meant putting his head even further above the parapet, and he hadn't found nearly enough courage yet.

Through the patio doors, he could see Cian and their father snapping at each other like hungry wolves. Seamus blamed Cian for the VSV debacle. Diarmuid wasn't privy to the specifics – only that it had been an expensive failure, and the slender-hulled super-boats had been hurriedly hidden away from the prying authorities. He took a last desperate gulp of fresh air while he could. "*Ah! Anseo faoi dheireadh. An dara lón díreach críochnaithe agat, a Dhiarmuid?* – Ah! Here he is at last. Just finished your second lunch, Diarmuid?"

His father teased the big man incessantly, but Diarmuid would take all the verbal cruelty the man could muster, so long as he didn't have to share the same room with these two for any longer than necessary.

It was only when Cian and Seamus were together that Diarmuid could clearly distinguish their auras. Though they shared the yellow and black, Seamus had memories of other colours within his swirling mess. The Seer could also recognise glimpses of red and green, but they had fallen sick from the purulent infection of the black, and Seamus's hues were muddying as they mixed in with his son's darkness. Cian's power was kept from complete shadow by a sluggish oozing of yellow from its centre – his beautiful voice.

Despite these subtle differences, their combined auras were painfully strong at this distance. Seamus had always known how to affect his eldest son and had used it as a weapon against him all his life.

"Don't look so worried, Diarmuid. I just wanted to catch up on the last delivery." Even now his father could make himself sound kind. "I haven't seen you for a couple of months."

"It went well." Saying as little as possible was always safest with his father.

Diarmuid waited. He wanted more air, but something about his father's expectant look kept him from leaving.

"We're closing the web. She'll be here before long, the *marked one*." Diarmuid's heart stepped up, and he knew his father enjoyed the little tease; both of them chuckled at his expense. "I'll let you taste her, son, but she'll be mine to keep."

≈

2

Diarmuid needed more than just fresh air after his ordeal. He craved comfort, and set off towards the cliffs to find it. Diarmuid wedged his bulk against the standing stone; the chair-shaped bulge towards its base enabled him to take his great weight off his legs without actually having to sit, as getting up was always more trouble than it was worth. This stone had been his friend since childhood; a lump of granite hauled down from the Wicklow Mountains. He knew the lines carved into it were Ogham, but didn't have a clue what the script meant.

It hadn't only been Diarmuid's backside that had worn the stone into a seat – he had an idea he was just the latest in a long line of loner-misfits who'd sought refuge here over the centuries. Settling back against the worn surface, Diarmuid turned to the west, searching out for the heartbeat of the Goddess. He didn't actually believe that an immortal sat beneath the Hill of Tara, but the immense power he felt coming up through his feet tasted undeniably female.

Most often he thought of her as a great moon, touching the earth at the sacred Hill and spilling her silvery-white energy along these tracks. The Irish government had cut, scarred and desecrated the land with their concrete and tarmac but the moon-powered roads were still there – if you had the power to see them. A yellow stick man on a wooden post advertised the trail as the 'Wicklow Way', but that wasn't the path Diarmuid saw at all. This was the Slíghe Chualann, one of the five ancient roads that began their life at Tara and fanned out to the compass points across Ireland. Superstitious folk talked of 'fairy' or 'corpse' roads but what they'd sensed were these prehistoric trails.

Diarmuid could vaguely feel the pull of the other four paths, but the Slíghe Chualann beneath him now was humming. She was calling him back to Tara, and someday soon he would go.

Home

Sioned thundered into the meeting, slamming the door back violently against its hinges. "The fleet have past Y Felinheli," she gasped; her eyes wild with frenetic expectation. "Bryn wants to know what to do. He wants to know whether or not to…"

"Send out both Demetae and Silurian clans – fully armed," Arwel cut in tightly.

"Armed? What do you mean? You're not seriously going to fight them?" Sioned asked, her excitement morphing into confused shock.

"No," Arwel answered, but he didn't seem totally sure.

"You want us to arrest them?" she stated with dumb disbelief.

"No. There aren't enough cells." He appeared dispassionate but Arwel's hands trembled as he spoke.

"But that's our brother out there…"

"Who could be a spy, Sioned." His voice rose before falling rapidly. "Any one of them could be."

"And they have two extra boats with them, Sioned." Ifan added quietly.

"But that doesn't mean…" Sioned protested in a whine.

"We don't know *what* it means yet. But until we do, and no matter how much it may hurt, we must treat the fleet with suspicion – even brutality if it comes to it." Ifan spoke with more authority now, gripping the table hard and easing to his feet. "Take your best fighters out there now, Sioned, and stand firm."

The young girl accepted the order stoically and ran from the room, leaving the community leaders to discuss their next move.

"We need to keep them penned into one area." Arwel looked at Mona. "But we'll have to test each of them separately. I don't want to let the spy know what we're looking for."

"I could pretend to test their combat skills. Perhaps they'll let their guard down during a bout." Tom started to wake and she rearranged him in her arms. "I don't know what else…"

Arwel nodded in agreement. "And it would give you a chance to see how they smell… if they smell of sulphur, like Gareth."

Mona concurred. It wasn't much of a strategy but it would have to do, given the lack of time before the fleet arrived.

"I'll join Sioned and Bryn on the front line," the Archdruid muttered ominously to the gathered leaders. "Everyone else should station themselves at the far end of the Hall, and wait for Mona's lead."

≈

The six boats were quickly moored alongside the jetty. They had finally come home, but the buildings of HMS *Conway* still felt out of reach. The protective lines of warriors hadn't budged an inch.

The ropes were made off, but not one of the passengers attempted to disembark. Dafydd hurled questions at his father from the bow of his boat, but the Archdruid merely responded by sending forward one of the girls. Cai's chest tightened; it was his own little sister, Sioned. He leaped up onto the jetty, arms outstretched.

"Don't come any closer, Cai." She held a sword in one hand and showed him the palm of the other. "There's a spy. We've been betrayed… betrayed and attacked." Her glance scanned the boats. "You're all under suspicion." Despite her bravado, his sister's eyes were shining with some awful news. "Can you get them to follow you straight to the hall? "Please, Cai," she begged. "Explain it to them."

It didn't take a lot of explaining, and pretty soon the returning

5

sailors collapsed and scattered themselves amongst the training mats in the Hall. They were hungry, thirsty and exhausted, but neither food nor drink was offered them. The silence was uncanny; the only sound a rustle of leathers as the armed women and boys trickled in quietly behind them. Positioning themselves against the walls, they surrounded the new arrivals, isolating them from the community beyond. No move was made to engage but they showed no inclination of standing down either.

Both sides were acutely aware of each other, and the air was thick with distrust. Cai searched for Mona, but there was no sign of her at all, and the foreboding deepened. He wondered where Mona was. What the hell had happened here? Dafydd stared longingly at his wife across the gulf of suspicion. Nansi had tears in her eyes but no children at her side. Cai blanched at the thought of a fight – a civil war within the *Conway*.

Eventually, Ifan shuffled forwards into the hostile emptiness of no-man's-land. Older and bent with grief for his eldest son, Emlyn, he lifted his hand to address them. Cai expected the Archdruid to talk; to explain the bizarre situation, but the silence dragged on as Ifan openly scruitinised each face in turn, both family and stranger.

Mona strode through the doors and Cai moved towards her on instinct. His whole body constricted with love.

Ifan continued at her signal. "All of you listen to what Mona has to say." Ifan's voice was harsh with bottled-up emotion.

Tom had taken ages to settle, and Mona hadn't been able to find anyone reliable to look after him. Everyone she trusted was in here, on her side of the room. Arwel hovered beside her, clip board in hand, but Mona instantly ceased to be aware of him at all because her brain could only contemplate one person in the room, and he stood on the other side of the divide.

Cai stood as near as he could to the demarcation line, and he was staring into her soul. The room swam, and his image bobbed up and down in front of her, as if he were still on the bow of a boat. Mona closed her eyes, drawing back from the brink. The room stopped moving and Cai's image sharpened.

When she spoke, her voice was crystal clear. "Throw down any weapons you have, and take a step back." A short silence was followed by much loud muttering and swearing. "Do it now," she barked, and the room was gradually filled with the sound of metal dropping to wood. Nobody said anything more, so she continued. "You will come with me – one at a time." She pointed past the double doors. "There is to be no talking or singing – in any language."

She sounded like a stranger to her own ears and while Ifan translated the commands, her gaze slid once more towards Cai. Mona couldn't tell what he saw in her eyes, but he didn't smile as he approached her.

Cai would be the first to be tested. His skin had turned a nut brown, enhancing the blueness of his eyes and making it hard for her to look away from them. Arwel cleared his throat, focusing her attention.

"Come with me, Cai." Arwel murmured trying his best to remain professional as he noted down his brother's name on the clipboard he gripped in front of him.

Mona followed them out of the Hall, battling to keep her mind on-task. He looked older and far more attractive than she'd remembered, and somehow they'd touched hands, the boundary between them blurring. It was only the slightest osf contacts, but it surged through her body, toes to teeth, catapulting a hallucination into her mind.

As blacksmith of the settlement, Meilyr knew the routine of early mornings: building the fire with coal and coke; creating and tending the heart of fire; regulating the airflow – feeding the beast. He understood the minute changes in the iron, from black through all the reds and yellows, to the whitest of heats.

He had the power to shape and fuse metal, with the strength of his right arm. Meilyr knew too well the screaming ache of muscles, the slick of sweat down his back, the quench and the satisfaction of a

7

finished job. He lifted the hammer high above his shoulder, before striking metal down on metal with controlled force; working quickly while enough of the cherry red remained.

Quenching the blade in the barrel at his side, he watched her saunter in through the smithy entrance and into the steam with the promise of more than lunch in her smile. "Come and get it while it's still warm."

It only took two strides to reach her, but Canaid whirled away from him with mischief in her eyes and the wooden soup bowl cupped in her hands. By the time Meilyr had wiped the sweat from his brow, his wife had abandoned the soup and twisted herself back into the circle of arms. Soft, hot lips fluttered around his neck and chest as he picked her up, the sweat of his labour mixing with her sweet, salty kisses.

Mona pulled her hand away before she saw anymore, and Cai frowned, then smiled at her. "You stayed." His statement was quiet, reverent, and Mona momentarily forgot what she was here to do. She hadn't prepared herself enough for the strange apparitions that sporadically haunted their touch. Arwel coughed, reminding her that there was no time for this now.

"Stand still," she commanded in a dispassionate tone. Cai seemed perplexed but nodded and Mona forced herself past him, sniffing the air for the faint smell of sulphur, but she breathed in only pure Cai – diesel, hardwood, sea.

"Did I pass?" he asked.

Cai's smile desiccated Mona into a dried branch; one more touch would snap her in half.

"Now we fight." She gestured to the mat, and Cai began the attack. Fast, furious and accurate. He had improved.

Arwel stopped the fight after only a few seconds. "Welcome back, Cai," he said, almost sobbing with relief and folding his brother against his chest with uncharacteristic intensity.

Cai held Arwel close and then released him, spreading his arms wide. "Mona," he whispered, but she'd reeled away from him and had already marched back into the Hall. "Mona, wait…"

8

"Let her finish the job, Cai." Arwel's voice was low and reassuring. "We'll talk later."

He followed Arwel's lead and took up position behind Mona, but Cai couldn't shift the seed of worry that had taken root in the pit of his stomach.

Mona faced the ranked warriors on the other side of the line, her stance wide and locked. "Next." Some of the Cornish men had started mumbling to one another.

"No talking," she snapped quickly, as she realised their conversation wasn't in English.

They stopped talking but one of the bigger men began trundling towards her. Mona couldn't see his face because it was obscured by a mop of greasy looking, blonde hair.

"Stand still," she ordered again, more harshly this time.

She wasn't sure how Arwel wanted to organise the testing. It was doubtful that any of the newcomers from Kernow or Galicia could be the spy, but it would be madness to leave them untested. The man hadn't stopped though, he hadn't even slowed and Mona sensed the change in her troops as they assessed the threat and reacted to him.

"I said stand still," she growled to the chorus of many blades being drawn. The approaching Cornish man was enormous. He had massive shoulders and great, big, muscly arms, and Mona instinctively tightened her core in readiness. The big man finally halted, only a foot from her, and the air between them sang with menace.

"Why? What are you going to do, Mo? Fight me?"

She stepped back at the precise moment her legs gave way. Cai caught and held her up, but Mona's attention was focused entirely on the huge man in front of her – a man who had just spoken with her brother's voice. He'd lifted his head and scraped away the hair.

Idwal's features were as familiar to her as looking in the mirror. Mona breathed in the scent of a long-lost home as he reached forwards and pulled her against him. Idwal patted her gently on the back with a soothing croon while her thoughts collided and backed up in her head.

Alive, I knew you were alive! Though that wasn't what Mona said as she looked up into his face, her mother's face.

"You left me. I've been on my own - for such a long time," she choked out; reliving the raw memory of that rejection all over again.

Idwal stood Mona back on her feet, and she saw him trying to formulate something. What? An excuse, an apology? But before Idwal could say anything at all, a loud caterwauling from the door cut him short. Mona realised with slow-motion alarm that her time had run out. She turned from Idwal and Cai to greet the young girl rushing towards her and carrying a screaming ball of fury.

"I'm sorry, Mona... I've tried everything," she spoke frantically. "But he was just getting angrier and redder. He only wants you."

"That's ok. You did the right thing." Mona thought she sounded surprisingly composed as she took her indignant baby from the girl, and walked from the hall.

≈

Rob had shared a bedroom with Mona for over nine months now, and they'd grown so close that he assumed he knew every nuance of her body language. It appeared he'd been mistaken. Rob had never seen her look at anyone like that. Every fibre of Mona's body longed for this man's touch; every glance demonstrated a palpable need for it.

Cai hadn't moved or reacted initially. His eyes were planted squarely on the closed double doors and he looked as if he might shatter into a thousand pieces at any moment. But as bewilderment was transplanted with anger, Rob watched the warrior's body bunch and clench, as if readying itself for combat. This Cai wasn't exactly the man he'd imagined, and certainly not as he was now, with Bryn and Dafydd struggling to restrain him. Mona had always told Rob she admired Cai's control, but this man was brutal, almost dangerous. Rob knew those eyes, though.

"Easy now, Cai," Bryn muttered, not unkindly. "Let her see to the boy. Just give her a minute."

Every one of the congregated fighters stared openly at Cai, and Dafydd belatedly took the initiative. "Congratulations! He looks a fine, strong lad."

Rob was aware the long-awaited reunion had not gone to plan, but this wild man seemed to be taking news of parenthood very badly indeed. A germ of dislike planted itself in his heart, together with a fear that he might lose Mona and Tom to a man who didn't deserve either of them.

≈

Fed and contented, Tom was fast asleep by the time Cai and Arwel burst through the door. Someone else must have waylaid Cai long enough for her to feed the baby, and she wondered who would have had the strength to contain him for that length of time. As he lunged into the room, Cai was panting hard, his eyes wild for answers he didn't want.

"That baby – it's yours?"

"Yes."

"You're its mother?" Cai asked as if there might, against all odds, be another answer. One that would make everything all right.

Ifan gasped for breath as he joined them, closing the door firmly behind him. The room was too small to contain the potent emotions swirling within it, and the threat of complete meltdown filled the air.

"Is he mine?" Cai's voice was barely audible.

Ever so slightly, Mona shook her head, and from the corner of her eye she watched Arwel slump against the wall in despair. As he did the maths, Cai stared at Mona with disgust and loathing. He looked ready to explode, but instead bolted for the door. Standing across the threshold, Ifan blocked his way.

"Wait! There's something we need to tell you – to discuss." Ifan glanced to Mona for back up but she couldn't breathe. There was a tight band round her chest that she couldn't seem to loosen.

"How old is it?" Cai spat, his eyes violent with hate and trained on her child.

11

"Tom is three months old," Ifan answered stiffly on Mona's behalf. Cai spun to face Mona and she could see that he had lost the battle for self-control. He was going to say it all now. "So what are we talking about, Mo, days? How many days before you started fucking anything with a pulse? Do you even know who the father is?"

Cai spat bullets of hurt, and it would have been better to look away or leave or do anything but sit there, with her son on her lap, watching the car crash of betrayal and hate. Arwel answered for her this time.

"Listen, Cai, calm down, it wasn't like that. And there are more important things to address now."

Unable to express himself any longer in English, Cai loosed a tirade of ragged Welsh at a stoic Ifan. The Archdruid took it all, and reached out as if he might still be able to calm the younger man. Arwel sunk to the chair in defeat.

"What did he say?" Mona asked him. In the eye of the storm now, she had regained some of her composure.

Arwel shook his head sadly – she didn't need to know, but Cai was ready to enlighten her. "*Putain Saesneg wyt ti* – I said you're an English whore. How many days did you last, Mona? I loved you. You bitch!" Cai was hurting. All his love was skinned and bleeding.

Vitriol was Cai's chosen weapon and bizarrely it was much easier to bear than tears or pity. Who was this man? Where had he been when she needed him? Brendan's posthumous words about calm and cunning whispered into Mona's ear, and she rejected them outright. Attack was always the best form of defence. Raging with her own anger, Mona advanced to within inches of Cai. She forced a strength she didn't feel into her voice.

"Yes, just days. I needed him. I wanted him. Do you want to know any more details or will that do for now?"

"Who is he? Where is he?" Cai wanted a fight, he didn't care who with.

"He's dead now," she spat.

The pain in his eyes was almost unbearable. "I hope he was worth it."

"Why did you say all that, Mona?" Arwel was staggered by her response.

"Because it's the truth."

Cai hobbled towards the door again, and he was still not allowed to pass.

"Stop, you must hear this, you must *understand* this," Ifan blurted out. "The man, Tom's father... he was from a rogue Irish clan. No one knows he's the father. And no one *must* know." He'd slowed up now, for the big finale. "I've let it be known that *you* are Tom's father, Cai. It's the only way to protect them both."

Deaf to Ifan's words, Cai lurched out of Mona's door without a backwards glance.

≈

Surging with hate, Cai found himself back in his old room. Before he could decide what to do with his pent-up aggression, his grandfather walked in and plonked a bottle of rum on the desk.

"I'm glad you're back home safe, son. I thought you might need this." Yes, obliteration – that's what Cai needed. Hywel filled two glasses and Cai finished the drink in a couple of swallows. Hywel refilled it. "You seem angry."

Rum and bile mixed in Cai's throat. "I'm fucking furious!"

Hywel took a sip of his own, biding his time.

"Mona's child..."

"Don't." Gritting his teeth, Cai slammed down his glass, and his grandfather held his breath.

"Ifan said..."

"Don't say another word to me about that slut and her bastard child."

Hywel backed away, palms outwards. "I'll leave you to it, son. I'll leave you be."

13

The old man left the room exultant. A year away had done the trick; the witch's spell had been broken. Now that Hywel had Cai back on side, it was time to straighten out his old friend Ifan on a few things.

≈

As Arwel had trailed after Cai from the hall, the noise of opinion and rumour hummed into life. Bryn came over to Rob, his face ashen. "Looks like Dad hasn't taken it too well. Do you think I should go and see if Mo's ok?" Rob asked glumly.

"No!" Bryn's response was almost hysterical. "Look around, Rob, people are going to talk. There will be gossip about you being Tom's father." They both knew that; the possibility had allowed them to be together for the last few months. Rob couldn't quite understand why this was relevant now, and Bryn explained. "If Cai thinks you're the child's father, he will want to fight you. He may try to hurt you anyway."

Cai hadn't impressed Rob so far, but this seemed a little far-fetched. "I'll just talk to him. Explain about Mo and me."

"No!" Bryn responded with the same vehemence.

"I won't say anything about us, don't worry."

"That's not what worries me." Bryn moved closer; alone, they would have kissed. "You wouldn't get a second chance with Cai. He could kill you, Rob." Bryn didn't want to think about a confrontation between the two men in Mona's life. "You saw him in here, it took both of us to restrain him. I won't be able to protect you from him. I cannot beat him in a fight."

Rob realised now why Mona had begged him not to move out. She had foreseen the entire catastrophe: Cai's anger; Rob's danger. Only Mona could protect Rob from Cai. "Promise me you'll keep close to her – until it all dies down," Bryn persisted.

"Of course," Rob replied, but that wasn't good enough for Bryn.

"Promise me," he demanded. Rob promised.

2

Reunion

It was inevitable the next intruder would be her long-lost brother. *Bring them on*, Mona thought. *I'm in the mood for a fight.*

Idwal filled the doorway for a second, before deciding to come all the way in. She'd already deposited Tom in the middle of the bed, keeping her hands free just in case she felt the need to strangle her brother. "So it's true? That's your baby? I mean yours and Cai's? That's what they're saying in the hall."

"And?" she replied, instantly defensive but almost eager for complete emotional annihilation.

"And nothing." He shrugged. "I mean, are you all right with that?"

"All right with that? Idwal, I'm twenty-two years old! Of course I'm not fucking all right with it, but it's a bit late now!" Suddenly she knew what he was going to say, knew he would lapse into some moralistic diatribe about being careful and making your own bed. "How dare you even think about spouting bollocks like that? How many women have you had in the last two years? The last month? How dare you judge me, you selfish, cowardly git. How could you leave me on my own? Didn't you ever think…?" She broke off mid-sentence, words failing her.

"Mona, Mona, I'm so sorry, come here." She remained stationary, and so Idwal moved forward to hug her stiffened body. "I had a letter, Mo, same as you. I'm sure they had to split us up after Mum and Dad… Brendan told me all three of you had died in the crash." He squeezed her hard and spoke into her hair.

"I miss them so much, Id… I miss them… every day," she confessed.

"Me too," Idwal whispered. They were motionless for a long time. "Still got it I see." Idwal tugged on one of the wires leading to Mona's ear.

"Of course," she muttered fiercely.

Idwal eventually peered over at the sleeping child. "So he's my nephew?" he said, smiling at his new little relative.

"Yes, I suppose he is."

"Can I pick him up, then?" he asked in a hesitant but perfect English accent. Mona passed Tom over to him, marvelling at how the mere sound of her brother's voice improved her mood. "Look, he's awake." Tom broke wind with a loud sigh and startled at his uncle's booming laugh. "Well he definitely takes after you digestively. Got Cai's eyes though." Idwal noticed her pain. "It'll just take a bit of getting used to, Mo – he'll come round."

Mona nodded dumbly and suggested that her brother have a shower.

≈

The first three rums had washed the bile from his mouth and warmed his stomach. Cai was becoming belligerent by the fourth, but at least he hadn't started crying yet.

He snatched the blue iPod from his back pocket and stood staring at it for a while – such stupid, fragile dreams. After dropping it on the side, he strode away, taking the half-empty bottle with him. What did he need? Another drink? A fight maybe? What he didn't need was to hear any more about Mona. The gossip in the makeshift prison of the Hall had been full of her heroic exploits. She'd broken him, destroyed him – she was a whore.

Arwel materialised up ahead, blocking his way back into the Hall. "I need your help, Cai. We've made no progress at all with finding…" Arwel lowered his voice, "the spy." Cai wasn't listening; he was drunk and determined to get past Arwel. "You don't need to go back in there. You've already been tested."

"Leave me alone. You don't know what I need."

"You've got it all wrong about Mona. He forced her. Please, just go back and talk to her. Please, Cai, just talk to her."

Drunk and out of control, Cai was only enraged further by talk of Mona. "Tell me, Arwel? How did he do that? Was he eight-foot tall with four arms?" Cai's breath was rank as he spat his conclusion. "There isn't a man alive who could force Mona to have sex. Now get out of my way or..."

"Ne be? Wyt ti eisiau cwffio – Or what? You'll fight me?" Arwel had shaped his hands into pathetic fists, but Cai would never be drunk enough to hit his baby brother.

"Get out of my way. You don't understand."

"I'm the same age as my dad when I was born. I know enough, Cai! Enough to know you're acting like a total prick."

Cai was too drunk to be shocked by Arwel's insult. Dragging him from the door, he flung the boy aside, and then let himself back into the big room.

It was clear from the party atmosphere that someone must have smuggled in some alcohol. There was a lot of raucous giggling from a nearby table, and Cai directed himself towards it. He knew now what he wanted, and from whom he could get it.

Carmen, Maria and the other Galician women were flirting outrageously with some of the Cornish crew. Cai dropped himself awkwardly on a spare seat facing Carmen. He recalled, with a sudden jolt, how beautiful she was. How her soft, curling hair, so luxuriant and heavy, draped down to rest enticingly above a pair of perfect breasts. Her laughing mouth was exactly the right shape for kissing.

There was a wolfish look in Cai's roaming eyes, and it didn't take Carmen long to respond to his come-on. Perching herself coquettishly on his lap, she allowed Cai to circle her tiny waist with his hands and pulled him into the soft curtain of her thick black hair. Heedless of the looks and comments he was attracting, Cai closed his eyes, breathing in the scent of her exotic femininity. They were both oblivious to the crude jokes and coarse banter of those around them. Leading Cai into a darkened corner of the Hall, Carmen encouraged him to explore as much of her body as possible through her clothes. Where Mona was hard and strong – too hard and strong – Carmen was soft and pliable. Cai had a year's worth of pent-up lust to burn off, and his need became so acute, so quickly, that he half-dragged Carmen from the hall to his room.

≈

Rob found Mona still and quiet. It worried him. Tom had fallen asleep at her breast and she stared dry-eyed into space. He kissed the top of her head, gently easing the baby from her grasp and into his basket.

"You knew he'd act like this?"

She nodded mechanically.

"But you still love him." It wasn't a question and she repeated the head movement. "He's a complete arsehole, Mo. Don't waste yourself on a man like that."

Rob knelt down in front of her on his knees, and she stroked his golden hair. "It's not as straightforward as that, my love." Mona sounded very tired.

"We don't need him, Mo. We're good parents to Tom, that doesn't have to change." Rob was so kind. So unbearably kind as he pledged his life to her son. "I know we're an odd combination, but all he needs is love and I've got plenty of that."

There weren't any tears. Mona had spent them all rehearsing for this day. "We'll be fine. It will all be fine."

Rob didn't contradict her lie. "Bryn's worried that Cai might believe the rumours about me… being Tom's dad. He thinks he may try to hurt me. He's mad, right?"

This information seemed to galvanise Mona. Snapping out of her reverie, she tucked her damp breast back into her bra. An anxious tone crept into her voice. "No. He's right. You're to stay by me at all times." Mona thought back to Hywel's many warnings and shuddered.

≈

Ifan opened the door expectantly when he heard Arwel's footsteps. "Well?"

Arwel shook his head. It was half disbelief and half shock at how badly Cai had taken the news. "He's angry and now three sheets to the wind." Arwel lifted his hands with futility. "He didn't listen to a word I said."

"Where is he now?"

"Consoling himself…"

There was an abrupt knock on the door and Ifan peered up at Arwel, hopeful that Cai had changed his mind and come to talk. But as Arwel pulled back the door Mona's brother strode in.

"Are you Ifan?"

The man spoke with supreme authority and the sudden influx of power caused the old man's scalp to tighten so quickly that his eyes watered.

"Yes, the *Archdruid*," he stressed the title and pointed to the teenager. "And this is my grandson and apprentice, Arwel."

"Pleased to meet you both." Idwal crushed each of their hands in turn.

"Can I help you?" Ifan asked, dabbing his eyes with a hanky. Idwal's power still invigorated his senses, but the old man was quickly acclimatising to it.

"Well, I wanted to find out what the state of play is… with this spy."

The Archdruid and his apprentice exchanged furtive glances, but neither responded to the big Englishman's question. "So, have you got any ideas?" Idwal's tone wasn't exactly aggressive, but he was expectant, demanding.

"We've been working on it non-stop… but with the testing of the fleet incomplete…" Arwel felt the need to defend their abject failure.

"So, have you got any suspects in the *Conway*?"

"Well, not suspects exactly…"

Idwal blew out in exasperation. "So just how long have you been working on this?"

"About a year," Arwel admitted.

"A *year*!"

Ifan had recovered enough to be thoroughly affronted by Idwal's high-handed manner. "It's a very painstaking process. We're going through arrivals with a fine toothcomb and cross-referencing…"

"Cross-referencing!" Idwal was aghast. "Have you tried a search? Questioning?"

"If we want your help, we'll ask for it," Ifan snapped.

"Fine," Idwal said, raising his hands in deference. "I didn't mean to offend, but I'm more than happy to help – if you need me." He backed out of the room and left.

"Arrogant, English arsehole." Ifan made sure he cursed the big warrior well after his footsteps had receded down the corridor.

Arwel smiled. "I like him – he's going to get things done."

≈

Despite the numbing effects of rum, Cai was desperate to bury himself in Carmen's body. She was small and light. So light, in fact, that he could throw her onto his bed with relative ease. She gave a little cry of alarm, but Cai didn't apologise; he was too busy tearing the jeans from her legs.

"Hang on, Cai." Her tone remained persistently seductive and she sat up to kiss him. Carmen's perfume made him gag. Her mouth stank and it wasn't a kiss he was interested in. Cai used his forearm to bat her backwards onto the bed. Her jeans were off now and he concentrated on ridding himself of his own. He already had the condom in his hand.

Lying back, Carmen squirmed in anticipation, clasping her knees together in mock demureness as Cai rolled the condom onto his erect penis. Impatient, Cai forced her legs apart without preamble, splaying her thighs out across the bed. "I'm not ready, Cai," she squealed as he spat on his hand, pushing first one, then two fingers inside her. When he deemed her wet enough, Cai plunged straight in. Pumping furiously, he climaxed with a shuddering groan no more than a minute later. Carmen was panting with need as he pulled out of her and left for the bathroom.

Moments later, he returned with another condom in his hand. Carmen gazed at him from the bed with a look that sought intimacy and affection as well as sexual satisfaction. Cai never wanted to see that look on a woman's face again. "Turn over," he commanded.

≈

Mona hauled Tom down the corridor and round the corner to Siân's crèche. She was using Tom's routine to root her in reality. The enormity of Cai's response had been overwhelming. Yesterday's confrontation had been worse than all nightmares about it, and Mona felt brittle but had no choice but to stay strong.

"You are a little fatty," she told Tom, marvelling at the density of his body. He stared back at her with those profoundly blue eyes, as if trying to understand what she said. "I'm not going to carry you all your life, you know."

She kissed the fat folds at his neck. When did they start to walk, she wondered, and talk? He had begun to smile, though rarely, and she wondered whether he was just a serious person or she was doing something wrong. Tom ate and filled his nappy just fine, as far as she could make out, and that's what everyone else seemed concerned about.

There was the normal crowd in Siân's extended rooms. A frisson of excitement from Sioned put Mona on the back foot.

"It came!" she squealed, moving aside to reveal a slightly battered but very serviceable pram.

Despite herself, Mona was pleased; he was getting too heavy for the sling. "Shall we see if he fits, then?" Siân asked, taking Tom from his mother and settling him in amongst the bedding.

Nia slipped an arm through Mona's during the experiment. "Want to talk about it?"

Of course. Nia had been in the Hall. She would have witnessed Cai's reaction. Sioned could contain herself no longer. "What did Cai say?" His sister still hadn't heard then.

"Well, it's quite a lot to take in. We've got some talking to do," Mona replied, cautiously. She was a rabbit in the headlights. How could she continue to lie to these women she loved – who loved her and who cared so much for her baby boy? Would it really be so dangerous to confide the truth? Or was it just too late now? Both Nia and Siân misread her blankness for pain. They needn't have; she'd already locked the damage away. Cai couldn't hurt her anymore.

"Why don't we test-drive the new machine, Sioned?" Siân hinted subtly. "He's all wrapped up now."

There was more fussing, but when they had left, Nia cut to the chase. "He's not taken it well, has he?" She didn't stop talking long enough to hear Mona's reply. "Ifan and Dafydd are arranging the farewells for Emlyn, Ieuan and the other lads… who didn't come home. They've decided to use it as an opportunity to break in the newcomers – after the testing, of course. Mam wants to give Emlyn a good send-off." Talking about the dead was a shortcut back to sorrow, and Nia paused. "Anyway, Mam said she wants to babysit Tom… that she doesn't really want to party too hard." Nia hesitated. "I thought it might be a wonderful opportunity for you and Cai to get to know each other again." Nia looked down into her twisted hands for a second. "And I'd like you to introduce me to your brother."

That cleared up a couple of things for Mona. Nia obviously hadn't yet spoken to Cai, and she would definitely be having a word with her brother – about keeping his hands off Nia.

"When is all this happening?" Mona asked, in as light and interested a tone as she could fake.

"It'll take a few days to organise and get the groceries in, but Saturday, we hope."

"Great. Can you tell your mum to feed him with the bottled stuff? I've got this testing to do."

≈

Mona jogged to where her brother had been billeted. Rapping hard on his door, she shouted, "Let me in, Id. We need to talk about the test today."

Idwal opened the door, wet from the shower, all towel and hair. Mona sat on the bed.

"There's got to be a better way of finding the…" he began.

"I'd really like your help today," she butted in. "With the testing in the hall… I'm going to do the sniffing; then we should split up and check out their fighting. It'll be so much quicker."

"What's this sniffing about? You've not fallen for all that magic crap, have you?"

Mona shrugged, not yet ready to discuss her opinion of magic. "Arwel thinks the spy might smell differently," she said vaguely, trying hard not to immediately divulge all her secrets to her brother.

"You *are* shitting me?" Mona merely shrugged again, so Idwal took the hint and moved on. "And why are we testing their fighting, for God's sake?"

"To see if they're any good." She rolled her eyes at the stupidity of his question. "It gets the selection process out of the way, a bit like a grading, I suppose. And I don't want any of them untrained for long."

"We could get Cai to help too. I've heard he's a handy fighter," Idwal suggested.

"We'll be fine." Mona's body language said anyone but Cai, and Idwal didn't push the point.

"You reckon they'll be back, then, the Irish?" Mona nodded, but her face twisted in a grimace. Her brother recognised the look. "I know, doesn't seem right… fighting the Irish. I keep thinking of Mum and Bren. Does anyone know what they're up to? Why they're after us?"

"No, not really. Arwel and Nia have got some theories, but…" Mona decided she'd said enough. "But we need to be ready, for when they come again."

"They're good fighters, my lot," he said. "A bit undisciplined, but…"

"Good isn't good enough, Idwal. We could be attacked at any time. As far as I can tell, they respect you, so I'm going to need your backing in there today."

"You're Jean-Luc and I'm Number One," he said with a wide grin.

"At last!" Mona managed to force a small smile. "Someone who speaks my language."

"Aren't there any Trekkies here, then?" Idwal asked with mock astonishment, and Mona jabbed her elbow into her brother's ribs, and almost laughed.

≈

Mona stopped in front of the training room. She actually felt nervous. "You'll back me up? No matter what?" she asked her brother.

"Man up, loser. It'll be a piece of piss." Idwal poked her in the back and she snorted at the familiar but forgotten quip.

Arwel was waiting inside, clipboard in hand and a face full of thunder. "They've been drinking all night!"

He sounded exasperated, but the scene in the Hall was about what Mona had expected. The stink of rum and unwashed bodies lay thick on the air. She was impressed the guards were still attentive, and nodded appreciatively at her troops. Dafydd and Dai were busy rousing people from their sleep, and Idwal started opening windows.

It took about five minutes before most of the returning warriors became semi-upright. There was no sign of Cai.

"Can you make sure everyone is still here?" Mona asked no one in particular. She scanned for Rob, and, seeing him behind Bryn, she breathed a little easier. Dafydd and Dai conferred and then Dafydd left the room.

Mona didn't rush the sulphur test. It was relatively easy to detect, even through a miasma of rum, but she'd been tricked before. Two lines formed in front of the siblings and they steadily worked their way through the new arrivals. Nursing hangovers, none of the new recruits were too difficult to overcome during the short fighting bouts. At every negative result, Arwel placed a small cross on his paperwork. There weren't that many more to test and he began chewing his pencil in consternation.

Mona was defending a rather sloppy kick to her left thigh when a beautiful but dishevelled young woman was ushered through the door in the company of Cai. The couple were holding hands. Mona froze for a moment, allowing the blow from the Cornishman to connect. Using the pain to clear her mind, Mona shook out the injury, reformed her stance, and quickly annihilated her young opponent.

Carmen didn't smell of sulphur; she smelled of alcohol, sex and Cai. She fought with Idwal very briefly, while Mona took a breather and a cup of water. A pain throbbed in her chest that had nothing to do with her recent exertion, but she got to her feet and spoke through it.

"You're fairly decent warriors, but that won't be enough. We will train you to fight more effectively and you will become battle-ready. Training will take place in here, *every day,* and there will be no more booze. Get cleaned up and rest. You're going to need it."

Mona strode to the door and Rob followed. She had Tom to feed.

≈

Sioned had expected to see Cai at training, and she'd slipped in just after Mona and Idwal had started the session. The young woman had been desperate to catch up with her brother as soon as he'd returned, but Siân had advised her to let him deal with the Tom situation first. Since then, there seemed to have been some sort of meltdown.

Sioned had been shocked at the rumour about Cai and the Galician woman, but she didn't believe it until they'd sidled in together. Then hope had turned to disgust. Sioned walked up to Cai slowly; he stank. "What the hell are you playing at?" She didn't even try to curb the aggression in her tone.

Cai didn't register her immediately, and Sioned couldn't be sure if it was the hangover or the fact he was burning holes into Mona with his stare. So she shook him. "Hi, Sioned." A glance up, but he couldn't meet her eye.

"Aren't you going to introduce me, Cai?" Even through the fuzz, he heard the tone in her voice, the assurance. She sounded just like Mona.

"Carmen, Sioned." The woman on his arm was equally stony-faced. "Sioned, Carmen."

Did he not know what Mona had done? Who she had become? Or did he just not care anymore? Sioned had always forgiven her brother everything, but now she knew better.

"*Mi fasa Mam mor falch* – Mam would be so proud." Sioned smiled sweetly, knowing exactly how much that would hurt him.

≈

Arwel trudged back to the rooms in a stupor; he couldn't believe how badly Cai had behaved at training. Not that Mona was blameless of course, but to flaunt the Galician woman had been cruel, vicious. Arwel was at a loss. Ifan looked up from his desk, a similarly dejected look on his face. "I'm having a drink," his grandad said, and raised the glass as if to prove a point. "Care to join me?"

Arwel didn't think that drinking was a solution to their problem. "No, thank you." He raised his arms in a helpless gesture. "What are we going to do now?"

26

Ifan answered with an unintelligible groan and sank his head in his hands. "We have to do something, Taid. She's vulnerable and we're no closer to finding the spy. Mona's completed the tests on the newcomers and found absolutely nothing. Which means, the spy must be..."

There was a firm rap on the door and Hywel strolled in. He glanced briefly at Arwel, and then proceeded to address Ifan. "Cai's not acting like he's the brat's father."

The old eyes twinkled and Arwel couldn't bite his tongue quickly enough. "Has he told you that?"

Hywel didn't deign to look at the youngster again.

"I know my grandson. Cai recognises the Englishwoman for what she is – a common whore. The child isn't his, and he knows it."

Ifan slammed his glass down, harder than he'd meant to, but it got the attention of both his visitors.

"Can you leave us, Arwel? Hywel and I need to chat."

Arwel had no option but to obey his grandad's order, and as he left the room, he could hear Ifan offer his oldest friend a drink.

3

Meeting

Cai watched Mona sweep out of the room followed by her big, blonde English lover. She'd said the brat's father was dead but more likely this was its sire – judging by the way he trotted out after her. Mona had said she didn't fancy good-looking men, and Cai grunted caustically to himself at the memory. She'd said a lot of things. He supposed she'd gone back to feed the mutant thing she'd spawned, and it made him nauseous to think of it suckling at Mona's breast.

At least she'd reacted to his entrance with Carmen. He was cruelly gratified it had affected her enough to make a mistake. That he'd seen pain, as well as shock in her eyes. Part of Cai wanted everyone to know the real extent of Mona's infidelity. That there were actually three men involved in this farce. If anyone asked, he might even tell them. Sioned, for one, needed to know her heroine was just a dirty little tramp. His sister had always been the one person in the world who had loved him, without question. Now Mona had even tainted their relationship.

There was a gentle tugging on his arm, and Carmen pulled him down to whisper in his ear. "I've been given my room; let's celebrate." She winked, tapping a bulging rucksack. "I've got everything we need right here."

Cai lay on her bed as Carmen chattered at him. She was putting things away and trying to engage him in general gossip. He tuned out effortlessly, but grunted from time to time, wondering when she'd stop fussing and start taking off her clothes. The violent sex of the night before had subsided into repetitious, ordinary sex and he was beginning to feel a little more sated. Carmen needed to stop trying to kiss and flirt with him, though.

"Anyway, what is it with her and training? She's just like a man. Does she ever wear anything apart from that awful combat gear? Of course the hair doesn't help. Have you ever seen her wear make-up?"

No, no, no! He was not ready to have a conversation about Mona with this woman. "Come here," he croaked, dragging her down on top of him and kissing her more roughly than he'd intended – until she stopped talking.

"I was going to have a shower," she protested half-heartedly as Cai removed her clothing.

"Later." Cai's voice was husky, his mind set on one thing only. Outside world forgotten, they were both soon absorbed in the rhythm of their bodies.

≈

When Hywel finally left his old friend's room, his mind was too full of revulsion to function properly. He wandered directionless through the corridors, resting his hand against the wall under the burden of this new knowledge.

Mona's bastard child wasn't his great-grandson; the truth was far more horrific. The baby wasn't merely tainted with her Saxon blood – it was an enemy growth, planted there by the visitor who had called himself Gareth.

Mona had bewitched Ifan entirely, and the Archdruid talked only of protecting her – protecting it. Hywel, though, knew where his loyalties lay. He knew they were all now in grave danger from Mona and the mewling beast. But he was alone. She'd managed to persuade the entire community of her innocence. How could they not see the Saxon army she was gathering around herself? First this Rob, then her brother. How could Ifan insist on it being coincidence, worse still, fate?

The old man paused, suddenly remembering he was no longer alone. There was one other who had broken free from Mona's enchantments: his grandson, Cai. Together they would destroy this alien threat.

When Hywel found Cai's room empty, his despondency didn't last long. He realised that Destiny had handed him the promise of revenge. To him and him alone, she had given this one last chance of redemption.

≈

Nia wasn't exactly stalking Idwal, but had been watching him at a safe distance from virtually the first moment she'd set eyes on him. Without doubt he was the epitome of Celtic manhood. The Latin text ran unbidden into her mind as she watched him now, manhandling the heavy mats:

'The Celts are tall of body, with rippling muscles, and white of skin, their hair is blonde... and they pull it back from the forehead to the top of the head and back to the nape of the neck.'

Idwal was pretty sure Cai had arrived and left again with Carmen. Not that he blamed him exactly – most men eventually left with her. Though things should be a bit different for Cai now. Shouldn't they? He hauled the last of the mats to the pile, looking forward very much to some lunch. Perhaps he should have a little chat with Cai?

"Ho, Idwal, cares Vona, Nia of-vy – Hello, Idwal. I'm Mona's friend, Nia. Have you seen her? I thought she might be here training."

"Um." Idwal was standing next to the most ravishing creature he had ever seen. She spoke Cornish in the most mesmerising accent. "Ho – Hello," he stammered. Everything about her was honey and caramel. She was golden and sparkling, her voice was...

"*Ytho, hy gweles a wrusta* – So, have you seen her? She's not with Rob or Tom."

Rob? Idwal pondered. Perhaps he'd been too harsh on Cai. "She could be in the canteen? We could look for her and eat at the same time," he replied in Cornish and smiled expansively.

"Perhaps," Nia agreed.

≈

"There's Bacardi in the bag," Carmen called from the shower. Cai rooted around in the carrier, finding the bottle and a bumper pack of condoms. He put them both on the side and collected a couple of plastic cups from the shelf. He had filled and finished one before Carmen emerged.

As the alcohol took hold once more, befuddling his mind, Cai's body slid easily into another state of arousal.

"I'm glad I bought the large pack." Carmen giggled, both flattered and amused by his constant state of readiness for her. "I'm a bit sore," she crooned. "Be gentle."

"I will," he lied.

≈

There was no awkwardness at all between them as they queued, ate and chatted. Nia decided it was because he was so similar, in almost every way, to his sister. Idwal decided he'd accidentally found an angel on earth, and that he absolutely couldn't foul up.

They were on a third cup, both reluctant to draw anything to a close, when Rob appeared with Tom. The baby was asleep and strapped snugly to his chest. He sat down slowly in the third chair, eager not to wake his load. After introducing himself, Rob appraised Idwal.

"You're so much alike. Though you're much better-looking of course."

Idwal laughed, but Nia chastised him fondly.

"Don't scare him off, Rob. We don't get enough visitors as it is."

"Idwal," he said, squeezing Rob's hand and introducing himself formally. "Nice to hear an English accent." Idwal grinned. "How's your Welsh coming on?"

"Not great," he sighed. "But at least I give it a go. Mo won't even consider it."

"Not surprised," Idwal tutted extravagantly. "She's never been one for languages."

"I reckon there's a bit more to it than that. She's definitely a bit touchy about it." Rob kissed Tom's head absent-mindedly.

Idwal grimaced – that sounded like his sister. "I've been hearing all sorts of wonderful things about you; looking after Mo, looking after Tom. I'm really grateful, you know."

"The knack of looking after your sister is to make her think she's looking after you. And to be fair, we've taken care of each other really…"

A burst of raucous laughter interrupted Rob mid- sentence. The sound came from an adjacent table, where a group of the newcomers were talking and laughing loudly.

"I reckon they've been at it all day, since first thing. Maria walked in on them not half an hour ago. Apparently Cai's got a bit of a reputation with the ladies here. Funny really, he always seemed a bit shy to me."

"I don't blame him. It's been over a year. I expect she's busy with the baby – and if Carmen's offering… lucky git!"

Neither Nia, Rob nor Idwal acknowledged the conversation, though Idwal decided privately that he would definitely be having a word with Cai.

"So, where's Mo now?" Nia piped up swiftly to prevent an awkward silence.

"At the range." Rob's tone was ominous.

"Oh." Nia was well aware of the foulness of Mona's mood if she'd resorted to throwing daggers.

"But there's some good news. She's finally agreed to let us take Tommy to the mainland for a day-trip."

"What!"

"It's ok – she only agreed we could tag along with Siân and Dafydd on the big shop for the party. I tried to convince her we were enough protection for old stinky pants, but she insisted on Sioned riding shotgun."

"What time are you off?" Nia asked. "I could really do with something from Superdrug."

Rob gave her a sympathetic smile. Nia still suffered terribly every month, and he knew what she needed. "Early tide. We'll have to hang around in Bangor till the shops open. And don't tell anyone else! It's not a normal run and we need to keep the requests down."

"Thank you," she said, stroking Tom's sleeping head.

≈

Mona wasn't surprised at the rustiness of her aim. But she kept at it, and by her second hour on the range she'd hit her stride. Learning to throw a knife so that it would kill someone took time and practice. Fortunately, you didn't need to think too hard, and hours could disappear, taking misery with them.

Since the arrival of Tom, she'd had very little opportunity to indulge herself – just a few hours here and there – but Rob had guessed her mood correctly today, and allowed her time off until the next feed was due. The sneak had struck a deal in return though, and just the thought of it made her go cold. Mona wondered whether she'd been too hasty in agreeing to the this trip. Rob didn't see danger or threat, and he was great with Tom, but could he really protect him? Dafydd would be there too of course, and Sioned was becoming a skilful fighter. On the other hand, the proposed trip meant both Tom and Rob would be safe from Cai for a few hours... and that was the clincher. They could have their outing.

Mind made up, Mona threw her final dagger of the day. It struck the target perfectly, right between the freshly painted, bright blue eyes.

≈

Rob had disappeared with alarming speed when Tom started making his little chuntering sounds.

"He's a lovely lad," Idwal observed as Rob raced away through the mess hall doors.

"He and Mona have really looked after each other," Nia agreed. "They're a great team actually, and they share an odd sense of humour." There was a brief silence before Nia broached the conversation they'd overheard earlier. "Cai's my cousin, but I will murder him if it's true – and it's bound to be true." Staring down at the dregs in her teacup, she continued. "I warned her about him, right from the off."

"I quite like him," Idwal said simply, and Nia gave him an icy stare.

"Cúchulainn," she snorted with a surprising amount of aggression.

"Cu who?" he said looking around, and she frowned at him.

"Cúchulainn, the great Irish hero." Idwal shook his head, nonplussed, and Nia sighed. "The Hound of Ulster?" She seemed a little disappointed. "So you don't know any more about Celtic culture than Mo."

"No, sorry. I've been in the army," he said simply. "And then on the run... when I got my uncle's letter."

"But you found Druids in Cornwall."

"I followed Brendan's instructions... and they led me there." There was a moment of quiet that Idwal tried to fill. "So this hero?"

"Hero or not, Cúchulainn *was* a hound where women were concerned."

Idwal began to feel uncomfortable. "And Cai?"

"King hound," she answered unequivocally.

"There was another nickname Glyn and Alun used for Cai..." Idwal said to change the subject.

"Cernnunos?"

"Yes! That was it." Idwal was relieved he'd managed to turn the conversation.

"Well at least sex and impregnantion were Cernunno's divine duty", Nia scoffed disdainfully. "Cai seems to approach it more like a full-time hobby."

"Well, I know they've got a baby together now." Idwal squirmed. "But there doesn't seem to be any... affection between them anymore. In fact, I got the distinct impression Cai doesn't even believe Tom's his."

Nia remembered the change that Mona had wrought in Cai during the few short weeks they'd spent together. It had been truly amazing to see his customary melancholy morph into smiles and laughter. Yet Nia knew her cousin too well. She had warned Mona about him *ad nauseam*, and in her heart she wasn't surprised by his behaviour, just disappointed.

"That's ridiculous! Anyone can see the resemblance. The problem is, of course, Mona loves him."

Idwal snorted. "I can't imagine that! Mona in love."

"I didn't say that, and anyway, have you ever seen them fight each other?"

Idwal didn't really know what Nia meant by her last statement, but thought it best to say nothing more on the subject. "Well, I suppose we could just sit here till dinner?" Idwal sighed.

"I'm doing some research in the library – such as it is," Nia answered promptly. "Is there any chance you can help me?"

"Erm, I'm not actually as dopey as Mona, but I'm no scholar either," he confessed.

"I'm trying to establish some specific links between a few ancient symbols and Mona's *mark*." She eyed him intently. "And I think you may be the next best thing."

≈

Bryn sat in the chair and Rob lay on the bed strumming.

"She's in pieces, and I don't know how to help her."

35

"She's not your responsibility." Bryn had accepted Rob's relationship with Mona, but he was not close to her. Bryn felt close to no one but Rob.

"I love Mona and Tom as if they were my own family. We are a family in a funny sort of way," he whispered. Bryn looked uneasy. It wasn't quite jealousy, but it was close. "How can she love a man like Cai?" Rob continued. "Didn't you see him with that woman? Mona's never been in pain like it. He could actually destroy her."

"No one can destroy her, Rob, least of all Cai."

"Are you talking about a different man?" Rob was irritated by Bryn's cavalier attitude towards Mona's plight, and Bryn knew it, knew his body language like a favourite album.

"Mona and Cai are thunder and lightning," he said. "It's old, old magic, Rob."

≈

Within seconds of walking into the library with Nia, it became apparent to Idwal that this was her private domain. It wasn't *the* library, it was *Nia's* library, and Idwal instantly began to feel awkward. She obviously hoped he could help her find answers and settled down immediately to search for a passage in a large volume – one of many. She was almost hidden behind the piles of books.

"So, I'm amazed you speak Cornish so well," she carried on conversationally, "bearing in mind Mona's trouble with Welsh. Have you managed to pick up any Welsh or Brythonic?"

If he smiled and nodded, Idwal thought, she might presume he'd understood her. It was clear from her pained expression that Nia hadn't fall for the ploy. So staring at the floor, he started to fiddle with a peeled corner of the table. "I'm sorry, Nia. Maybe I'm not the best person to help you; you've lost me already."

He's going to leave, Nia thought suddenly. She'd always used her intellect before to discourage unwelcome attention – and it had been a great tactic, had worked every time. But she didn't want Idwal to go. "There's no reason you should know this stuff." She stood up so he could see her. "Perhaps I should just give you a potted history and we can look through those references another day."

"Sounds like there might be an exam at the end of it," he said softly.

Nia's smile froze – was he joking? She couldn't tell, as he still seemed to be finding the table very interesting. Then he lifted his head, eyes brimming with the strange humour he shared with his sister. *Please stay,* she chanted in her mind. "Idwal, I'm a geek. All this stuff." She flailed her arms in random directions. "I'm obsessed. This is all I do." It sounded too much like a confession, and now he was laughing at her, or at least doing his level best not to.

"So how bad is it, Nia? Do you have to sneak back here in the early hours for a fix? Or are you just a binge reader?"

Nia found it impossible to stop herself smiling. "Bit of both actually."

The silence wasn't awkward now, just expectant. "Come on then," he groaned. "Looks like I've got a lot of catching up to do. Why don't you start at the very beginning, and assume I know nothing."

Nia was delighted, and began to ask some simple questions. "You're almost fluent in Cornish now. When did you start learning it?"

"About eighteen months ago, I suppose. I picked it up quite quickly." He shrugged at her supportive smile. "It's easy when you're immersed in it. The lads speak Cornish all the time."

"Except when they need to speak to another Celt." Idwal was slightly taken aback by Nia's sharp tone.

"But *you* speak both Cornish and Welsh… don't you?" Idwal asked, tilting his head to one side. "How many languages can you speak?"

Nia's immediate instinct to give the facts unequivocally stalled. Maybe confessing her fluency in all five Celtic languages might be a mistake on this occasion. "I get by," she replied noncommittally

"And Mo's been here over a year. Hasn't she learned any Welsh at all?" Idwal asked, shaking his head.

Nia raised her eyes to the ceiling. "No! Unbelievable, I know! She still can't speak a word, and we've all tried to help her."

"She's difficult to teach." Idwal obviously spoke from bitter experience and Nia nodded vehemently in complete agreement.

≈

When Nia began the lesson, she decided against a chronological history. "Nothing was ever recorded contemporaneously, so most of it is detective work and myth. And I know we're always talking about being Druids, but that's not strictly true either. However, we are Celts." There was a schoolmarmish tone to Nia's lecture that Idwal found completely beguiling. As she warmed to her theme, her face lit up with excitement. "Somewhere around 1200 BC, the Iron Age began in Britain. The whole of what is the UK and Ireland now was made up of tribes, mainly Celtic in nature. People used to think the Celts were a single race, but it's more likely they were diverse populations of people, who shared a broad culture and language. That would seem to make sense..." Nia waggled her head from side to side as she weighed up how much detail to include. "As the archaeological evidence shows, the Celts ventured out in every direction from Central Europe. They covered all of Britain and a huge part of Western Europe, even parts of Spain. Clearly not one race."

Nia spared Idwal a quick glance to check he was following. Assured that he was, she launched back into her sermon.

"I'm simplifying horribly, but the European Celts were called Continental and those in Britain and Ireland were called Insular. The Insular Celts were subdivided into the Brythonic-speaking: Welsh, Cornish and Breton. And the Goidelic: Irish, Manx and Scottish – Gaelic if you like. Do you see?"

Idwal did, but thought he'd try to show off something he had actually learnt on his travels. "What about Galicia and Asturias? They're Celts."

Nia looked fit to burst with glee at his question. "Ah yes! The Galician Problem." She almost swooned. "Academics are locked in fierce debate about the inclusion of those two nations into the Celtic family. The basis for the argument is the..." Nia glanced at Idwal. "Any way, I'm going off topic. It's complicated..."

"But what do you think, Nia? Are they Celts?" Idwal moved forwards, just grazing Nia's personal space. She lost her train of thought, her reason scattered. "I...er...what was I saying?"

"Galicia, Asturias..."

"Yes, of course they are." She stared into his eyes for slightly longer than she needed to. "Anyway." She shook her head. "As I was saying... Druid is too simplistic, because that is not *all* we are. It's widely accepted that Celtic society was roughly divided into three groups: a warrior aristocracy, an intellectual class, and then everyone else. Druids were part of the intelligentsia, which was itself subdivided into three: Bards, Ovates and Druids proper."

"Yes, Cai mentioned something about this: Bards – singers and poets; Ovates – healers and doctors; and Druids, who were the priestly magicians." Idwal laughed and wiggled his fingers melodramatically, as if casting a spell.

"Priestly magicians, I like that," she chuckled. "Though Paganism is more of a way of life than a religion. We celebrate nature essentially, and a great deal of our spiritual life is bound to the changing of the seasons. Ceremonies are held in our sacred sites: Bryn Celli Ddu, Barclodiad y Gawes and Din Llugwy... of course... though we mostly celebrate our rites here..." For some reason, Nia found herself studying the shape of his lips. "We honour our ancestors there, drawing on their wisdom and strength at the appointed times: Imbolc, Beltane, Lughnasadh, Samhain." She cleared her throat. "There are the Solstice festivals in Summer and Winter, together with the Autumn and Vernal Equinox." Idwal was watching her intently, and Nia looked away before she lost her train of thought again. "Without doubt, we've been trying to preserve our Druidic abilities for millennia. But of course, that's no good on its own. You need to have protection. You need to eat."

"So you're saying we're like... tiny individual Iron Age tribes, scattered around what's left of the Celtic lands?"

"I suppose I am." Nia seemed impressed with his overly simplistic analogy.

"And has it worked? Have we protected those... abilities?" Idwal asked, sceptically.

"No!" Nia practically exploded with enthusiasm. "We're in massive magical decline. But Mona... Mona is *everything*."

"What, my sister Mona?"

"As far as I can tell, she's the culmination of warrior aristocratic and Druidic talent... she's some sort of key."

"But she can't even speak Welsh!"

"I know! It's so exciting, isn't it?" Nia beamed.

Idwal couldn't see it. However, he hadn't failed to notice that Nia had gradually moved closer and was now almost within touching distance. He felt a desperate urge to reach out, but she was just too wonderful to frighten off. "Carry on," he insisted.

"So, the Romans demolished the Continental Celts and moved towards Britain." Her seriousness drew Nia even nearer. "They were intent on destroying Anglesey – Ynys Môn – as it was supposed to be the centre of Celtic Druidic activity and learning. And they did of course."

While she thumbed through pages for a quote, Idwal studied her, admiring the curling, honey-coloured hair as it spilled across her face and books.

"Here it is. It's only Tacitus, and there's no knowing if he used eyewitness accounts, but it is a source of sorts:

'*On the coastline, a line of warriors of the opposition was stationed, mainly made up of armed men, amongst them women, with their hair blowing in the wind, while they were carrying torches. Druids were amongst them, shouting terrifying spells, their hands raised towards the heavens, which scared our soldiers so much that their limbs became paralysed. As a result, they remained stationary and were injured. At the end of the battle, the Romans were victorious, and the holy oaks of the Druids were destroyed.*'"

"But that wasn't it for us. How come?"

"If Mona had been there, what do you think she would have done, Idwal?"

"Fight." There was no hesitation.

"What about Tom?"

Idwal tried to imagine how his sister would act. It was easy. "She'd have sent him away. They would know about the invasion beforehand. It wouldn't be a surprise."

Nia clapped her hands together. "Yes, she would. *She did.* Mona sent us away when the Irish invaded. It's not too big an assumption that, back then, the children, some teachers and even some warriors would have been preserved by sending them away. Somewhere safe. The Romans never conquered Scotland or Ireland, and I believe they were sent there. Christianity did its fair share of Druidic persecution later on, but still, that's my basic point."

"And after a certain amount of time…"

Nia nodded. "We started to come back."

Idwal couldn't quite see why. "Why here, why Anglesey?"

"Anglesey, Ynys Môn, has been called '*Môn Mam Cymru* – The Mother of Wales'. That's not a geographical point." Nia seemed to think she'd made a joke and Idwal smiled out of courtesy. "Because of our magic!" she grinned impishly, and Idwal's breath caught. "At the risk of sounding like a nineteenth-century Celtic romanticist, some people have even argued that Ynys Môn might be Avalon – from Arthurian legend and Grail mythology."

Idwal didn't laugh, but he wanted to. It was all getting very weird.

Nia continued, unperturbed by his scepticism. "The word *Avalon* comes from *afallach* – rich in apples – and Ynys Môn was known for apple production at one point."

"So is Kent. Arthur could have made his home on the Isle of Sheppey." Idwal couldn't help the little joke, but Nia didn't seem upset.

"Yes, I grant you it's a bit tenuous. Interesting though." Nia finished with a yawn. "What time is it?"

"Three-thirty."

"In the morning?" Nia was astonished.

"Here, let me help you clear away. I'll walk you back."

"Thanks." Nia dimpled.

"No problem. I don't want you stumbling across any Romans."

4

Decision

Hywel couldn't find enough spittle in his mouth to moisten an envelope, so he folded the note to Ifan and laid it on his neatly made bed.

The old man couldn't actually look at the dagger without imagining it disappearing into his daughter's chest. He hadn't ever known why he'd needed to keep the evil blade. Until now. It had been stored in this room ever since his precious daughter, Rhiannon, and her husband, Gwilym, had died upon it. Its hiding place had remained a close-guarded secret, surviving countless searches over the lonely years. It was only now Hywel understood the reason behind the most recent search. Not for stolen gold, but for evidence of the spy. The spy who strutted openly through these corridors, suckling her vile offspring.

When he finally picked up the dagger, Hywel felt the justice of his resolution all over again. This was the only weapon in the *Conway* that could overcome Mona's grisly talents. He'd also need it to dispose of the Englishman in her bed – who would no doubt attempt to protect the evil tick at her breast.

The corridors of the *Conway* were rarely completely empty, but Hywel thought his best chance lay in the small hours before dawn. His grip on the dagger tightened as he stole his way towards Mona's room.

Pausing outside her door, Hywel collected himself. Speed and savagery would be his only hope. There was the sudden sound of footsteps in the corridor behind him, and Hywel placed his hand on the handle. It lurched away from him as the door was opened from the inside. Standing in the doorway, with his back to Hywel, was the English giant. He was facing Mona's bed and talking. "Come on, Sion, we need to get a move on."

The sound of his granddaughter's name in Rob's Saxon mouth enraged Hywel, but even in his fury he registered the deliberately hushed tones. Mona and her offspring were obviously still asleep. Decision made, Hywel struck out with the dagger as hard as he could, plunging its blade into the Englishman's back. His body awash with sudden, unexpected pain, Rob staggered, and then fell to the ground.

Hywel stepped quickly past him, hurrying across the room towards the sleeping mother and child. From somewhere behind him, Hywel heard Sioned's shriek of surprise and horror, but the old man was only an arm's length away now. He pulled it back, ready to strike.

Rob began to screech as he crawled across the floor, grabbing for Hywel's feet. The commotion woke Mona, giving her time to free a leg from the bedclothes and kick the cruel blade aside. Rob tried but failed to hold on to the old man, who wriggled free and thrashed his way towards the baby. Mona seized him by the shoulders as he spat and foamed.

"I know it all now. I know what it is. It *needs* to die." A desperate final strength bloomed in his wiry sinews, and Hywel flung himself at Tom, his teeth bared.

Mona felt the heat in her hands and tried to rein in the destructive impulse, but nothing could quell the rush of energy surging through her. As she watched, helpless, Hywel's body superheated, and then exploded. Sioned started to scream.

≈

44

Waking in the early hours, Cai felt sick and sore. A glance at another empty bottle told him why. In between periods of sexual frenzy, he had more or less slept and drunk away a whole day.

Lying in Carmen's bed and looking up at the ceiling, he started to think again. His certainty in his love for Mona had sustained him for a year. He hadn't even considered that her feelings weren't the same. It really had just been sex for her, and the irony of the situation hit home. Maybe that was why he had fallen for her.

Glancing over at Carmen, he realised that whatever magical control she had over other men, it clearly didn't hold as much sway with him. Cai didn't even think he liked her particularly. When she wasn't speaking drivel, she was gossiping. He knew he could spend another full day in bed with Carmen and still feel just as unfulfilled. Cai felt a sharp pang of conscience at the thought. He had used her enough already, and too roughly.

Predictably, he found himself wondering about Mona's relationship with the Englishman. Somehow, Rob didn't really look man enough for Mona, and he certainly didn't move like a fighter. Cai could probably hurt him if he got the man on his own. Almost immediately, Cai pictured Mona defending her lover against him. The thought of fighting her in earnest was a cocktail of lust and hatred injected directly into his bloodstream. It was an aphrodisiac more potent than anything he'd felt over the last twenty-four hours with Carmen.

Fantasising like this was bordering on madness, and Cai knew he had to leave. Logistically, that wasn't a problem for him anymore. He could easily stand on his own two feet in the outside world. Cai could find work in any office and fuck women in stationery cupboards, like he should have done with Stacey. All that misplaced honour annoyed him now and he craved a way out.

There was no way he could stomach living in the same building as Mona and her new family. There wasn't anything keeping him here any longer, apart from Sioned, of course, and Taid. Returning to Eigg and the English couple wasn't really an option in his present state of mind, but he could crew his way around the world. He'd overheard some talk about it, from snatched conversations on the south coast. Rich men paid good money, even to deckhands. You lived on the boat and went to fabulous locations, where the possibilities for exotic sex were limitless. Cai knew he'd be an engineer in no time – and that could be a very good wage indeed.

Leaving the community would create a mountain of bureaucratic grief, but in his mind, Cai had already escaped. After extricating himself gingerly from Carmen, he dressed and moved soundlessly out of the room.

"So... Carmen?" Cai didn't turn all the way round to look at Idwal. Just a glance over his shoulder assured him the big man meant business.

"What do you want, Idwal?" he asked wearily, guessing the answer.

That answer never came, though, because a familiar scream pierced the early morning quiet. Cai and Idwal reacted to it simultaneously – sprinting towards the sound, which had now morphed into panicked shouting.

Even before Cai skidded round the last bend, he knew it was Sioned. His sister continued to scream and struggle as Cai caught her by the shoulders, a second later. Sioned pointed towards Mona's door, but Idwal had already smashed his way through it, into the smell of burning and tragedy.

Through the gap, Cai saw Rob lying across Mona's floor, either dead or unconscious. She shouted instructions to her brother while shoving the child into his arms. "Check him for burns," she ordered.

Cai watched in horror as Mona dragged the bloody clothes from the man's body and heaved him against her, as quickly as his dead weight would allow. She knelt beside him and cradled Rob in her arms. Her eyes were closed and she was murmuring into his hair. Floating all around them were grainy remains of ash, and Sioned's babbling now made sense. The ash was his taid. Mona had just slaughtered his grandfather.

46

Still holding Sioned tight to him, Cai forced her away from the carnage and out into the corridor. People were starting to gather and react. Someone took Sioned from him, and sometime later he found himself looking up into Ifan's sad, old eyes.

"Come… see me." The old man's words were fumbled through his tears.

Cai was left alone again, slumped bonelessly on the ground. He had finally found the energy to stand up, when Idwal emerged from the room. They stared at each other for a moment. The enormity of the situation was slowly dawning on Cai. His taid was dead. Mona had murdered him.

"He tried to kill them," Idwal stated.

Was it some sort of excuse for the murder of the man who'd loved him all his life? "Really? Did you see it, Idwal? Were you there?"

"How dare you fucking…" Idwal clenched his teeth and fists.

"What! How dare I what? Question Mona? Isn't anyone allowed to do that anymore? She's just killed my grandfather!" he screamed hoarsely.

Idwal took a great stride towards him. Lifting Cai by the scruff of his neck, he swung and crashed him against the door. Immobilised, Idwal grabbed him by the shirt and delivered an efficient jab to his head. Cai crumpled to the floor, knocked out momentarily.

"Stop!" Mona staggered from the bathroom. Idwal had witnessed her drawing poison from Rob and vomiting up some repulsive black gunge. Finally emptied of the venom, she'd caught her brother lamping Cai on the jaw. "What have you done to him?" She fell to her knees beside Cai, touching the planes of his face to feel how badly he was hurt. "He's out cold, you bloody idiot. He's unconscious."

"He needed teaching a lesson," Idwal growled back. But the anger had gone and regret had already started to replace it.

Mona could afford to touch Cai, now he was unconscious. The brave, beautiful man she might have loved and had now lost. She stroked his hair, wanting to kiss him, even though she knew she couldn't. Mona launched her fury against her brother instead. "This isn't you, you're not like this. He didn't attack us. For Christ's sake! I've just killed his grandad. Can't you cut him some slack?"

"Mo, he's sleeping with Carmen. He's cheating on you."

One last stroke and Mona's hand reluctantly left Cai's hair. "No," she sighed. "Not cheating. We might have had something before he went away. That's..." Mona finally made it true by telling someone else. "That's gone now. And I know he's with Carmen." She exhaled her regret in a lumpy sigh. "I don't blame him. She's pretty, she doesn't have a baby, and I very much doubt she can burn men alive by just touching them." Mona huffed one humourless laugh. "I can really see the attraction."

"Please don't joke about this, Mo. Tom's his son and I haven't even seen him look in the boy's direction, let alone pick him up. I know it was a shock, but he's just got to man up about it."

Mona closed her eyes and got to her feet. Cai didn't deserve that one. "It's more complicated than that."

"Then tell me. Maybe I can help." Idwal pulled her to a chair and, weakened by his concern, Mona was almost tempted to tell him everything.

"I don't... I won't destroy him, Idwal. Anyway, he's better off with Carmen. They make a good couple." She paused; this might be a good time to talk about her plan. "I need to leave here, Id. I've wanted to go for a while, but I promised Cai I'd wait till he got back. That doesn't really matter anymore." She stole another glance at Cai's inert body. "We could leave together now. I've got the money from the house in Kent. We could travel the world: America, Australia..."

"Yes," Idwal answered, but he sounded strangely reluctant. Mona was surprised; he'd been here only a couple of days. "Let's talk about it later. I think you're still in shock. I bloody well am."

≈

Cai lay on his side where he had fallen. He'd been knocked out for a few seconds, hurt and dazed, but he was no longer unconscious. Having heard their conversation, he wished he was.

5

Facts

Eventually, two crotchety old blokes had forced Idwal out of Mona's room. He'd wanted to stay and help her, but they made it clear he wasn't welcome and he didn't want to start another fight. So he just paced up and down outside in the corridor for a couple of minutes, hot, trembling and helpless. Idwal wanted to understand what had just happened. How his sister had so effortlessly incinerated an old man. The smell of the vile, black vomit burnt the inside of his nostrils, and he'd had to swallow back his own nausea.

He needed some answers, and though Nia wasn't likely to be in her library just yet, Idwal decided to go there anyway and wait for her. When Nia did arrive, her face was raw from crying.

"It was self-defence." Idwal rose to his feet in a rush, making Nia jump. "He attacked Tom." Nia held a hand over her mouth to stop the sobs, but she nodded; she knew the truth from Sioned. "I don't understand what she did. How can she…?" His hands flopped to his sides. Idwal was truly lost. He was actually frightened by what he'd just witnessed.

"It's all right, Idwal."

He shook his head manically from side to side. "No! It's not all right. She burnt him alive, Nia, with her hands." He held his own out in front of her to illustrate his disbelief. "What is it?"

Nia took his hands and steadied them in her own tiny pair. "It's magic." She smiled.

Idwal frowned and tried to close his mind as well as his eyes. He didn't want to even contemplate the idea of magic, but he was running out of alternatives.

"I don't believe in magic, Nia."

She laughed. "Well, I think it's high time you started." Idwal pulled away from her and spread his arms across the table for support. Nia tried to calm him again by rubbing her hand over his back – it was massive.

"So it's a weapon? She's a weapon?"

"It's an instinctive reaction to threat. I haven't been able to get much more out of Mona than that. I don't think she believes in magic either." Nia sighed. "She doesn't understand how or why it happens, and I've got a suspicion she's frightened of it – for that very reason."

"And the vomit?"

"As far as I can tell, that is a more deliberate act. She draws out the poison through touch and regurgitates it somehow."

"And it doesn't affect her? The poison?"

Nia shrugged. She didn't have an answer. "I only know that it works." Nia's delicate shoulders moved up and down under her summer dress. "She healed me last year. I would have died without her help."

Idwal searched Nia's soul with the briefest of glances. "Have you any idea how mad this sounds, Nia? She's my baby sister."

For the second time in a day, Nia found it difficult to concentrate. Under Idwal's scrutiny, her thoughts felt disordered and chaotic. Struggling to compose herself, Nia re-told the story. "The blade was impregnated with a chemical compound the Irish have started using. That very blade killed Hywel's daughter Rhiannon – Cai's mam." Nia couldn't believe how darkly the tragedy had ended. "He must have kept it."

"Why kill Mona?"

50

"He didn't trust her. He was frightened of her," Nia answered Idwal's questioning glance. "Her power terrified him," she sighed. "That and her relationship with Cai."

Idwal's hands left the table and gravitated to the top of his head. He knitted them together at the reminder. "I just hit Cai." He put his head in his hands, but peeked through the fingers to see her reaction.

"Good," she replied sharply. "He's hurt Mo badly enough."

"Actually, she seems all right about it," Idwal said quietly.

Nia made a noise of disbelief. "She *seems* all right about a lot of things. Mona often wears a resolute face to mask her pain."

Idwal recognised the wisdom of her words and, decision made, he finally sat down. "Look, Nia, are there any books in English on this stuff? I'm not convinced about this mumbo jumbo, but perhaps I should do my own research."

Agreeing, Nia delved directly into a pile of books. She eventually came up for air with an armful of volumes. "This is all background stuff – the most important texts are in Irish and Welsh. You're bright, you're already improving with spoken Welsh, and I'm sure you'll pick it up in no time, but you need to read those first, ok?"

≈

Cai stumbled back along the corridor making for his own room and desperately trying to eradicate the horrific images from his mind. But they were indelible: his grandfather's ashes strewn over the bed as Mona resuscitated her lover; Mona's hands in his hair; her words to Idwal; Mona leaving. He bounced from one side of the corridor to the other. It was part hangover, part shock and part head injury, and he didn't see Ifan until the Archdruid was upon him.

"I know you've been avoiding me, boy, but I need to talk to you."

Cai registered very little apart from the curt tone and the word *boy*. "Not now you don't."

It was a warning of sorts, but not one Ifan took seriously. The old man had already grabbed his arm as he pushed past. "Yes, *now*, Cai."

A surge of vitriol flared in Cai and he pressed the old man to the wall. "Not if it's about Mona or Taid I don't. Now leave me…"

"Mona hasn't told you everything you need to know," Ifan fumed, cutting across the younger man. "And don't you dare tell me you don't want to talk about your grandfather. We need to talk – now."

Ifan wasn't up to striding anymore, but he gave a good approximation of it, leaving Cai stooped and alone in the corridor.

≈

The knock at Ifan's door came earlier than expected. The Archdruid thought Cai might have washed and changed first, but it was the same stinking, soiled creature who slunk into the room, and lowered himself into the armchair opposite. It wasn't until Cai reached for the mug that Ifan noticed his black eye.

"How did you get that?"

"Idwal," Cai grunted between sips.

"It was only a matter of time, I suppose."

Cai shrugged wearily in agreement.

"Hywel was my friend for over sixty-five years." Ifan began. "Don't think the last two hours haven't been torture. I knew him better than anyone."

Ifan clearly wanted to talk about Taid. He had something to say and thought Cai needed to hear it.

"Apparently, Hywel didn't know about the run to the mainland today. He would have had an easy time of it if both Mona and Rob had been asleep. It was that big curved knife, so your sister said… I knew he'd changed since your mam and dad…" Ifan stopped talking and bent low over the desk. He cried soundlessly, tears seeping from his eyes and onto his thermal vest, but Cai couldn't seem to find the emotional energy to comfort him in any way.

"How did he think he could get away with it?" Cai asked eventually.

"He didn't. It was essentially a suicide mission." In a strange way, it relieved Cai that his grandfather hadn't planned on sailing away into the night. "He left a note and I've read it and reread it, trying to discover a hidden meaning amongst the rambling," Ifan added quietly.

"I don't want to read it," Cai said. "Just tell me." He could see the letter on the desk, written in his grandfather's impeccable handwriting, but he couldn't bring himself to reach across and pick it up.

"Hywel believed he was doing his final duty by killing Mona. It was to protect us from her – and Tom." Ifan bowed his head. "I'm rather afraid all this may well be my fault, having confided my fears in my old friend. It seems he left here intent on murder."

"So he's not the spy? I thought maybe…"

"Yes, in a way I was hoping I could find evidence of that. However, I'm very much afraid your grandfather was just a sad, old man, driven to madness by grief… doing what he thought best in the circumstances. Our spy is an altogether more capable threat. Someone who has the ability and freedom to travel and deliver information."

"I'm sorry?" Cai squinted through the fug of pain and confusion. "How can killing Mona save us?"

"Think about it," Ifan snapped. "She bears the *mark,* the *mark* of those who killed his daughter. Can't you remember the fear she provoked last year?"

Cai's feelings about Mona were so far out of whack that it wasn't a question he could answer accurately, but, yes, he could remember the fear. "But she fought against the Irish when they attacked. Didn't she prove herself then?"

"To a certain extent, and Hywel may have believed in her innocence until the end of his days; if I had only kept my mouth shut." Ifan groaned with regret. "I made the mistake of telling him about the boy's father. It seems that was the last straw, and he became determined both of them should die."

"You said only the four of us knew," Cai challenged the old man.

Ifan banged the desk, slopping his tea. "I was at my wits' end with your behaviour. I needed help. Mona needed help. I wanted your taid to talk some sense into you. You'd even ignored Arwel."

Ifan deflated, his temper spent. "I was wrong to confide in him, and now I fear we've run out of time."

"For what?"

"To help Mona. To stop her before she kills us all."

Cai's mouth opened and shut several times before he could get any words out. "So you're saying Taid was right... she is... one of *them*?"

Ifan shook his head and took a long, deep breath, dreading the task ahead. "For all her talents, Mona has a very sizeable Achilles heel. It was something I became vaguely aware of last year, when Nia sang in the chapel. Throughout her life, Mona has struggled with language; it somehow slides over her brain. However, when Welsh or indeed Irish is spoken directly to her..." Ifan frowned as another thought came to trouble him. "Or when the emotions behind the words are suitably powerful – she can be overcome by them. It is as if the... sentiments contained in the words are channelled directly into her brain. When Mona is in thrall to their power, it is possible to make her feel, and consequently do, anything." Ifan paused to let the information sink in. "I hadn't told anyone about my suspicions, not even Hywel, but when Gareth arrived here, he knew exactly how to use Mona's weakness against her. He had the most beautiful speaking voice, for which I'm sure he was especially chosen. Somebody else, our spy I suppose, must have been taking notes as well. In the short time he was here, Gareth spoke or sung continually, especially around Mona. It distracted her senses, making her blind to any threat. When entranced in this way, Mona can be persuaded to do anything, and even feel good about it while it's happening."

"Who was he?" Cai finally asked, not sure he wanted to know the answer.

"A week or so after you had sailed, Gareth arrived here with Rob. He had all the information, knew all the names – the spy is thorough."

Cai winced again at the betrayal. "So if Gareth already knew about her weakness, this Rob..." Cai swallowed, finding it hard to say the man's name, "can't possibly be the spy?"

Ifan shook his head, very slowly. "I don't know, son. Absolutely everyone is under scrutiny." Ifan stopped talking and stared into space, lost in a web of ignorance.

"Gareth?" Cai reminded him quietly.

"He was friendly and popular," Ifan began again, his voice hushed. "He sang beautifully. Mona didn't have much to do with him, as she was absolutely determined to get the community fighting fit and ready for battle – but he kept… finding her. In retrospect, I realise he was singling her out, softening her up and testing the theory. She went to bed early most nights, and it wasn't until the party, on his last night, that Gareth made his move."

Ifan shifted a couple of times in his chair. The atmosphere in the room felt charged and oppressive. Ifan was clearly reluctant to continue, but having gone this far, he had no choice but to do so. "We found her… afterwards. Physically, she wasn't badly injured – just some minor bruising."

Cai wanted him to take the words back, to *unsay* them. "No." Cai shook his head emphatically. "No, that's not what she said… Mona said they had a relationship, that she wanted him." Cai found himself standing and clutching the sides of the desk.

"No, Cai. That wasn't the way of it."

"Not Mona. Not…" His mind was finding it hard to handle the enormity of the situation. He wanted to scream and cry and beg for it to be different.

"She doesn't consider it to be rape. Mona is acutely aware that she wanted him at that moment, that she welcomed him. It has affected her mentally. Mona is very unused to feeling vulnerable, and yet he cut straight through her defences using only words."

"Why did he do it?"

"He was probably sent here to kill her and… got carried away. Though we'll never really know. Maybe it was just because he could. Regardless, the instant he lost concentration, the spell was broken and she killed him."

Cai didn't want to think about that moment. The ejaculation and orgasm followed by the horrific, burning death, but it was not an image that could be easily dispelled. Ifan still talked. "It was well organised really. He could kill her and leave on the early morning tide as planned. As it happened, we let his mooring ropes go and no one was any the wiser. Gareth had said his goodbyes, and even our spy must have been fooled for a while."

"But you were suspicious? You followed him?" Cai's voice began to break.

"No, that was Arwel." Ifan's sudden smile was a strange mixture of indulgence and regret. "He is a truly amazing young man, and completely dedicated to Mona."

Cai tried again to shake the image of Gareth's post-coital death from his mind, but failed miserably. He felt tortured by the hopeless regret that his brother had been there to save Mona when he had not.

"The ease with which she can be compelled to do... the most awful things... is extremely dangerous. I tested her myself." Ifan's tone became ominous. "She would have willingly poured a kettle of boiling water over Tom, when he was just a few days old. I'm even sure I could have made her enjoy it." Ifan countered Cai's shocked look. "I had to judge how badly affected she was!" He shook his head again, this time in shame. "Since then we haven't had a civil word. In fact, I have feared for my life on occasion."

Another horrible truth had started to dawn on Cai. Hadn't he used the same tactic on Mona last year? Cajoling her with Welsh when he knew how strongly it was affecting her? Enticing her outside to betray her with a kiss.

Ifan continued, his tone relentless. "If Mona is capable of killing her own child, do you think she would stop at you or me? You haven't seen her in the teeth of battle as I have. She is absolutely capable of destroying our entire community, with a few well-chosen words and backup from our enemies." Ifan looked deep into Cai with his beady old eyes. "When you decide to snap out of your self-pitying wallow, take a moment to look at her properly. You'll see not just exhaustion and pain. Mona's frightened."

"So what can we do? How can we help her?" Cai asked automatically, then froze as he realised the alternative. "Or do you mean…?"

"Kill her? Yes, it is an option. I know she's considered it. She won't kill herself now, though for a while I wasn't entirely sure. And if you factor in Tom…"

"But you *have* considered it, haven't you?"

"Yes, and Mona knows it. That's why she's so isolated. She keeps Rob close, and he's a big help with the boy of course, but her paranoia extends even to Nia – and possibly her brother now. I know she trusts Arwel, and he would never harm her."

"*Dwi ddim am ei lladd hi* – I'm not going to kill her, Ifan, if that's what you're going to ask of me." Cai suddenly backed towards the door, a painful obstruction in his chest. His conscience fled from the disgusting thought.

Ifan sighed. "Even I'm not that much of a monster." *Are you sure?* said a tiny voice in the old man's head. *What if the plan fails?* "Sit down, Cai. It's a lot to take in – so much has happened." Ifan shuffled round to the kettle to give himself something to do. "Are there any questions you want to ask me?"

"I need to know why I'm the father. Wouldn't it be an easier lie to use Rob, if they've been… together for a year?"

There was a slight pause. "Well, a couple of things made you the best choice. Most importantly, it was common knowledge that you were intimate with Mona right up until the call came. The timing was fortuitous, and the boy has your colouring." Ifan looked across at Cai hopefully. "There isn't a chance he *is* yours?" Cai laughed, without a shred of humour. "Something funny?"

"We only spent one night together." The memory of it had kept him going for a year.

Ifan allowed him a moment's pity. "Yes, that is tragic, son. But it doesn't change the facts. Rob and Mona didn't become… close until the pregnancy was some way along, and there was no other candidate." Ifan shrugged his small, fragile shoulders. "As far as I can tell, Mona has never talked about you being the boy's father, to anyone. She was furious when I suggested it, even though I explained my reasoning."

"Your reasoning?"

"If the father's identity were known, the consequences could be grave for both of them. How many of us have lost our loved ones to this rogue Irish threat? Would Siân understand, or Sioned, if they found out that the little boy they love so much… is essentially their enemy? What if they learned of Mona's weakness? Could you guarantee that no one else would act as your grandfather did?" Ifan sighed and lowered himself onto the bench by the kitchen. He looked small and weak for the first time Cai could ever remember. "No. Someone else had to be the father, so it was you. I started spreading gossip about you being the boy's dad as soon as I learned of the pregnancy." He paused to study Cai more closely. "You should also know I told Mona to lie to you. To tell you Tom was yours."

"I would have believed her," Cai laughed, wanting to cry.

"It would have been easier all round," Ifan huffed. "Hywel need not have died." Cai put a hand up to his forehead and Ifan's tone softened. "Tom's middle name is Cai. I noticed it when Mona registered him in the book."

Cai felt a lump forming in his throat, but fought against it.

"Mona hasn't been able to confide in anyone, apart from Arwel, and he's only a boy. There's been an air of mystery and gossip surrounding Tom." Ifan sighed, rubbing his tired eyes. His tone hardened again in accusation. "Which you have now fuelled further by your behaviour with this… Carmen woman."

Carmen. A relationship Cai had thrown himself into so effortlessly, without once questioning Mona. He had wanted to hurt her so much. "Why didn't she tell me the truth, about Gareth, about Tom? Was it *just* pig-headedness?"

Ifan's slight nod gave Cai the impression that might have been part of the reason. "Mona's not used to being vulnerable, and you know she can't abide pity, but there may be more to it than that." He rubbed a hand back and forth across his stubbly white chin. "She's afraid – of you and for you, I think. Remember her power has killed three men now – of its own accord apparently. Mona fears she might kill you, if you're a threat to her baby."

"And she loves it, the child?"

Ifan stared stonily at Cai, but didn't answer.

"Is there another way we can help her, send her away...?" *She wants to go anyway,* Cai thought. Though the idea of her alone, somewhere in the world without him, felt very wrong somehow.

Ifan nodded vigorously. This was the nub of his plan. "I believe if we can train her mind, we might be able to reach past the barrier and teach her to fight it. Nia, Arwel and I have all tried, but she's almost impossible to teach." Ifan rubbed his shoulder at the memory of a particularly difficult lesson. "I was going to ask you to try, one last time, but with everything unfolding as catastrophically as it has..." Ifan creaked to his feet and took both mugs to the sink. "Mona doesn't trust me anymore, and I doubt she thinks highly enough of you to consent to these lessons, but there's just no one else." He lifted an arthritic finger. "One thing's for sure. It must be done in absolute secrecy. We must keep it from our spy."

Cai considered the task ahead as a problem to be solved. He needed to get Mona to agree to his help, and if that failed he would have to force her. "I'll talk to her," he said confidently.

Ifan looked unimpressed. "And if that doesn't work?"

"We promote her to War Chief!" The idea had come from nowhere, but as all the pieces slotted into place, Cai sat bolt upright, a sudden look of enthusiasm on his face. He spoke intently, though mindful of the need to be diplomatic. "If you step down as Archdruid, Dafydd will have to step up, leaving War Chief for Mona." Ifan didn't comment but allowed Cai to expand on his scheme. "Dafydd won't have time to train Mona, but *I* will, and we can use the new post as a smokescreen – that is, until you find the spy."

Ifan nodded sadly. It wasn't much, but it gave them some

breathing space. "We'll need to get someone in to help with day-to-day management. Arwel's up to his neck in paperwork and…"

"Idwal," Cai interrupted him.

"But he's…"

"I know, but at least he's attempting the language, and he's capable."

"Arrogant, English shit," Ifan muttered.

Cai felt his swollen eye. "He's ok."

Ifan sighed. Arwel liked Idwal, and the boy wasn't often wrong. "I suppose we'll have to trust him," Ifan decided, rapping the desk in agreement of Cai's plan. "But no one is to know about Mona's lessons, not even her brother. I've been far too trusting already."

Cai's mind was awhirl with activity. Having come up with a plan, he was eager to help Mona as best he could. "How long have I got?"

"I don't know – a few days maybe. Not long, and if it doesn't work…" Ifan left the sentence unfinished.

6

Fear

On leaving Ifan, Cai had intended to go straight to his room for a shower, shave and change of clothes. To his surprise, however, he found himself outside Mona's door. After hesitating briefly, he appalled himself by knocking on it.

Cai half hoped, half feared Mona had changed rooms in the aftermath of Hywel's attack, but after a short wait, Mona opened the door. She didn't slam it in his face, as he suspected she might, but backed away to stand defensively in front of the two sleeping figures on the bed. The light inside the room was dim, but Cai could see it was Rob, lying with Tom in his arms. He was as big and handsome as Cai had feared, and even in sleep, Rob held the boy as if he loved him. As if he wasn't holding another man's child.

Despite suffering a range of contradictory emotions, Cai had to acknowledge that Rob had all but laid down his life for Mona. Perhaps he wasn't such a bad choice for her. Wrenching his eyes from the intimate domestic scene, Cai surprised himself still further with his next words. "I could have been anyone. Why haven't you got someone posted outside the door?"

Mona had just woken up. Cai had caught her off guard and she hadn't yet had time to organise her reactions. She gave a little cough to try to buy some.

"You're right. I'll get Bryn to find someone."

"Good." Cai wanted to beg for her forgiveness, to murder again the man who had violated her, to do anything to have her back. But as he moved towards her there was no let-up in her defensive posture. Cai's head drooped. Did she really consider him a threat to her family? They both found it easier to concentrate on a point somewhere on the floor between them. "I'm not here to harm you, Mona, I just need to talk to you."

"So you've spoken to Ifan?" Her voice was quiet and hard.

"I'm sorry for the things I said. They were unforgivable." Cai waited for his forgiveness nonetheless; for her to tell him it was ok. But she didn't. "You should have told me the truth," he finally said.

Cai hadn't moved, but he seemed nearer, more menacing. "I didn't lie," she growled. "It's not like I've forgotten. I know what I felt. He didn't rape me. He just talked to me and I *wanted* him. I wanted to have sex with him... you don't understand."

At that, Cai met her eye and moved forwards – a clear, implied threat. "I could make you feel the same way by speaking two words to you, right now, and we both know it."

Mona gasped and stepped back. There was a frailty in her grey eyes that Cai hadn't seen there before.

"How dare you threaten me?" she whispered through clenched teeth.

Cai held her eye for a second longer. She would never tell him what had truly happened in that room. He sat down heavily on the edge of a chair, a waft of his own stench nauseating him. How had something so wonderful ended like this? So much wasted love. Elbows on knees and head in hands, Cai spoke wearily and quietly. "Only Ifan, Arwel and I know who the child's father is and how he managed to get to you. No one else. I'm the only one who can help you now."

"Or hurt me," she croaked, turning away from him. Cai reached out instinctively, catching her wrist.

The fire crackled amiably between them tonight. The blacksmith's family lived in a portion of the workshop. It wasn't as comfortable as the Archdruid's roundhouse, but warm, dry and filled with love. Canaid sang as she soothed their youngest child against her. Meilyr had a whittling knife in his hand, but stilled his work while he listened to her throaty sweetness. She sang a tale of love and loss drawing tears of wonder from the young blacksmith's eyes.

Mona wrenched her hand back hastily. "Get...get out. Just leave me alone."

≈

Cai stood in the shower until the water ran cold, stunned by the intensity of this second strange encounter. There was an uncomfortable familiarity about both the setting and characters that populated this tale. He pushed it away, allowing Mona's troubles to play through his mind. The grim truth was that he had left her unprotected. If he had been here when Gareth came sniffing around, Mona would have been safe in his bed, in his arms – not forced to breed some mutant progeny. Rob had been there for her since then, and Cai knew in his heart he'd lost her. But that didn't mean she had to die. Mona might not want his help, but that was what she was going to get.

He needed to speak to Sioned, but now she was sixteen, his sister had her own room, and he didn't know where to find it. Eventually, Cai tried his aunt.

"Siân, it's Cai," he said, knocking softly at her door. Sioned surprised him by opening it herself and then squashing him with an almighty hug. They'd been through this before, and as long as they held on to each other, they would cope. Cai knew he could survive his grandfather's death, but his mind couldn't seem to comprehend the loss of Mona.

After he'd outlined the basic plan, Sioned appraised her brother coolly. "Mona told me you might act like this, and I didn't believe her."

Cai shook his head at the enormity of his recent failings.

"Anyway, it's not me you need to speak to. Al's your man."

"Al?" Cai asked, confused by the name.

"Oh," Sioned replied, not wanting to revisit the nickname saga. "It's a long story, but you need to speak to Arwel. He and Mona are very close. You might just have made an enemy for life."

≈

Cai found Arwel studying in Ifan's library. He looked up and then straight back down at his books. "Have you come to debrief me about the attack? I need to know everything: the boats, the tactics, the numbers, the fighting. That's the key to getting hold of this bloody spy," he muttered fiercely.

"Later." Cai coughed. "I've come to ask for your help."

"I've got nothing to say to you." Even as a kid, Arwel had never had much of a temper, but Cai could see he was desperately trying to control it now. "I think you should go."

"I want to teach Mona – to help her fight the problem."

Arwel instantly grasped how much of the truth Cai now knew. "She's impossible to teach. We've all tried. Anyway, I thought you were too busy with Carmen."

Cai had no option but to let it go; he'd find another way without Arwel's help. He turned to leave. "Why do you want to help her anyway?" Arwel asked calmly.

Wasn't it obvious? Cai frowned. "I love her."

Arwel nodded. "And Tom?"

"He's not my son," Cai said quietly, and Arwel closed his eyes.

"That didn't seem to bother your parents, Cai. I always knew they loved me." He buried his nose back in his books. "Grow up," he murmured, not quite under his breath.

≈

Nia found herself studying Idwal as he read. He was far too big for the plastic chair, and his great, long legs were much too thick to fit under the desk. The muscles in his thighs were nearly too powerful to be contained by his training leathers. His presence provoked unfamiliar stirrings in her body, and she felt her cheeks burn with embarrassment. After re-reading the same sentence again and again, Nia gave up and took a good long look at him.

Idwal was blonde, a reddish-blonde, and his hair was a lot longer than Mona's. They shared the same bone structure and their eyes were exactly the same colour. Yet Mona didn't make her feel like this: like a silly little girl, trembling and fluttering.

Nia had a strong compulsion to push Idwal's hair out of his eyes for him. She was about to do so, but was stopped short by the sound of his loud, bellowing laughter breaking across the silence.

"Listen to this," he chortled. "'*According to Aristotle, most belligerent nations were strongly influenced by their women, but the Celts were unusual because their men openly preferred male lovers.*'" He carried on reading, the smile still in his voice. "Apparently, this bloke Diodorus said '*though Celtic women are beautiful, men prefer to sleep together, and young men will offer themselves to strangers and are insulted if the offer is refused.*' Rob will love this."

Nia was giggling herself by now. "There *is* evidence of strong male bonding rituals."

"I'll bet there is! It's amazing any of us survived, if all the men were busy *bonding* with each other."

Nia scrambled for a book, holding her hand palm outwards to keep Idwal quiet until she'd found her quote. "Ok, this is a comment on the sexuality of Celtic women by Cassius Dio." She coughed melodramatically. "'*A very witty remark was made by the wife of Argentocoxus, a Caledonian, to Julia Augusta. When the empress was jesting with her, about the free intercourse of the Celtic women with the men of Britain, she replied: "We fulfil the demands of nature in a much better way than you Roman women; for we consort openly with the best men, whereas you let yourself be debauched in secret by the vilest."*'"

The topic of discussion had made Nia flushed and excited. Looking at her, Idwal marvelled at how small and perfect she was. He wanted to pick her up, but feared he might break her. "I'll concede that one, but I'm on the hunt for more male bonding."

They tried to concentrate for a few minutes longer but were soon forced to give up – both craving further interaction with the other.

"So what is Mona's other power?" Idwal hadn't thought to ask before.

"Well, fighting." Nia seemed puzzled. "Surely you've seen her fight?"

"Not since she was sixteen, and I used to beat her fairly easily then. She can't have improved that much."

Nia didn't try to hide her grin. "I'm so glad she did." Her smile faded. "We'd have been lost... when the enemy came."

"What's this Irish feud about, Nia?" Idwal had wanted to ask her thoughts on the subject for a while now.

"Arwel thinks..."

"But what do you think?"

Nia shook her head. "I don't think it's an Irish feud... it's not a nationality issue, it can't be. We're all a Celtic jumble here, pretty much a mixture: Irish, Welsh, Cornish, Manx – it keeps the gene pool healthy." She flicked her eyes up to Idwal and flushed unexpectedly. "My nana came from Galway."

"So what is it?"

Nia seemed reluctant to answer, but did eventually. "It's just one family."

"My family?" Idwal challenged her gently.

"Yes, your family. And I can't help but think it's personal... some sort of vendetta..."

Before she could explain further, there was a knock at the door. A community meeting had been set up following Hywel's death. Rumours had been flying about and people needed reassurance. Idwal was surprised to learn from the messenger that he'd been asked to join the committee meeting beforehand.

"Mona needs to be there." Nia stood up, all business once more. "Shall I go for her, Id?"

How come his nickname had never sounded so lovely before? Perhaps it was her accent. "No, I'll get her. See you in there." He rose to leave, but Idwal didn't want to go just yet. "Can I take a couple of these with me, for a bit of saucy late-night reading?"

Nia blushed violently and looked down. *Oh no*, he'd pushed it too far. She was embarrassed and upset and Idwal had the horrible feeling he'd blown it already. But Nia raised her head and gave Idwal the most level stare he could ever remember receiving.

"Here," she said, handing him a small slim volume. "Try Gwerful Mechain. Her erotic poetry is extremely powerful."

Before he could respond, Nia was nose down again in a book. He edged towards the door, now flushing furiously himself.

≈

Idwal was both shocked and pleased to see the stern-looking Bryn striding towards Mona's door. "Good thinking, mate."

"Not my idea, but I agree." Bryn looked tired and drawn.

The sound of wailing told Idwal everyone was awake, so after knocking perfunctorily he walked straight in. The sight of Mona – haggard, washed out and grey – came as a physical shock. She moved round and round the small room, jiggling Tom rhythmically in a vain attempt to quiet him. "Oh, thank God you're here," she said, lurching forwards. She spoke in an undertone, just loud enough to be heard above the din. "I've lost my milk. It must have dried up when I healed Rob. I've been trying for the last few hours…" There was pain as well as tiredness in her voice. "Please go to Siân; she'll know what to do. I can't leave Rob, and Tom's starving."

Idwal couldn't get over how fragile she seemed. "You're ill… you look ill. Get back to bed. I'll take Tom to Siân, then bring you something. What do you need? Food or…"

"No!" she shrieked. "I can't let you take him. Please help me,

Idwal." She squeezed her eyes shut. "Just get the milk and come back. And don't let anyone come with you." Mona was certain. "I can't face them, Siân, Sioned… not yet."

"They don't blame you."

Mona grimaced. "Come back soon, please."

≈

"Hurry up, Id, *hurry up*. Stop crying, Tommy, *please, please stop crying*," Mona whispered into his hot, angry head, her own tears of frustration and exhaustion absorbed by Tom's thick, dark hair. The baby had sucked and gnawed at her all day and she was sore and ravaged. But Tom was still hungry and his rage was unabated despite her pleas for calm.

When Idwal returned, he walked towards her with his hands held up in the surrender position. He was talking, but she couldn't hear him over the wailing. The next instant, he was swept aside by Siân, who wore a grimly efficient expression. She made Idwal sit down in a chair with both bottle and child, and when Siân was happy that Tom's uncle wouldn't choke him, she faced Mona.

"Come here, my love," she murmured, enclosing Mona in her soft arms. "You don't have to do this on your own. Let me help you."

Siân had come armed with healing tinctures and herbs. She administered them to Mona as the baby gulped his way into sleep and silence.

"I'm sorry about Hywel," Mona croaked. "I didn't mean to kill him."

"Sioned told me what happened. She saw it all…"

"But…"

Siân shook her head. "You need to sleep," she crooned, settling Mona down behind the recovering Rob.

Siân, however, didn't know what Mona knew. Once again, she had been overcome by the force of her untamed power. Moreover, it appeared to be growing inexorably in strength.

≈

Idwal and Siân were forced to take Tom into the committee meeting with them, where they found everyone else waiting. "Mona can't make it, she's… sleeping," Siân announced.

Cai scowled at her from across the room, but she chose to ignore him. Siân had no time for her nephew – not now he'd let Mona down so badly.

"Not to worry," Ifan said kindly. "I'm sure you'll keep her up-to-date – and Bryn too. I hear he's standing sentry." Ifan coughed to change the subject. "The facts about Hywel's death," he began, his brisk, chairman-like tone failing to conceal the quaver of emotion in his voice. "Hywel entered Mona's room early yesterday morning, expecting her to be alone and asleep. He meant to kill both Mona and her baby. Luckily, she wasn't alone. Rob was awake, and took the brunt of the attack. Though he used the corrupted blade against Rob, Hywel was no match for Mona, whose unusual power we have previously witnessed."

Having given them the basic facts, he paused before disclosing more. "It seems he used the *very* blade that killed his own child. The reasons are obvious: one touch with the tainted metal would be enough to kill even Mona. He could not have hoped to beat her otherwise. Rob, though weak, is well, as the steel has lost a great deal of its potency over the years." He coughed, that part of his performance done. "I have here the letter Hywel left for me – for us. It explains his actions to the community." Ifan passed the note to Dafydd, who, having already read it, passed it on to Siân. "I have lost a brave son and a good friend." Ifan now began his prepared speech. "And I am not the man or leader I once was. I feel it is now time for me to pass the Archdruidship on to Dafydd."

Dafydd's stony expression concealed what his heart knew. He was not ready to accept this post, and he never would be.

"As I'm sure you understand, the transition period will involve training and change. This change will affect the chain of command within the *Conway*. As I will need to spend some considerable time with Dafydd, I would like to ask Idwal to act as an interim manager – for the continued smooth running of the community."

Idwal had been ineptly trying to rearrange Tom into a more comfortable position. "What?" he asked, stunned.

"You're an obvious choice." Ifan looked to both Dafydd and Cai, who nodded their approval. "You're a leader and a good organiser. However, you will need local knowledge, so I've asked Nia to give you some assistance in this area."

Idwal glanced over at Nia and felt his face flush again.

"Mona will replace Dafydd in military command, and Cai will be her second. Bryn will have to hold the fort for a little while – until everything is resolved."

This was unexpected news, and there was a ruffle of alarm, which Ifan dealt with smoothly.

"Not many of you were here when we were attacked. Mona is the natural choice as our War Chief, with my grandson's help." He smiled wanly at Arwel. "Cai can give her support with the training, and provide information on the newcomers. I have full faith in Mona – if we have to deal with another threat."

"What if she refuses?" Idwal said, speaking to Ifan but with one eye on Cai. "She's pretty weak at the moment, and there's Tom. It's a lot to ask."

"Which is why I've asked for a support team around Mona and Tom. Siân and Sioned are willing to give her as much help as she needs in the coming days – until things stabilise and Rob is better. Cai is content with his subordinate role."

Cai again gave his agreement with a curt nod. "I'm sorry for burdening you in this way," Ifan continued quietly, "but I can no longer shoulder the responsibilities of my post. If the committee agrees, I shall perform my final act as Archdruid at my son's passing rites on Saturday."

≈

Mona woke to the sound of light but insistent knocking. Rob had begun to improve at last, but he wouldn't have the energy to get to the door. She felt washed out, but she was better off than Rob, and shuffled across the room to answer it. Bryn's expression was taut and his eyes full of worry.

"Is he awake yet?"

Mona nodded and let him in. "I'll leave you to it," she said, shambling towards the bathroom.

Bryn's hands trembled as they smoothed back the golden hair. When Rob's eyes finally fluttered open, Bryn's filled with tears of relief. His head dropped to Rob's chest, where it rose and fell gently with his breath.

"I thought you were gone," he whispered.

Rob ruffled Bryn's hair weakly. "I'll never leave you," he murmured, but was already drifting back into sleep again. Bryn kissed him lightly, and then let himself out.

≈

Ifan had said his final piece and left, leaving the hard work of negotiation still undone. Nia joined Idwal and took Tom from him. He looked relieved.

"How come something so little gets so heavy so quickly?" he said to mask the strange fluttering in his chest.

"Not so little any more, are you, Tommy boy?"

The baby sighed and nuzzled at Nia's neck, happy with her familiarity.

Nia seemed unaffected by Idwal's presence. "Are you ok with all this?" he asked. "I know you've got your own work. I don't want to be a pain."

"You'll get the hang of it soon enough," she replied helpfully. "I'll just point you in the right direction. I know what you need. Ifan's already briefed me."

Siân joined them with Hywel's final letter in her hands, and a look of deep sadness on her face. "He still believed Mona was evil." She shook her head in disbelief. "That it was his duty to save us from her – or them, in fact." Siân waved the paper. "Hywel describes Tom, his own great-grandson, as being more of a threat than Mona."

Cai watched them from across the room: Mona's loyal few. He knew he had to face them now or admit defeat right away. They seemed to huddle closer together as he approached. "I'd like to speak with you, all of you, if that's ok?"

Idwal braced himself for a confrontation, but Cai kept his body language submissive and his tone conciliatory.

"I'd like to ask for your help in convincing Mona to work with me. I know she won't want to, but I believe she's the right choice for the job, and she will need my help... initially at least."

They didn't trade glances, but Cai felt they wanted to. Idwal was the first to speak. "Look, Cai. You haven't exactly impressed me as far as Mo's concerned. She's not very strong at the moment. Maybe if we wait a while."

"There's no time," Cai blurted out. "I know I've been a shit over the last few days, but things have changed now, and I can't get to see her without your help."

This time they did swap looks, and it seemed to Cai that Idwal was softening, even if his cousin and aunt weren't.

"I don't think you realise how upset she is," Siân said with a resigned sigh.

"I'm not going to hurt her anymore, Siân. We just need to work a few things out."

She studied him sideways for a second. "Ok, you two take Tom back to her. I've got to rearrange my shifts. Good luck," she added unpromisingly.

The men were left alone together. Siân had handed Cai a large padded bag and Idwal gingerly accepted back his nephew.

"I told Mona about Carmen," Idwal mentioned as they walked at a snail's pace through the *Conway*'s corridors.

Cai nodded. "She only needs to agree to my help. Carmen, Rob, they don't matter." *I just need to sort this out,* Cai thought.

Idwal paused, struck by a sudden thought of his own. "What do you mean – Rob?"

"Well, I'll have to talk to him. Explain that it's only work," Cai clarified. Though he'd secretly hoped Idwal might have been able to smooth things over with Mona's partner. "I suppose we should try to sort out something between us… about Tom as well."

"You're not joking, are you?" Idwal seemed stunned.

"About what?"

"Mona and Rob aren't a *couple*, Cai. He's gay."

Cai didn't have time to process this information. They were at her door and Idwal asked him a question.

"So how are we going to play this?"

"I don't know. Are you sure he's gay? I mean, have you asked him? How do you know?" he hissed.

"Hi, Mo, where's Rob?" Idwal improvised as he walked in with Cai trailing behind.

"He's a bit better." Mona wasn't looking at her brother. "Gone for band practice."

"Someone should be guarding the door," Cai growled immediately, glaring at Mona. The room smelt of illness and fear and he had a powerful urge to open all the windows. Mona was curled into an armchair, arms wrapped around knees and head resting on top. She looked frail and frightened.

"Right then!" Idwal said with forced jolliness. "Let's have a little chat."

Mona carefully unknotted herself and got slowly to her feet. She moved purposefully towards Idwal, clearly intent on getting Tom away from him. Her brother pointedly ignored Mona and placed the baby straight into Cai's arms.

"You get the mugs, Mo. Cai can hold him for a minute."

The child was hot and dense, like holding a heavy, sleeping piglet. The head didn't seem adequately attached to the shoulders. Cai couldn't work out if Mona's inward breath was due to fear or anger, but he resisted looking up to find out, concentrating instead on organising his arms so he could hold the child without dropping it.

It seemed difficult to believe a kettle could take so long to boil, but while they waited, Idwal got everyone sat down and outlined the essentials from the meeting. Skilfully, he made Ifan's decision to resign as Archdruid sound perfectly reasonable and straightforward. Mona hadn't been taken in, however.

"No."

Idwal's eyes flicked to Cai's – trouble. "No what?"

"I'm not ready to take over from Emlyn, from Dafydd." Mona was not interested in the promotion. "Give it to Bryn. Anyway, I'm leaving."

"Ifan thinks you're up to it," Idwal responded carefully.

Cai knew that was a mistake, as soon as Idwal had said it. He could see the sharp suspicion in Mona's eyes and the new wariness in her posture. There was a trap here somewhere and she could smell it.

"And what's your story, Cai? How do you think you'll be able to help me?"

"I'm not bad at strategy. I've learned a lot this year from the boys and…" He cleared his throat. "I'd like to spend some time with my son." *Check.* Cai had won over Idwal, which of course was the entire purpose of the visit.

"Come on, Mo, give him a chance." Idwal tried for cheery again. "I'll break his skull if he upsets you, don't worry." But the joke fell flat, as Cai and Mona locked eyes over Tom's head.

Mona was speechless with both fear and fury. Cai wanted more access to them and it made her sick to think why. Hywel had warned her often enough about his capacity for revenge. After all, what additional proof did Cai need of the danger she posed? She'd just murdered his grandfather.

"Give me my son and get out." Her words were slow and deliberate. An atmosphere of menace filled the room like a choking cloud, and Mona no longer looked fragile.

Cai, though, remained seated, refusing to move.

"No! We have to discuss this now." She advanced on him, ready to fight for her child. "Not while I'm holding Tom," Cai barked back. "You might harm him."

"Come on, Mo. He's got a point. Let's not lose our tempers," Idwal muttered condescendingly.

How had Cai manipulated the situation so cleverly? How had Mona become the danger to Tom? She had to appeal to her brother.

"Idwal, you don't know all the facts." Could she risk everything and confide in him? A look at Cai told her the truth. She was trapped.

"Don't I?" Idwal replied slowly, eyeing Cai suspiciously again.

"Tom isn't Cai's son." She'd said it out loud at last. Cai had now bleached white with rage, but she carried on talking, explaining. "That's why he's so angry." Mona's volume had risen, but she wasn't yet shouting.

Cai stood suddenly, jarring Tom from his sleep. Idwal could not know the truth – not yet. "Then who is his father, Mona?" Cai asked, in a frantic effort to put Idwal off the scent. "Is it Rob?"

Idwal breathed again. *Rob* – it had been a simple misunderstanding. The tension in the room had begun to affect the baby, and Tom started to make sounds of distress. "It's ok, Mo, I know why Cai's angry," Idwal tried to reason with her.

But she wasn't taking any notice of her brother because Cai was getting closer. Tom squirmed and Cai didn't know how to control the jerking movements, so he just squashed the baby tighter until he reached Mona. "You're right to be frightened of me," he whispered malevolently as he passed her the child.

After Cai had slammed the door behind him, Idwal rounded on Mona. "What the hell was all that about?" Mona was trying to calm Tom and didn't answer. "Did you know he thought Rob was your boyfriend?" Idwal ploughed on. "That's why he's been so upset. I can't believe you would taunt him like that." Mona infuriated him. "I know you're angry, but that's inexcusable behaviour. Can't you see how much he wants to get to know his son?"

Mona was at a loss. Cai had somehow won over her brother. "Just promise me you'll never leave him alone with Tom."

"Don't be so…"

"Just promise me," she begged.

≈

Cai outlined his plan on the way to the canteen.

"That's quite complicated." Idwal blew out a long, whistling sigh. "A lot could go wrong and, anyway, why go to all the bother? I mean, I think she's the best person for the job, but if it's you or me, what's the real difference?"

Cai sat with his head in his hands at the table. He had fallen at the first hurdle.

"There's more to this than Tom and the job, isn't there?" Idwal asked gently. "Why didn't you just talk to her about Rob? Then all this could have been avoided. It's pretty obvious how you feel about her."

"So you'll help me?" Hope renewed, Cai sprung back into life again. He had to go. There was so much to organise before the dedications on Saturday. It only gave him thirty-six hours.

"You have to end it with Carmen," Idwal said firmly. "I'm not going to all this effort without that guarantee."

Cai agreed without hesitation. Ending it with Carmen was the least of his worries.

≈

Rob had only been allowed to leave their room after Mona had given him a final health check and a warning to stay clear of Cai. He agreed, desperate to see Bryn but nervous at what he might find.

"Come in." Bryn's voice sounded soft and desolate.

Rob held his mandolin aloft. "Would music therapy help?"

Bryn tried to smile, but it didn't really work. He lay on the bed, hunched and awkward. "I've been trying really hard not to have a drink." Even the confession annoyed Rob, and he couldn't help but let out a deep sigh. "I thought he'd killed you. And I'm sure now," Bryn continued in a whispered monotone.

"Sure about what?" Rob moved nearer, still clutching his mandolin.

"That I can't... I can't actually exist without you."

Bryn's words tightened Rob's throat, and for a split second, Bryn looked at Rob as if he *had* lost him, as if he had already died. "I love you... you're the only person I have ever loved." He swallowed loudly and with some difficulty. "You're the only person who has ever loved me."

Bryn was a man of very few words and, though sure of his love, Rob had never thought he would hear it expressed so starkly. Placing the mandolin gently on the chair, he settled down next to Bryn so they lay facing each other on their sides. Rob's nearness alone was enough to make Bryn relax and unwind. He gradually allowed Rob to pull him in, head against chest. Rob sang as he soothed him, a short, simple lullaby repeated over and over until Bryn fell asleep in his arms.

Mil harddach wyt na'r rhosyn gwyn,
Na'r rhosyn coch ar ael y bryn,
Na'r alarch balch yn nofio'r llyn,
Fy maban bach.

You are a thousand times more beautiful than the white rose,
Or the red rose on the brow of the hill,
Or the proud swan swimming the lake,
My little baby.

Knowledge

Now Idwal was legitimately allowed to spend time with Nia, he intended to throttle back any advances or risqué jokes. He had never met anyone quite like her before, and for the first time in his life he wanted to play by the rules. Behaving was hard, though, when you didn't know what the rules were.

Nia was ready and waiting for him in the library, all clean and fresh. If anyone had asked, Idwal would have said she smelled like a flower and looked like an angel. Putting such thoughts aside, Idwal told her about his conversation with Cai.

"Seriously? All that nonsense, because he thought she was with Rob?" Nia sounded disgusted at her cousin's stupidity. "All that... with Carmen?"

Idwal nodded. "Though to be fair, he's never really met Rob. I don't reckon they've ever actually spoken."

Nia wasn't impressed. "He could have asked Mona. He could have talked to her."

Nia shook her head in despair, and Idwal hoped she wasn't damning men in general. "Mona isn't exactly blameless either, you know," he insisted. "She could have done some explaining." Idwal scrunched up his face in consternation. "I'm beginning to think Cai may actually be in love with her, though I can't see why. You should have seen the way she looked at him when he asked for more contact with Tommy. She even made out he wasn't Tom's father."

Nia raised her eyebrows, but it was too ridiculous a notion to consider. "I'll help with Cai's plan," she complied reluctantly. "And I'm sure Mam and Sion will too – if you have a word with them." Nia instantly became business-like. "But we've got a lot to get through now."

Idwal found everything easy to understand. Nia noted down any ideas he had on improvements to the smooth running of the community. A transitional period was clearly needed. The tribal system had worked well, but it was uncertain whether or not it could continue, now the fleet had returned.

Early on in their conversation, Idwal had been shocked to discover just how removed the Welsh Druids were from mainstream British society.

"That's why we need to maintain a strong community here. The only real way to survive is to stay below the radar, to rely only on ourselves. No one is registered with any type of government organisation, which means no driving licences or passports, no bank accounts," Nia explained clearly.

"What about education? Surely you'd have to be registered at the uni?"

"Children are taught here and to a high standard, but inevitably there are people who need to take their studies further. We still need doctors and dentists, other professionals too. We have sympathisers in almost every field you can imagine, but living in the real world requires documentation – so we use false papers and addresses. That's where the cottages at Swnt come in – it's a whole fictitious extended family. All legal, all false."

"And they come back here, once they've finished their studies?"

"Not always, we occasionally lose some. There are always going to be those who prefer to integrate with the outside world. But the security of our community is paramount, and there are strict protocols about leaving and joining. And once you leave there's no coming back."

Nia explained about the hierarchy within the *Conway*. "The Archdruid has the final say in virtually all matters – though a good leader considers the opinions of his advisors: War Chief, Bard and Healer."

"So who's…?"

Nia rolled her eyes. "This is where it gets complicated." She sat up to explain the recent history. "Emlyn was next in line to be Archdruid."

"Would he have been any good?"

Nia angled her head in thought. "I'm not sure."

"Then why was he chosen?"

"In times gone by, the choice was made through talent, but now…"

"You've no way of telling," Idwal finished for her. "Is it always a man?"

Nia shifted uncomfortably. "I haven't known a female Archdruid – though there's plenty of evidence they existed." She sighed sadly. "It's a struggle to just survive here, and we've fallen into the same trap as all women; bringing up children and keeping everything going. Sacrificing personal ambition for the good of the community – the bloodlines are all important.

"Bloodlines?"

"Yes. We've kept records… about magical bloodlines. The strongest are mated together…"

"What?" Idwal's eyebrows had shot up in amazement.

"That sounds a bit clinical. What I meant to say was…"

"So you have control over everything… all of it? Even love and marriage?"

"That's a little more complicated, but, yes, it's imperative we preserve the line."

Idwal looked incredulous and Nia tried to steer the subject to more mundane matters, but he remained dogged. "It's like selective breeding, isn't it?"

"Yes." She'd lost the battle. "I suppose it is – in a way."

"So, Tom is just the sort of baby you'd want, the child of two powerful Druids."

"That wasn't the committee's initial reaction to the pregnancy." Nia rolled her eyes at the furore. "Cai has always been destined to mate with Cerys, actually." Idwal just blinked. "And you're using the term Druid too loosely," Nia continued, oblivious. "I don't even know what Mona *is*, and Cai is almost completely warrior class. He has a lot of Silurian in his make-up." Idwal raised his eyebrows again. Rather than answer him directly, Nia sought refuge in a nearby book. "According to Tacitus, members of the Silurian tribe usually had a dark complexion and curly hair. Due to their appearance, Tacitus hinted they might have crossed over from Spain at an earlier date."

"Sounds like Cai. And were they particularly bloodthirsty?"

"Oh yes." She scanned down the text. "The Silures fiercely resisted the Roman conquest, waging guerrilla warfare against their invaders under Caratacus. The Roman leader Ostorius stated publicly that they should be either exterminated or transplanted, so great was the danger they posed."

"So, on balance, Tom might be able to handle himself in a fight. He looks like his dad – as far as I can tell, but do you think he'll have this *mark* thing?"

"I don't believe the *mark* is genetic." Nia said this as if she hadn't quite made up her mind on the subject. "But that's the most amazing thing about genetics. No one knows! It's just stored in his DNA. Tom could be really good at ballet for all we know."

Nia didn't mean this as a joke, but Idwal seemed to find it hugely funny. "Sorry, Nia, I was imagining my sister's reaction when Tom confesses his love for ballet."

"But that's it of course. Mona will bring him up to be interested in the things she is. It's the nature–nurture debate. Of course he'll be a good fighter, with Mona as his mam."

"And what about Cai? Will he be part of their life, do you think?"

It saddened Nia deeply that her cousin had abandoned his

son, and she sighed. "I never thought him capable of acting quite so badly. How can he not love Tom? He's the most wonderful child."

≈

Cai needed to get the Carmen business out of the way. He wasn't alarmed by the prospect, but it was never pleasant and he half-hoped she wouldn't be in. When she opened the door to him, Carmen had an expectant glint in her eye, and she instinctively slid her hands around his waist. He looked down at her.

"I've come to talk."

"Not your normal style, I'll admit, but we can give it a go first, if you like."

He unclipped her hands. "I've come to apologise really. I want to say sorry for getting drunk... and using you."

"Ah, so it *is* true. Mona's bastard is yours and now you're trying to play happy families."

"We're going to have to work together, and I want to get to know him. I'd like to help her out, if I can."

Carmen shook her head with a mixture of disgust and shock. "Didn't she just kill your taid?" Cai froze at the memory and forced himself to remember the circumstances. "Didn't she burn him to death with her bare hands?"

"So I hear," he said quietly.

"And you still want her?" Carmen was astonished. She had fully expected Cai to come running back to her after this recent turn of events.

"I want to help her," he corrected.

"But she knows about us." Carmen took a wild stab in the dark. "And she won't let you back into her bed until you give me up. Am I right?"

Cai groaned inwardly. Even if she understood, he didn't think Carmen would care. "It doesn't matter. I just wanted to say sorry."

"Sorry for what? Being so rough?"

"Yes, I'm sorry for that too."

Carmen cast him a longing look. "I didn't mind," she whispered.

Cai put his hands in his pockets and shuffled to the door with an awkward shrug.

"You can come back here whenever you need to. What she doesn't know won't hurt her," Carmen called after him.

≈

Arwel trawled through the paper trail – again. The answer was here. It *had* to be here, hidden among the mountainous piles of evidence. But he just didn't seem to be breaking any new ground. On paper, everything pointed to Mona. Arwel wondered, not for the first time, if she could be playing an exceptionally clever game of quadruple cross. Yet again he dismissed the idea. Mona didn't have the capacity for such deceit or planning.

Dafydd and Cai had provided him with all the information they'd gleaned from the voyage. Their talk of tracking devices might be a possible lead. He stared into the sea of black and white print in front of him, eyes glazing over as he did so. His thoughts turned to Cai and the outlandish plan for aiding Mona. Arwel still felt a burning disappointment whenever he thought about his adopted brother. He'd even tried to put himself in Cai's shoes, but there was no way Arwel could have behaved like that to Rhona – even if she had borne another man's child. Arwel and Rhona loved each other. It was simple: she was his haven of calm. When he fell into her softness each night, he was at peace. Rhona was love.

It wasn't the same for Mona and Cai. They were a storm at sea. Cai had begged Arwel to speak to Mona, to make her see sense. Cai didn't want to waste time and energy on tricking her if he didn't have to. And Arwel *had* tried, but the violent clash of their emotions had been overwhelming and left him gasping for air. He might as well have tried to reason with a hurricane.

Eventually, Arwel had agreed to help with Cai's elaborate plan, as it seemed the only way left. Though he held very little hope it would work. After all, Cai had never really seen Mona in action.

≈

Mona was starving. Her self-imposed exile in the room had left her reliant on others for meals, and nobody had bothered bringing anything for ages. Reluctantly, she strapped Tom in the harness and went hunting in the canteen.

It was early – too early for a cooked breakfast, but she found some cereal. Mona ate quickly, wanting to be out before everyone else arrived and before Tom kicked off. She was still there when Cerys and Gwen wandered over with their trays, bleary-eyed but seemingly pleased to see her.

"Where have you been hiding, Mona?" Cerys nudged her playfully, and then pressed a finger on the baby's nose. "He's a cute little thing."

Mona shrugged and grunted, not knowing how to answer. So much had happened that she couldn't articulate any of it.

"Don't feel bad about Hywel. We've all heard what happened," Gwen said, smearing butter on her toast. "Miserable old sod," she added with a cheeky wink.

"Here," Cerys said, putting down her coffee and wiggling her fingers in Tom's direction. "Let me have a cuddle." Mona heaved the sleeping lump into her arms and he woke up on cue. "Oh!" Cerys said, looking down at his blue frown. "He really does look like…"

"So!" Gwen interrupted Cerys's potentially awkward observation. "Is he a good sleeper?"

"Yes," Mona said, glad of Gwen's thoughtfulness. "At least, I think so."

"He's a real poppet," Gwen said, rubbing her hand over Tom's chunky arm.

Conversation turned easily to the Passing Over ceremony. It would be Ifan's last grim job as Archdruid to lay the spirit of his son to rest, along with the youngsters who had perished on the voyage – and now Hywel. The rite would be held tomorrow. Both Nia and Rob had been asked to sing, with Bryn providing the drum percussion. The evening wake would be an opportunity to get to know the newcomers properly and the excitement in the air was tangible. The women gossiped about dresses and who fancied whom.

"What about you, then, Mo?" Cerys asked simply, despite Gwen trying to kick her under the table.

"Don't worry, Gwen. I know about Carmen." She grimaced at the women. "It's probably for the best."

"He's a total snake, if you ask me," Cerys said unequivocally. "We thought he'd really changed, didn't we, Gwen?"

Gwen didn't have the opportunity to answer because Alun swooped down on her from behind and nuzzled her neck. "*Bore da, cariad* – Good morning, my love," he said before nodding awkwardly to Mona.

To her surprise, Mona felt glad to be with people again, but took this as her cue to leave. Glyn was on his way over with Cerys in his sights.

Mona took Tom back into her arms and wandered away. Not relishing a return to the loneliness of her room, she ventured outside to brave the elements. Watching from a vantage point by the jetty, Mona could see quite a few people building the bonfire for the ceremony. She would have liked to attend the funeral rites tomorrow, but didn't know how she might react to the sound of so much Welsh, especially on such an emotionally charged occasion.

"So! You're outside at last, you slacker." Idwal came bounding up from the bonfire, topless and sweaty. Mona didn't want to look down at the shoreline, just in case she saw Cai in the same state. "How's Mr Stinky Pants?"

"Asleep. Leave him that way."

"You're not still grumpy about yesterday?"

"A bit. What time is it in the morning?" Mona could never stay angry with her brother for long. She doubted if anyone could.

"Sunrise. You coming?"

"I'd like to, just to hear the singing. Have you ever heard Nia sing?"

To her amazement, Idwal's face turned an unprecedented shade of beetroot. Mona's heart sank. She'd dropped the ball – this wasn't supposed to happen.

"Please, *please* don't tell me you've already gone in for the kill with her. Nia is not like *normal* girls. She doesn't get the way it works."

"I haven't done anything of the sort, Mona." He sounded indignant. "We're just friends and I'd appreciate it if you didn't lecture me about affairs of the heart. It's not as if…"

But Mona had heard enough, and started to make her way back inside. There was nothing else for it; she would have to warn Nia about her brother directly. Taking immediate action, Mona made a bee-line for the Hall. Nia would most probably be practising for her performance there.

Mona had guessed correctly. However, there was more than a simple musical rehearsal in progress. Barging through the double-doors, she managed to launch herself into a full-on run-through for the entire ceremony. All the protagonists were present, including Cai, whose glare she tried and failed miserably to avoid.

Mouthing an apology to Nia, Mona fled from the Hall, desperate to get away from Cai. The thought of him, the sound of him, the smell of him. She'd lost more than her confidence since Hywel's demise. The steely resolve that had served her so well had started to creak and crumble. Mona was beginning to lose her only real coping mechanism for dealing with him. And he knew it.

Cai caught her a few strides away from the door. "Mona."

She faltered at his light touch on her shoulder, because it was loaded with another febrile vision.

Seven of them had taken the cwrwg out to sea; six men to row and Canaid to keep their rhythm steady with her song. The magic in her chanting had lured fish to their nets and the sea coracle returned to the sandy beach fully laden with its catch. As the water beneath them grew shallower, the rowing ceased as all the men jumped into the sea simultaneously, pushing the boat as far up the shelving sand as possible. Only then did Maelgwn shout his orders. Though older than Meilyr by a few years, the Archdruid was strong and nimble. His dark eyes glittered with arcane power and he wore authority around his neck in the form of two torcs: one of silver and one of gold.

"Take these, you oaf," Maelgwn shouted to the blacksmith, flinging a string of fish in his direction.

Meilyr caught and carried two strings as he watched the Archdruid help Canaid from the coracle, catching her tightly around the waist and easing her slowly down the front of his body until her feet reached the shore.

"I didn't realise there was a rehearsal." Mona gasped, bewildered by the return of the anomalous visions.

Cai shrugged. He either wasn't interested or couldn't speak. The last time they'd been this close, Arwel had been forced to step between them.

"The new troops need a workout." He sounded strained, but Mona couldn't tell anymore if that was normal for him. "Can you help Idwal after lunch? I'm too busy."

That was it? He didn't want to talk about the bizarre story unfolding between them? Or yesterday's charade in front of Idwal? The near violence in front of Arwel? Two could play that game. If he wanted icy civility, she could give as good as she got. "What time? I'll have to get cover."

He glanced down at Tom, who was flapping his arms and legs in Cai's direction. "Two till four. I've asked my sister to have... Tom." Cai appeared to have difficulty saying her son's name without grimacing. Turning away, he walked back to the rehearsal.

Mona thought she might actually be starting to hate him.

≈

87

If she was going to fight this afternoon, Mona knew she would have to limber up. Luckily, Tom performed all his requisite bodily functions without fail, so she was able to prop him up in the middle of the room while working through her patterns.

As she sang along to her movements, he became more excited and interested, his blue-eyed stare no longer quite so sombre. To entertain him, Mona began to exaggerate both her movements and their accompanying soundtrack. By the end of the warm-up, Tom was smiling and flailing his arms about as if in response to her patterns, but she couldn't be sure. What she *did* know, as they left for lunch, was that she was more than ready for a fight.

Sioned joined her and Mona squeezed the girl's hand. "How are you?"

"I'm fine now. I'm doing a bit at the ceremony." She lifted her chin and changed the subject. "You're looking better. Cai said you were doing some training."

"Are you sure you don't mind looking after Tom? I don't want your brother bullying you into a chore."

Sioned looked at Mona in puzzlement. "Cai can't make me do anything I don't want to." She smiled into the baby's face. "And anyway, he is my nephew, Mona. I love him. Tom's never a chore."

Again Mona felt the sharp, stabbing pain of deceit.

"I'm so sorry about your taid."

"I was there. I saw what he did," Sioned replied plainly.

Mona didn't want to broach the subject of his letter or mention madness. She strongly suspected Hywel had been of sound mind, even if no one else seemed to think so.

Mona raced to the training room. It was as if each step towards the room freed her, but it wasn't just that. Each step away from Tom released her. Mona didn't doubt her love for her child, only the endurance of her sanity. The web of lies and fear she had woven was slowly beginning to choke them both. She needed to let some of those stitches go.

Sioned could protect him. She'd been well trained, but could she fight and beat her brother? An image of Cai ripping her son from

Sioned's arms caused Mona to stumble, but she forced it from her mind, staggering onwards to the training room.

≈

A mere glance at his body language told Mona that Idwal was in an ebullient mood. She walked in to find him larking around with a few of the new recruits. Idwal was good at being daft. It was almost an art form.

She trotted up to him. "Am I late?"

"No, but we're all ready, limbered up and everything. You've just missed Cai."

"Did he say where he'd be?" *Killing my son*, her paranoia screamed.

"Well, no, but he did suggest that you and I could give the demo and then take questions after. '*Could Mona have salvaged some pride and scored maybe once?*' That sort of thing."

She couldn't help but get caught up in his mood.

"Ok, but we'll need a wager. Like the old days."

"Oh, I see, hankering after some fizzy cola bottles, are we?" He squeezed his eyes to a slit. "Or is it a KitKat you're after?" He looked up, theatrically drumming his fingers against his chin. "But you realise you have to *win* to obtain the victor's feast?" Their banter had attracted a small audience, and Idwal was beginning to really ham it up. "How about, if I win, you have to wear a pink frilly dress to the party on Saturday. And if you win…"

"You'll have a haircut," Mona finished with a flourish.

Idwal half closed his eyes again, weighing up the odds. He had beautiful gold hair, which hung almost to his shoulders. Mona didn't really want it cut, because it was so much like their mum's.

"You're on," he said, all business.

≈

Cai had eventually managed to push the strange narrative aside, but a niggling understanding had started to seep into his mind. He would have to consult Nia, but not yet. Discussions about possible past lives could wait. He had a job to do and stood now, out of sight, watching their easy playfulness from outside the Hall door. He couldn't help but grin. Mona's own smile was one of the most wonderful things about her. It lit her up. It lit him up.

He still had a ridiculous amount to do, but there was no way he was going to miss this. Cai had to know if Mona had any weaknesses left for him to exploit.

The siblings had both stretched out and bowed. Idwal's stance was relaxed while Mona's just seemed relaxed. Bryn was reffing: five bouts of two minutes each.

Cai didn't think Idwal even saw the first kick. His sister was lethal and focused. Every time Idwal might have scored a point, Mona forced him backwards with a series of pinpoint-accurate blows. Cai found it hard to be objective about her fighting, but he could see that each tiny movement was correct, her core balance immoveable even to the tilt of her head. She tore through Idwal's defence: jab, block, punch, kick, kick, block, punch. She was mesmerising. It was beautiful.

The last time he'd seen her fight, Emlyn had been her opponent. Mona had improved since then, and Idwal, winded from the off, couldn't manage a single point. But if he was put out at being so soundly beaten by his little sister, he didn't show it. In fact, he was extremely magnanimous in defeat – once he could breathe and speak again.

"You are the best bloody fighter I've ever met," Idwal wheezed, picking her up with a one-armed bear hug.

"I'm just frightened to death of pink," she laughed.

"You're not really going to cut my hair?"

"A deal is a deal, I'm afraid." She squinted at him. "You're not reneging, are you?"

Eventually they got down to training. Mona had the capacity to remember each of the moves and countermoves in any bout she'd been involved in or had witnessed. It was the way her mind worked. The fight wasn't just a string of moves. It was a garment that she could unpick.

Cai needed to tear himself away, but all he wanted to do was stay and watch. She repeated the bout in slow motion, asking questions, getting answers, and making them understand. Having gathered the information he needed, Cai reluctantly left.

≈

Idwal, though astounded by her fighting, was much more impressed by her technical knowledge and coaching methods. The new recruits were easy to teach now. They all wanted to improve and the session went well. Even Carmen and friends showed a grudging respect and knuckled down to the drills. Idwal was sensitive enough to encourage them into his group.

There was plenty of joking on the way to the canteen at lunchtime and mostly at Idwal's expense. He didn't seem too put out, but didn't waste any time in telling Tom that his nasty mum was a bully. Mona told Tom to ignore his uncle, whose beautiful hair was still in jeopardy.

Nia reacted with uncharacteristic vehemence to the possibility of the haircut. Tom started whinging, but Rob produced a bottle and Mona began to enjoy the relaxed camaraderie among her friends.

"I know! Let's see what it's like in a ponytail." Mona had her hands around her brother's sweaty hair in an instant. "It could do with a wash, you gremlin."

"Stop her, Nia." Idwal bleated in mock desperation.

Nia, however, took the request more seriously. "If you're intent on the wager, I suggest Siân actually cut his hair, Mo."

Mona studied the red gold locks in her hands and let them fall. "Ok. You win. No haircut, but you owe me – big time."

"What?" her brother answered, relieved but now wary.

Mona closed her eyes, as if trying to conjure an impossible task

91

for her brother to fulfil. "Gin," she finally said, laughing. "And tonic and ice."

There followed a chorus of vocal agreement, which died a death as Cai marched in. He chucked a filthy look in the direction of their little group and Mona inched a step nearer to Rob.

"Have you got everything organised for Saturday?" Mona asked Rob as she watched Carmen glide to Cai from the other side of the canteen.

"Yep, and I'm feeling good," Rob answered, as he watched Cai ignore Carmen and stalk towards Dafydd. "It'll be one hell of a show."

Everyone looked like they had somewhere else to go – apart from Mona. Rob hurried back to work while Sioned was lured away by a brave suitor. Mona sat alone with Idwal and Nia, and she felt like a gooseberry.

"*N'ôl at waith felly, Nia?* – Back to work then, Nia?" he smiled cheekily at her, and Nia beamed back at him like a proud school teacher.

"I don't bloody believe it!" Mona was floored that her brother had spoken in competent-sounding Welsh.

"What!" he said defensively. "It's easy enough if you put your mind to it." They both got up, but Mona didn't move. "You coming with us?" he looked down at her mischievously. "Or do you want to sit here on your own like Billy No Mates?"

Mona didn't want to be alone, and stood up with a grumble. "All right. But you can stop showing off right now." She passed it off as a joke but the less Welsh she was exposed to the better in her opinion.

≈

Idwal and Nia seemed at home in the library, each with their own little research area and pile of books.

"What are you working on?" Mona asked as she settled Tom on her lap in the corner.

"Your *mark*," Idwal replied.

"Oh, *that*."

"Come on, then, let me have a look." Idwal held out his hand. Mona raised her eyebrows in irritation, but rolled slightly to fish the metalwork from her back pocket. She threw it across the room to him and he caught it effortlessly.

"Ouch!" he said, juggling it forwards onto the desk like a hot potato. "It stings." He touched the metal again tentatively and the sting turned into a searing pain, travelling up through his hand and screeching around his body. "What the fuck?" he hissed, chucking it away from him and across the desk.

Mona held her breath and stared at him, remembering her own initial, excruciating encounter with the *mark*. "You all right?" she asked carefully.

Idwal seemed pale and trembling, but he hadn't passed out. "Yeah," he said shakily and blew out slowly. "Went right through me." He shuddered, frowned and shook his head. "What's that all about, then?"

He looked at Mona for an answer, but she just shrugged and fiddled with the baby on her knee. Nia, however, was overjoyed at his reaction.

"I know! It's worse than static, which makes me think it's some sort of capacitor – a battery."

"But how…?" Idwal looked at Mona, but she'd kept her head down.

"I've got a theory." Nia had retrieved the iron symbol from the table-top with the tip of her pen. "I'm not entirely sure, but I think Mona introduced her natural magic… " A glance at Mona forced a change to the word. "Energy into the thing while she made it. Almost like a trickle charge into a starter battery." She studied Idwal to see if he was keeping up. "I believe that when Colm attacked her with it, still hot and alive with her… energy, it acted as a jump-start to her power – igniting and magnifying her in-built talent."

Mona snorted at the explanation.

"Don't be like that, Mona," Nia lectured. "You know how important it is to discover its origin and meaning."

Mona sighed heavily and bounced Tom up and down for a bit.

"Why don't you want to find out, Mo?" Idwal asked, genuinely curious about her reticence.

"I don't know."

"Liar!"

Mona scowled. "I don't want Nia to find any more bad news for me."

Nia looked shocked. "Is that what you really think?"

"No, not really, but if you keep digging I'm frightened of what you might find. It's not a gift." Mona remembered all the times her power had been activated, each man she'd killed. "It's a curse and I can't control it."

Nia wanted to continue the discussion, but Idwal, seeing how ill at ease it made his sister feel, decided a dramatic change of subject was called for.

"Seen any good games recently, Mo?"

Mona's face lit up at the mention of her beloved sport. "What I wouldn't give to see a decent game of rugby. It's hard to believe we're in Wales, isn't it?"

"Actually, although rugby is often thought of as the archetypal Welsh sport, it's played mainly in the south of the country."

Mona stifled a yawn at Nia's contribution. "What was the last game you saw, Id?"

"I caught most of the Six Nations in Cornwall. Wales did well." He grinned boyishly at Nia. "Roberts and North are on form, as is Halfpenny." He winked at Mona. "No Grand Slam this time, though."

"What's the Grand Slam?" Nia chipped in, to Idwal's obvious disbelief.

"I know," Mona agreed, shaking her head with mock pity. "So sad. How did we do?"

"Not bad. It's a young side, but good, I reckon…"

"What do you mean by *we*?" Nia asked a bit snippily.

"Well, England…"

"I can't believe you still think…"

"Anyway, back to the rugby," Idwal said quickly. He pointed at his nephew. "We'll have to find a team for you to join, sunshine."

Mona laughed. "I've been thinking exactly the same thing." She distorted her features into a melodramatic grimace. "Or he might end up playing *football*."

At the mention of the F-word, Idwal shuddered with disgust, and they both laughed at their private joke.

"Why do you love rugby so much?" Nia studied the siblings.

Mona looked confused by the question, in a way Idwal did not. "Actually, I've given this a lot of thought," he muttered sheepishly. Both women twisted around to hear his words of wisdom. "It's in our blood. A bit like your magic, Nia."

Mona winced at the word, but Nia ignored her.

"Surely if it's a Druidic… sport, we'd play it here – and we clearly don't." She frowned, not sure where Idwal's argument was going.

"You don't play it because you don't need to," Idwal continued. "Rugby is a game played by Celts who aren't allowed to fight with swords anymore. It's the only battlefield left that's still played on earth – mud. Where men and women can still grapple and fight without armour." Idwal smiled at his own romanticism.

But Nia was nodding now, as if agreeing with Idwal. "You have a point. But am I right in thinking the Six Nations now include Italy?"

"Yes," Idwal replied, a little deflated. "You've always got an answer, haven't you, Nia?" he sighed.

"And there's Australia, New Zealand and the rest of the southern hemisphere…"

Idwal cut her off, embarrassed now by his impassioned outburst. "It's just a theory," he mumbled.

After picking up Tom, Mona walked over to her brother and ruffled his still sweaty hair. "I loved watching the big games on the telly at home. The build-up before the game, Mum and her special rugby snacks; Dad and Bren." She laughed at the memory of their rivalry. "One in the red corner; one in the green corner."

Idwal put an arm around his sister, drawn into the shared memory. "The beer and the singing. What was that song Bren used to sing, Mo?"

She did remember, and it was a happy thought, but also drenched in loss. Mona couldn't afford to dwell on the past, so she merely shrugged. "You're such a good number eight, Id. I used to love watching you play. Do you remember that game against Essex…?"

Nia put up with a half-hour or so of rugby stories before settling down to study again. Mona felt she should help with the research and asked if she could join them.

"You never know. There may be something you've missed." They both stared at her, mouths agape. "Shut up, you two. I *can* read!"

≈

According to the texts, there were several different manifestations of power. They mostly involved telling the future, predicting the weather, and eating all or odd parts of bulls.

"Why are most of the references Irish?" Mona asked at one point.

"There's a lot more original material in the Irish texts, and the bulk of Druidism is based there." Nia launched into teacher mode. "Remember, the Irish weren't Romanised. They had longer to survive before Christianity arrived."

Idwal and Nia seemed happy to sit and read forever, but Mona had had more than enough, and urged them to join her in the canteen. They were late into supper, and Cai pounced as soon as they were through the door. After directing an icy-blue stare towards Mona and Tom, he ignored mother and son completely, firing a question at Nia and Idwal.

"There's a last-minute issue with the wake. Can I have a quick word?" Cai was insistent, so they quickly moved off with him to another table.

Mona tried not to listen too hard to the Welsh whispers around her, but she was unable to resist staring at Cai. The veins and tendons in his forearms were bulging with some recent exertion, and his body had a rigid, unbending look to it. Despite the symmetrical beauty of his face, he exuded a rough and earthy sexuality. Mona was only one of several women in the room, including Carmen, who covertly studied Cai. She watched the Galician woman join him after he'd finished his little meeting with Nia and Idwal. The pain in Mona's chest flared and she dragged her eyes away as she saw Carmen glide her arms around Cai's waist. Mona made herself join the back of the food queue, and when she could bear to look again, both Cai and Carmen had left the canteen. They didn't seem to spend much time together in public. Presumably all the action happened at night behind closed doors. A sharp jolt pierced Mona's body as she remembered, in exquisite detail, her one and only night with Cai.

8

Plan

It was nearly midnight and Cai was running on fumes. His mind feverishly worked through the various permutations of the plan. Only one major issue remained unresolved, and he reluctantly moved his thoughts to the boathouse. Get that done and then sleep. He'd only manage four hours if they started the ceremony on time, but it would just have to be enough.

He met Carmen, drunk and swaying on her feet, as he turned past the accommodation wing. Cai's heart sank as she approached, and he realised their relationship hadn't really come to a conclusive end yet. Carmen's attempts at a public reunion in the canteen had irritated him. He was stupidly busy and too tired to endure a scene, but as she approached, Cai saw what was coming by the mad look in her eye. He'd found himself in similar situations too many times before.

"I just don't *get* it!" Her voice was amplified by the booze she'd drunk. "What do you see in that warrior queen bitch?"

"*Ssh*, come on now, Carmen, you've had too much to drink. You don't know what you're saying," Cai said, walking towards her and gesturing downwards on the air with his hands.

"I *do* know what I'm saying." If anything, Carmen shouted even louder. "I'm saying you should be with *me*. We have much more in common. You're beautiful," she said, poking him lightly in the chest.

"And I'm beautiful." She twisted the same finger towards herself. "Mona is a man in disguise. She fights like a man and she talks like a man." Her eyes widened in mock comprehension. "She *is* a man... so what does that make you?" She grinned at her conclusion. "You've stolen that baby from somewhere to mask your little secret." Carmen clearly thought she'd been quite funny and congratulated herself with a cackle.

Cai didn't see any point in arguing with her, but was staggered by how bitter she seemed to feel. Grasping her by the shoulders, he began to ease Carmen back towards her room, leading her down the corridor in a precarious shuffle. "You don't mean those things."

"I'm only warning you, Cai. She's a complete cow and she's tricked you into staying with her by getting pregnant. Everyone thinks it. They're just too frightened to say it."

"*Stop!*" he barked harshly. The truth made Carmen's accusation intolerable.

Hearing the anger in his voice, Carmen's bravado cracked. Breaking down, she began to sob piteously into his shirt. The fight had gone out of the young woman, and as the crying subsided he was able to lead her gently to her room. After making sure she was lying on her side, Cai turned off the light and left her to sleep things off.

≈

Following further *mark* discussions after supper, Mona was late making her way back through the *Conway* to bed. They'd talked things over endlessly in the library, and every lead had ultimately come to a dead end.

Tom seemed quite cosy in the sling, and she recalled a phrase her mother had used: "*You could sleep on a washing line, Mojo.*" Until she'd had Tom, Mona had never completely understood what her mum had meant. She smiled to herself, thinking of other sayings, which for the first time had started to make sense.

There were raised voices in the corridor ahead. Late-night assignations were common now that the fleet was back, and often loud, especially on a weekend. Mona couldn't help but admire the directness of Druidic sexuality. It had its rules and ceremonies, but none of those things were bent on perverting sex into a weapon or a sin. Unfortunately, there would always be some on-going drama; no matter how liberated a community appeared to be.

The shouting ahead continued for a little longer, but then ended in a soft whimpering. Mona rounded the corner in time to see Cai gently holding Carmen against him before easing them both into her room.

In an instant, Mona's mind filled with the thick green poison of jealousy. It slid through her vascular system, infecting reason and contaminating it with hate. Vicious, septic thoughts made her muscles quiver with a desire for violent action. Despite the child at her breast, it took every particle of self-restraint to prevent Mona from kicking down Carmen's door and ripping the rutting lovers to pieces. Pulling herself together, she walked on past the room, carrying both Tom and the wreckage of her self-esteem with her.

≈

Rob had asked her several times to come to the Passing Over ceremony. In the end, and against her better judgement, Mona had promised she would. He seemed uncharacteristically nervous about singing the *cerdd farwnad* – the elegiac musical lament. She knew his performance with Nia would be exquisite and that this might be dangerous for her. So, to be safe, she put wax plugs in her ears to keep out the sound.

With Tom on her chest, Mona put on a cloak and trekked over to the shore. The ceremony was well underway by the time she reached the boathouse. She had decided to watch from the periphery, not knowing how welcome she would be, given the circumstances of Hywel's death.

Despite having lived in the *Conway* for an entire year, Mona had managed to avoid a good many of the Druids' ceremonies. She understood their connection to the earth and seasons through their festivals. The Beltane celebrations in May had been a real eye-opener. However, since learning of her vulnerability, both Mona and Arwel had thought that attending the Pagan rites wasn't worth the risk. Having missed Nesta's Passing, she had no idea how the Druids dealt with death and grief. Arwel would have warned her to stay away, but she was already here now.

Watching today from her vantage point, Mona was struck by the formality of the service. It might be a load of superstitious nonsense to her, but to those on the beach it was a crucial rite in their spiritual lives.

Leaning into a doorway to escape the wind, Mona concentrated on Ifan as he started to call the 'Corners' and asked the 'Watchtowers' to assist. Nia had explained to her once that the Watchtowers provided protection for the participants during the ritual and were asked to leave once it had been completed. Mona had never thought to ask what they needed protection from.

Ifan performed his final task as Archdruid with confidence, power and solemnity. He always moved slowly, but today he glided with an almost regal dignity. Ifan was the white-cloaked focal point in amongst the flapping black of the congregation.

The first corner he called was the East, symbolised by Air. The second, South, represented by Fire. The third, West, by Water. The last was North, and Earth. No one talked or even whispered. Not a cough or a baby's cry could be heard from anywhere. All present were under Ifan's thrall.

Cai spoke for his grandfather and for Ieuan, which surprised her a little. Dafydd spoke for Emlyn, and he appeared to be completely wrecked by the experience. Mona hadn't really known the three lads Dafydd had sent home to protect the *Conway*. They'd never arrived, and everyone knew they'd met their end on the ferry home from the Isle of Man. She knew the ones left behind, though: their mothers and fathers, siblings and sweethearts – those who spoke for and mourned the young men.

The wind was strong and the voices on the shore spoke in hushed tones. Mona's earplugs blocked out any sounds that might have reached her, giving the whole ceremony the appearance of an elaborate mime. There were no bodies to anoint, purify or burn, but a fire on the foreshore nevertheless crackled and shone in the first light.

≈

Cai was relieved to see that Mona had stayed away. It meant he could concentrate on his eulogies. They were all short, and soon the drum began and the voices lifted. Rob started in a whisper, gathering the sadness in his voice and weaving it around the mourners. As he plaited his voice with love and loss, it grew deeper, richer and almost overpowering, even in the vastness of the shore. It was a relief, at last, to hear Nia's bright, high, crystal-clear tones, which tempered and tamed the power of Rob's voice, subduing it into harmony.

Despite the beauty of the performance, Cai had weightier issues on his mind. Mulling over the tasks ahead, his eyes were drawn to the boathouse. Leaning heavily against a doorjamb was a cloaked figure he realised was Mona. Studying her, Cai could see she was struggling to stay upright and had begun to slowly slide down the door. The emotion in the air was palpable and Cai became instantly aware of the danger facing her. He couldn't risk anyone seeing her in that state; he'd worked too hard on the alternatives. With deliberate calmness, Cai inched away from the fire and the crowd. After backing out of the circle, he turned and sprinted up to the boathouse door.

The hooded cloak covered Mona's face and body completely. She now lay unmoving on the floor, and Cai peeled back her hood. One look at her, and he became caught up in the ecstasy of her pain.

Tears had soaked the child strapped to her body, but her eyes still held oceans more. What Cai saw was pure and magnificent grief. Grief that had been collected from all those present, distilled through the music, and then poured unfiltered into the depths of Mona's soul. Cai couldn't allow the sight of Mona to move him, and he took a deep shuddering breath before pulling her to his side and steering her through the doorway.

As they moved inside the building, further away from the sound of the singing, Mona slowly began to come round. However, the grief still crippled her and impeded their progress. Cai was forced to literally drag her through the deserted corridors of the *Conway* and back to her room. He unstrapped the sleeping boy as gently as he could and laid him on the bed next to his mother – noticing the wax earplugs as he did so. They obviously hadn't worked, and Cai was irritated by her lack of caution.

Mona said nothing, but stared wetly and relentlessly at Cai. It was only at that moment he completely understood the full extent of Mona's vulnerability. In her right mind, she would never have allowed Cai to touch either her or her boy. She would never have let him wipe the tears from her face, or sit so close to her on this bed. If he wished, Cai would be free to harm either of them now and Mona would be powerless to stop him.

The thought was shocking. Moving away, he watched her from the armchair until the singing had stopped. When the noise outside ceased, Mona closed her eyes and entered a deep sleep.

With the crisis averted, Cai left to deal with one more task.

≈

In a few hours, the charade would be underway, and Cai prayed his nerve would hold. He met Idwal at ten to run through any last-minute issues before his appointment with Dafydd. There could be no errors.

"Went well this morning. I couldn't believe the singing," Idwal mumbled. "It broke my heart."

Cai's head shot up. Could Idwal be affected in the same way as his sister? He cast his mind back to the ceremony on the foreshore. No. Idwal had grieved, but it wasn't the same.

"I didn't see Mo there. Bit early for the squib, I suppose…"

Idwal was procrastinating; he obviously had something to say and was finding it difficult to do so.

"What is it?" asked Cai. "Is there a problem?" He had staked everything on this plan and wasn't ready to tolerate disappointment at this stage.

"I fought Mona yesterday."

"Yeah, I forgot to ask, how did it go?" Cai lied smoothly.

"She's like… it's like…" Cai understood Idwal's inability to describe the experience. "I couldn't see how she'd done it… not until she freeze-framed the fight afterwards. Anyway, I just wanted to say… that I understand why she has to be the military leader. It's obviously some sort of divine calling for her. Not only the moves or training, but a whole strategy and… I reckon she's some sort of warrior goddess."

Cai laughed, despite his jangled brain. "You've been spending too much time with Nia."

Idwal laughed along but flushed a little.

"I'm afraid I set you up, Id. I suppose I could have told you, but would you have believed me?"

Idwal shook his head ruefully and scratched the back of his neck awkwardly. "Probably not." He coughed. "Apparently watching you two fight is a bit of an event."

"Is it?" Cai asked, not lying now. He hadn't realised other people had noticed.

"So I hear." Idwal shuffled his feet, clearly agitated. "Anyway, everything is set for tonight and we're all ready, but if it doesn't work out, we should just let it go… until she comes round on her own. I'm finding it really hard… you know… going behind her back like this. And after yesterday… I'm fearing for my life!" Idwal spoke with a chuckle, but Cai got the message.

"Don't worry. I know this is our last chance."

≈

Mona and Tom had both been a bit damp when they woke up. She didn't have to wonder why, because she could remember every second of time that had passed: from the moment Rob started singing until he closed his mouth. The earplugs hadn't worked. His voice had overpowered everything and dragged up all her buried sorrow: her parents, Brendan, the loss of Idwal, the loneliness, Gareth's voice, Cai's love – and his betrayals.

Mona had been broken to pieces by the music, lost entirely to its sadness and heartbreak. Coming round, she'd become aware of Cai's presence: holding her; wiping her face; staring at her from the armchair across the room. His expression had told her how helpless she'd become, that he could reach over and smother them both – and there would be nothing she could do to stop him.

It was his hard, grim, dry eyes she remembered best, the dawning intelligence in them of how vulnerable she truly was. It had been a chilling warning, and in her head, Mona had already prepared to leave. Even if Idwal decided to stay here, even if she and Tom had to survive on their own – it had to be safer than staying here.

≈

Cai struggled in through Emlyn's door, weighed down with a ton of baby paraphernalia. He didn't believe a small child could possibly need all this stuff, but Siân had assured him otherwise. Dafydd was already there, running his finger over the spines in the bookcase.

"It's like a museum," he whispered. "The old man has left it like a shrine."

Cai eased his burden to the ground and faced his uncle. "There's nowhere else, Dafydd. Look at all this stuff."

Dafydd scanned the baby junk. "Yeah, I remember those days." He smiled and picked up a little vest. "No, I don't mind, Cai. I just can't see the point."

Cai had spent enough time in his uncle's company to recognise an impending lecture.

"Don't get me wrong, I can see Carmen's appeal, and I've never really got to the bottom of how I feel about Mona. But…" He shook the little vest. "What about the boy, Cai? He's your son, for fuck's sake."

Cai snatched the little garment from his uncle and chucked it back on the pile. He was sorely tempted to tell Dafydd the truth and wipe the judgemental expression from his face. "That's why we're here," he growled stiffly instead.

"Do you *really* think you're going to persuade Mona to move in with you?" Dafydd was almost incredulous. "Even after your little fling with…"

"We'll be sleeping in this bed together tonight," Cai replied tightly as he started to pack away some of the clothes.

After a moment's silence, Dafydd chuckled and clapped a conciliatory hand on his nephew's back. "I like your optimism, Cai, and I suppose if anyone's got a chance, it's you."

Dafydd stayed to help with the reorganisation by clearing out his dead brother's clothes from the remaining drawers.

"I'm not sure about being Archdruid, Cai. It was always Em's job really."

"You'll be fine," Cai muttered, though he didn't entirely believe that to be the case.

Dafydd grunted, not taken in. "How's Arwel's investigation going?"

"He's tried everything, and I don't know if any of the information I've given him will help. Why, what have you heard?"

"Nothing much." Dafydd shrugged. "Bryn reckons there's still the odd foray into the strait… that the Irish can't seem to keep away. And the rumour mill hasn't stopped."

Cai looked up questioningly – he hadn't heard any gossip.

"Nansi says there was a visitor back in the summer, Gary or something. He said he came from Pentre Ifan, but his accent was thick Gwent."

Cai swallowed before answering. "And people think he was the spy?"

Dafydd nodded. "Or Rob. They both arrived at the same time apparently."

"True," Cai agreed, looking out of the window. He could only think of the tasks still ahead of him – he really needed to get hold of Mona's mp3 player. "But in truth, the spy could be any one of us."

9

Party

It was lovely to see familiar faces at supper. Nia and Sioned were both a little pink and breathless.

"Been practising," Sioned explained through her apple pie. After shovelling it down her, she raced off before Mona had a chance to ask her what for.

"Must dash, Mo. There are a few last-minute changes to talk to Rob about. I'll come by at 6.30. We can get ready together." Nia kissed her cheek and left before Mona had a chance to decline the bizarre invitation.

This party was becoming more than a little crazy. Mona glanced around the canteen; neither Cai nor Carmen were anywhere to be seen. She suppressed a sudden rush of jealousy. It was about time she got Tom's things together.

≈

Siân arrived promptly to pick up Tom. Surprisingly, she seemed eager to leave directly, even turning down the offer of a cup of tea. Mona would have loved her to stop and chat for a while, but Siân was obviously keen to get going. She was on the cusp of leaving, when Mona had a sudden change of heart.

"Do you know what? Let's forget it. I'm just going to turn in," Mona sighed, sure now that she wasn't up for any celebrating.

Siân's face fell and she clutched at Tom. "No!" She looked panicked for a split second. "Come on, Mona! How often do you get the chance to really enjoy yourself? This Cornish lot look like fun. Go on and get ready. You'll have a lovely time, I promise."

"Ok," Mona relented, kissing Tom's fat cheek one last time. "Be good," she warned him, still considering playing truant from the party. Too late, Siân had gone and she'd just passed over her last chance to duck out of it.

The promise of dancing raised Mona's spirits, and she searched for the mp3 player with the intention of getting herself in the mood for a boogie. She couldn't find it in any of the usual places, however, and by the time she'd fruitlessly scoured her room, it was getting late. Now quite irritable, Mona undressed, had a quick shower, and padded over to her underwear drawer for a clean pair of knickers.

Nothing. The drawer was empty, as were the drawers above and below it. Hadn't she just been through these when searching for the mp3 player? Looking round the room, Mona noticed a pile of new clothing that had appeared on her bed, presumably while she was having her shower: a black dress, some rather ornate underwear, a pair of stockings and a pair of high-heeled shoes.

"Ha bloody ha, Idwal Jones. *You wanker!*" Mona shouted, knowing the culprit would want to be near enough to appreciate her reaction. She looked round for the clothes she'd just discarded, so she could find her brother and kick him up the bum, but they too were gone. Mona was left with two options: tracking the swine down through the *Conway* dressed in a towel or actually putting on the clothes he'd left out for her. She chose a third option, wrapping herself in the towel and getting into bed with a book that she was far too pissed off to read.

Eventually came the tentative knock she'd been expecting. As the door eased open, Mona threw her hardback at it so ferociously that the door was forced shut again. "Piss off, Idwal," she shouted.

The door opened again to reveal Nia, with Sioned in tow. "Don't blame your brother. It was all my idea," she squeaked, not sure if it was safe to come in.

"What! Why?"

"Oh, I don't know." She shrugged her shoulders pathetically. "We've all had such a rotten time recently. I thought it might cheer us up, and I suppose I wanted a night to remember."

Mona's anger began to dissolve in the face of Nia's disappointment. "What, by laughing at me in a ridiculous dress? *Stockings* for fuck's sake!"

"It's not ridiculous. It's rather beautiful and expensive," Nia chided.

"Oh, come in, then," Mona finally said, more gruffly than she actually felt by now.

Both visitors perked up a bit and settled on the edge of her bed. Nia rummaged through a large bag. "Besides, I've come bearing gifts." To Mona's amazement, Nia produced a bottle of gin, which she held aloft triumphantly. "Idwal's made good on his side of the deal."

"Tonic, ice and glasses as well," added Sioned, smiling and holding up her own offerings.

Mona relented and settled down with her friends for a drink. "You look really beautiful tonight, Sion," she said, gazing admiringly at the young woman's creamily freckled skin, dazzling blue eyes, and dark, curling hair.

Sioned's eyes sparkled. "You're only saying that because I look so much like my brother."

"Sioned," Mona sighed. Maybe this was the time to put her straight about the romantic hopes she held out for them. "Your brother *is* a beautiful man and a good one too, in many ways, but a year is a long time and he's got someone else now."

"That's just sex," Sioned answered bluntly. "I know how he looks at you."

Mona shuddered at the thought. "Where's that drink, Nia?" she asked.

They sipped their G&Ts in silence for a while. The taste was everything Mona remembered it being.

"Not too much for you, Sioned. You're going to need your wits about you looking like that," teased Nia, who also looked extremely glamorous.

"Who do you take after?" Mona asked, all irritation gone with the swallow of gin.

Sioned frowned, trying to remember. "Eyes from Mam, hair from Dad. But I probably look more like him."

"Idwal is the spit of my mum, except for, you know, being manly and all."

"She must have been a very beautiful woman," Nia said quietly.

"She was. I take after Dad," Mona giggled, but the girls exchanged meaningful looks and she knew what was coming next.

"Come on, Mo, let me do your make-up," Sioned coaxed. "We'll be three killer babes."

"Two killer babes and a musician," Nia muttered.

Mona squirted a mouthful of drink across the duvet as she laughed. "That was actually funny, Nia. My brother is having too much of an influence on you."

Nia coloured and dimpled like a Victorian heroine. *Oh dear god no*, thought Mona. Sioned was still jiggling up and down on the bed. "Please?"

"Ok, all right. But if I let you do my make-up, can I wear my jeans?"

They both shared another one of those looks. "Not really the effect we're after," Sioned whined.

Mona took a long hard look at the dress. It was everything she was not, and in a strange way, it unnerved her. "Fine, but I'll need another drink if you're going to pour me into that dress. Where did you get it anyway? It looks new."

Nia held her still while Sioned applied the paint.

"I don't know why you're so reluctant, Mona," Nia declared. "The application and enjoyment of cosmetics is a great tradition among the Celts."

Sioned rolled her eyes and Mona smiled. "*Keep still* or I'll jog the line," she nagged.

"Especially among the men," Nia added dreamily.

"Why don't you play dolls with Idwal then!" Mona mumbled through closed lips, and was appalled to see Nia blushing at the mere mention of her brother. "*About* Idwal…" Mona tried.

"Keep still!" Sioned moaned.

≈

After about another half an hour of faffing, all three women made their way towards the festivities. Progress was slow, as Mona found walking quickly in heels a challenge. However, she was learning fast and worked out that the heels made her hips sway of their own accord. So, she thought, it was not some strange female alchemy as she'd always imagined – just anatomy and physics.

Mona had been given a pendant necklace to wear: an elegant clock mechanism that had been expertly converted into jewellery. It was exactly the right size and shape to cover her *mark* and she loved it. As they made their way down the *Conway*'s corridors, Mona toyed with the metalwork obsessively; she'd never felt quite this exposed before and was thankful the Hall lights would be low.

Idwal stood up as the women approached. "Mona, you look…"

"I'm just wearing a dress, Id," she said, embarrassed but quite pleased at the strength of his reaction.

"You look lovely."

"At least it's not pink and frilly," she quipped, unable to accept the compliment graciously.

Nia put the alcohol, tonic and ice on the table, and then walked over to the band, which was already warming up with some Celtic swing. Mona smiled at the sound of the music – she might not have such a bad night after all.

Idwal's eyes remained riveted on Nia, even after she'd taken up her place on stage. Eventually, Mona felt she should intervene.

"You shouldn't let Nia take the rap for you."

Idwal shrugged nervously and Mona fidgeted; the dress restricted the movement of her ribcage, slightly compromising her breathing.

She couldn't help but look around for Cai. Although pleased not to spot him with Carmen, she felt somehow upset at not seeing him at all. She wondered briefly if he had volunteered for the defence crew. Scanning the room again, Mona spied Carmen. The young woman wore a stunning tight pink dress, which accentuated every curve of her body, and emphasised her sultry colouring. She'd arrived late, making a spectacular entrance with her attractive friends. They'd all settled down on a large table with the Cornishmen, but there was still no sign of Cai.

Sioned and a group of other sixteen-year-old sirens were breaking hearts *en masse* nearby. She looked over from time to time, as if to check that Mona was enjoying herself, but she and Idwal were left sitting alone for the most part. Nia, Rob and Bryn joined them from time to time as the band changed and the music evolved.

Mona made a concerted effort to breathe less deeply than normal, due to the tightness of the dress, but eventually she was forced to stand up to release the pressure on her midriff.

"Well, you've had your fun. Give me back my jeans and I'll get changed in the ladies."

Idwal caught her hand and towed her back to her seat. "Come on, Mo, man up. The dancing will start soon."

Mona groaned. The stockings were making her legs feel itchy. "I can't dance in this! It's like a bloody corset," she whinged. "I can't move my legs." She shuffled as if to emphasise the point, but gave up and sat back down.

Idwal glowed each time Nia returned to the table. In the end, Mona decided to broach the subject – once Nia was back on stage with the band.

"You really like her?"

"Who?" He smiled, and then sighed. "She's so…"

"Clever?"

"Kind. I was going to say kind, but ravishing, clever, magical, talented; they'll all do." He sighed again, longingly. "And before you say anything, Mo, I know. I know what you mean now…

about her being special. I'm absolutely not going to make any sort of move."

"Pull the other one," Mona muttered.

"No, not this time. It's not like that – we're just good friends." He gave a small, sincere smile. "I won't hurt her, don't worry."

They were joined by a couple of the Cornish crew. Cadan and Peder banged their pints down on the table.

"Hello, Chief," Peder said to Mona. "Anyone sitting here?" He sat down next to her anyway, without waiting for an answer. Peder was a big lad; about six foot seven and built like a second row. He'd come over to flirt, having had a little Dutch courage. "You look really nice tonight," he said, placing a large tanned paw on top of her hand.

"Thanks, Ped," she replied, keeping it light. "What do you play: four or five?"

"How did you know I play rugby?"

Peder had a delightful smile, and Mona thought how nice it would be to be wrapped up in those lovely big brown arms. But she couldn't possibly allow Peder near her. If Welsh and Irish affected her so catastrophically, Cornish or Manx or Scots Gaelic would no doubt have exactly the same effect. Mona could never afford to love any of these Celts – and that crushing reality reinforced her decision to leave. Mona swallowed back the loneliness. She had Tom and Rob.

"You move like one… and you've got fat ears," she joked to Peder, determined to keep sadness at bay tonight.

≈

There was a loud squeak of interference from a speaker – *a speaker?* A muffled apology was followed by a wave of exquisite dance music. Mona stared at Idwal. "My music, my player… I love you!" She kissed her brother hard on the cheek. "Let's dance," she said, dragging him off his seat.

Buoyed by the familiarity of the soundtrack, Mona launched herself at the music and danced – in spite of the dress, stockings and shoes. Idwal cavorted alongside her in his own equally unique way – and Mona felt happy. Track after track of energetic pop and rock filled the night. This wasn't such an awful party, after all.

"I can't believe how much rubbish you listen to, Mo."

"Shut up, Id, you know how much Mum loved this one."

He hugged her instinctively. Yes, he remembered.

"Ok, I'll give you that one. But no one can dance to *this*."

"No," she laughed. "But we can die trying."

The Cornish boys were game, but the indigenous Welsh were a little more reticent. Mona couldn't help but wonder whether the dour influence of the chapel in Wales had tempered their innate Druidic flamboyance – or they just didn't like her taste in music. It didn't bother her. She didn't care and she didn't want to stop. Indeed, Mona was most put out when Idwal started dragging her back to the table – *way* too soon.

"Come on, Mo, we need to hydrate. Anyway, they're all getting a bit soppy now."

"I don't have soppy music on my machine I'll have you know..." Mona was jerked bodily back onto the dance floor by a pair of strong arms. "Hey, Ped, that's..." But she knew it wasn't the Cornishman. Mona's body had opened like a flower at Cai's touch. He held her in a tight grip, forcing her body hard against him and preventing even the slightest movement. Cai had finally made his attack, but her body's instinctive compliance to his had scuppered any chance of Mona defending herself. She was caught, caught fast in his grasp.

Cai spoke quickly and harshly into her ear. "Don't talk, just listen." She didn't talk. "Stop trying to think of moves to counter me. You're in a full body grip. And even if you could get far enough away from me..." he swallowed, "you won't be able to execute a decent move without ripping your dress to your thigh... or showing off your exotic underwear. Nod if you understand."

The machine played an even slower number, and Cai moved them around in some sort of time to it. He rearranged his hands over her back, sliding them to her waist with far too much pressure. Mona nodded. "I'm going to explain this very briefly, and I need you to listen carefully. Only then will I loosen my hold." His breath was hot and angry on her face. "You are our Achilles heel, Mona. And only four of us know the truth of it. Ifan and Arwel have failed, but I'm going to sort it out."

She stiffened and he guessed why.

"I'm not going to hurt you." But his aggression increased if anything, and he pulled her even harder against him. "I'm going to find a way out of our predicament… I'm going to teach you the language, so that you can defend yourself against it. We've only got a week, and it will be extremely hard work." He paused to swallow again before continuing. "No one must know what we're doing… which is why we have been given our new jobs."

Peder and Carmen danced close by, but Cai didn't seem to notice – he merely carried on squeezing and talking.

"Our jobs are cover… for us to spend the necessary time together. Even Arwel has no idea who the spy is, so we can't trust anyone, not even your brother. Nod if you understand."

She nodded. The combination of tight dress and Cai's even tighter squeeze made her feel light-headed and woozy, giving everything around her a surreal, dreamlike quality. "This little charade is our reunion. You and I are moving into shared accommodation tonight. It will mean I can protect and teach you at the same time." He took a deep breath. Mona was finally back in his arms. "At the end of this song, I'm going to kiss you, and at the end of the next song, we're leaving together. Nod if you understand."

She was rigid from fear and lack of air and didn't respond quickly enough. Cai crushed even harder and she nodded.

"I'm going to ease up now, but I need to know you're not going to try anything."

Mona nodded several times, desperately needing to fill her lungs with air.

Cai slackened his grip and she sagged while gulping in the precious air. Though not pushed up against him as much now, his hands had started to rub up and down the length of her body from

116

her shoulder to her bum. When he deemed she'd got her breath back sufficiently, Cai dragged Mona back up savagely and kissed her, bruising her lips and hurting her neck. The strains of a familiar love song forced their way through the tinny speakers, and the irony wasn't lost on her. It had been playing when he'd first kissed her in Moelfre. Kissed and betrayed her. The most romantic moment of her life, shot to pieces with the rest of it.

"Good." Cai had pulled away, just far enough to talk and breathe. Like Mona, he was panting. "So far it's all been me, so you're going to have to... put your arms around my neck and kiss me. After that you can ask your questions, but only until the end of this song; then we're leaving."

Cai released her arms so she could ease them around his neck. She obeyed woodenly, pulling his head towards her and giving him a numb, blunt kiss. His eyes were cold and hard and her mind worked through to the endgame. What happened after the week was up?

"You still haven't got this, Mona, have you? We have an audience and they need to believe that you want me enough to take me back, now, *tonight*." He glanced over to her friends, where they sat in judgement. "You're displaying about as much life as a rag doll. Now kiss me as if you want me, or your brother will come over and ask me to stop hurting you." Cai talked into the curve of her neck, his lips spitting the words against her skin. It might have seemed to an onlooker that he was kissing her tenderly. "I really don't want to resort to talking you into it, but I will – if I have to. I've worked too hard for this to fail now."

Mona's next kiss was every bit as brutal and violent as his, and she hoped it passed for passionate. At the end of it, she still hadn't thought of a way out. He'd sewn up all the loose threads.

"Better," he admitted. "We've got another minute. You can ask a question now, but as soon as the song ends, we're walking over to the table and making our excuses."

"What about Tom?" Was all Mona could think to ask.

≈

When Mona had first walked into the Hall, Arwel heard Cai's breathing stop. The dress he'd bought for her revealed everything Mona always kept hidden. The breadth and strength of her shoulders, the flare of her breasts and hips. Mona's ankles and calves were exposed for the first time and Arwel found himself mesmerised by the muscle definition in her lower leg. The dress covered Mona's body from sternum to calf, but it enhanced her curves so much that Arwel found himself blushing. Cai had groaned, unable to take his eyes off her.

"I can't do this. It's not possible," he'd muttered.

Arwel had criticised the stupidity of his plan often enough over the last few manic days, so why had the thought of failure only just occurred to him now?

Cai had sat immobile in a dark corner of the room for two hours, eating her alive with his eyes as she gyrated to the music. He wasn't alone in his appreciation – the big Cornish lad kept trying to dance with her, lunging towards her waist to see if she'd respond. It had been difficult for Arwel to gauge Cai's reaction to this new suitor, but when the appointed time had come, he'd gone onto the battlefield and executed the planned move perfectly. A textbook body-lock disguised as passion. Arwel hadn't bargained for the brutality of the attack, and he had no idea how the rest of her friends were ever going to see it as affection.

Arwel joined the others as nonchalantly as he could. He was the only one who knew the full importance of the struggle taking place on the dance floor.

"She doesn't look happy," Nia whispered. "That's not a happy Mona face."

"I think it's only shock. He has grabbed her out of the blue," Idwal said. He really wanted this reunion to work. They all watched in silence for at least a minute, and even Idwal was beginning to have his doubts when Cai caught Mona's head in his hands and kissed her soundly. Idwal held his breath – if she didn't deck him now, things might turn out ok. He released his breath as Mona returned the kiss. *Twice.* "See, everything's fine."

Rob still looked uneasy, but there were tears of joy in Sioned's eyes, and Nia also seemed much happier. Arwel, though, felt sick to the stomach. In his heart of hearts he knew he had betrayed her utterly.

≈

"We're picking Tom up from Siân on the way to our room. You can say your goodbyes to him tonight," he informed her tightly and Mona gasped.

The song ended and he yanked her along by the waist. *Goodbyes?* She could make a move, now that he only had one arm in full contact, but he'd read her mind and squashed her closer to him.

"As long as my brain and voice still work, there's nothing you can do… so don't even think about it."

They had reached the table and were facing her friends. Mona was still in shock and Cai did all the talking – in Welsh, to push home the point. Their expressions ranged from the embarrassed to the jubilant, but Mona noticed how Arwel deliberately avoided meeting her eyes. Cai had needed help to execute this plan, and his adopted brother had the face of a Judas.

A short time later, Cai marched Mona down the corridor to Siân's. No one said a word until Siân answered the door. Her eyes widened with surprise at first, but she was soon gazing with affection at the newly reunited couple.

"You're earlier than I expected. He's just gone off. You know he'll be fine here overnight if you… want some time together."

"No, we'll take him with us," Cai answered assertively, squeezing Mona to him and kissing her head lightly. "Won't we, *cariad*?"

Mona nodded dumbly in response to Siân's instructions about bottles and next feeds. Yet as soon as Tom was back in her arms, she felt fire re-enter her bloodstream. Her feet hurt terribly in the ridiculous heels, but at least she was no longer being route-marched.

Mona turned automatically towards her room, but Cai pulled her back in the opposite direction.

"We're in Emlyn's old rooms. There's a study."

Cai said nothing more until he'd unlocked and opened Emlyn's door. The room was lit by dozens of tea lights in glass jars and there were bunches of flowers in random jugs all around the room. Mona looked at him in amazement.

"Sioned," he explained tightly, dropping down Tom's bag in a small kitchen area.

Cai's attitude had changed since they had left Siân. He now treated her more like a recently caged lion, keeping his distance and watching her every move. "You arranged it all? *Everything?* This stupid dress? Even my music?"

"I had a lot of help," he replied curtly.

Mona didn't know what to say. She'd been completely deceived by her friends. Tom moved and she rearranged him against her, using his reassuring weight to anchor her.

"They only agreed because I made such a big deal about wanting you back. It's not their fault." Cai swiftly defended the traitors. "You should know that your brother was extremely upset about the... subterfuge."

"I bet he was," Mona muttered into Tom's soft, sweet hair. "Arwel? Rob? Nia too?"

"Mona, they want you to be happy. I just convinced them you would be. Don't blame them." Cai's tone was militant, but weary.

"And at the end of the week?"

"I'm having a brew." He ignored her and walked to the sink.

"What then?"

"Don't you dare ask me that!" He slammed his fist down on the counter, making her jump. "Not without trying first." His aggression had returned in full. "If you weren't so bloody stubborn, there wouldn't have been any need for all this."

Mona wouldn't budge from the most important question. "And Tom?"

Cai made them tea; all the while explaining, as calmly as he could, what would happen. It was proving very difficult.

"Each day we'll go to breakfast together. We will train in the morning, but after lunch we're in here, where we'll work for as long as we can on the language. Supper will be brought to us, and the next day... we start again. *Until you can fight this thing on your own.*" He put the milk away. "Our cover has two parts, so we'll have to do some military stuff with Dafydd. Arwel is going to monitor your progress in the language and report back to Ifan."

Mona frowned at the turncoat's name.

"We'll need to be affectionate towards each other in public, but that will apply only when we're not training. Nobody would believe you'd let your emotions get in the way of work." He had it all worked out, down to the last detail.

Cai handed her the mug and she cuffed it away harshly, spilling scalding tea over his shirt and smashing the china against the wall. He flinched, stiffened, and then practically spat the last detail of the week's arrangements at her.

"Tom will be staying with Siân for the entire time."

"No!"

"No what?"

"He has to be with me at night."

"You're going to need a clear head. You'll need a full night's sleep. I won't allow it."

Mona was desperate. "Please, Cai, if I've only got a week left with him."

"No, you can say goodbye tonight." He was immoveable. "All your clothes are in the right-hand drawer. I'm getting changed for bed... so I'll use the shower first. I won't be long. There's a basket for your child."

Mona's mind had been focused elsewhere, and she hadn't realised until now that there was only one bed in the room.

"You'll be completely safe from me." Cai smirked viciously at her panicked look. "Don't worry."

There was a cruel edge in his voice she'd heard there before. His tone implied that he'd never even found her attractive.

≈

Once in the bathroom, Cai leaned back against the door. The spent adrenaline in his body had left him feeling weak and nauseous, and he was shaking quite badly. Holding the sink for support, he pressed his forehead onto the reviving chill of the porcelain. Against all odds, he'd managed to control her, but there was still a long way to go. Attacking Mona had been horrific, but letting her go had been much worse.

He showered quickly – suddenly unsure about leaving her alone. Perhaps he should have locked her in? Mona was still standing in the room when he opened the bathroom door, but Tom was now cocooned between two pillows. He looked very small in the double bed.

Mona had a toothbrush and pyjamas in her hand and watched him solemnly.

"You have to unzip me. I can't, I've tried."

No, no, no. I can't do this, not now. "Ok, turn round." Cai managed to sound irritated, almost bored.

The zip ran right down the back of Mona's dress, from the neck at the top all the way past her bottom. The hook and eye mechanism at the top was the most awkward, but the zip slid easily enough, until he reached the middle of her back. At this point, the pressure of her chest stretched the dress tight. As he passed the restriction, the top of the dress started to fall forwards under the weight of her breasts, revealing a black lacy bra, knickers and stocking tops.

With rigid self-control, Cai ignored the curve of Mona's back and bottom, and walked straight past her to the far side of the bed. He got in, closed his eyes and lay still – his entire body alert to her every sound and movement. Cai could feel her pent-up violence as Mona balled up the dress and threw it against the far wall.

"And I want my bloody music back!" she spat before blowing out the last candle.

Cai ignored her body heat as she slid into bed next to him, cradling the child in her arms.

≈

As soon as Cai had dragged Mona away, Idwal and Nia let out long sighs of relief. Turning to each other, they laughed at the symmetry of their reactions, both equally glad that the ordeal was over.

Mona's playlist had come to an end, and the band had reclaimed the stage again. Idwal could tell how much Nia loved the Celtic sounds by her tapping foot. Surely an innocent dance wouldn't be inappropriate?

"I'm not one for proper dancing, but would you mind if I had a go at throwing you round the dance floor?"

"I'd love to," she answered, and he took her hand.

It was that point of the evening when people had stopped caring what they looked like on the dance floor and were simply enjoying themselves. This made things easier for Idwal and Nia, who were fumbling to adjust to their very different sizes and styles of dancing. But after some initial confusion – whether Nia should stare straight ahead into Idwal's midriff or crick her neck looking up into his eyes – they were soon locked together in their own intimate world. Talking constantly, Idwal forced Nia's gaze upwards towards his face.

"Don't worry about Mona. If she didn't want to go with him, he'd be in no doubt of it by now. I've been reading your books, and I reckon she's the reincarnation of Boudicca."

Nia didn't laugh. How did he manage to get it so wrong? *Every single time?*

"Well, she could be. Reincarnation is a big part of our belief system. Though she's reminding me more and more of Medb."

"*Ooh*, I know this one," Idwal said quickly, shutting his eyes to recall the memory. "Medb, warrior queen of Connacht. Enemy of Cúchulainn, and all round nasty cow."

Nia glanced up in shock. "I didn't mean…"

"I know, I know. Anyway, I added the last bit." He chuckled and Nia felt the vibrations in her bones.

"So you're a bit like Buddhists?" he asked, picking up on the only reference he'd understood. That Buddhists believed in reincarnation was the only thing he knew about their religion.

"Not really." Nia tilted her head to one side, in the way Idwal always found so endearing. "We haven't got a religion as such, and we don't actually know what our forebears believed – though now we follow a broadly Pagan pattern with a smattering of gods and goddesses. However, many of us believe in the transmigration of the soul – that after death, it passes from one body into another."

Idwal had simply been trying to make conversation, so Nia would be forced to look up at him. He smiled at the seriousness of Nia's response, making her blush with embarrassment as she realised her mistake.

"I'm sorry, Idwal," she groaned. "You were just chatting." Nia touched her head to his chest in despair.

Idwal desperately wanted to hold it there, against him, but he was pretty sure this would constitute a breach of the rules.

"I need help," she muttered.

"You're perfect, Nia."

Eventually, the music ended and the band packed up. Nia knew now that she wanted Idwal to walk her back to her room, to kiss her at the door and then take her to bed. Unfortunately, the Cornish cohort was coming over and too soon, Idwal was dragged away from her.

≈

Nia lay awake for a long time, pondering the difficulty of practical, rather than theoretical, biology. Did she want to have sex with Idwal because her body screamed to carry his babies? Or was it her fixated mind that demanded this of her, because his genes might hold the possibility of magical power? There was an outside chance it was because he was gorgeous, kind and funny.

Whatever the reason, it was new and real. Nia wasn't a virgin. She'd come to an arrangement with Ieuan when she was sixteen. She hadn't really wanted to, and only went along with the ritual because she thought it an important rite of passage. Nia hadn't enjoyed it and since then had thought of sex as one more sport she'd never be any good at. Idwal was the first man she had ever reacted physically to, and the sensation was starting to overwhelm her whenever they were together. Even now, the memory of Idwal's proximity made her feel weak and fluttery.

There was a loud giggle right outside her door amid a wave of drunken shushing. The voices suggested a combination of Cornish lads and Galician women. There was a thrilling, erotic lilt to the exotic accents of the latter, and Nia understood why Cai had succumbed so easily to Carmen's charms.

"Can I interest any of you lovely ladies in a little nightcap?"

"Ha! Move along, Peder. Anyone seen where Idwal went?" The Galician woman made an appreciative purr. "My gods, the things I could do to that man."

There followed a chorus of robust feminine agreement.

"What! That pretty boy! What you need is some proper Cornish muscle." The women laughed cruelly and Peder sounded a little despondent. "Anyway, I thought Carmen was working on him again, now Cai's... moved on."

"Oh, she's always working on someone," another sensual female voice added. "As far as I can see, he's fair game."

"So that's not a *no*, then, is it?" Peder wheedled. There was more giggling and they moved away.

Nia sat bolt upright in bed, her heart hammering against her nightdress. She found it difficult to think. Was this horrific sensation jealousy? She stood up and paced back and forth across the room – stopping dead in her tracks as the realisation hit her. *Galicia.* There had always been questions asked about the inclusion of Galicia in the roll call of Celtic nations, and Nia had been curious about the women's credentials. If there was a Druid community on the Iberian Peninsula, it must be tiny – so tiny, in fact, that it must be in dire peril of extinction. The women weren't here on a gap year. They were here to find a solution to their impending doom. They were here to find viable Celtic mates – the more powerful, the better. Carmen had tried and failed with Cai, and now she was after Idwal. It was the next logical step.

Nia whirled into action. She had no time to waste against far more experienced competition. Neither Idwal nor Carmen had been part of the group outside. What if the Galician siren had already made her move?

Nia readied herself quickly and set off towards Idwal's room before she could change her mind. It wasn't until she had knocked on his door that her fear found a tangible form. Idwal hadn't once made a pass at her – during all their time alone together. Nia knew he was as experienced as Cai, so his failure to act couldn't possibly have stemmed from lack of confidence.

There was no answer. Relieved and appalled in equal measure, Nia turned away down the corridor. She had gone only a few yards, however, when the door creaked open behind her. In the doorway stood a bleary-eyed Idwal, a sheet wrapped tightly round his body.

"Nia?"

She could see his brain working: *Mona, Tom.*

"Is there a problem?"

Nia tiptoed back to his door, her face telling him not to panic. "No, I… I only wanted to talk to you," she whispered.

"Yes, of course. Come in."

Nia could see she hadn't totally allayed his fears, and he stood apprehensively just inside the room. He kept it extremely tidy and organised – his army training, she guessed, but it was a real change from his sister. Idwal arranged the sheet a little more decorously, but she could see he was naked beneath it and the knowledge excited her still further.

"I'm sorry to wake you. I know it's very late... I mean, early... I just..."

He was standing quite near her now and she didn't have the first idea how to behave, but he seemed to be waiting for her to explain herself, and she was normally so good at that. For once, words didn't seem appropriate, and with sudden rashness, she opened her cloak and let it drop to the floor. Underneath, she was completely naked.

"I'd like to have sex with you."

Idwal's eyes were wide with shock. Nia had expected that, but she had hoped her nude presence would soon lead to physical intimacy between them. It didn't, and the shocked look remained on his face.

Idwal realised he was staring, but it was hard not to. Nia was completely and utterly naked. His body had already reacted to her offer, but forcing his mind in a different direction, Idwal started to question Nia's bizarre behaviour. He wondered briefly if she was drunk, but dismissed the idea straightaway and tried to formulate another reason. Seconds ticked by and Idwal remembered how to breathe. It would only take the gentlest of touches to break the spell and draw Nia into his arms and bed, but that would totally annihilate the regulations he'd set in place for himself. Eventually, she started to shiver, so he picked up her cloak and, very gently, placed it round her again.

"You're getting cold."

Nia squeezed her eyes closed and bolted for the door. She didn't get far though, because Idwal put out one of his big arms to stop her and then lifted her up into both of them.

"Let's get some sleep. We'll have a chat in the morning."

Idwal lay her down on his bed and then joined her. She curled up against his chest and he kissed the top of her head.

10

Pretend

Cai woke in the early hours to the sound of hideous screaming. It took him half a minute to realise it was the baby and not a full-on nocturnal attack. Sitting up in bed, he saw only Mona's back as she swayed and jiggled and shushed. The child would calm down for a while, and then let off again, as if it had been stabbed. The high-pitched screeching tore through Cai's brain until he thought his eardrums would burst. He wondered, not entirely flippantly, whether the yowling would breach 'Noise at Work Regulations' in an engineering workshop. The caterwauling didn't seem to bother Mona, though. She appeared completely focused on trying out different remedies, including massage, to relieve whatever pain the child was suffering from. Cai watched for a while, unable to think of anything at all to say or do. He actually wanted to shout at the child to stop it screaming, but somehow, during the mayhem, he managed to fall asleep again.

Cai woke at his normal time to find them both sleeping in the armchair, and covered with Mona's cloak. He made the bed, hoping the noise would wake her. It did, and by breakfast time they had all arrived at Siân's door. Just before he knocked, Cai slid an arm around Mona's shoulders. She flinched, but didn't shake him off.

The baby still whimpered a little in its sleep and grimaced from time to time. Cai couldn't work out if last night was normal or if the child had been really sick. If it *was* ill, that would put a real spanner in the works.

"He might have colic. He had a really bad night," Mona told Siân as soon as she appeared at the door.

Cai breathed a sigh of relief. At least last night was an anomaly.

Siân took the baby in her arms with a delighted look on her face, as if she hadn't seen it for weeks. "I'll get Hefin to mix something up and I'll massage him with some lavender. It's nothing to worry about, love," she reassured Mona with uncharacteristic kindness. "It'll take a bit of time for him to adjust to the formula." She was clearly a little concerned for Mona, who looked drawn.

"Any chance you can keep him tonight, Siân?" Cai asked boldly.

"No problem," she answered instantly, running the back of her finger gently across Tom's fat cheek. "It might be for the best, until the powders start working."

They left for breakfast and Cai took hold of Mona's hand as they entered the canteen. There weren't many recruits up yet. Cai had organised a normal start this morning, but there were only just enough participants to validate a training session. Neither Rob, Nia nor Idwal were at breakfast, and Mona sighed thankfully. Sioned came in shortly after them, however, and ran over straightaway.

"Did you love the candles and flowers, Mo?"

The young girl's misplaced excitement threatened to blow the lid off Mona's self-control. Cai crushed her hand, too tightly, in warning. "They were perfect. How did you know?" she croaked.

"Just skill, I guess." Sioned winked and started walking away.

"You haven't seen my mp3 player, have you, Sion?"

"Dewi must still have it." She smiled at Mona with love. "See! Wasn't it a brilliant party? Gotta go. You would not *believe* all the gossip from last night." She rolled her eyes conspiratorially and flapped her hand. "I'll tell you later."

Mona's hand pulsated as Cai released it and the blood began returning to her fingers. She was spared further conversation with him by Arwel's arrival. It was his betrayal that had hurt her the most.

"How could you?" she accused him bluntly.

Shamefaced, Arwel mumbled something incomprehensible at the floor, and Cai was left to answer on his behalf.

"None of this is Arwel. It's all me, blame me."

Cai may have been a good tactician, but Mona knew the timbre of Arwel's work. She just looked away from both of them to her throbbing hand.

≈

Once inside the training room, Cai abandoned any pretence of affection. Mona started breathing normally again, not counting her breaths in and out in order to remain in some sort of control. She allowed herself to sink deeply into the rhythm of her patterns, and with each completed move, she felt her confidence returning. After finishing the routine, Mona was more ready to fight than train.

Dafydd arrived a little late and dishevelled. He took a second to look at them and winked, impressed by Cai's victory. "Surprised you two are up."

Cai tried to smile knowingly, but didn't risk any more physical contact with Mona – not now they were in this room. They made their way to the circle and Mona started the class.

"We're going to work this three times, but limit the moves. So, kicks only in the first bout, punches and chops in the second, and close contact wrestling in the third. First to three should do it. Watch carefully, and we'll discuss all three at the end." She looked each of the warriors in the eye. "You're going to need to create the best combinations of moves for yourselves. Sometimes we're restricted to a single type of action, so it's best to be prepared." She then spoke to Cai. "Ready?"

Mona knew Cai had improved and that he was now an extremely competent fighter. But there had always been an extra element to her fighting – an ability to channel every particle of her being into combat.

As she faced Cai now, Mona could feel her rage, fear and humiliation turn to fuel. She would hold back enough not to break his bones, but there would be pain. Her strategy was simple: incapacitate her opponent in the first bout with three carefully placed kicks.

Mona began by inflicting painful blows to Cai's left thigh, right knee and right hip. The punches and slaps thrown in the second round weakened these targeted areas further and caused pain and winding to his chest area. By the time they reached the wrestling stage – Mona's weakest discipline – Cai was tottering and off balance.

He'd sustained substantial damage to his load-bearing thigh and knee. Mona used her speed to capitalise on this weakness, because even in his current state, Cai was the stronger, heavier fighter. Mona couldn't help but admire his stoicism. He didn't cry out once, and even managed a mangled smile as she helped him to his feet.

At first, the class seemed stunned by her brutality. There was a shocked silence in the training room and it required some prompting to get them to answer appropriately.

"What does that teach you?"

"Be first with the kicks?" came a tentative answer.

"Yes, Cadan, be first with the kicks!"

≈

Nia was grateful to be still wrapped in her cloak when she awoke – and that she was alone. Thank the gods Idwal had had the decency to slip away quietly. What on earth had possessed her to behave so rashly?" It had all seemed so straightforward in the early hours of the morning. She would die of embarrassment next time she saw him.

The noise of the door opening warned Nia that her death was imminent.

"Morning! Look, breakfast." Idwal was eating some sort of pastry, while holding more of the contraband aloft. His words were a little muffled and Nia couldn't meet his eye.

"I'm so sorry about last night. Please don't ever tell anyone. Not even Mona." She stood up and began inching towards the door.

"Don't go. Can't we talk about it?"

Nia looked at him then, but her eyes were full and her voice wouldn't work.

Grasping her by the shoulders, Idwal sat her down on the edge of the bed, and then knelt down before her. He smelt of toothpaste and pastry. "What happened?"

Nia decided she might as well tell him the truth. It was as mad as any fabrication. "I heard some women talking about you. They had... designs on you, and I didn't like it. I'm not very experienced and I just thought... I thought it as good an approach as any." Her voice lowered in volume. "I didn't realise you didn't feel the same until it was too late." Idwal was right: talking was better and, when her voice worked, her eyes were dry.

"Nia!" Idwal's voice turned soft with wonder. "Mona warned me to stay away from you, said she'd kill me if I... upset you." He barely breathed, hardly daring to believe his luck. "I was trying to be a gentleman – for the first time in my life."

She grabbed his hand. "I'm completely out of my depth, Idwal. I've never actually wanted to have sex with anyone before, but each time I see you – it's all I can think about."

He instantly wanted to laugh at this clinical self-assessment, but he held back; she was extremely vulnerable.

"I know you want to laugh at me, you brute. I can feel it." Nia poked him in the shoulder and he did laugh, but it was such a lovely carefree sound that she soon joined him.

"*Ti yw'r ddynes fwya anhygoel i mi gyfarfod â hi erioed* – You're the most wonderful woman I've ever met."

He leaned in to her gently, pushing back her curtain of hair. "I'm going to kiss you now and I'd be grateful if you didn't make notes."

≈

132

Cai found walking to lunch extremely difficult, but he suffered in silence, even managing to fuss and kiss Mona a bit as Sioned joined them.

"How are you today?" she asked them both with a glint in her eye. Sioned had been on patrol during Cai's humiliating punishment and was none the wiser.

Mona put her hand on Cai's injured thigh, rubbed its length brusquely and left her hand there. She was viciously delighted as he gasped.

"Wonderful, and you?"

"Ok," she grinned smugly. "Though it's been like a ghost ship here. Most of the men got stuck into the bitter with the Cornish boys and haven't come round yet." She paused for dramatic effect. "And both Nia and Idwal are missing!"

Her eyes flashed and Mona's heart skipped a beat. So it was too late; her brother had caught Nia. Mona wondered gloomily if their relationship would end in a similar car crash to hers. Sioned had noticed the pause.

"You don't seem happy, Mo."

Mona shrugged and glanced at Cai. "Oh well, we'd better get to work," she said, slapping her hand down hard on his damaged limb.

≈

Cai didn't even try to keep up with Mona on their way back to the room, and staggered in five minutes behind her. No longer able to keep up the pretence, he eased himself onto the bed. He hoped he wouldn't pass out from the pain, and prayed that if he did, she would think he was sleeping.

"I'll get us set up in the study." Mona sounded breezily business-like. "What do we need for the lesson? Pens, paper, books, or would you prefer more traditional instruments of torture?"

The pain was too overwhelming for Cai to attempt a response. When he did eventually look up, Mona was holding the *mark* above him, her eyes closed. Cai briefly passed out, but came around seconds later to the sensation of his trousers being pulled down. With a loud yelp, he moved quickly to cover himself.

"Lie still," Mona commanded, her voice full of exasperation. "I'm not going to cut it off."

Cai's left thigh was in a bad way, with a huge amount of trauma in his muscles. He tensed as she closed both hands over the damage; he felt a tugging then a freezing, then a blessed numbness. She moved to his knee and repeated the sequence. By the time she'd repaired his hip and chest area, Mona's breathing had become heavy and laboured.

"Sleep now," she managed, before crawling into bed next to him and collapsing.

≈

A knock at the door woke them. It was Sioned with their evening meal. She giggled scandalously as she spied her apparently naked brother in the bed.

"You said you were going to come to supper!" She grinned cheekily, clearly delighted with the reunion. "Anyway, Siân says Tom's fine and you might need this to keep your strength up."

"Any sign of my music player yet?" Mona asked, deflecting the banter. It was silly really, but she felt the loss of her little machine keenly.

"No, not yet," Sioned replied. "But I'll check around. It's got to be here somewhere."

≈

Mona set the food down in the study, and once dressed, Cai joined her. They ate in silence, avoiding each other's eyes, as if they'd just shared some embarrassing intimacy.

Mona spoke first. "I held back today, Cai. I know what will hurt, what will break, and what will kill. I realise you've got your own weapon against me, but don't ever threaten me with it again. Remember, you would have to be conscious to talk."

He nodded, and they continued in silence for several minutes more. Cai spoke next, his tone conciliatory. "Thanks for healing me." Mona dismissed his awkward gratitude with a shrug. "You weren't sick?"

"I wasn't drawing poison. I just put some of my life force into you. It drains me, that's all."

Cai nodded as if he understood. "You can sleep if you want. We don't have to start straightaway."

"I'm fine." Mona took the empty plates into the tiny kitchen and washed them. "We can work till midnight, and then I'm going to bed." She sighed in despair, thinking of the hours of failure that lay ahead. "But I have to warn you: Nia, Arwel and Ifan have all tried to teach me this infernal language. There must be something wrong with my brain. I will work, but I'm not optimistic."

Mona did try, *really* hard, but the Welsh words just seemed to slide through her memory. She would get a word or phrase and hold it, repeat it even, but teach her another and the first would slip away. Like magnetic poles meeting, each new word would repel the last, and by midnight they were both exhausted.

≈

"Idwal... Id." He was asleep, with Nia wrapped in the huge heaviness of his arms. *"Idwal."*

His eyes stayed closed, but a faint smile flickered around his lips, so she began speaking.

"I've had an idea."

The smile widened, but his eyes remained shut.

"I think you *do* have magic, just like Mo. Sex is your power."

He tried not to laugh, but it was hard work. "That's very kind, Nia, but I'm fairly sure that I'm a pretty average sort of lover."

"Oh?" Nia's mind played over the extraordinary day she had

spent in Idwal's bed. "Do you mean that's how everyone feels when they have sex?"

"Pretty much. *Ssh*, go to sleep. Sleep time."

Nia found his words hard to believe, as she recalled the wave after wave of exquisite energy that had wracked her body; from extreme tenderness to violent passion. "I can't believe I've wasted all this time studying! Why didn't someone tell me you've all been doing this – feeling like this?"

Idwal's eyes were open now, staring into the warm brown of hers. "I'm very glad no one did. I'm glad you saved it all for me."

"And you've been having sex like *this*, with all the women you meet, for years?"

There wasn't any point denying it, but Idwal wasn't sure he liked the direction the conversation was taking. "Not all of them, and not all the time, but... yes."

"Well, whatever you lack in natural talent, you've certainly made up for it... with dedicated practice."

I'm being funny, she thought. As he chuckled, Nia wiggled an arm free so she could touch his chest, and Idwal closed his eyes again.

11

Healer

Both tutor and student were more than ready for the canteen early on Monday morning, having given up any pretence of progress at midnight.

Mona was humiliated by her inability to learn Welsh, and it rankled her that Cai was now fully aware of her intellectual feebleness. Added to which, there had been a twenty-minute farce of avoiding body and eye contact as they prepared for the day ahead. It wasn't merely the acute embarrassment of sharing these small rooms. Any slight, accidental touch between them could spark off those unwelcome apparitions, and yet there appeared to be no categorical trigger-point.

Mona remained tetchy at breakfast, and she pulled her hand away in alarm as Cai attempted some false affection. "If we were in an actual relationship, I doubt we'd do all this touching and holding of hands."

Cai stopped trying immediately. "We can cut it out now Sioned has seen the evidence with her own eyes."

Mona was proved right. The word had indeed spread, and there were lots of knowing little smiles at breakfast. As Nia and Idwal approached, they weren't just holding hands but glowing with happiness. Nia looked beautiful, as always, but content and at ease in a way Mona had never seen before. She seemed unable to stop smiling, and Mona realised instantaneously that this was the genuine thing.

"You're a dead man, Idwal Jones!" Mona joked, but watching the couple gaze at each other reminded her so poignantly of the looks her parents had shared, she knew they were going to be happy ever after. "Don't name any of your children after an island," she warned them, and they beamed at each other again. "I don't suppose either of you have seen my mp3?"

Neither of them had and they promised to look, but she couldn't imagine that happening. They'd lost the ability to see anything but each other.

≈

Mona could feel Cai's reticence as they neared the training room, but he seemed resigned to more punishment. Now that he wasn't touching her all the time, Cai's presence was almost tolerable, though she resented the way her body constantly responded to his – especially to his smell.

There was a full house this morning, and Mona got them sparring in groups of four. Carmen and Maria were grouped with a couple of Cornish lads and their light-hearted, flirtatious chat stuttered to a halt as Mona approached to assess their progress.

While watching their form, Mona found herself studying Carmen's small, curvy body instead of her core stability. She wore a skin-tight, plunging bra top and matching leggings. The woman had a stunning Latin face, tumbling dark curls, full breasts and a tiny waist. Somehow, and without her permission, Mona's imagination conjured an embarrassingly vivid image of Cai and Carmen writhing in the throes of passion – every part of them locked together in ecstasy.

Swallowing a slug of green poison, Mona forced her gaze away. As she moved on to the next group, Carmen muttered something to the men that elicited a round of chuckling. Mona felt the green snake in her belly writhe to strike. With effort, she moved to the door, desperate to get out before her violent desires overwhelmed her.

Cai looked a little awkward as Mona passed him, and she guessed he probably conjured similar images each time he saw the beautiful

Galician woman. Mona remembered their very brief affair last year and wondered if Carmen would last the full two weeks. Perhaps she was exotic enough to be the real thing this time.

"I've got to check on Tom; see you back in the room at one," she told him as she left.

≈

"I love to watch her fight," Peder said to no one in particular as he stared after Mona's disappearing form. "She's just so..."

"Raw? Dangerous?" Cadan interrupted, hands on top of his head and breathing hard.

"It's more than that, though, isn't it? It's like she's designed to fight. Not only good, but perfect."

Carmen scoffed, harshly. "She's plain at best, and just look at those shoulders. I swear she's broader than Cai." Carmen was irritated by the attention Mona received from some of the men. She was not an attractive woman. So what if she could fight?

Cai watched Mona leave. She seemed a little upset, but it was hard to tell. He wasn't entirely happy with the awestruck tone of the Cornishmen either. Carmen slipped her arm nimbly through his. It was a mistake, she realised, as he drew his arm back with equal haste. "Are you trying to upset her?"

"What? Do you think she'll threaten to kill me?" Carmen asked acidly.

"No, I think you'll hurt her feelings."

"So, she's let you back into bed with her now – after she's beaten you black and blue. Tell me, Cai, how rough does Mona like her sex?"

Carmen allowed herself a satisfied giggle. She had an audience, but nobody else laughed. Cai walked away from her and out the door without another word.

≈

Idwal and Nia had discussed the difficulty of working together in a confined space, and the reality wasn't nearly as easy as the theory. Fifteen minutes after arriving in the library, and Nia had already looked up from her tome.

"Are you trying not to think about sex?"

Idwal chortled; he'd thought he was prepared for any of her eccentricities. "That's a pretty regular part of my life," he replied with an overdramatic sigh.

"So, how often do you think about sex, on average, in a day?"

"Aren't we supposed to be researching the *mark*?"

"You're prevaricating."

"I don't want to get into trouble," he said. Nia laughed and they managed another hour.

Idwal found he'd finally exhausted all the texts in English translation, and he started thumbing through some of the innumerable volumes in Welsh. He had never encountered written Welsh before, but had started to pick up the spoken language very easily, and the words on the page were starting to make some sense. He concentrated his efforts on a tale he knew well: *Gwenllian the Brave*. Maybe it was because he'd so recently read it in English, but Idwal seemed to know where he was in the story.

"Are you understanding any of the Welsh text?" Nia asked.

"I might well be."

"Thank the gods for that. It's so difficult thinking of you as being English."

Idwal bridled a little at Nia's words. "Why? It's where I was born and grew up. You might have this whole Saxon-hating thing a bit out of proportion."

"You've read the histories; you know what controlling monsters the Anglo-Saxons have been, Idwal." Nia snorted. "*Idwal Jones*, very English," she continued to mutter loudly.

"Don't be like that. I'm proud of being English."

"*Proud?* Are you mad?" Nia stood up and Idwal sensed her outrage. "Think of the word for England: *Lloegyr*, the lost lands." She trembled with emotion and pointed at her books. "The English word for *Alba* is Scotland; for *Kernow* it's Cornwall; for *Cymru*, Wales; for *Éire*, Ireland." Nia counted the names of the Sea Kingdoms out on her trembling fingers. "*Breizh* has become Brittany and *Ellan Vannin* is now called the Isle of Man." Nia only paused long enough to suck in a passionate breath. "They've annihilated all but one of those languages. But while they lived, there was one word for the English common to every single one of them: *Sais* – Saxon. And it *wasn't* a compliment."

"Nia…"

"No, Idwal. We've been bullied for centuries. Pushed and squeezed into the furthest points on these islands. There are sixteen million Celts left in these lands and only two million still speak any sort of mother tongue." Nia stuck her chin out and her nose back into her book, but Idwal tapped her knee.

"Come on, Nia. Can't I just be Idwal?" He gently pulled her chin up with a finger. "Mum and Dad never mentioned Wales or Ireland – apart from the Six Nations of course, and that normally involved singing rather than speaking."

Nia's curiosity overwhelmed her anger and she looked up. "Did they sing well?"

"My dad did. He could make a lot of noise," Idwal answered truthfully, and she smiled.

Nia had an agenda though – if Idwal could sing, her life might very well be complete. "*Fedri di ganu* – Can you sing?"

"I too can make a lot of noise. Would you like to hear?"

"Yes, please." Nia crawled onto his lap. "I'm so sorry, Idwal. You can't help who you are." She touched his face lightly. "I don't care anyway. I'd like you even if you were Roman." Nia grinned shyly and Idwal took the opportunity to kiss her.

"Ok. But I reckon it's only fair on the rest of the *Conway's* inhabitants if you judge my voice in private."

Idwal carried her out through the door, gazing down at his amazing find.

"Mmmm. I think that may be wise – if your voice is anything like your sister's…" Nia was about to say more, but suddenly stiffened board-like as a searing pain shot through her abdomen. In response, she curled into a ball, horrifying Idwal, who had registered the pain through his arms.

"*Bloody hell*, Nia! What was that?" He put her back down carefully.

Nia blew out in short bursts, trying to regulate the intensity of the pain. "It's ok, it's just… my period. It's a lot harder than it used to be." There was another attack, then a short reprieve. "It will pass shortly, just keep talking to me."

He didn't talk, but moved both hands over her abdomen. "Unzip your skirt. I need to touch your skin." The pain had washed over her again, incapacitating Nia, so he did it himself. "It's like knives in there – all hot and inflamed." Idwal didn't know how or why he knew that; he merely wanted it to be cool and calm. As his hands moved across her body, Nia felt a gentle, knitting pressure followed by a welcome numbing sensation. Slowly, her body began to unclench itself.

≈

Cai found himself jogging by the time he reached their room. To his relief, she was still there, rummaging around on the floor and picking up clothes.

"Are you ok?" Cai asked as casually as he could.

"Yes," she lied. "I just remembered Nia said she would do my laundry if I got it to her at lunch. It's all changed since… Nesta died." The motherly queen of laundry was the last person Mona wanted to think about. She couldn't possibly divulge that particular weak spot to him, so she continued crawling around until she found the lone dusty sock she sought.

"I'm sorry about Nesta." Cai coughed. "I'd heard you two became close." He didn't want to upset Mona further, but Cai felt like he needed to say something to her. There couldn't possibly be any more clothes under the desk, but she didn't come out.

"She was good to me," Mona answered. *And to anyone else who needed a mum*, she could have added. Mona and Arwel had shared her love.

Mona's body language screamed at Cai to leave her alone, so he scanned the floor for any more of her clothes, and spied a pile in the far corner by the kitchenette. It was the black dress he'd bought her, with all the underwear balled up inside it. He remembered her flinging it across the room on Saturday night, right after he'd helped her out of it. The memory caused an embarrassing physiological response. As luck would have it, Mona chose that moment to get up and walk over, forcing Cai to hide his embarrassment with the bundle of clothes.

Mona had fabricated a smile, attempting to mask the sadness she felt over Nesta. "What have you got there? Oh!" Mona stopped when she saw the dress in his hands. "I'm sure Nia or Siân can straighten it out a bit. Someone else will be able to use it." Cai didn't answer, he seemed a little on edge, so Mona carried on talking. "Using the dress to incapacitate me worked well. I was completely disabled by the tightness of the skirt across my thighs and calves."

Cai tried to swallow as his mouth dried out further.

"It was constricting across the ribcage, preventing me from breathing properly. I couldn't take down a full breath; get the oxygen to the muscles – very clever." She recalled how well Cai had executed the attack sequence, though there was always room for improvement. "And it was a good hold, but if you had twisted your wrist slightly it would have compromised my balance – as well as everything else. Here, let me show you." Mona reached for his hand, which he quickly snatched away.

"No! No, that's fine. We need to get on, or we'll miss Nia."

She shrugged and held out the bag for Cai to drop the dress in, but he paused. "Do you mind if I keep it?" he asked.

"No, of course not." It was much too big for Carmen, she thought.

≈

143

Nia met them as they were walking in. She flashed a quick, unspoken message to Mona with her eyes.

"We need to talk," she breathed into the back of Mona's neck in the lunch queue. "About Idwal."

Mona's heart sank like a stone, wondering what on earth she could mean.

Nia spoke uncharacteristically bluntly to Cai. "I need Mona for half an hour after lunch – woman stuff."

Mona thought Cai would put up more of a fight, but he didn't. He had been quiet since training, and it dawned on her that he was probably missing Carmen. The green venom roiled, but she held it at bay. They were getting on much better, now he was being reasonable, and Mona resolved to tell him she didn't mind him spending his nights with the Galician woman.

≈

Idwal waited for them in the library. He'd managed to ease the cramps in Nia's stomach and she seemed to think it was some sort of miracle. It was madness of course; Idwal knew he was no medic. A-level biology was as far as he'd got, and though he recognised it might have something to do with his genetics, he also wondered if it might just have been a coincidence. Idwal didn't have to wait long before Mona barged through the door, eyes wide with expectation.

"Don't get too excited, Mo. It could have been luck."

She ignored his protestations and examined his hands. "How did you feel when it happened?"

"I don't know."

"Try to remember. I haven't got much time."

"Nia was in pain and I just wanted to help." He closed his eyes, trying to remember the sequence of events. "I touched her, and I felt her pain."

"You were in pain?"

"No, I only registered the intensity, and then I investigated it somehow."

"And?"

"And…" He shrugged. "I just thought about calming it down." He turned to Nia. "I haven't fixed you. It'll come back… next time."

"How do you know that?" Mona asked, and Idwal scrunched up his face.

"I don't know. It sounds mad, but I can sense it, almost *see* it." Idwal's gaze moved back and forth, trapped between the two women. "I'm not sure what happened…"

"Let's see." Mona ignored his doubts and rolled up her sleeve to reveal a bruise on her forearm. He touched it. "What do you see now?"

"Nothing." And it was true – whatever he'd *seen* before had vanished and the bruise remained a purple blotch on his sister's arm. Mona seemed relieved and Nia disappointed. "False alarm," Idwal said, smiling.

≈

Cai wracked his brain while he waited for Mona, trying desperately to think of another approach he could use to get the Welsh to stick in her head. He'd attempted traditional teaching methods, and as she'd predicted, the result had been a fiasco. Cai had even considered dealing with it as an engineering problem. There *was* a way. He just had to find it – and by Sunday. He'd fetched up his sketchbooks from the voyage and rifled through them for inspiration.

Mona burst into the room a little out of breath. "Sorry. It took longer than I thought. Let's get started."

"Ok. We're going to try a different approach today. We'll see how you get on using visual triggers." Mona could see a number of beautiful technical drawings, spread out across the table with Cai's neat, clear annotations in the margins. "I want you to think of these words as machine parts. Maybe we can build phrases and sentences like sorting out the engine of a bike."

For the first time since attempting to learn the language, Mona felt positive. This sounded like the nearest thing to a solution she'd come across. "Brilliant. Let's go."

≈

It was an excellent plan, and by rights, it should have worked. Mona had a good grasp of engineering and a capable mind, but as the minutes and hours dragged on without success, they both became despondent.

"Let's take a break," he muttered.

"I'm fine to carry on," she growled back, stubbornly.

"Well I'm not," Cai retaliated, his patience finally fraying.

The atmosphere in the room had changed from optimistic endeavour to irritated weariness, and Mona felt her failure and his disappointment deeply, and she shoved the sketchbook away from her in frustration.

"I don't know why you don't all speak English anyway. Welsh is such a stupid bloody language," she grumbled belligerently.

"What did you say?" Mona knew she'd insulted Cai by the way the blood drained from his face. "How dare you?" he bellowed, shocking Mona rigid in her seat.

"I only meant..."

"I know what you meant, Mona. You're not just stupid – you're ignorant. How much do you know of our history?"

Mona was taken aback by his sudden vehemence.

"Well, Nia..."

"Not enough, obviously." Cai was furious. He clearly didn't want a discussion, so Mona rose slowly from her seat to leave. "Sit down and listen to me, you arrogant bitch." Cai shoved his weight against her shoulders, forcing Mona to sit back down and listen. "For centuries, England has punished, legislated against, and ignored anyone who's dared use their own language." His voice was quiet initially, but the volume rose with his indignation. "Gaelic, Cornish, Manx – they've nearly all gone. But some of us held on to *our* language, *our* history, and passed it down to *our* children – despite the continual struggle and abuse." Cai's passion made him breathless, and he pointed at the Moses basket. "Whatever else your son is, he's a *Celt*. I don't care if it's Welsh or Irish he's taught, but it's his birthright to speak it." Cai's tirade was winding down, but he hadn't yet finished. The emotion in his voice had morphed into wonder. "Welsh is not *just* a language, Mona. There is a quiet resistance in each word uttered – every syllable. It is mighty and beautiful and it is *still* here, even after all this time, and if we stop fighting for it now, it will die."

Mona kept her eyes lowered as Cai stormed out of the room, slamming the door on his way through. She was thoroughly ashamed of her ignorance – on all counts. He'd probably left to get some fresh air and to stiffen his resolve. Mona was painfully aware of how frustrating her denseness could be for her tutors.

With nothing else to do, she started to thumb through the sketchbooks he'd left out. They seemed to be a series of visual diaries chronicling Cai's year away – and they were exquisite. There was a detailed drawing of a Thames sailing barge, together with a whole assortment of different vessels, some marked with technical annotations and others clearly drawn for the sheer aesthetic pleasure of the task. Mona became lost in the pages, and she found a small but precise drawing of a clock mechanism, hung from a chain. The drawing showed Welsh text round the outside of the clock with her name hidden inside the main body of the piece. With a surge of affection, Mona realised that *Cai* had made the beautiful pendant for her. It was the only thing she'd wanted to keep from Saturday's debacle.

In another sketchbook she found more technical notes and drawings, which she might have been able to understand, given a degree in electronics. In amongst all the dryness, she found several pages of drawings, dedicated to a woman with incredibly large breasts. The bloom of affection faded, but only a little – she'd known all along what to expect from Cai. Mona reopened the sketchbook containing her pendant and traced the lines of the drawing with her index finger.

As Cai came back in through the door she deftly flipped back to the barges. He looked contrite. "I didn't mean to lose my temper."

"No, I'm sorry. I *am* ignorant and stupid. Though I did try to warn you. I'm so dense, light bends around me."

Cai didn't even laugh at her joke, and there was nothing else to say. After two days of hard work, there had been absolutely no progress – at all.

"These drawings are lovely, Cai. Where did you see these boats?"

"They're barges, from Holland, but I found them on my journey." He seemed a little mollified. "People, families, live on them."

"Really?" Mona peered a little closer. "That sounds like fun."

"It does," he agreed, twisting the sketchbook between them. Mona couldn't help but admire the tapering shape of his hands and fingers. "They used to be cargo-carrying and people convert the holds into living accommodation... I thought you'd like them."

Forgetting the circumstances, Cai and Mona began to talk as if they liked each other. "They're a lovely shape," she said. "Though I bet they're difficult to steer." She tapped the page. "Looks like all the engine is in the back?"

"I know!" he chuckled. "I think you'd have to get some sort of bow thruster fitted."

"What's one of those?"

"Well, it's an extra engine up at the bow. Makes manoeuvring easier."

"I see." She nodded. "I bet they're a bugger to park. Clever." She peered at the drawing again. "Diesel or electric?"

"You can get both, but I thought a hydraulic system might be an interesting way to go."

Mona wasn't too clued-up on hydraulics, and she would have loved to have spent an evening learning more. It wouldn't have solved her immediate problem though, and the moment passed. "I suppose we'd better swot up on the military notes for Dafydd."

When not trying to learn Welsh, Mona was a different person: quick and interested, giving alternative viewpoints on everything Cai had to say.

"Well, that's it really." Cai stretched out, forcing his triceps to contract. Mona looked and then looked away. "You've got it all down. There's nothing more to say."

"Nothing more to say, *Chief*," she teased. He did laugh, but it was fairly hollow. There remained one more avenue to try, Cai thought, but Mona wasn't going to like it, and any reference in that direction was virtually taboo between them. Mona glanced at the time.

"We've missed supper again." She yawned. "I get so sleepy in here."

"Are you calling me boring?"

She found it difficult to tell whether Cai was joking. His delivery was always so deadpan.

"Only when you try to teach me your language. It makes me drowsy."

His heart raced a little and he sat upright – should he use this opportunity to tell Mona his plan? But Mona was already ahead of him; not angry, as he would have guessed, but terribly, sickeningly afraid.

"You don't know what it's like, Cai. I get completely overpowered."

Mona didn't look up, and he instinctively put a hand over hers. "I know you're frightened, but we're running out of time here. I only want to protect you. You must know that by now."

She flipped his hand off hers, thankful that his careless touch hadn't sparked any more irritating visions. "I need to think," she said, standing abruptly and walking straight into the bathroom. Cai went in search of food. Mona's mood always improved after eating.

The shower woke her up. Mona knew, as Cai did, that it was the only real route left open to them. Days were slipping by and she had to know what to expect at the end of the week – if the lessons failed. There was quite a lot she needed to negotiate with him, and Mona realised, by the end of her shower, she was holding a pretty good card. *Bloody hell – no clothes.*

"Cai," she called. No answer. "Cai!" Again, nothing.

Mona opened the door slightly and peeped through the crack. The room was empty. She didn't want to put her dirty clothes back on, so after wrapping the towel around her, she dashed over to her drawers. "Why do I always leave laundry so long?" she muttered to herself.

A solitary pair of last-resort pants stared up at her, along with a very old pair of tracky bottoms and a style of T-shirt that she shunned because the neckline showed her *mark*. She'd have to put the dirty bra back on.

Mona was closing the drawer when Cai came back in with food. "Back in a minute. Smells good," she gabbled and raced back to the bathroom.

The five more minutes it took Mona to get dressed were welcome to Cai, who used the time to try to regain control over his palpitating heart. The image of her wet body wrapped in its small towel was unshakeable, as was the rippling flow of muscle in her back and legs as she ran. His self-control took another pounding when she rejoined him. Instead of her normal combat clothes, Mona now wore a pair of low-waisted leggings and a T-shirt that either belonged to Sioned or had shrunk in the wash. His eyes were drawn instinctively to her *mark*, causing her to put her hand over it self-consciously.

"I told you I hated laundry," she quipped, but felt more exposed than she'd bargained for. "Have you got something I can borrow? You always seem to have clean clothes."

"That's because I do my laundry every week," he tutted. Cai found a shirt that covered her, making them both happier.

He didn't push the point, but was more than ready to talk when she started the negotiations. "I think if we try this approach... we must concentrate on subjects you feel strongly about but that don't affect me at all." Cai agreed, and she continued. "If there's any sort of progress tonight, I want Tom back." She put up her hand to prevent him from protesting. "Don't worry. If he has a bad night, then I'll forgo training and sleep for a bit. And…" She paused. "And I want to talk about what happens on Sunday… if even this doesn't work."

"I've got a few subjects in mind, actually," Cai replied. "So we'll be playing it really safe, and you're absolutely right: I am pretty boring. You know?" He smiled. "I can get really quite excited about the Stirling engine."

"I knew it! Geek." Mona kept her tone light, but she waited for his reply.

"Agreed about Tom. I can look after the bigger babies, no problem."

"And?"

"I've readied the *Marc'h* for you. There are supplies, some cash, blankets and clothes on board. I'll take you as far as the mainland and you can go on by train." It was a hard thing for him to say, knowing it would be the last time he would ever see her, but it was better than the alternative. He'd wanted to send her to Eigg, but Dafydd would know to look there.

Mona was stunned by his compassion and couldn't think of a response. "What does *Marc'h* mean?" she asked, filling the silence.

"More lessons?" He smiled sadly.

"It just sounds English. I thought…"

Cai took up a pen and wrote down the word.

"Not Roman. Not English. It's a Breton word, but there's so much meaning in it."

Mona frowned and Cai wrote down another word: *Mark*. Mona's hand touched the cloth at her chest, but Cai shook his head.

"No, Mark the man, a Cornish king, *Margh, or March* in Welsh, uncle of Tristan, husband of Iseult – the Hound of the Sea." Cai smiled and Mona held her breath. "Cornish, Breton and Welsh share a root language, Mo, but they also share some folklore. In the Welsh version of the tale Mark has the ears of a horse – a play on words because *March* means horse in Welsh."

"That's too much in just one word," Mona whispered in wonder, and Cai agreed with a proud smile.

"It's a clever, beautiful language."

"It is," she agreed, directing the full wattage of her smile at him for the first time in over a year.

Cai wanted to reach a hand across the table, but restrained himself. "The Irish clan know about you now, and if they found you here, they will keep looking until they find you again. You could never come back, Mona." He frowned. "Though I would tell Idwal eventually, give him a meeting place and a time, somewhere in the future."

Mona was quiet for a while. "And Ifan?"

"What can he do if you're gone?"

≈

Arwel held Rhona in her sleep. He'd managed to engineer them a tiny room of their own. It was only just large enough for a bed, but that was all they needed. They would handfast at Lughnasadh, in a little over a week's time. He knew it would cause no end of trouble, but that wasn't the only thing keeping him awake tonight.

Something about the information he'd been sifting through stuck in his mind like a splinter. The more his brain rubbed over the idea, the nearer he came to pinpointing the snag – the spy.

There came a soft but insistent knock at the door, and when he failed to respond quickly enough, a voice called out. "Arwel!" Sioned's voice was demanding, not playful. Work, then, he thought – an emergency. He didn't invite her in, but shot through the door, closing it behind him swiftly before her sharp eyes could catch a glimpse of Rhona.

"What's the problem?"

"I'm not entirely certain, but Dai thinks he might have picked up some talk about VSVs over the radio."

Arwel's heart clenched. They'd got away with it for a week, but the enemy had to know the *Conway* had been reunited. It would be utter foolishness for them to attack now. There was something fundamental he was overlooking, but his brain hurt from thinking. "Who have you told?"

"I've come straight here. I didn't want to disturb Mona and Cai – just in case we're wrong." A ghost of a smile twisted her lips as she stared meaningfully at his door.

"Come on," he said, pulling her away. "Let's get to the control room."

Bryn and Dai were both there and Arwel realised it must have been shift change. "All I heard was 'four pointy hulls', then nothing. I didn't ask too many questions." Dai sounded worried.

"Find out everything you can," Arwel urged. "It's not over."

Bryn looked up in grim agreement and Sioned sighed. "What do they want with us?"

≈

Mona and Cai had assumed the careful non-contact distance adopted during the last catastrophic set of lessons. He also made sure they were sitting down on opposing sides of the desk.

"I'm going to start talking, in Welsh, about some pretty ordinary things. After a while, I'll introduce a level of intensity to a certain word. You need to tell me what you hear and feel and we'll go from there. If you don't like what's going on, bang the table – before it gets too much."

Cai started speaking. As always, Mona's eyes were drawn to the movement of his lips as they formed the unintelligible words. His mouth moved differently when he spoke Welsh, she noticed; there were soft 'll's from the side and rolling 'rh's. Suddenly, and without warning, she realised that Cai spoke of barnacles – more than that: about how he hated scraping barnacles off boats. She felt his frustration at the endlessness of the task. She felt his resentment at the stubborn molluscs as they dug in to the hull, the sharp pain of his knuckles as they scraped against the skin. She gripped the table and he stopped talking.

"*Barnacles*! You hate them. *So much*."

"Yes," he chuckled. "I do. How do you feel?"

"I understood the sounds, and then some words attached themselves to that meaning. Am I making any sense?"

"No! No not at all, but that doesn't matter. So, can you tell me any words in Welsh, barnacle or boat, for instance?"

"*Cragen crâch* and *cwch*," Mona answered promptly, and Cai's heart sang with sudden, unexpected hope.

"Ok, next time you start to feel it… try to block the effect. Fight it if you can." He was eager to make progress.

"Can you try something you dislike a little less?"

Cai merely nodded, intent on the experiment, and began to speak again. Her mind filled with the texture of soft, white processed bread, cloying her mouth and sticking to its roof. Knowing this was the idea to catch and grapple with, she concentrated hard on holding it in place.

It was exhausting work and slow, but they made concrete progress. Mona knew the word for bread, and she could still remember the words for barnacle and boat. At the same time, she could sense a slight grinding in her head, as if a great, big, loose tooth had been wobbled. They should stop soon. She'd reached that sleepy point when her own demons began to flood in. Still Cai talked, his voice hypnotic, erotic, sensual. *Bang.* He stopped talking.

"What was that?" she asked.

"I was describing some fight moves."

"No more of those, then," she stated unequivocally and slumped forwards, exhausted but relieved.

"Shall we get Tom?" Cai suggested.

Mona jumped up for the door before he could take another breath.

≈

Mona used a system of pillow walls and buttresses to pen Tom in on the bed while she organised his life. Cai couldn't help thinking there must be a more efficient method of ensuring his safety.

"He really needs some sort of small chair," he mumbled, mostly to himself. "Something that provides a bit of support but allows him to look around. Shouldn't be too hard to make."

"It's called a bouncer, I think you'll find," Mona said, shaking a bottle of milk. "I've put it on the list for the next mainland trip. There's quite a decent Oxfam there. It shouldn't cost much more than a fiver."

Cai left them to it, making himself scarce in the bathroom. Mentally, he prepared himself for the charade of indifference that watching her undress required. Unusually, though, both mother and child were already in bed and asleep when he returned to the bedroom.

He was grateful for the reprieve, and pulled back the bedclothes on his side of the bed, only to discover that Mona's shorts had ridden up to reveal her right buttock. She lay facing away from him, on her side with one knee bent. Cai tried not to look at where the folds of material disappeared in between her legs – but it was too late. Mona's vest had twisted with her movements and the side of her plump, white breast strained around its edge. Only her arms had any summer colouring, but they seemed dark in contrast to the baby's tiny hand lying across them. Tom lay cocooned in Mona's arms, his head against her heart. Cai found it difficult to define the strange, conflicting emotions he felt, but jealousy was definitely among them.

With great effort, he replaced the sheet and tried to think of anything but the aching, which now throbbed through his body. There was no way he'd be able to sleep next to Mona tonight, so he got up and left the room.

Cai had only taken a few strides down the corridor when he realised that he'd left them unguarded. Cadan was the first sober recruit he could find, and Cai promised him a late start at training in exchange for guarding their door. It was an easy task: act as an armed guard with no one in or out. Cai set off for his workshop, pleased to have thought of an achievable goal and a distraction from Mona.

By two in the morning, he had worked out a basic design and cutting list, but needed more practical information. Cadan stood up as Cai arrived back at the door.

"Thanks, Cad. I'm going to need a guard for a couple more nights – around about the same time. Can you sort it out with some of the lads? I don't mind who, as long as they're sober." He clapped Cadan on the arm and pushed down on the door handle. "See you at ten for training."

Cadan regarded Cai with a funny expression – disapproval maybe – but he was too tired and preoccupied to care. "Your boy got a bit fractious tonight. Sounded like your missus could have done with a hand in there." There was that look again.

"Oh, he's often like that. I don't think it's serious. Anyway, Mona knows what she's doing. Night, then."

Careful not to let his eyes be drawn under the sheets, Cai banked a wall of cushions between him and Mona, then fell asleep thinking of how to attach a swivel mechanism to a hardwood frame.

12

Treasure

Neither Tom nor Mona stirred at the alarm, so Cai left them undisturbed in bed. By the time he was ready to leave, they were still dead to the world, and Cai spent a minute or so watching Mona's sleeping face. He'd been careful never to stare while she was awake. Though sure that Mona's face hadn't changed, Cai found it hard to remember her as plain. It wasn't that he thought her beautiful now – she was just Mona and just right.

He needed to speak to Rob about the baby chair mechanism, as his designs were getting more elaborate by the minute. "Can I have a word?" Cai asked him tentatively at breakfast.

Rob appeared to have made a full recovery, but seemed thinner and tetchier. "I haven't seen her music player," he replied blandly.

"No. That's not what I was going to say."

"So what is it?" Rob asked, reluctantly settling down next to Cai with his muesli. "Is everything ok?"

"Tom had a bad night again, so I've left them in bed." Cai felt awkward about asking another favour. He knew Rob remained sceptical about him. "I need your advice about a bouncer chair. Tom needs one, or something like it, and I think it would make Mona's life a bit easier. I want to help her and it seems a good way."

"Yep, great idea." Rob pushed his untouched breakfast away. "But she'd probably settle for a hand with the night-time feeds at the moment." There was an irritated edge to Rob's tone and Cai looked stunned.

"But I'm not qualified to do that."

"You're his dad. That's the only qualification you need."

Cai didn't look convinced. "I'm trying to keep it a surprise, so don't let on. Is there any way you can meet me in my workshop tonight? About 10.30? It should only take a few minutes."

"Ok," Rob grunted, shaking his head at the cereal box as Cai trundled off to the training room. "See you there."

≈

Idwal knocked again; perhaps he'd been too tentative the first time.

"Come in, Idwal." Tucked up in bed, Nia looked very pale and small. Idwal beamed sunnily at her, pleased to have tracked her down to her mother's rooms. Siân came through from the tiny kitchen with a drink for her daughter, and she smiled awkwardly at Idwal. He knew Siân was trying to come to terms with their relationship, but it would be hard for her to let Nia go.

"I'm off, then," she said quietly.

"I'm not staying, Siân," Idwal replied hurriedly. "I was just worried when Nia wasn't at breakfast."

"*Plis nei di aros* – Please stay," Nia murmured from beneath the duvet. As Siân left, she patted Idwal with strained affection.

"How bad is it?" he asked, smoothing Nia's hair back.

"Bad."

"Can I help?"

She moved her head to nod, but had to squeeze her eyes shut as another wave of painful cramping overwhelmed her. Idwal moved his hand under her nightdress. She was so tiny that it covered her abdomen entirely. Somehow, through his fingers, he was able to see clearly the inside of her pelvic area.

Admittedly, most of what he could see was a confusing muddle, and Idwal was forced to draw on distant memories of A-level biology diagrams before he could make any sense of it. Nia's cervix, uterus… but there was a tangled mess either side that looked to be the source of the problem. If he concentrated really hard, Idwal could somehow clear away the inflammation.

In his mind's eye, Idwal could see tiny little threads emanating from his fingers into Nia's body, but when he lifted his hand to look, it seemed entirely normal. Placing his fingers back down on Nia's flesh, the threads became visible once more. Concentrating hard, Idwal used the force of his mind to push them into an inflamed area. Nia froze as he did so, but he gently repeated the process over and over until she began to feel better.

"You should sleep now. I'll be back later." He kissed her forehead and she sank into a deep sleep. As Idwal left for the library, something nagged urgently at his mind.

≈

Before beginning the lesson, Cai asked everyone at training about the missing mp3 player.

"Who's lost an mp3? I thought we weren't allowed anything like that here?" Carmen piped up, but Cai ignored her and continued with the session.

As Cai gave out the practice moves, one of the younger Cornishmen sidled up to Carmen at the back of the training room. "You are a wicked little tart."

She raised her eyebrows in surprise, but still remembered to shrug nonchalantly.

"Don't play the innocent! I've spoken to Cadan myself. How did you manage to lure him back? You two must have had a full-on session. Cai looks totally knackered."

Carmen quickly grasped what she was being accused of, and played along so she could find out more.

"You know how it is." She smiled and pushed her torso towards him. "I'm totally irresistible."

159

"Word is he's made the same arrangement for the next couple of nights." The young man sniggered like a dirty schoolboy.

"I'd better have a little nap this afternoon, then." Carmen fluttered her eyes at him from beneath her dark lashes. "I can't even remember what time he left."

"The early hours, Cad said. You naughty little minx."

≈

By lunchtime, Carmen had made sure everyone knew about Cai's alleged infidelity. When she sat herself down next to Peder in the canteen, he was surprisingly offish with her. It didn't take Carmen long to figure out why.

"It's only that I feel sorry for Mona," he mumbled. "What with the baby and that."

"Well, I shouldn't really gossip…" Carmen lowered her voice and Peder leaned in. "Cai doesn't actually want anyone to know, but *he* thinks Mona's got the hots for someone else. He doesn't reckon she's interested in him anymore." She winked at him and his face lit up. "I think I might know who she fancies, Ped."

"Not me?" His eyes widened. "Don't be daft." Carmen merely smiled and nodded her head wisely. His ego did the rest. "She *was* quite friendly with me on Saturday night," he mused. "Just before Cai whisked her away, that is. I thought I might have been in with a chance at one point."

"Why don't you put your name down as guard tonight? You can ask her yourself," Carmen suggested innocently. Peder smiled back at her and she nodded knowingly.

≈

Mona was exhausted, despite having only just woken up. She'd deposited Tom with Siân and had shuffled in late to lunch. Her head hurt, but it wasn't a headache. Cai's lessons were having a

160

really strange effect on her brain. Even the conversational Welsh that she'd heard spoken around her all year had started to disturb her. The sound of Welsh had been a constant babble of water over stone, but now the squabbles and chit-chat of her friends had a frightening intensity to them, and she moved away to a space on her own.

Carmen noticed that Mona sat by herself at lunch. Cai was deep in discussion with the gorgeous but shy Rob, a couple of tables down. Her brother and the wet librarian were nowhere to be seen. So Carmen made her move. There was something *off* about Mona, like she had a migraine, or something. *Babies.* She shuddered. Carmen was well aware of what was expected from her back home, but it was her life, her choice and her body – babies could definitely wait. By the same token, Carmen didn't feel sorry for Mona: she was just a stupid cow who'd got carelessly pregnant.

Although not ugly, Mona was big and very unfeminine. It upset Carmen to her core that Cai had been unmoved by her own beauty and talents. If he didn't want her, then she'd make life as difficult as possible for Mona. At least it would provide some entertainment on this godforsaken rock.

"Back late last night, wasn't he?" Carmen said conversationally. Lost in her own thoughts, Mona hadn't even noticed she had company, and jumped on hearing a voice beside her. Carmen repeated the question, Mona's silence telling her all she needed to know. "He's coming again tonight, if you'll pardon the pun. Probably more than once; he's like a machine once he gets started, don't you find that?"

Carmen could see Cai was winding up his conversation with Rob. Knowing that he'd be likely to come over, she got up and left Mona to it. Carmen doubted there would be fireworks immediately, but felt a definite sense of satisfaction as she sauntered away.

≈

Following her tête-à-tête with Carmen, Mona felt an urgent need for some fresh air. Walking past Cai, who was still with Rob, she remarked as casually as she could, "I'm going for a walk. Be back in a while."

Rob knew Mona's body language too well for her to completely disguise her anguish from him. But she nevertheless smiled at him over Cai's head – she missed his company badly.

"Sounds like a good plan," Cai replied, distracted by Rob's new, much simpler ideas for the baby-chair. He could get everything finished tonight.

The fresh air revived her. She hadn't trained or fought since the day before yesterday, and Mona needed to kick-start her brain into gear again. Something about working with Cai in that room made her sleepy and strangely submissive.

Carmen had goaded the green monster in Mona's belly, and the bitch's words had upset, but not surprised her. The Galician woman clearly resented Cai's absence and his puppet show with Mona meant he'd spent all his waking hours with her over the last few days. Trying to be objective about their relationship, Mona understood that Cai, of all people, needed to have sex. Perhaps she was just hurt that he hadn't mentioned he was going out? Then again, it wasn't anything to do with her – maybe he was just being discreet. She had to remind herself to distinguish reality from pretence.

Mona wasn't sure why Carmen had felt the need to mention their liaison last night. Maybe she really was just a nasty piece of work. On a more pragmatic note, it might make Mona's life easier if some of Cai's sexual tension could be dissipated. She certainly didn't need any more of those unwanted emotions slipping into her mind from his during their interminable lessons.

There was a chance this new method would work, and she had to stick with it. They had only five days left, and regardless of her initial misgivings, it was clear now that Cai wanted to help. Carmen's poisonous remarks had confirmed something though. Mona and Tom were leaving on Sunday, regardless of whether she'd been cured or not.

≈

Cai had opened every one of the windows and he'd put a glass of water on Mona's side of the desk. He smiled as she let herself in. He really was the most attractive man she'd ever known – no wonder Carmen didn't want to share him.

"How do you feel?" he asked.

"*So* sleepy. The windows are a good idea." A wave of sensual lethargy had descended on Mona the second she'd stepped over the threshold.

"More dislikes today. Negative is better than positive with you. It's easier to avoid potential pitfalls."

"Yep, excellent idea."

Cai admired her bravado, knowing Mona was still petrified of what might happen next.

≈

There weren't a great many biology books in the library, but Idwal had read and reread what was there, several times, in his quest to help Nia. She sat beside him now, lost on a literary trail of her own. She looked utterly delightful when she studied, he thought.

"So what have you discovered, Dr Jones?"

Idwal snorted, feeling a bit Harrison Ford-ish. "Not much," he lied. "How about you?"

"Actually, I might just be onto something. Do you remember the story of *Gwenllian the Brave*?" She knew he did, and forged ahead. "Well, apart from the fact she's rumoured to be one of the authors of the Mabinogion, I've found something else." Nia flicked and rummaged until she found the section. "Gwenllian was beheaded in front of her son, Morgan, who was then captured by the Normans, but managed to escape. It appears he also became a bit of a writer." She kept her finger on the page but stared directly at Idwal. "He's interesting, because the whole family were thought to be Druids – a bad thing to be at the time."

"No shit, Sherlock!"

Nia frowned slightly but ignored his strange epithet. "Morgan went into hiding but continued to write. I've always found his stuff a little odd, eccentric, but there are references that keep cropping up about Ynys Môn." Idwal raised his eyebrows. "And some sort of *treasure* or *gift*."

"You think there may be buried treasure here?"

"It could explain the interest. It's only a lead, but it does carry on in other texts for the next few centuries. An exciting little topic to get obsessed about, don't you think?"

"Nothing better than a little bit of healthy obsession. Talking of which…" He picked her up and dumped her on the desk. "Time for the next round of treatment."

"I'm fine." She struggled weakly.

"No lying. It's pointless. Keep still and flat."

Nia puffed in exasperation. "You sound just like Mona. You're a terrifically bossy family, you know."

Idwal smiled down at her, and then closed his eyes to concentrate. The more he concentrated, the more he saw. Everything seemed normal until he moved his little threads past the uterus and onto the fallopian tubes.

Neither of Nia's fallopian tubes resembled the drawings he'd spent the whole afternoon studying. Hers were flattened and stuck, all the way up to the ovaries. Idwal focused his power on a tube, to study it closer and maybe see if he could just unstick the walls from each other.

Nia screamed in agony. He'd got carried away trying to repair her; he'd been too brutal. Without the slightest idea how, Idwal instinctively flooded her body with a powerful soothing balm, relieving the pain he'd caused her with his mistake.

"I'm fine," she gasped. "Sorry I screamed – it was a bit of a surprise, that's all."

"Nia…" He stopped. How could he tell her what he feared? That she might never be able to have children. "Let's get out of here. Let's take a walk."

≈

The sunny day had brought a lot of people out. Up ahead, Idwal could see Tom's battered red pram parked near the beach, and from the shore came the sounds of squealing and laughter. On a rare dry day, Sioned and her friends were enjoying an afternoon off by the water's edge. There was no sign of Tom, and Idwal upped his walking speed towards the pram.

"Don't worry, Sioned adores Tom and she's always very careful," Nia reassured him.

He slowed with mock nonchalance and Nia stifled a laugh. "I'm not worried." And he wasn't now, because Idwal saw a guard stationed at Tom's side in the guise of an extremely gangly teenager.

"Afternoon, Arwel," Nia chimed as she peeked inside the pram. "Can I pick him up?"

Arwel struggled to his feet, *Gallic Wars* in hand. "Only if he's awake. It took me ages to settle him."

Tom was awake and Nia gave him a cuddle. In the light of what he had to tell her, seeing Nia hold Tom affected Idwal quite powerfully.

Sioned spotted them from the beach and came bounding over, flushed from the sun and slightly damp. "I'll take over now, Al."

"I'm ok here," Arwel said. Sioned shrugged and turned her attention to Tom.

"Does Mona know he's out here?" Nia asked a little pointedly.

"No, and she doesn't need to. He's got sunblock and all sorts on. Fresh air is good for babies, isn't it, Al?"

Arwel nodded. He always agreed with Sioned.

Idwal noticed that Tom twisted in Sioned's direction as she spoke, and mentioned it.

"Of course he did! He loves me because I'm his favourite aunty," Sioned said proudly, squashing her face next to Tom's and angling them both towards Idwal. "Can't you see the family resemblance?"

Idwal puffed, as if in despair. "I certainly can, poor little chap."

Sioned gave him a mock sneer, and Nia, ever the diplomat, intervened. "He looks like both sides of the family. It's only his eyes that make him look more like Cai."

Sioned reluctantly agreed. "I worry he might grow up to be as serious as my brother."

"I hope not," Idwal said quickly. "That would make him ugly, boring *and* difficult."

The sneer from Sioned was far more genuine this time, and Nia mediated again. "Actually, it's a really powerful combination… in mere stubbornness alone."

Nia had meant it as a joke, but her brain directly raced off, analysing Tom's genetic inheritance.

Just to be safe, Sioned rescued the baby from Nia, who'd entered a state of intellectual reverie. "Don't listen to them, Tommy. You won't be stubborn." Tom reacted to Sioned by hooting and bashing out at her face. "You're my little treasure," she said, trying to catch his flailing fingers in her mouth.

Nia was thunderstruck. "What did you just say?" she demanded of Sioned.

"Nothing… I just said…"

Nia had already turned and raced away up the beach. Idwal raised his shoulders in a brief apology to Sioned and chased after her.

≈

"Shall I close the windows?"

"*No!*" Mona's eyes were drooping.

"It's getting a bit cold in here, Mo. I'll get you a jumper." Cai could feel the chill on his arms, and was convinced Mona would too. He let her rest while he made the coffee, and then returned to the table with a jumper and mug in his hands. "Thought we needed a caffeine boost. Mo?"

She'd fallen asleep on her arms. It was probably a bit too early to stop, but there wasn't any point in carrying on like this. Cai decided to call it a day. "Come on, Mona. We'll leave it for now. You did well today." He knelt down by the side of the chair and put his arm around her shoulder. "*Ti wedi cael digon; gwely i ti cariad* – Come on, love. You've had enough; let's get you to bed." Cai gently pulled her up.

Mona's arms and shoulders were cool and bumped with gooseflesh. She was almost standing when she opened her eyes to him – eyes full of desire. Mona had already pressed her body up against his before he'd managed to stop talking, her lips mere millimetres away from his own.

Cai closed his eyes and sucked back his words. Mona lurched away, embarrassed and shocked. She sat on the edge of the bed, one arm curled around her stomach, the other over her eyes. "That was a close one." Mona rubbed her face, mortified.

"I'm so sorry, Mo. We should have stopped earlier. I'm tired too and I got used to speaking in Welsh…"

"Don't worry about it," she muttered. "I'm going to pick up Tommy." She stood up briskly and went to the door. Mona knew this would be a good time to let Cai know that she'd be ok with him sleeping at Carmen's; being incarcerated with them wasn't fair. "Don't feel like you have to stick around here for us, you know. We'll be fine on our own." Mona found she couldn't quite say the actual words of release.

Cai felt a little hurt. Was Mona more upset about his mistake than she'd let on? "Has it got worse since we started today? I thought we were making some progress," he asked quietly.

Mona still appeared more than a little awkward. "I think we are. It's just affecting me more deeply. There's a constant low-level sleepiness and…" She coughed, remembering her conversation with Carmen. "As soon as you say anything with any sort of… anyway, it's much… worse. I'm afraid we might have disturbed something. Perhaps we should…"

"I'll be a tyrant from now on," Cai interrupted her. "I'm sorry, but we can't give up. There's just too much at stake."

≈

By the time Idwal reached the library, Nia had already started flipping through books and rummaging amongst piles of volumes. She knew he stood behind her but didn't wait to give him an explanation for her hasty flight from the beach.

"I'll get you a pile of books to read through… and you might want to get some snacks up here. I think it's going to be a long haul." She'd become frenetic, and spots of colour dappled her cheekbones.

"Nia, I need to speak to you. It's important…"

"As important as Tom's life?"

Idwal hadn't been expecting that. What he had to say could wait. "What am I looking for?" he said, rolling up his sleeves.

"Do you remember what we talked about earlier?"

"Gwenllian?"

"Yes, her son's writings. Something is beginning to make sense." She checked the spines of books perfunctorily and placed them on his growing pile. "We're looking for anything that mentions *treasure* or *gift* or *prize*. If we can get all the references together, I might have something."

"How does this treasure affect Tom?"

She stared up meaningfully. "If I'm right, Tom *is* the treasure."

≈

Cai pottered in the kitchen, waiting for Mona and Tom to settle before he could slip out. The pair fell quickly into sleep, but there wouldn't be a guard outside the door for another twenty minutes or so. He sat in the armchair again and watched their sleeping forms, as they breathed as one.

Tom reminded him of Sioned when she'd been a baby, but only because she was the only other baby – apart from Arwel – that he'd had much to do with. He'd started to think of Tom as Mona's child now, rather than as an evil alien being sucking the life out of her. Cai couldn't see what it was about Tom that made the rest of his family adore him, but there was no denying he was a large, handsome, healthy baby. He also enjoyed watching the interplay between mother and child, the constant tenderness between the two. Mona was always touching and kissing him, without even consciously thinking about it. Sometimes when she looked at Tom, Mona seemed to be witnessing some sort of miracle.

Peder turned up for guard duty this time. The Cornishman wasn't chatty, and Cai was pleased. He wanted to finish the chair tonight and wondered what he would learn from Rob.

≈

"Is that it?" Rob had given Cai a sketch of some metal tubing and fabric.

"Yeah. That's all you need. You were overcomplicating it."

"Bit of a trait of mine, I'm afraid." Cai rubbed at his brow reluctant to ask yet another favour from a man he barely knew. "Is there any chance you can stay here with me and get it finished? I can weld the steel, but could use a hand with the fabric."

Rob rolled his eyes, but had obviously anticipated Cai's request. Reaching inside his bag, Rob produced not only fabric and needles, but also a flask of coffee and a packet of biscuits.

They worked quickly, Rob suggesting adjustments as Cai fashioned the tubing. The flask came out as soon as the metalwork had been completed.

"I want them back, you know. You can't keep them to yourself." Rob kept the tone light, but meant what he said.

Cai suddenly realised that Rob resented him at some fundamental level. "Can't we share them?"

Rob's stare was stony. "Can you?"

"We're working hard... very hard. It should all be over by Sunday."

There wasn't yet animosity between them, but a definite edge had crept into the room. The men were both quiet for a moment, and Cai had the feeling that Rob had something to say. But he kept his silence and it was Cai who spoke again. "You and Mona get on really well, don't you?"

Rob looked up from his stitching, wanting to say something, but he simply gave a nonchalant shrug and got back to work. Cai laughed dryly, resigned to the fact.

"What?" Rob asked.

"You don't trust me."

"No, I don't. I'm not even sure I *like* you." Rob had said it now; there was no point in stopping there. "You've been a complete shit to her. The rest of them may have fallen for it, but I haven't." He threw down the fabric. "You waltz back here and *literally* whisk her off her feet." Cai cringed at the outburst. "And I *still* can't believe she's taken you back after the way you've been… carrying on with that Galician bitch." Rob had really warmed to the subject. "I mean, how well do you really know her, Cai? I know her. I love them in a way you can't even comprehend."

Rob was right. Mona remained a mystery to Cai on many levels, but Rob didn't have all the facts. "I don't suppose it's been easy for you – being part of this."

"Part of what? Being a gay man in a homophobic, macho community?"

Cai gave a wry nod. He hadn't expected their conversation to take this turn. "Yes, I can see that," he muttered.

"But don't tell me?" Rob whispered through gritted teeth. "You can't bring yourself to talk about it."

He was aggravated enough with Cai to voice every ounce of his frustration tonight.

"I'd be lying if I said this was comfortable for me…" Cai replied carefully.

"Honest I suppose," Rob interrupted as he savagely stabbed needle into fabric.

"Truth is Rob, I don't care whether you're gay or not. You took care of Mo when I…."

"Don't give me that crap, I didn't do it for you," he snapped. Nothing Cai could possibly say would matter now. "She's cried in her sleep, *every night*, for the best part of a year. Did you know that?"

Cai closed his eyes shut against that news.

"No," Rob said, crushing the material in his hand. "I thought not." Rob hadn't finished yet. "I don't like this power game you're playing. You know, I really thought Mona was invincible, but now I'm not sure. I think you could actually destroy her." Cai met Rob's glare, but he was implacable. "I'm asking you not to. I'm asking you nicely *not* to hurt her. If you can't hack it, then you should get out now. Don't stay for Tom's sake." Rob paused for breath, fixing Cai with his stare. "I know you're his father, but I delivered Tom, I love him, and I'm more than capable of being a good father to him – for the rest of my life."

Having had his say, Rob smoothed out the crumpled fabric, letting the tension in the air dissipate. "Look, I don't want to upset you. Just think about what I've said. I'll get her through it; only don't… drag it out." He coughed, slightly embarrassed by his emotional outburst. "And now for the fabric. Watch and learn, young Padawan."

Cai found he couldn't laugh at this Mona-ism, but they set to work again.

≈

Tom's colic had improved, but out of habit, he still woke at 1.30 in the morning with a half-hearted squawk. Mona had the medicine ready, and hoped to settle him without a full-scale battle. She stood up to soothe and shush him, explaining softly that he was much better and it was definitely time to go back to sleep.

Mona felt enormously sleepy herself, and the low-level arousal, which had been with her all day, was still present – even without Cai around. It was as if the big wobbly tooth in her head, disturbed by their progress, had started to release waves of eroticism. Mona hoped

Cai's exertions tonight would emancipate her tomorrow. But thinking about what he was up to with Carmen only served to arouse her further.

Tom's mewling had died down to the odd sigh and whimper as she lay him back down on the bed. Mona readied herself to slide in beside him, when there was a knock on the door.

"Everything all right in there, Mo?" It was Peder. How strange!

She opened the door. "Yes, fine. He's asleep now." She put a finger to her lips and made a hushing sound, then smiled lightly. "What are you doing here?"

"Cai asked me to keep watch while he… popped out." Peder gazed into her eyes and they both knew what he meant. "I'm sorry. I don't agree with it. Not with you and the little fella."

"Don't worry, Ped. It'll sort itself out."

"I could beat him up for you," he joked.

"No." She shook her head and smiled sleepily. "You couldn't. You're still far too unstable in your core."

Mona didn't ask him in, but she sensed Peder wanted her to. He looked at her mouth, then down at her chest and back up again. *Dear God, don't say anything to me in Cornish*, she thought. The slightest Celtic whisper would send her over the edge.

"Mona." Peder only breathed this one simple word, but it was drenched in pity, frustration and desire. Mona was no match for its might in her current state and that one Celtic word was enough.

≈

"Thanks, Rob… it's great. I just wanted to say…" Cai felt he owed Rob some sort of explanation.

"Ssh! No more talking. We'll talk later; when I'm not falling asleep. Go!"

Rob pushed Cai out of the workshop and he started back down the corridor towards their room. Cai was happy with the chair. It was a bit of an eyesore, but it would do the job and he really wanted

Mona to like it. Peder wasn't outside the room and Cai cursed him –
he shouldn't have left his post.

Opening the door quietly, Cai was shaken rigid by what he saw.
Peder had pushed Mona up against the sink, and one of his great big
hands roamed her body. The other hand drew her head tight against
his. They were kissing each other passionately, and he kept whispering
her name – over and over again.

Cai staggered headlong into the room, abandoning the chair as
he did so. At the sound, Peder twisted to face him. But it wasn't
Peder who Cai stared at – he was looking straight at Mona and she
revolted him. "Mona! What the…"

"Don't start *that*." As the Cornishman spoke, Cai was forced to
refocus. "Don't sound so fucking hard done by, mate. Everyone
knows where you've been."

Cai frowned in confusion as he watched Mona push Peder away
and rake shaking fingers through her hair. "What do you mean?"

Peder squared up to Cai, who was still watching Mona. "There's
no point in denying it. Carmen told me herself."

"Carmen?"

Peder laughed harshly. "You're fucking unreal."

Tom started to cry and Mona flipped. "*Get out!*" She shoved
Peder so hard that he lost his balance.

"But Mona…" He made another gentle approach and she shunted
him away again, even harder this time.

"Get out! *Now*! Both of you."

Mona's initial shame had been replaced by red-hot fury. Suddenly
wary, Peder backed away towards the door. After a final hard glance
at Mona, Cai also strode out, the sound of Tom's screams chasing
after him down the corridor.

≈

Mona couldn't control her anger and as a result failed to settle Tom.
No amount of shushing or swaying would convince him to calm

down; he even refused a bottle. In desperation, she tied him against her in a sling and attempted to walk away his cries. At first, her wandering was an aimless, rage-driven journey through the *Conway*'s corridors, but after five minutes of seething anger, Mona realised she had a destination in mind.

It was only after Mona had knocked on Carmen's door that she knew what question to ask. "Come in, Cai," came the sensual invitation. Mona's intended question disintegrated like smoke, and she bulldozed her way into Carmen's grotto of love. The room was lit with tea lights and was thick with the heavy scent of joss sticks. On the bedside table sat a bottle of rum and several packets of condoms.

Carmen herself was stretched out on her front; her curvy, undulating body temptingly displayed through a fine veneer of silk. Buds in her ears led to a small battered mp3 player, which she instinctively clenched tighter as Mona entered.

"That's mine." Mona's reaction was primal, and as Carmen skittered backwards on the bed, Mona caught hold of the front of her flimsy nightdress – which ripped like a cobweb.

"Take it! You fucking brute." Carmen yanked the earphones from her head and flung them at Mona. "No wonder Cai's so rough," she spat, while pinching together the remains of the nightdress over her full, brown breasts.

"You stole it!" Mona accused.

"I found it and kept it. There's a difference," she shouted back, giving up with the nightdress and covering her nakedness with the bed-sheet instead. "You shouldn't neglect things you care about, Mona. People will take them from you."

Tom had been quiet throughout Mona's grabbing assault, but he started to sob again in the bitter silence that followed. His head was hot and damp with tears. Tom didn't need to be here, caught up in this squalid, sordid little story. Mona didn't need it either. How had it come to this? Squabbling over music players – fighting over a man? Mona pulled Tom from the sling and held him close to her heart, soothing, stroking and swaying into his shuddering neck.

"I don't care what you do with Cai," Mona whispered as Tom's eyes finally closed. "Just keep the fuck out of my way." Mona didn't want to be here when Cai came in, so she stuffed the music player into her back pocket and headed out.

≈

Desperately needing some fresh air, Cai stomped out of the *Conway's* main doors and into the salt wind of the strait. Unfortunately, Peder was still following him and *still* talking.

"What do you mean, she's not interested in me? It certainly felt like it back there."

Cai clenched his whole body in an effort to stop himself decking the Cornishman. "Trust me, she's not."

"You can't have them both. That's not fair." Peder sounded a little childish, but he obviously believed what he said.

"Look, Peder. I'm not with Carmen. It was a one-night thing – a mistake."

"So where have you been for the past couple of nights?" It was more of an accusation than a question.

"In my workshop. I've been making a chair for Tom... with Rob."

Peder looked shocked, then angry, and then awkward. He leant up against the boathouse wall and swore. "*Fucking evil cow.*" He dragged both hands through his hair and then down his face, shaking his head slowly. "She said Mona fancied me. She said you two were still at it. I felt sorry for Mo, and when she came to the door, I..."

"Did you speak to her in Welsh?"

"No, I can't speak Welsh," Peder replied, looking confused.

"Cornish, then?" Cai asked bitterly.

"No, I just said her name and..."

"Is that all? Are you sure?" Cai was trying to piece together events. How could she have been affected so easily? Surely just saying her name couldn't have pushed Mona over the edge? It would have happened before now. His mind wandered back to their conversation this afternoon. The lessons were working; she'd said so. Then he remembered her wanting to give up. They'd disturbed something. *Mona*, he thought. That one Welsh word might have been enough. Cai kicked the timber wall and then pummelled it with his clenched fists.

"I'm sorry, mate – I had no idea." Peder straightened and raised his chin. "You can take a clean swipe at me. It's nothing I don't deserve." Cai shook his head and sunk down to the ground, sitting on his haunches. After a minute or so, Peder joined him.

"So, it's pretty serious?" he enquired gently. Cai didn't think he could respond appropriately to an understatement of such magnitude. "Does she know?" Peder asked cryptically.

"Know what?"

"How you feel?"

Cai was puzzled. Mona wasn't a stupid woman, despite her inability to learn Welsh. She would have worked it out by now. "I assumed…"

"*Ah!* Big mistake." Peder sucked his teeth and shook his head. "I'm not saying I know a lot about relationships, but that's rule number one. Tell them how you feel." He looked at Cai with a sliver of pity. "Or at least tell them who you *aren't* shagging."

The truth flattened Cai. "Mona thinks I'm still…"

"Carmen's made it her business to let everyone else know. I doubt she left Mo out."

Cai bounced up onto the balls of his feet. "I should go and tell her… let her know."

"What are you going to say?" Peder also moved to stand, but more slowly. Cai shook his head, still unclear how to explain himself. "Let's have a walk round the block – get it straight in your head before you say something *really* stupid," Peder advised gravely.

≈

Mona could see, think and act freely now. Being incarcerated with Cai and his language had weakened her. He'd had her in a full, sensual body grip, and the more progress she'd made with the Welsh, the more vulnerable and pathetic she'd become. One word, one *fucking* word, was all it took now. Things were getting worse not better. Now they were apart, she could look ahead into a future with Cai and see a diminished, weak and totally reliant woman. Not the person Mona ever thought she'd be.

Even if the situation with Carmen were resolved, there would be other women, other fights. Mona saw clearly that she had only one choice to make if she was going to survive as herself – as Mona Jones. She sat Tom in the new bouncer she'd found just inside the door, and she set to work.

The letter to Cai was the hardest, but those to her friends and brother weren't easy to write either. Once she'd finished, Mona packed a rucksack and holdall with warm and waterproof gear, then stuffed as many nappies as she could in afterwards. Away from the constant churn of Cai's emotions, she was able to plan her getaway calmly and methodically.

≈

The first signs of dawn were glimmering in the east as Peder and Cai approached the ornate double gates at the entrance to the *Conway's* compound.

"You could always try the comedy angle. Mona might appreciate that." The men stood close enough for Peder to catch Cai's look of incredulity. "Or maybe not," he chuckled.

"What about Carmen?" Cai asked, and it was a loaded question.

"Let me deal with her," Peder grunted ominously. "She needs setting straight."

Cai sighed with regret, but it had been good talking to Peder. He gazed up at the mottled sky, preparing what he had to say to Mona. A slight movement in Cai's peripheral vision hooked his interest, and he twisted to peer into the half-light. Nothing stirred, but he walked towards the shadows anyway, squinting to eliminate excess detail.

A sudden explosion of noise and power erupted from the ground, and Cai was knocked backwards by a double-barrelled kick to the chest. Cai knew he'd been winded, even as he flew backwards through the air. Peder attempted to grapple with the attacker, who spun and dodged through the large lock forward's grasp and was already showing the Cornishman a clean set of heels. Peder shot off in pursuit, but his prey was quick, nimble and making yards with every stride.

Cai dragged himself from the ground, rasping harshly, but he could see that Peder was losing the foot race to the gates. Still gasping for air, Cai launched into a desperate sprint, passing Peder as the big man ran out of steam.

Up ahead, Cai's attacker had thrown himself at the gates and had started to scale them with graceful ease. Approaching at speed, Cai launched himself after the perpetrator, flailing an arm desperately at one of the man's trailing legs. His hand snagged an ankle and he held on for grim life. The wiry strength of his opponent was immense and he used his other leg as a weapon, striking down at Cai's head over and over again in an attempt to dislodge him. Cai dug in and reached up with his other hand, using his full body weight to try to topple the other man from his perch.

The attacker was getting nowhere with his assault on Cai's head, and turned his attention to the hands that clung to his lower body. Tearing and pummelling, he managed to free one of his legs, and set to work on the other. In desperation, Cai windmilled his dislodged arm around in a big arc, hoping that his clenched fist would find a large enough target to cause damage. His flailing punch crashed into the soft tissue between the man's thighs. The intruder, who had been trying to hoist his leading leg over the top of the gates, doubled up in agony, completely incapacitated by the sudden, searing pain between his thighs. Seizing his advantage, Cai crawled up the man's body, arm over arm, until he straddled the gates alongside him. His opponent was weakened and nauseous from the vicious blow, but Cai made sure of his gains by thumping his assailant in the face.

After the second jab, the man began to slide off the gates in slow motion, knocked out by the force of Cai's punch. Swearing and cursing at his over exuberance, Cai leant forwards, desperately grabbing at the man to halt his descent. His weight had passed the tipping point, however, and Cai was pulled down with him. Both men tumbled off the gates towards the ground.

≈

Nia had fallen asleep into a really large volume. It must have happened fairly recently because Idwal was sure she'd answered him not five minutes ago. After scooping her up, he carried her to his room. The movement woke her and she snuggled into his chest. "What did you want to tell me… before?"

"It can wait till daylight." Idwal wasn't sure whether he was just being a coward now. He knew the news would be catastrophic for Nia. It would be for any young woman, but Idwal realised that it jeopardised any future they might have together. Nia would do what was right for the community, and by those rules it would be essential for Idwal to father viable heirs.

The task of shattering her ignorance weighed heavily on his mind, and Idwal couldn't really sleep at all. So he left her nestled in happy ignorance for as long as he could, then took to the corridors in search of solace.

13

Recognition

Cai fought to keep on top of the other man's body as they slid and fell towards the ground. Peder crouched beneath them both, waiting to adjust himself at a millisecond's notice. He concerned himself mainly with breaking Cai's fall and the trespasser's head took another sickening smack as it collided with the ground.

"Is he alive?" Cai asked as he checked his own body's damage.

Peder took a while to find the pulse at the man's neck. "I think so. You ok?"

Cai's head had taken the brunt of the intruder's blows. Several large lumps were forming on his skull beneath the hairline. "I'll live," he said, getting to his feet. "You'd better get Bryn down here, or whoever's on duty." He stared pointedly at the big Cornishman. "Leave Mona be," Cai warned in all seriousness.

Peder's eyes became large and innocent before they developed into a wink and a grin. "Aye, aye, Chief."

Shaking his sore head, Cai began to pat the assailant down for weapons and clues. He found some chewing gum, something that looked like a shoe-horn, a packet of cigarettes and a ticket for the late morning ferry to Dún Laoghaire. He also discovered a small knife, wedged into the back of the man's belt. Cai handled this with extreme care, fearful it might be another toxic blade. He didn't have sufficient time or energy to strip the man, but had rechecked his vital signs before Bryn and Arwel came running into view.

"Is he still alive?" Arwel shouted, even before he'd come to a standstill.

"He's bashed his head, but he's still breathing." Cai looked at Bryn, who stood still and silent, staring down at the unconscious intruder intently. "How did he get past?" Cai asked.

"I have no idea," Bryn replied dryly, and Cai knew that some poor negligent sentry was in for a tremendous bollocking.

"Have you searched him?" Arwel asked.

Cai showed them his finds. "Careful with the blade," Bryn barked, though Cai had already taken the precaution of wrapping it in his jacket. With a final stare at the limp body, Bryn marched off. "I'm doubling the sentries and making a sweep of the entire compound."

Arwel shone a torch onto the booty, studying the plastic and ticket with a keen eye. "Irish," Cai stated rather than asked.

Arwel waggled his head. "Most probably, though we'll find out more when he comes round." He cast a slightly disgruntled look in his brother's direction. "You could have been a bit more careful." Arwel missed Cai's stunned expression because he'd started to fiddle with the strange curve of plastic.

"It can't be a shoe-horn," Cai told him. "It could be some sort of key."

Arwel agreed to some extent. "Mmm, it's quite thick. And there's…"

"Come on, Al, get the other end." Cai pointed at the body. "We need to get him inside."

"Peder and Idwal are on their way," Arwel answered without looking up. He was still enormously distracted by the black plastic shape in his hand. "They'll be out in a minute."

≈

At Arwel's request, they installed the intruder in the underground cells. Idwal and Peder had stripped the man, but they hadn't found anything else on his person. He'd groaned a few times during the process but hadn't come round fully. Idwal was examining the man's head, and tutting. "I don't reckon he'll be of any use till the morning."

Cai had a banging headache himself now, and cradled his skull as the conversation swirled around him.

"Someone should stay with him overnight," Bryn grumbled. He had calmed down a bit after the additional sweep, but remained belligerent.

"I don't mind keeping him company," Idwal offered, giving himself an excuse to put off his impending chat with Nia.

"I'll stay with you," Bryn growled.

Idwal didn't argue, and sat down next to Cai, waking him from a doze. "You all right, mate? Ped said the little weasel kicked you in the head."

"Mmm," Cai answered. Talking was far too complicated.

Without warning, Idwal's fingers crept gently around Cai's cranium. "Let me have a feel."

At first, Cai was confused by the sensation of subtle, gentle relief flowing through him, but then the realisation hit him with a sudden jolt – Idwal was a healer, a *proper* healer. Idwal pursed his lips and shook his head; he clearly didn't want anyone to know. Cai nodded, reassuring Idwal that his secret was safe.

"You should get some sleep," Idwal said after a few minutes. "Arwel wants you here for the questioning."

"How long have you...?"

"I don't know, it comes and goes. I'm not sure what it's all about." He lowered his voice. "Something happened when I picked up Mona's metal knot... like it bit me." He shook his head. "Could be a coincidence, but..."

Cai felt the lumps on his head, noting how much the swelling had subsided. "That's a lot better, thanks."

Idwal smiled back wanly. "How's Mo? You two getting on ok?"

"Well, we've still got a few things to talk about..."

"Tell me about it!" Idwal sighed, thinking of Nia. He stood up, reminded of the difficult conversation to come. "Still, I'm glad you managed to talk Mo back round. She already had her bags packed, you know."

Cai sat bolt upright, suddenly worried. Could Mona be leaving right now? "What time do you want me back here?" Cai asked as he bounded to the door.

Arwel looked up from his ponderings, still clutching the plastic. "After breakfast should be fine."

≈

Cai realised, as he ran, that he had no idea of the time. Mona could have been gone for hours. Perhaps he should go to the boat shed first? No, he was panicking. He'd hidden the keys and she wouldn't have the first idea where to look.

Despite Idwal's ministrations, Cai still felt light-headed. His face ached like hell and his body was reluctant to obey orders. As he approached the door of their room, there was a hammering thud behind his eyes. A line of light below the door gave him sudden hope. She was still there. Cai barged in through the door and fell at her feet.

Mona was dressed in full combat gear, a sword at her side, Tom strapped to her chest, and a hooded cloak wrapped around them. She was the embodiment of a Celtic warrior queen – glorious and deadly. Cai wanted to remain where he knelt, and beg her to stay, but stood instead, straightening up and closing the door behind him. Mona dropped the holdall and closed her eyes, the key to his grandfather's boat clenched tightly in her fist.

"Why now? Why not Sunday?" Cai asked breathlessly. "You won't make it on your own." But even as the words left his lips, Cai knew they weren't true. Mona would always survive, no matter what.

"I'm not *me* anymore, Cai. I can't live like this. I'm powerless when I'm with you. Those lessons have changed me… I'm just an extension of *you* and *your* feelings." Mona's words were coming out in short whispered breaths. "I left a note. Please read it when I'm gone."

Cai shook his head, twisted the key in the lock then put it, very deliberately, into his pocket. He walked past Mona to the bed, resisting the urge to physically restrain her. There were letters laid on top of the bedcovers and he found the one bearing his name underneath her precious music player.

Mona hadn't dared to look, but she knew what he was about to do. "Please don't read it now."

Cai sat on the bed and read. After a long silence, he coughed. "Your music?" he asked.

Mona didn't need to hear the pain in his voice to understand how deeply he was hurt. She could feel his emotions dragging her down into their maelstrom, pulling her relentlessly into his agony.

"I thought you'd remember me – when you listened to it. I wanted to give you something..."

"I don't need your bloody music." His words were strangled with sorrow. "You're carved into me, into my soul."

Mona needed to leave now, before it was too late. Another minute would be too much for her. "Please let me go – you're killing me. There's something happening inside my brain; you've loosened it, and I just can't... take it anymore. I've got to get away from you. *Please*. Let me go."

Cai got up from the bed, and moved to stand between her and the door. He had the letter and mp3 player scrunched in his hand, and was getting even nearer. "If you touch me now... I will dissolve," Mona panted.

Cai reached out, grasped her by the shoulders and then pushed the hood back very slowly. Her grey eyes spoke of vulnerability and exposure, but he'd lost the ability to think straight. Cai was a Welshman and he could only speak these words in his mother tongue. He moved his lips to her ear. "*Dwi'n dy garu di, Mona Jones* – I love you, Mona Jones, and you're never going anywhere without me."

The rotten tooth in Mona's head broke free of its roots. The pain and poison were too much for her and she fell forwards, unconscious, into Cai's arms. He lowered her gently to the end of the bed, careful not to crush Tom, who'd started to stir. Staring down at her prone form, he began to pace the room, wondering what on earth he should do next.

14

Mistress

Bryn and Idwal were sitting either side of the captive's bed. Bryn stared down at the still sleeping man with obvious loathing.

"How's Rob?" Idwal asked softly. Bryn's head shot up in panic, and Idwal smiled at him. "He's a lovely man." Idwal grinned, and Bryn finally gave him a small shy smile.

"Yes," he croaked, "the best."

"And he's fine? Fully recovered?"

"I don't know. He's still getting headaches, and..." Bryn was interrupted by a long moaning sound from the prisoner between them. He stood up and drew his sword, passing it to Idwal. "I'll go for Arwel and Dafydd. Just don't take any chances with him. Ok?"

Idwal stood poised over the groaning man, short sword drawn. He didn't look particularly dangerous, but Peder had described Cai's struggle, and Idwal didn't want to risk a confrontation with the wiry prisoner.

"Where's my stuff?" the man asked, the instant he was aware enough to speak. Idwal wasn't surprised by the Irish accent, and didn't answer his question. He'd had enough military training to know the rules. "Have you any water here? I'm parched."

Idwal passed him a cup of water as Arwel had made it clear he wanted the man hydrated for questioning. Although handcuffed, the Irishman drained the water without difficulty, and then scanned the cell until he'd spied his belongings.

"I've got breath like shite – won't you pass me my gum, big fella?" The man winked cheekily.

Idwal didn't react or move an inch, but remained impassive; both eyes and sword steady. The captive stared longingly at his stash, but Idwal had no intention of handing anything over. The gum and cigarettes could easily be poisoned, and they were all looking forward to getting some answers out of this man.

Sitting up gingerly, the prisoner blew out with a long whistle. "It's hot as fuck down here." He began unbuttoning his shirt, and Idwal moved a step nearer, the blade still balanced. "Easy now, I'm just trying to cool down…" the man forced an easy smile but his eyes were drawn in panic to the pile of possessions on the table. Idwal caught a glimpse of a rippling blue light, emanating from the curved plastic object.

"What's that?" Idwal asked, motioning towards it with a quick shunt of his head.

The captive puffed. "Give me my gum and I'll tell you," he said; his tone a mixture of boredom and insolence.

Idwal backed up and felt behind him. The object was heavier than it looked and Idwal felt a tiny vibration in his palm. He risked a glance down just as the cell door creaked open. Bryn, Arwel and Dafydd began filing in, and Idwal held up the black curve in his hand. "It lit up and…"

"*Stop him!*" Arwel shouted, and Idwal whirled to see the captive crunching down savagely at some beads on the necklace at his throat. His face was purple and bloated, and the prisoner frothed at the mouth, his body contorting in pain. Idwal lunged at the man, intending to snatch the beads from his mouth, but a big arm pulled him back.

"No! They're poisonous. Keep back." Bryn yanked Idwal away and spread his arms wide, shielding everyone behind him from any possible threat.

The man didn't take long to die, but it was pitiful to watch. After witnessing his final death throes, they all felt sickened; his body had evacuated its contents and the room now stank.

Idwal was mortified by his stupidity. "Arwel, I'm so..."

"Forget it," the young man said, clearly furious. Idwal then faced Dafydd, who clapped him on the shoulder. "You weren't to know. Get some sleep and we'll talk later."

Idwal was embarrassed. Of course he should have known. He was a trained soldier; he'd learnt all about hidden poison capsules. It was the exact copy of a suicide practice employed by captured Tamil Tigers. He felt like a complete idiot.

"So what did it do?" Arwel asked gruffly, holding up the plastic and looking Idwal in the eye.

"It lit up and vibrated," Idwal said, then gasped at his sudden intuition. "Like a phone!"

Arwel nodded slowly, twisting it around in his hands.

≈

After finding his bed empty, Idwal tracked Nia down to the library. He was furious with himself, both for his monumental stupidity and for letting Arwel down. She looked up, blessing Idwal with a warm, victorious smile.

"I've gathered all the evidence together for Ifan, and I've found an incredible piece of information about the *mark* in the process... what's wrong?"

Nia was stunned by Idwal's news about the intruder. "What did he want?" Idwal groaned at Nia's question. "Sorry," she said quickly. "I mean... does anyone have any idea?"

"*No!*" he shouted, unleashing his anger on her. "I fucked up, remember?" Nia recoiled from his rage, and Idwal felt an immediate wave of remorse. Tired, ashamed, and still dreading what he hadn't yet told her, Idwal fell to his knees before her. "I'm sorry. I'm just so... angry." She soothed his golden hair and kissed it. "Will you marry me, Nia?" She blinked slowly, like an owl, and he stopped breathing. Nia didn't answer and he started to panic. "I haven't actually got a ring, but I'll get you one... you know, eventually..."

"I don't understand," she said. "Why so quickly? Why now?"

"Please. Just say yes," he begged.

Nia very much wanted to say yes. However, that wasn't the way things were done in the *Conway*, and what she did eventually say sounded a little pedantic. "We call it handfasting here, and we don't normally use rings – though some do of course."

"Is there a big difference?"

"There is for people like us in the community."

Idwal sighed. He had already failed. "In what way?" he asked wearily. He could guess the gist of her reply, if not its exact wording.

"There are certain criteria. You should know. I've explained before."

Nia's cold pragmatism rekindled his anger. "And what if we don't want children?"

"Don't you?" Nia looked at him quizzically.

Idwal had no other option now but to tell her the truth. "Nia, I think it extremely unlikely that you will ever be able to conceive a child." He tried to break the news as gently as possible, but his voice was laced with anger at the injustice of the situation.

"What?" Her voice sounded so small.

"I could try to repair the fallopian tubes. But it would take a long time and cause a lot of pain." His expression creased in defeat. "And it probably wouldn't work."

Nia didn't respond initially, but he could see she'd already worked through the implications of what he'd told her. In an instant, she became reserved and distant. Gently pushing him away, she stood up. "Thank you for your offer, Idwal, but I cannot accept."

"Nia, it's just us. I..." Idwal stopped himself saying the words '*I love you*', because how could he? They'd only just met, and yet here he was on his knees, asking her to marry him. "Please..." he said instead, but she was already walking away from him and out of the room.

≈

Mona came round with a start. She was vaguely aware of time having passed and immediately wondered whether Tom needed feeding. As she did so, she realised with a jolt that he wasn't in his usual place, in the crook of her arm. Panicking, she leapt upright and fumbled for the bedside light.

With the room lit up, Mona could see Tom's tiny form lying flat against Cai's chest. Cai himself was asleep on the chair at the end of the bed. Her heart stopped lurching wildly, though she still made sure that both man and baby were breathing normally before getting into her pyjamas. Her head ached and there were tramlines criss-crossing her body from where she'd fallen asleep fully clothed.

Cai's arms wrapped around the boy instinctively as she tried to gently prise Tom away.

"It's ok," she whispered. "I've got him. You can go back to sleep."

Cai struggled to pull himself upright in the chair.

"What time is it?"

"Not yet morning. I passed out." Mona talked in an undertone, not wanting to wake the baby.

"Mona. I need to explain."

She shook her head gently. "Later. We should sleep now." Cai looked at the bed and then at Mona. There was trauma and a deep, gritty tiredness in his eyes. "Come to bed," Mona said as she snuggled under the covers with Tom against her shoulder.

The early hours had turned into morning proper, and though still shattered, Cai had woken at his usual time. He suspected Mona would also stir shortly, but at this moment in time she lay extremely close to him. So close, in fact, he could very easily manoeuvre his body to lie against hers. He had an overwhelming urge to kiss her exposed neck and jawline, but just made do with touching her shoulder. Mona twisted, Tom still in her arms, to face him. She frowned as she touched a finger to his forehead.

"You're bruised."

If Cai told her about the breach in security, Mona would be up and out of the room in an instant. There were more than enough people in the cells already and he really needed to talk to her. Something significant had happened last night, but he had no idea what.

"*Cymraeg*, Mona." He said the words gently to gauge her reaction, holding her hand against his head.

"*Pen*," Mona answered, with neither fear nor anger as she traced her index finger from the bruise on his forehead through his eyebrows and down the length of his nose. "*Trwyn*," she breathed. She brushed her thumb across the width of his lips. "*Ceg*." Cai closed his eyes in relief and pleasure. When he opened them next, Mona was holding her hand against Tom's fat tummy. "*Babi*." She smiled. "*Fy mabi bach* – My little baby."

Cai nodded and smiled back, laying his hand on top of hers. "*Fy mabi bach*."

Tom started to squirm, and Cai scooped his arm around the fidgeting infant, still amazed at what a monumental task it had been to quieten him last night. He kissed the boy's head, finding he quite liked the smell of the soft dark hair. Mona got out of bed and headed for the discarded bags on the floor, looking for a full bottle. She wore a vest and shorts, and her braless breasts moved enticingly beneath the thin material, nipples erect in the early-morning chill. Watching her, Cai felt like he might explode.

When he emerged from the bathroom, Cai was disappointed to find Mona wearing a jumper over her vest, but also amazed that she'd managed to feed Tom and clear away the previous night's mess.

"I'm sorry about all that. I'm not familiar with the technicalities." He gestured towards the numerous soiled nappies in the bin bag. "It's amazing how much such a small body can produce." Talking about Tom was easier than discussing last night. "Caring for him really is quite complicated, isn't it?"

Tom decided to emphasise this point by trying to stuff an entire foot into his mouth and choke himself.

"Not complicated," Mona said with feeling. "Just endless and constant. In one end and out the other." Mona pulled the foot from his mouth and kissed it. "Siân says it will get better when he starts doing more stuff." Tom had a go with his other foot and Mona tickled it. "It's an awful thing to admit, but sometimes I can't wait to go training, just to get away from… all this. I don't know if that's a normal way to react, or if I'm not actually doing it right."

To avoid mentioning last night, Mona had confessed more about her insecurities than she'd meant to. Suddenly self-conscious, she told Cai to put the kettle on and disappeared into the bathroom.

≈

Tom didn't like being left in the chair, and strained upwards with his arms and body until Cai picked him up again. He was then forced to make a cup of tea while holding on to the boy, which was an education. His hands full, he found it necessary to employ parts of his body – chin, mouth and elbows – not ordinarily required for such a routine task. Tom seemed quite happy to be constantly positioned and repositioned like a boneless cat. Just as long as he was held.

Cai balanced Tom on his knee facing him. The boy stared back at him sombrely through his big blue eyes. Cai couldn't tell whether they were exactly the same colour as his own, but they were remarkably similar. It wasn't too strange that people had assumed Tom was his son.

Mona took Tom from Cai and planted him in the little chair. "I know you don't want to talk about yesterday, Mona, but it was a last resort." He remembered the letter and his throat constricted. "I can't let you…"

"Shush, Cai. I know what happened." She sat on the end of the bed so that their knees almost touched, then leaned forwards, holding his head on both sides as if willing him to understand something vital. "*Dwi'n dy garu di, Cai Owens* – I love you Cai Owens."

To hear her finally speaking his language after all this time – and with an accent and intonation nearly matching his own – came as an enormous shock to Cai. Taking her hands from his head, Cai grasped them tightly; too tightly, in fact, if they had belonged to any woman other than Mona. "How much do you understand?" he asked.

"It's not like magic, you know," Mona said with a wicked grin. "I can't just speak perfect Welsh." She rolled her eyes.

"So what happened?" he asked.

"I don't know. I've been surrounded by it for so long." She pointed both index fingers towards her temple, as if they were guns. "You dislodged something, and it all came flooding in." Mona grinned again like an idiot.

"So, we've done it?" Cai got up and clasped her shoulders. "You're... cured?"

Mona's smile changed into a frown of consternation. "I don't know. I'm not sure." Cai sat back down, biting his tongue. The only way to know for sure would be to conduct an empirical test, but he wasn't about to propose that.

"Perhaps you should test me?" Mona asked warily.

Cai shrugged. "Maybe we should wait until..."

"Just get on with it," Mona blurted.

"Ok." Cai stood again and coughed. He opened his mouth.

"What are you going to talk about?" Mona interrupted, clearly nervous.

"Do you want me to do this or not?"

"Not," Mona confessed, and then changed her mind. "No, I do... just stop, you know, if..."

"Trust me." He gave her a reassuring squeeze. "But try to fight it." Mona nodded. "*Cau dy lygaid* – Close your eyes," he crooned, and she did. "*Cusana fi, Mona* – Kiss me, Mona."

Cai stopped talking, but Mona's mouth had latched onto his before he'd had a chance to pull away. There was a knock on the door.

"Back to the drawing board," he muttered as Arwel let himself in.

≈

When Nia finally left her mother's rooms the next morning, everything seemed much clearer in her head. Siân had not reacted as Nia might have guessed, and between them they'd eventually come up with an alternative solution. She found Idwal asleep on the floor outside her bedroom, his great long legs curled up to create less of an obstruction in the corridor.

"Come in with me," Nia whispered, resisting the urge to cry.

Idwal sat on the bed in silence, looking lost, until she climbed onto his lap and straddled him. Taking his head in her hands, she began to talk. "I explained the situation to Mam, and before she said anything else, she asked me if I loved you."

Idwal swallowed, knowing he would get the truth, like it or not. "And?"

"I told her I hadn't thought about it. But then I *did* think about it. Being with you makes me happy, Idwal, happier than I've ever been in my life." She kissed him very softly.

"So you've changed your mind?"

"No." She smiled sadly. "But I've come up with an alternative." Nia took a deep breath. "That we stay together until you need to produce an heir. And when you *do* handfast, we can come to an arrangement. I will share you, if your wife can."

Idwal was baffled by her plan. "I want you, Nia. I want to marry *you*, not anyone else."

"You're going to be Archdruid. You may not want children now, but that time will come. Everyone will expect it."

"Then I won't be Archdruid. It's easy."

Nia shook her head. "No, Idwal. The job chooses you. It's already happened – can't you see that? Dafydd doesn't want the job. It was never his to begin with."

Idwal sat up and held her waist. "If you want children, we could adopt." He was aware of the pleading in his tone, but she repeated the head movement.

"I won't handfast you, Idwal Jones."

Idwal was maddened by her implacability. "But what? You'll be my mistress?"

"Polygamy has been traditionally commonplace in our society, Idwal. There's no need to be so prim and Christian about this." She was aware his anger had now turned to disgust, but still Nia would not budge. "*Does yna ddim dewis* – Take it or leave it."

15

Revelation

"Dead Irishman?" Mona squawked when she overheard Arwel's breathless debriefing to Cai.

Arwel stared at her open-mouthed. "You can understand Welsh?" His eyes chased back and forth between Mona and Cai, and then he clapped his brother on the shoulder with immense pride. "So you've cracked it?"

"Not quite," Cai mumbled, scratching the back of his neck. "But it's a big breakthrough."

Mona flushed slightly at Cai's evasive response. Suppressing any unsettling thoughts, she turned on Arwel, her eyes full of unanswered questions. "So did you get *anything* out of him before he died?" she asked, after he'd given her all the relevant facts.

"No." Arwel shook his head but pulled something from his pocket. "But I think this is his phone." He put it on the table between them.

Mona stared at the piece of plastic, then up at the men, in disbelief. "Really?"

Arwel shrugged. "I wondered if you could try to take it apart, in your workshop," he asked Cai, who had picked up the flat object and was examining it intently.

"I can give it a go." Cai didn't sound too hopeful, and he looked over at Mona. "But I'm not leaving you here on your own again."

Arwel was surprised at the authority in Cai's voice, and even more surprised that Mona seemed willing to accept it.

"I'll go and see Rob," she replied quietly.

"Good idea," Cai answered as he stood up. "Make sure you're armed." Mona lifted her shirt to reveal several weapons, and Cai smiled approvingly.

≈

"Hello, Stinky," Mona sang as she put her head in through the gap. She couldn't get any sense out of Rob for the next five minutes. He had taken Tom from her and was drowning the baby in affection. "Where's Bryn?"

Rob rolled his eyes. "On patrol – *again*. He's taken the breach as a personal affront." He hoisted Tom into the air and blew a raspberry against the folds of his neck. Tom squealed with joy. "I've missed him so much," Rob sighed, between the kisses and squeezes.

"And I've missed you," Mona said, grabbing her friend around the waist and crushing the air from his lungs.

Rob turned to her with worry in his eyes. "Is everything ok? I mean, he's not…"

"It's complicated." Mona sighed. She knew Rob would try to wheedle her into leaving Cai. "I'm… it's… hard when he's with Carmen," she admitted. "I'm finding it hard to share him, even though…"

"Carmen!" Rob's face had paled. "The complete shit!" Rob frowned. "But he… I really thought…"

Mona gave him a sad little half-shrug, letting him know she was upset but didn't want to talk about it. Rob fixed his attention on the baby, and changed the subject. "How do you like the bouncer?"

Mona frowned at the odd turn in the conversation.

"Yeah, it's great actually, really sturdy. Dafydd must have paid much more than a fiver for it."

197

"But Dafydd didn't buy it, Mo. We made it." Rob was beaming at her and so she smiled back.

"Who's we?"

"*I* made it – with Cai." Rob seemed confused. "Didn't he tell you?"

"No. When did he find the time?" she wondered out loud.

"It only took two nights." Rob rubbed his lips over Tom's hair. "He'd overcomplicated it, but I put him straight. We finished it last night…"

"What time?" Mona asked, the timescales suddenly making sense.

"I don't know – late. Can't have been much before one in the morning. Why?"

"Stay here," Mona growled. "I've got to have a word with someone."

≈

There was no answer at first, but Mona tried again, and this time the door opened. On seeing her, Carmen backed away into her room. "I'm not afraid of you," she gasped, clearly petrified.

"Big mistake," Mona snarled, letting herself in.

Carmen scrambled back into bed and pulled the duvet around her for protection. "What do you want now?"

"Cai hasn't been with you for the last two nights."

Carmen shrugged. "He's obviously stupid as well as blind."

Mona hadn't met anyone quite like Carmen before, and she failed to understand why the woman had gone to such elaborate lengths to upset so many people.

"What are you playing at?"

"Isn't it obvious?"

"No," Mona answered instinctively, but another glance at the woman's taut expression suggested an answer. "You've got… feelings for him?"

Carmen barked mirthlessly. "Feelings…? I don't know if that's what you'd call them, but I suppose it's the nearest I've got."

"So how did you think it would end?"

198

Carmen lifted her delicate shoulders again and shook her magnificent hair. "I'm not sure. Not like this, anyway."

"Why don't you just leave?" Mona asked wearily.

"I haven't got what I came for yet," she answered spitefully. If Carmen was affronted by Mona's directness, it didn't show, and she was equally blunt back. "I've never felt like that with a man before. I liked it when he hurt me."

Mona's eyebrows rose. "He hurt you?"

"He was rough. I liked it." Mona didn't know how to respond. "I have power over men, and I don't over Cai. It's refreshing." The woman genuinely confused Mona. "Men fall in love with me; not the other way round," she spat. "I knew I wouldn't get him back – not with the way he is around you. So I just mixed things up a bit. Ped's a stupid, great lump, he just took it too far," she sulked and pouted.

"Did you tell Peder I fancied him?" Mona asked slowly.

Carmen's answer came with a cruel smile. "I'd love to know what Cai sees in you." She took her time assessing Mona's appearance. "You must have some pretty powerful magic to disguise all that." She chuckled. "I mean you're not exactly…"

Mona needed to leave.

≈

Tom slept and Mona paced. There had been a breach in the *Conway*'s perimeter, and everyone but the War Chief was doing something useful. Mona felt she should be with Bryn on patrol, or quizzing Arwel about the dead man, or bollocking her brother for his stupidity. She didn't allow herself to consider what she'd like to do to Cai, but every glance at the baby's bouncer reminded her of him.

In the end, she decided it would be best to just thank Cai for the chair and avoid any mention of Carmen. No sooner had he returned, however, than her body began buzzing with expectation. Mona started folding clothes to distract herself, while Cai sat down, drumming his fingers on the table.

"It must be a new generation material," he mused. "There's a textured panel on one side. I should be able to get into it... but I can't." There was a long silence as Cai pondered the possibilities.

"So what's the plan?" Mona asked, as soon as she'd run out of clothes to fold.

She had broken his train of thought and he glanced at his watch. "Dafydd's called a meeting in about an hour's time. We'll have to take Tommy along, I'm afraid." He cleared the table. "And in the meantime..." Cai gestured to the chair. "We've got work to do."

≈

Ifan just couldn't muster up any energy. Without an official role, he was impotent to deal with the latest incident. A deep-seated sense of powerlessness had sapped his body of its strength and vigour, so with nothing better to do, he'd retreated to his bed, where he relived, over and over, his many past failures.

The imperious rapping on the door reminded him of Mona. "Ifan? Are you in there? It's Idwal."

Close, Ifan thought, as he shuffled across the room to unlock it. Ifan opened the door just a crack. He wanted to get back to bed and continue wallowing in his misery.

"I'm not feeling very..."

"Tough," Idwal grunted, forcing his way in and past the old man. Ifan could see his strong magical aura glowing in the centre of the room.

"I'm not in charge anymore," Ifan whined, easing his tightened scalp with a quick massage.

"Everyone's up to their necks with this break-in and I need advice."

Ifan's eyebrows rose. The Englishman's tone wasn't exactly beseeching. "And?"

Idwal let the old man have it all, in one breath.

200

"Nia won't marry me because she's infertile. I want to know how to change her mind – if there's a way."

"Are you sure…?"

"Positive."

"How…?" But Ifan didn't need to finish his question. The answer was obvious. "You're a healer?" Idwal nodded curtly. "Show me."

Ifan lay back on his bed and Idwal looked down at him. "Where?"

"You tell me," Ifan replied simply.

Idwal closed his eyes and picked up Ifan's hands, trying to see inside the old man's body with his strange second sight. It didn't come initially, but after a few minutes, Idwal began to see the problem. Ifan's body was peppered with large areas of painful inflammation – hands, knees, hips and spine. Cartilage had disappeared between his joints and every movement forced bone to rub against bone. He worked at first on the old man's spine. It would be impossible for him to create cartilage, but Idwal found he could soothe the inflammation by sending little capillaries of power over and around the swollen areas.

By the time Idwal had finished treating the old man's damaged body, he was stiff with inactivity himself. He opened his eyes to see Ifan in tears. "Did I hurt you?" he asked with concern.

Ifan shook his head and pressed the young man's hand. "Thank you," he breathed, feeling pain-free for the first time in decades.

"You know it's only short-term relief, don't you?"

Ifan nodded and smiled beatifically. "Go get your girl, and we'll have a chat."

≈

"It might be safer to start again with my *dislikes*." Cai didn't make any more reference than that to Mona's previous failure, and she spent the next ten minutes or so blocking some of Cai's odd bugbears.

"Ok," he said eventually, glancing down at his watch and grinning. "Well done. Now let's progress to some *likes*."

"Music?" Mona said daringly, having been boosted with confidence.

Cai pursed his lips in mock horror and shook his head. Mona couldn't work out whether he was joking or serious, but her heart skipped a beat.

"I think I can handle a little chat about the Rolling Stones," she probed mischievously. Cai merely raised an eyebrow in an exaggerated, flirty manner, and she chuckled.

Cai liked making things: working out the design; making the cutting list; shaping and fixing the metal. He enjoyed the solitude of the workshop at night, and the sensation of tools in his hands. The work gave him a sense of deep contentment. It would, he thought, be an excellent emotion with which to test out Mona's new-found resilience.

To begin with, Mona found the sensations he described intoxicating. Concentrating hard, she found that by half-registering the language, she could begin to appreciate Cai's emotions rather than experience them directly. The tactic became her new plan of attack: listen to the music of the language rather than the lyrics.

Cai showed her the tempestuous waters of the Ynys Môn coastline. And a little boy, safe and warm in his *dadi*'s arms as he learnt to wait. For the weather, for the tide. Mona felt Cai's mind as an older boy, grappling with the language of the wind. Learning, trying and failing. She felt the years of hard work in his aching arms, and finally shared his joy the day he managed to tame the wind with his sail. It was a struggle, but Mona managed to keep the sense of his story without being overwhelmed by the sentiment.

"What's the word for sailing, Mo?" Cai tested her warily.

"*Hwylio*," she answered promptly. "*Hwylio ar y môr* – Sailing on the sea." Mona beamed proudly.

Each time Cai took a break, Mona felt the urge to close her eyes for a rest. It was exhausting work.

"Mona," he said, nudging her gently as he resumed his seat opposite her.

"You shouldn't speak to me in Welsh when I'm not ready." There was a smile on her lips, but her eyes stayed shut.

"I only said your name. I can't say it any other way." He defended himself with the same teasing tone.

"Can't you?" she asked, stretching her arms so that her midriff became momentarily exposed.

"I can," he swallowed, admiring the sliver of flesh. "But it's not advisable right now."

"Actually, that's not a bad idea," Mona gasped with sudden inspiration, sitting up and pulling her shirt back into place. "It will be so much quicker. It's a Welsh word. It will work, I'm sure of it. It worked with Ped…"

Cai shook his head mournfully. "Not a good idea."

"*Yes!* Yes, it is. I did really well with the metalwork, and the sailing – didn't I?" she asked with a grin, wanting to touch his hand with her fingertips, and not really remembering why she couldn't.

"Ok," he agreed reluctantly. Something safe, then, he thought, preparing his chosen trigger. "*Mona.*"

She gasped at the ferocity of the anger he'd felt – the disgust, when he first saw Tom. She'd been ready for anything and this was easier than it could have been. Mona had already heard the melody and concentrated now on blocking the emotion. She smiled at her victory, but became angry all over again about the way Cai had reacted to her son.

"There was never any excuse for feeling that way about Tom. None of this is his fault."

"I behaved appallingly," he conceded quietly. "I'll never forgive myself." Cai scratched at the wood with his index finger, struggling with the strangeness of what he was about to admit. "You could have lied to me, you know. I would have believed you – if you'd told me I was Tom's father."

Mona had never wanted to have this conversation with Cai. "We both know the chances of that being true are…"

"I would have wanted to believe it. You could have persuaded me."

Mona couldn't find her voice.

"How sure are you that I'm not – his father, I mean?"

"Don't do this, Cai. Please."

He closed his eyes. "Just tell me."

"I'm fairly confident he's not yours."

"But not completely certain?"

Mona forced out a breath, half annoyance, half something else. "No. Now can we please carry on with the language lessons?" she insisted. "I'm getting the hang of this, and we can't stop now – we've only got ten minutes left."

Cai smiled fractionally, then closed his eyes and took a deep breath. "*Mona*," he breathed out.

He was cold, drowning, slipping. Terror had seized him, and Cai knew the next desperate gasp for air would mean seawater and death. Fear turned to relief, as strong hands and arms dragged him back up to the air.

The silence stretched on. "That's not how I remember it," Mona eventually rasped out.

"I would have drowned, Mona. No doubt about it." If anything, his voice was even croakier than hers. Cai reached over the desk to hold both her hands. "I never said thank you."

Mona squeezed back. "Thanks for Tom's chair."

Cai opened his mouth to speak, to explain. He wanted to talk about Carmen – Mona could see it in his eyes – and she changed the subject, lightening her tone.

"So, I've blocked you at least twice now, you slacker."

"Yes, well done." Cai allowed her the change in mood and gave her an evil smirk. "But we're moving up a gear, so get ready."

Mona panicked and procrastinated. "Wait, I'm not ready. What time is it?"

"We've still got five minutes." Cai smiled encouragement at her across the desk and she inclined her head nervously. "*Mona*," he growled again, projecting all his pent-up lust at her in both syllables.

The force of the attack knocked her back against the chair, and she closed her eyes to break their connection with Cai's. Gripping the table edge for support, Mona put everything she had into blocking the emotion, holding and holding and holding.

"*Paid a gafael yn y bwrdd, Mo* – Take your hands off the table, Mo. I want you to unbutton your shirt." Her hands shook with the effort of resisting Cai's voice. "Just one little button, Mona," he crooned. "I want to see your breasts. I want to hold them, feel them in my hands. I want to kiss them." Cai was breathing hard and Mona was lost. He intensified the note of desire in his voice. "Undo the buttons, Mo." *She's mine*, he thought.

Mona's shaking hands fumbled with the task. She opened her eyes wide and gazed directly into his eyes, and a grin bloomed all over her face as she fastened the shirt buttons all the way up to her neck.

There was no time for Mona to bask in her victory. The door opened and a tousled blonde head poked into the room. "You're late," Arwel scolded.

≈

Before they walked into the meeting, Arwel reiterated the importance of keeping her new knowledge of Welsh a secret, and Mona nodded in agreement.

It wasn't a well-attended gathering. Idwal was meeting Ifan with Nia to discuss how best to contain the news of the incident, and Bryn continued to patrol manically. It felt strange that only Dafydd, Cai, Arwel and Mona were left to consider the breach, but it made pretending not to understand the language easier.

While the main meeting was held in English for Mona's sake, whispered asides and comments naturally took place in Welsh. Cai was right: it was a beautiful, lyrical language and she loved the sound of it in her head and mouth.

"They want something," Arwel said. "Our visitor was a scout." He held up the black rectangle. "And this is his phone."

"What do they want?" Dafydd asked and Arwel shrugged. He either didn't know or wasn't saying. It was difficult to know with the wily youngster.

The meeting rolled on, though no one seemed to have any firm knowledge to bring to the proceedings. Cai hadn't managed to crack the technology, Arwel couldn't come up with any suggestions, and Mona was mesmerised by the sight of Tom in Cai's arms. He'd insisted on taking charge of the baby so that Mona could concentrate and catch up. But watching them together had the opposite effect on her.

Ifan burst into the room, followed closely by Nia and Idwal. Nia had been crying, but Mona didn't have a chance to ask why, because Ifan was talking to her, low and breathless – as if he'd been running.

"Have you succeeded?" he almost begged. "Can you fight the language?" he asked again, immediately.

"Yes." She frowned. "What is it? What's happened?"

Mona looked nervously across at Nia, where she was enveloped in her brother's arms. Ifan had moved across the room and was whispering urgently into Arwel's ear. The expression on his grandson's face changed from intense curiosity to deep concern. Both men turned to stare at Tom, and Mona's body filled with adrenaline.

"What! What is it?" she roared.

"I'm going to have to tell them," Ifan concluded.

His grandson wasn't so sure. "What about the…"

"The spy isn't our biggest worry anymore."

Arwel weighed up his grandfather's words and reluctantly agreed. He asked everyone to sit down. Cai placed himself next to Mona as Ifan began to talk.

"This isn't going to be pleasant listening – for any of you, and I'm just giving you the facts. If we need to discuss anything, that will come later, understood?" There was murmured agreement, and Ifan started to talk. "A few days after the fleet left last year, we had a visit from a man calling himself Gareth. Although purporting to be Welsh, the man was in fact Irish – from the rogue clan."

Mona heard Nia's shocked gasp, but she couldn't bear to raise her eyes from the tabletop.

"I have no doubt his visit was orchestrated by our resident spy." Ifan looked helplessly at the assembled faces, hoping he wasn't talking directly to the traitor. "At the end of his stay here, he attacked and impregnated Mona, though she managed to destroy him in the process."

Mona could hear Idwal's devastated response behind her, together with a groan of realisation from Nia: the mystery illness, followed by black moods and withdrawal. Cai held Mona's hand beneath the table and Ifan resumed.

"As soon as Mona's pregnancy became apparent, I let it be known that the child was Cai's. It was a huge deceit, and one Mona did not agree to." Ifan cast a stern glance in Mona's direction, which she either didn't see or ignored. "Even after I convinced her about the danger of revealing his real father."

"Danger?" whispered Nia.

"This child is the offspring of our enemy." Ifan pointed harshly at Tom, and Mona felt an urge to attack the old man again. "Would you have loved him as you do with that knowledge? Would your mother? Would Sioned? No, he is the progeny of those who killed your father, Nia." Ifan threw his accusations around the room. "They killed your parents, Cai, and yours, Idwal. They killed your brother, Dafydd." Ifan now directed his ferocity at Cai. "I told one other person, and he tried to slaughter the boy."

"Just one man?" They could hear the incredulity in Idwal's voice. "But surely, Mona… how did he…?"

"Mona is an unparalleled warrior, Idwal, but for all that she has an awful vulnerability." It was hard for Mona to hear her weakness laid bare in front of her friends and peers. To hear Ifan explain how a mere whisper could turn her into a weapon capable of destroying everyone she loved. Of how she had almost killed her own newborn child.

"So the spy knew of her problem? How?" Dafydd asked, shell-shocked by the latest revelations.

"Clever, perceptive – I've no idea. We've spent a year trying to find out." Ifan clasped Arwel's shoulder in solidarity. "But in truth, we're no nearer to identifying a suspect than we were at the beginning."

Idwal suddenly stood up, a terrible thought hatching in his head. "You're going to neutralise her," he blurted, lurching forwards.

"Calm down, Idwal. She's safe from me." Ifan shook his head in painful disgust. "Though I can't say I haven't lain awake trying to weigh her life against that of our community." Ifan ignored Idwal's stunned stare. "Cai has been working with Mona over the last week, trying to find a cure for her condition, but time is against us." He gave Cai a sad little smile. "I assume you would have let her go if there hadn't been any progress. I knew you could never harm her."

"Test me now." Mona's belligerence pushed her into confronting Ifan.

"Mona," Arwel warned.

"No, Arwel," Ifan said, easing a small knife from his belt. "We have to know now. We're running out of time." Ifan handed Mona the dagger and slipped straight into his native tongue.

"*Cymer y gyllell, Mona* - Take the knife, Mona. One flick of your wrist and I'll be dead. *Do it.* You know you want to. Revenge for Tom. For all the pain I've put you through; all the pity from Cai; all the ridicule from other women." Ifan paused for breath before spitting out further provocations in Welsh. "The deceits I've made you carry. How will Sioned react when she discovers Tom isn't her nephew, but the spawn of her enemy? Yes, Mona, pick it up. It will be easy. It will be right."

Mona leaned in to Ifan, their noses virtually touching. Her Welsh wasn't completely accurate, but there was deadly force behind her words.

"*Basa mi fasa yn hawdd iawn* –Yes, it would be easy. One day maybe, you old git, but not today." She slammed the point of the weapon into the wood between them.

"Do not dare to judge me, Mona Jones. Not until you've been forced to make some of the choices I've had to. Don't you dare..." His rage abated, and Ifan sagged forward.

Mona stepped back and reached for Tom. She was hot and trembling, but Cai didn't give the baby up. Instead, he pulled Mona into his shoulder and kissed her head.

"I need a drink. Anyone else care to join me?" Ifan asked his stunned audience. Arwel retrieved a bottle of rum and gathered together some dirty, mismatched shot glasses.

The tension in the room eased slightly, and Idwal walked over to Mona. "I… I just don't know what to say. I'm so sorry… Mona." Idwal gazed at Cai. "You always knew he wasn't yours?" Cai nodded, but Idwal kept moving his eyes between man and boy, amazed.

"People see what they want to see, I suppose." Cai said as Tom reached up to grab at his nose.

That tiny gesture was almost too much for Mona, and she moved stiffly over to Nia. "I would have helped, Mo," Nia said. She stood stock-still. "You should have told me. I would have loved him just the same."

"You did help. If it wasn't for you… all of you…"

"I'm sorry," she repeated woodenly.

Bored of fiddling with Cai's face, Tom started to bounce up and down in his arms making squawking noises and throwing his weight around to let everyone know he was ready for his five o'clock feed.

They all sat in silence for a moment, listening to Tom's frenetic gurgling and gulping.

"I'm afraid there's more to discuss," Ifan announced after taking a sip of rum. "And I'm glad you're now sitting as you are, because it demonstrates my next point." He drained his glass and continued. "Please don't think I'm prying when I ask this question, but can you please tell me, Nia, exactly when you fell in love with Idwal?"

She felt too emotional to be embarrassed and answered thickly. "The very first moment I saw him."

Ifan nodded. "And you, Idwal, the same?" He nodded meekly, his arm still wrapped around Nia.

"Mona?"

Mona remained rattled. "I know what this is, Ifan. Your theory about selective breeding. People attract people. They fall in and out of love all the time. It doesn't mean anything."

He treated her outburst with patience. "Answer the question, please, Mona. Can you pinpoint a time when you first felt strong feelings towards Cai?"

"When I fought him for the first time, I suppose." It was more of a growl than a whisper. Mona wasn't about to confess anything in front of a room full of people. Ifan made no comment, but glanced towards Cai.

"What's the point of all this?" Cai said, equally uneasy about public declarations of affection.

Ifan grunted at both of them. "My point *is*," he stressed gruffly, "that none of you are particularly susceptible to… well… romantic inclinations, let us say. How many of you have ever felt like this about anyone before?" He didn't wait for an answer. "I'm sure these powerful connections occur for a reason – to create a stronger bloodline – and that the introduction of an outsider into a community is often the catalyst." Ifan had emphasised the point vigorously with his arms, but now let them hang loosely by his side. "Some of us believe it could be the reincarnation of soul mates meeting again. And contrary to Mona's accusation, I don't consider it to be a breeding programme, but I'm pretty sure someone out there does." Ifan's deep, heavy sigh signalled the approach of more bad news. "Mona, I hate to have to tell you this, but I now believe that Gareth was sent here not to kill you… but to impregnate you." Arwel stared at her with helpless pity. "Someone in Ireland sees your power not as a threat, but an opportunity – a chance to create some sort of perfect Druid, the pinnacle of our kind. And with Tom, they think they may have succeeded."

Mona couldn't speak, couldn't breathe, couldn't move. Cai answered for her, jumping to his feet. "He's only a baby, Ifan. Where did all this come from?" His eyes whipped around the room. "How come you think this, all of a sudden?"

Ifan's eyes swivelled towards Idwal, who answered Cai's question slowly. "I've been helping Nia research the *mark*." He sounded weary. "As you know, she's been working on it for a long time." Idwal smiled down at Nia, but she didn't reciprocate the glance. "So much is hearsay or half-forgotten lies, but something kept cropping up in reference to that symbol... something along the lines of a *treasure*, or a *gift*."

Nia stepped in, unable to abide Idwal's inaccuracies any longer, despite her strange mood.

"We thought it was an artifact of some kind. Yet there were certain phrases that kept re-appearing: '*centuries of love to make this gift live*', '*living treasure*'. Ifan believes that even if the stories aren't true... someone from this clan in Ireland believes them and is using Mona to fulfil their prophecies."

"And what do you think, Nia?" Cai asked calmly.

She grimaced. "We discovered that Mona's *mark* isn't a sign of evil after all, but rather a sign of power. It's a little like the swastika, originally a Buddhist sign of peace, before the Nazis corrupted and tainted it." Nia's voice grew stronger and more confident. "I'm presuming that as word of your *mark* spread from the spy back to Ireland, they would have recognised it as their sign. Its origin is not common knowledge, though someone else may have read the same texts and knows the truth."

Ifan looked into Mona's terrified eyes. "We're not saying Tom is anything other than a normal child, Mona. But that it may be someone's *obsession* to turn him into something else."

Cai was already there. "They want to bring him up in their power; they will come here for him." He glowered at Ifan. "When?"

"They will wait until his dependence on Mona has lessened. Am I right in thinking you have stopped breastfeeding?" Mona was unable to speak, but managed a slight inclination of the head. "And it's common knowledge?" Mona's face fell, and Ifan closed his eyes. "Any day, then. We've already seen the scout and there have been sightings in the strait. They know our strength – we should expect numbers."

Cai was already thinking, planning, and this time he didn't stop Mona from easing the baby out of his arms.

"Mona is no longer vulnerable. They won't be able to use her anymore and the informer can't know that yet."

Ifan looked dubious, but Idwal was becoming more confident, buoyed by Cai's optimism. "Yes, Mona can fight. We're a strong community, and with more of us trained…"

"Your powers aren't that of a fighter, Idwal," Ifan warned.

"Powers?" Dafydd asked.

"I'm a healer." Idwal sounded almost apologetic, and glanced at Nia, who continued to avoid his gaze. "I've learnt that if I lay my hands on someone, I can know the workings of their body. I can feel, virtually see, illness or disease and sort of repair it. I can… send out tiny lines of energy, like blood vessels of life force. It's not perfect yet, but I've been practising."

Cai was still calculating and now started to delegate. "From now on, Tom is with one of us constantly. If we're training, then you and Nia are with us in the room. No one else is to take responsibility for him." He pointed at Idwal. "Can you get hold of Bryn?" Cai shook his head in irritation. "Get him to calm down and take some sleep. Double the twenty-four-hour sentry shifts… and we'll need to find where the scout got in." His head snapped up. "Check all land and sea approaches." Cai turned earnestly to the new Archdruid. "Dafydd, can you contact the coastguard and crew for constant updates on shipping activity?"

Dafydd stood up, happy to have a job to do.

"I'll get them monitoring traffic from the Irish ferries through Holyhead as well," he added, as he left at a trot for the radio room.

Cai began to pace. "We have to find out who the spy is and neutralise them. There's no way we'll be able to keep any of this activity quiet. Can you continue to work on that, Ifan?" The old man agreed. "Nia, can you help Arwel cross-reference times and dates of arrivals of everyone here?"

"I've already…"

212

"Well do it *again*. You might have missed something," Cai barked in exasperation.

Then he looked at Mona. She had positioned Tom over one shoulder and absent-mindedly kissed his ear while massaging his little body. She seemed utterly oblivious to everything else.

≈

Tom normally fell asleep after his afternoon feed, but the unfamiliar room, and the tension within it, had made him anxious. As Mona patted and kissed him, he became more relaxed, and it wasn't long before she felt his soft even breaths, warm and comforting, against her neck.

Mona's own heart rate, however, had lurched to overdrive, and she felt incapable of thinking anything through properly – there was no time left to run or anywhere left to hide. A warm, dry hand touched Mona's cheek. There was kindness and love in Cai's face.

"It will be all right, Mo," he said.

Mona looked round – everyone but Cai and Ifan had gone. "What's the plan?" she made herself ask.

"It's all under control. We just need to…"

"That test you did earlier, Mona." It was Ifan who'd interrupted, but gently. "You did well, and I can see you've made immense progress, but…"

"But what?" Her earlier blind panic had been replaced by a desire for action.

"But we both know you can counter aggression with aggression – easily. I think we should test your real weakness, Mona."

They both glared at Ifan for a long, hard minute before Cai nodded. "I'll test her for you. You hold Tom," he said, taking Tom from Mona and passing him over the desk.

Cai held both her hands, soothing her knuckles with his thumbs. "I don't want him to hear. It's too personal," she whispered.

"Ifan, you're going to have to trust me. My words are for Mona only." Cai spoke to Ifan, but his eyes never left Mona's face.

"I understand," Ifan answered, and settled back in his chair with the sleeping baby.

"Are you ready?" Mona smiled back – of course she was ready. Tom's life depended on this. She could do anything. Cai wasn't sure he was ready, but cleared his throat and moved closer. Only Mona could hear his words now. Their proximity added a dangerous new dimension to the test. For both of them.

"*Mona.*" She had already started blocking. "*Gwisga'r wisg nes i brynu i ti* – I want you to wear the dress I bought for you. I felt your heat through it, when I forced your body against mine on the dance floor." Cai licked his lips. "I could feel your hips pushing into me, your breasts against my chest."

Mona had become a sculpture, unmoving, eyes closed.

"Do you remember how I had to unzip it for you? How it fell forwards… and open as I pulled the zip down your back and over your hips?" Cai reached a trembling hand towards her waist. "You stood in front of me… in just your underwear, and I wanted to turn you around… I wanted to touch you." Cai inched incrementally closer. "I wanted you to kiss me as I pulled you in. I wanted to trail my hands down your shoulders to your waist, so they could hold you here." His hands slunk from Mona's waist to her bum. "*Mona…*" Cai's voice lowered to a plea. "It's agony for me to lie next to you every night and not be allowed to touch you. Please…"

Cai moved nearer again but found himself held and stopped, pushed back from Mona by an arm's-length. She released his hands and took two clear steps backwards before facing Ifan.

In mangled Welsh, she spoke clearly and without emotion. "*Digon da i ti?* – Good enough for you?"

Cai staggered upright again, holding on to the table to collect himself.

Ifan seemed awkward and apologetic. "Yes," he croaked.

Firmly and decisively, Mona extracted Tom from the ex-Archdruid's arms and headed for the exit. She'd already started to leave the room when Cai called after her, but Mona didn't stop.

"She needs some time alone, son. Leave her be," Ifan said softly.

"But…" Cai looked to Ifan for the answer.

"It's just the way she is," the old man said.

Cai breathed out shakily and slumped into the nearest chair, massaging his eyes.

"I may have underestimated you," Ifan said, smiling at Cai. "You're a much better man than you know."

"No, Ifan. I'm a truly desperate man. I've had to have the restraint of Pwyll."

Ifan acknowledged the literary reference with a grim smile. "You've done well. You've made me proud."

Cai chuckled dryly as he got up and walked to the door. "It will all be fine. It has to be."

Ifan smiled back, and it was only when he could hear Cai's receding footsteps that the old man allowed his head to sink into his hands.

16

Panic

Cai woke as Mona creaked open the door. Tom was curled, hot and damp, against his chest and it was just dawn. "Where have you been?" He found it an effort to open his eyes.

"The armoury," Mona answered while filling the kettle and Cai wondered if her hands were shaking, or his eyes weren't fully focused yet. Mona was dressed for battle and wore a knife belt, populated with nine throwing knives. There were two short swords at her hip.

"I've just spoken to Dafydd about the invasion."

"What time is it?"

"Ten past five."

Cai couldn't keep the irritation from his sigh. "You're panicking, Mona. Calm down."

She was strung out on worry, and his patronising tone tweaked the thread a notch tighter. "Panicking!" Mona leant over his prone body, shouting as loud as her whisper would go. "They could be here any day, any minute. There are no lookouts, no radio shifts, nothing."

Tom started to stir and Cai hissed back. "I took care of all that last night. Everyone knows what they're doing and everything is in place."

"Dafydd didn't say…"

"It's five in the morning," he grouched.

"What does that mean?"

"It means come back to bed before Tom wakes up."

Cai's responses were getting snippier – a combination of tiredness, worry and frustration – and it fuelled Mona's retaliation.

"You have no idea how I feel about Tom. How can you?" The volume of the whisper hurt her throat and the tension of her balled fists ached through her arms. "He is my life, my *whole* life. If anything happens to him, I may as well curl up and die." It was only blind fear that kept back the sobs now.

"You cannot afford to overreact." His reply was measured and slow. Cai thought she might hit him then, but she took it out on the bag of clean washing at her feet – kicking it violently.

"Don't use that tone with me. I'm the bloody War Chief," she finally shouted.

"See you in the training room, *Chief*." Cai extricated himself from Tom and was out of the door in seconds, slamming it behind him.

≈

When Tom woke up, Mona carried him down with her for an early breakfast. Last night's fear of imminent invasion had altered into paranoia. Anyone of these people could be the spy. She was supposed to hand her son to Nia and Idwal at breakfast, but could she be handing him straight into the hands of the enemy?

Nia reassured her, and Idwal told her to pull herself together. They would take Tom with them to the training room. Idwal ordered Mona to shower, change out of her combat gear and back into training gear. Everything needed to appear calm and normal, for as long as possible. She saw the logic and agreed. Mona was capable of taking orders from anyone but Cai, it seemed. She'd been manic this morning but might just be able to put it all into perspective in time for the emergency meeting this afternoon.

≈

Running the aggravation out of his system was a good idea, but it wasn't working as well as usual for Cai, and he was still furious with Mona, even after the second lap of the *Conway*. Of course he knew how much she loved Tom. She was completely obsessed with the child. If there had ever been any room in her heart for him, Tom had replaced that quite convincingly.

Cai could sense her pulling away from him, avoiding any nuance of contact. Now that the language barrier had been breached, he feared she didn't want or need him anymore. Besides that, Mona was acting irrationally, hysterically even, and he had never seen her like it before. The enemy would come, there would be a fight and they would win. That's how she should think, if she was going to be any sort of decent War Chief.

Thankfully, there was no sign of Mona or Tom when Cai returned to the room. He wrenched off his sweaty clothes, still edgy with aggression and stormed into the bathroom.

Mona was stepping out of the shower and corralling her thoughts as Cai opened the bathroom door. He hadn't seen her naked body for a year, and in that split-second revelation, his fury turned to lust and then back again in an instant, as she reached for the towel.

"*Paid* – Don't do that," he bellowed, snatching it out of her hands.

It was just dawn as Meilyr reached the burial chamber of his ancestors. He stroked the huge capstone reverently, remembering the souls of those who'd touched this earth before him. The blacksmith's step then lightened as long legs strode out the short distance from the stones to his settlement; home to Canaid and the children. He'd got a better price than expected at market and had made good time back, despite the weight of the provisions he carried.

It was early; even too early to hear the staccato pecking of the hens, but Meilyr heard another sound as he crossed into the compound. He caught the rhythmic music of lovemaking; the gentle groans and gasps of which were coming from inside the smithy.

"*Dos oma* – Get out," Mona screeched back, pushing his hand away violently. When he didn't, Mona marched hastily past him.

Cai barked something unintelligible at the top of his lungs and the bathroom door shuddered with the violence of the kick he gave it.

≈

Neither of them dared utter a word to the other about the unravelling yarn they were witnessing. The darkening storyline fuelled the acute tension between them, but both Cai and Mona knew they had to project a united front at training. After all, knowledge of the impending invasion was held by only a very few and they couldn't afford to spread alarm.

Cai was rigid and terse. He took charge as soon as everyone was paying attention. Mona anxiously waited for her brother and Nia to arrive with Tom, and she rushed to them when they did – fifteen minutes late. Her paranoia had ratcheted up again in the training room. It was unlikely to be anyone in here, but you never knew, and Mona began scrutinising each face, searching for tell-tale signs.

Idwal nudged her. "Pay attention! He's talking about something new." How long had she been out of it? "You're on, Mo. You're doing the demo," Idwal prompted.

"What's it about, what did he say?"

"I don't really know. Something about using people's weaknesses against them."

It was too late. She was on the mats and Cai had already warmed up. How long had it been since she'd performed her patterns?

"So, keep in mind what I said," Cai advised the class. "It's an important lesson."

Mona had missed something. She'd broken her own golden rule about preparation, and only had the time it took for him to speak the last sentence to warm up. It wasn't enough, and he was still angry.

"So how are we doing this?"

"Weren't you listening?" He worked an angry muscle in his jaw. "One fight, first to five." Cai cracked the knuckles in his hands as he whispered into her ear. "I won't be fighting fairly... after all, I doubt the enemy will."

"Of course," she swallowed.

The first two points were easy. Mona knew he'd try to grapple and get close enough to speak. And despite everything, it was glorious to be sparring with him again. The intensity of his fighting thrilled her like music. He was so natural – more of a defensive fighter than her, but powerful and deadly.

She made contact with his ribs for the third point, but too late, she realised he'd lured her in with the false mistake. Cai took the punishment, but was poised to strike as she overextended. She gave away three clear points in succession as he closed for the kill – hip, thigh and shoulder.

Using the last point as purchase, Cai drew her in to grapple, and in her haste to disengage, Mona blocked and parried until he had forced her up against the training room wall. Their ribcages were touching intermittently as air was dragged through parched lips and rasping throats. She had nowhere to go and he was too close to kick or punch.

Their harsh respiration was the only sound in the room, until a single clap broke it. Shortly joined by a tentative second, and then the entire training room began applauding Cai's momentous victory.

The sound of clapping replaced the buzz of blood and adrenaline in Cai's ears. He found himself still pressed hard up against Mona, and when he glanced into her eyes he found something dark in them. Cai peeled his body away from hers, and Mona slid down the training room wall.

"You beat me," she managed, still not in control of her breathing. "People don't beat me."

"I'm not people," Cai panted, hands plaited behind his head to expand his lung capacity. It was a few seconds before he realised that Mona had already gone.

≈

"Well?" Nia asked, as Mona slid down the back wall. Idwal shifted Tom around in his arms. He was still dazed by the fight he'd just seen – he was almost embarrassed by its intimacy.

"I see what you mean." He rejigged Tom. "Cai will have to watch out now, though. My sister doesn't like to lose."

"It didn't look that way to me." Nia spoke under her breath. Tom was all arms and legs and odd angles. "Are you all right with him? He doesn't seem too comfortable."

Idwal peered down at Tom who dangled a bit, but looked fairly content. "You're ok, mate, aren't you?" He blew a raspberry on the baby's neck, and Tom liked it.

"He laughed, Id." Nia smiled. "Do it again!"

Mona found them entertaining her son when she reached the back of the room. It was only fair for Cai to finish the lesson, and Tom smiled when he saw his mum.

"I can't believe he beat you." Idwal couldn't help saying it, even with a helpful nudge from Nia.

Mona ignored him. "What's wrong Nia, why were you…?"

"I'm fine," Nia answered bravely.

It was clear to Mona that Nia was far from fine and that she didn't want to talk about it. Mona didn't push the point, but lowered her voice to speak to Idwal.

"Can you have a feel around in my head… to see if I've completely broken through the… barrier? I think it still needs some work."

Idwal handed Tom to Nia. "I'll make it look like I'm inspecting a head wound." He glanced at her with a smile on his lips. "Did Cai get you there? Or just everywhere else?"

"Ha, ha," she obliged without a trace of humour.

Mona felt a freezing sensation rather than pain, but when he released her head it was a relief. Idwal tutted. "Cai wasn't mucking around, Mo. He really made contact… you're quite badly bruised, you know."

"Nothing that a shower won't sort out." Idwal lifted a bossy eyebrow. "Ok, if it gets too bad I'll come for some medicine. Did you find it?"

"Yes, it's a strange thing. Like a window you've punched through. I've only tidied up around the edge a bit. I don't want to mess with the brain too much though - especially yours."

Cai arrived by her side, not exactly ebullient with victory but slightly less dour.

"I've just talked to Dafydd. He's given the all-clear for the next hour, and if anything changes he'll send someone." Cai made an effort to sound business-like.

"Good," Mona said before looking at Nia. "Is there any chance you two can keep hold of Tom until after lunch?"

≈

It was an uncomfortable walk back to their room. His anger had finally abated but Cai sensed, correctly, that Mona wasn't interested in idle banter or a fight analysis.

He hadn't played fair, using the threat of the language to panic her into moves she would never normally make, but he wasn't sorry. Knowing Mona, she'd already fixed the problem and would be plotting a revenge attack. He'd have to have his wits about him at all times, and his ribs were already desperately sore.

Mona stood quietly beside him as he unlocked the door and pushed it open to let her through. Expecting her to take the first shower, Cai walked into the tiny kitchen and ran a glass of water from the tap, trying to gauge her mood. Realising, after a few more seconds that Mona still stood behind him, Cai tensed and whirled at her, ready for the strike. However, she remained stationary in front of him, awkward somehow.

"You did well today," she told him.

Mona's body language baffled him. She seemed to be trying to hug and hide herself simultaneously.

"I didn't fight fair." Cai tried a small smile and she closed her eyes but opened them almost immediately.

"No, it was a solid bout. You're an excellent fighter."

"Are you angry with me?" Mona shook her head, a tiny, sad movement and the silence was deafening. "I thought I'd be happier about beating you," he muttered.

"You should be euphoric." And despite her strange mood, she growled a challenge. "Enjoy it. It won't ever happen again."

Cai took a tentative step towards her and she seemed to tense up. "I don't want to beat you, Mo. For crying out loud..." His voice was just about audible. "*Ti'n gwybod be dwi isio* – You know what I want."

Mona's eyes were clamped shut and her arms tightened around her waist, but she nodded. Her body language made sense now. Mona didn't want him, and she was trying to tell him so. A sickness coiled in his gut.

The few inches between them were an impassable barrier, but she could feel him testing the edges. Cai smelt strongly of sea, sweat, diesel and desire. The tightening in her stomach was almost too much to bear.

"*Dwyt ti ddim isio fi* – You don't want me." Cai's voice sounded dreadfully quiet and she opened her eyes to catch the pain of rejection in his.

She swallowed. "I do want you... but I just... I don't know how anymore."

The rigid cage of her arms stayed in place as he broke through the barrier, putting both of his arms around her. She allowed her forehead to meet his shoulder but was glad for the distance her arms still provided. "I've had a baby, Cai. And it's not only my body that's changed... I'm disconnected somehow... I can't let go. The last time I had sex..."

"Ssh Mona, no." He rocked her as he'd seen her rock Tom. "I won't hurt you, just please, please..." Cai's words ended in the soft kisses that he placed in her hair. He released her and moved his hands to her shoulders. Mona knew he was going to dislodge her arms, and after a few seconds of half-hearted resistance, she found herself pressed against him. The sensation caught in her throat this time. She breathed out as he absorbed some of her tension, but her arms still hung fisted at her side. Cradling her head against his chest, and holding it there, Cai continued to rock her.

"Can I kiss you?"

A slight nod allowed him to ease her head back and he saw the fear in her eyes. "I don't want to burn you."

"I'll take my chances," Cai whispered.

The feel of his lips against hers dragged a gasp from them. Cai nudged at her mouth gently but with increasing force until he had opened it fully with his insistent lips. Her fists began to unfurl as his urgent tongue deepened, then slowed and finally disappeared, leaving behind an ache she felt between her thighs. Mona heard the unzipping of her combat vest but was completely absorbed with the sight of Cai's mouth as he concentrated on his task – the tip of his tongue poking between his lips with the effort. After easing the vest from her shoulders and letting it drop, Cai discarded his own.

"Lift up your arms." His voice was still a whisper but a command rather than a request.

The thin material of her base-layer was drenched with cooling sweat, and it clung to her body obstinately. By the time Cai had rolled it up over her head, the exposure had made her shiver. Cai dropped the damp material to the floor, closed his eyes and hurriedly whisked off his own tight garment before returning to her bra. Mona thought vaguely that he might undo it, but he moved both hands slowly, reverently, until he held a breast in each hand, gently caressing each nipple with his thumbs through the black fabric. Smothering a whimper, Mona concentrated on his mouth again, watching as it joined his thumbs at her nipples. She licked her lips in sympathy as Cai's tongue skated over and over, round and round, until she had to close her eyes and reach for the support of Cai's hips. The intensity suddenly spiked as he released each breast from its cup and resumed with mouth on flesh this time. Mona's pelvis flexed abruptly against Cai's, finding his erection. Releasing Mona from her bra, he drew her naked torso into his and held her still for a long moment, rubbing his hands up and down her back while whispering something against the hollow of her neck. It may have been her name. The bra fell to the floor between them as he took one of her hands and led her to the foot of their bed.

The short journey relieved the white noise singing in her ears and she endured another jolt of embarrassment as Cai looked directly at her. His desire clouded the blue and her hand automatically reached up to cover her *mark*.

"*Gadael i mi dy weld* – Let me see you," he croaked, taking her hand away before placing both of his at her waist. Cai moved them slowly down either hip, and then behind to hold her bum. Mona was lost again to the surf in her ears as he began to knead her buttocks, using them as leverage to ease her hips in and against him. He pressed his mouth to hers, consuming her senses entirely again.

"*Gorwedd i lawr* – Lie down." Cai had unbuttoned her trousers and pulled everything down to her knees while she had been lost in his mouth and touch. She looked on in a daze as he unzipped her boots and peeled off the last of her clothing.

Mona lay alone on the bed. She was aware with one part of her mind that Cai was fetching a condom, but a larger part of her brain, had succumbed to fear in his absence. Mona had killed Gareth. He had died during orgasm. Was there a chance her body would react that way to Cai if he hurt her?

Mona was curled up around a pillow when he returned to the bed, her eyes shut, as if battling some internal dilemma. As he lay down next to her, Mona's eyes opened. "*Paid a fy mrifo i* – Please don't hurt me," she said. "I can't control my power." It was somewhere between an order and a plea and he nodded, gently tugging the pillow out from between them.

Cai wore only a condom now and the sensation of his hard nakedness against hers was intoxicating. Mona's hips began to gently rotate as Cai sought her mouth again, one of his hands held her head while the other kneaded and probed. Mona gasped as Cai's hand reached between her legs. He moved his palm against her pubic mound, his fingers lying across the entrance to her vagina.

225

"*Wyt ti'n barod* – Are you ready?" he murmured, his lips at her ear.

"*Dwi ddim yn gwybod* – I don't know." Her voice was a cracked pant, and Cai moved his hand from between her legs to place a finger gently on her lower lip.

"Ssh," he soothed, and pressed his forehead against hers. "*Na i ddim dy frifo di, Mona. Ddim rwan, ddim byth* – I will not hurt you, Mona. Not now, not ever."

Cai's face was so close that all she could see of it was blue – she was drowning in his blue. His lips met hers with such acute tenderness that a sob almost rose in her throat. Cai's tongue edged between her lips again and the intensity of the renewed pleasure dragged Mona's eyes closed. Cai began to move his tongue inside her mouth, slowly, too slowly, and her pelvis pushed forwards to meet his as he kissed her deeper and harder. Mona's arm roamed his back and thighs, pulling him down against her, pressing his body into hers. She felt his penis rubbing at the lips of her sex.

"Please, Mona, please," he breathed.

Cai rotated his hips gently, straining visibly with hard-fought control. The ligaments in his neck were taught and his body shook. Their combined breath turned into a single gasp as he pushed into her. Watching for any signs of pain, he stopped, but Mona's eyes remained shut and he flexed again, deeper. Her hips responded and he filled her, stilling entirely as he reached his final destination.

There wasn't enough control in his body to formulate another question, but he interpreted Mona's body language as indication that he could begin to move. Cai tried to maintain a slow and gentle rhythm but before long he was lost in the glory of loving her. His mouth needed to taste hers and his hands worshipped everywhere they touched.

The urgency grew as Mona's body began to answer his in full, bucking and twisting. Drinking him down and eating him alive. Cai felt her muscles tensing, beginning to break free of all restraint. Mona's body lurched, bowing up off the bed towards him, sucking his entire essence into her. Waves of ecstasy crashed through him until he found himself finally still, finally sated.

≈

"They'll come looking for us you know."

"Don't care," Cai said, watching his hand as it slid down the length of her thigh "Can't stop now." Mona lay naked in his arms and nothing else mattered.

"You know, I'd have put you down for a full-back, possibly a fly-half with your clothes on. But I think you could be a back row player. You've got great shoulders."

Mona was talking in Welsh and it was unbelievably arousing. She'd said something about rugby, and he giggled.

"What?"

"I don't know."

"Tell me."

Cai experienced the vibration of her speech through his lips. The feel of her nakedness against his chest was unbearably acute. "I just like the way you speak in Welsh." His lips had a life of their own and seemed unable to stop, until they had mapped the length and breadth of her body.

"Welsh! It's a piece of piss!"

He could sense her grin through the English one-liner. "What does *that* mean?"

"Piece of cake. Simple. Easy peasy, you know," she said, idly tracing a pattern on his back with her fingertips.

"So why don't you just say that?"

"Because it's funnier." She looked down at his confused frown and sighed as she kissed his forehead. "You wouldn't understand."

"Oh wouldn't I?" He beamed at her mischievously. He could sense her grin. "Don't get cocky, Jonesey. Your grammar is appalling." Cai resumed his kissing, and each time he kissed the *mark* his lips jolted with the static shock of power.

"I'm ever so pleased I didn't burn you to death." Mona waited for a response, but his lips were too busy. "It's so hard to get good subordinates, you know." Cai paused in his soft nibbling and bit her quite hard. "Ouch! Careful number one," Mona warned playfully before running both her hands through his curls. "You're a wonderful teacher, thank you."

"*Mae dysgu yn magu gwybodaeth* – Teaching is learning," Cai said simply. But he could see Mona was confused. "*Dysgu* means both teaching and learning in Welsh," he explained.

"Well at least that's *not* confusing." She rolled her eyes and he tickled her, his hands beginning to explore again. Mona thought she should really make a concerted effort to stop him this time or they might never leave the room. But his hands did still, and Cai became thoughtful.

"You don't want to talk about them, do you?"

Mona knew who he meant and shook her head stubbornly. "Doesn't sound like it's going to be a happy ending."

"No," he sighed, laying his head against her thigh. "They're old names, though. Can you guess what they mean?"

Mona stroked his hair and looked to the ceiling for inspiration. "Well Canaid's something to do with singing…"

"Good." Cai beamed. "And what about Meilyr?"

"Not the foggiest."

"Meilyr." Cai rolled the Welsh around in his mouth. "Very old name." He frowned fractionally. "It means a lot of things, but maybe… man of iron, in his case"

"Mmm, it sort of suits him. What about the other one… Maelgwn?"

Cai's face contorted at the name.

"Don't tell me… it means more than one thing."

Cai nodded slowly. "Though Prince of wolves seems to fit." He sighed deeply. "Do you want to hear a theory?"

"No, but I expect you'll tell me anyway."

"I think they're us… that we were them."

"I *knew* you'd say something like that. Do you have any idea how ridiculous you sound?" Mona cuffed him gently around the head. "Talk about ruining the moment!"

"I'm sorry." He kissed her stomach. "It's just... it's like when you smell something... and it transports you straight back to a specific moment in your life... "

"It seems to happen when we're angry with each other," Mona said as the thought occurred to her.

"Some of us believe that our souls endure, Mo. That they can live on when... "

"Don't get all weird and Pagan on me, Cai Owens."

Mona made a joke of it. The strange storyline made her uncomfortable and she clutched desperately at straws to change the subject.

"Tell me about your music," she blurted. "You've been very cagey, and I'm beginning to worry. Come on," she cajoled, "tell me."

Cai reluctantly stopped the kissing and supported his weight on an elbow. Mona was astonished to see him looking embarrassed.

"Didn't Nia explain about the significance of music in our culture, Mona?" Her creased brows told him that Nia had said nothing on the subject. "Maybe she should have. It's... it's an intensely personal question and well... I'm not sure I'm ready for that level of commitment." Cai looked down and Mona froze as he carried on speaking. Her very newly discovered world, wobbled violently on its axis. "Unless that's what you're asking." He glanced up again with a burning blue gaze. "*I ni gael priodi* – For me to handfast with you?"

"No... no! I just asked about your music. Sorry, Cai... I didn't mean... I didn't know..." He had really good control of his face but Cai's shaking stomach muscles gave away the laughter and she whacked him on the shoulder. "You total git, that's not funny."

Cai did laugh now, and even though it was at her expense, it was a joyous sound. "You should have seen your face," he chortled.

Mona inched to the side of the bed muttering, "Oh yes, very funny." But she laughed along and wasn't quick enough to make it all the way out of bed before he dragged her back in. "Cai, you have to let me go," she sighed from the safety of his arms.

"Will you stay if I sing you a song?" He looked so happy that she had to kiss him, but the kiss deepened again and she feared another descent into paradise.

"*Dim ond un gân–* Just for one song."

Cai released her and lay back, closing his eyes but holding on to her hand, he cleared his throat. Mona didn't really know what she'd expected – a joke song in his current mood. And maybe it was, but as the first notes came from his mouth, she was entranced. Cai's voice was quiet and husky, but the words and tune were perfect. He sang in English and Mona didn't recognise the song initially, as he'd slowed the tempo considerably.

'*Guide me Oh thy great Jehovah, pilgrim through this barren land...*'

Everyone knew this hymn, *Cwm Rhonda*, the unofficial Welsh anthem, but she had never heard it sung like this before. It was sultry, sexual and totally unchristian. Mona was scandalised, despite herself.

'*I am weak, but thou art mighty;*
Hold me with thy powerful hand.'

She could feel his voice gaining in power and vibrating through her body. It was cool silk. It was warm, grainy honey.

'*Bread of heaven, bread of heaven,*
Feed me till I want no more
Feed me till I want no more.'

Cai couldn't manage the next two verses because Mona had crawled on top of him and claimed his body again.

17

Treachery

The war council took place in Ifan's rooms, as the warriors had commandeered the training room where they were preparing their weapons and bodies for the onslaught.

Cai was talking through the plan in Welsh and Mona made the mistake, earlier on in the meeting, of watching him while he explained and argued. He was grim and succinct but watching him talk reminded her of how recently and where his lips had kissed her, how his hands had explored. At one point their eyes met and she'd responded with a spasm, as her body remembered his song. Cai had invented his own secret weapon against her.

As she wasn't supposed to understand Welsh anyway, Mona forced her mind to wander. Something niggled at a corner of her brain. It was all too easy, too straightforward. Cai's plans were thorough, but text-book.

There was a strong likelihood they were sharing this room with the spy, and she felt sure they were still being played. Arwel had been trying to decipher this riddle for a year and Mona knew he had little chance of cracking it in the next twenty-four hours or so. Was it too late for her to find out who, or try any misdirection? In truth, it probably was, but she'd been pondering on it long enough for a scheme to come knocking.

The plan began to take shape as her eyes flicked across the faces in the room and back to her sleeping child. She registered all but saw nothing, until she noted the shabby music player on the table in front of her. Mona grabbed it up and squeezed it as her resolve hardened. Nobody was above reproach, and Ifan beside her made a small cough as he read her scribbled list. Catching her attention and raising an eyebrow, the old Druid stared into her eyes and nodded his approval. He subtly passed her the key from his pocket. They were on the same track, but she had to act soon. Mona leaned in. "Tell Cai I had to go."

As she left the room, Idwal followed and Mona sighed – not wanting to rehash the same argument again. "It's the only way, Id." She took the offensive, not looking back as she strode onwards. "It's a double wall of protection for him, despite what you think."

He listened as they fell into step together. "I know what it is, Mona, you're wrapping us both up in cotton wool. Cai too if you could get away with it."

"That's not true. He's only delivering Tom down to you and Rob. Cai stands more of a chance if it comes to close contact. Tom will be safer with Cai. We've considered every option."

"Hey." He caught her arm. "Slow down. I know you're off somewhere, but I wondered if we could have a minute." Idwal appeared a little embarrassed.

I'm in a hurry, her brain screamed. "Is it Nia?"

"Just come in here a minute." They were standing by the library, and he pulled her inside. "I'm... I've asked Nia to marry me. Except they don't call it that here... handfasting is what they call it. Did you know that?" Idwal was blithering and Mona squished Tom a bit in her exuberant hug, though he didn't wake up.

"It's funny, but sometimes when I see you and Nia... it's exactly like the way Dad used to look at Mum." The lump in her throat was too complicated to decipher.

"Nia's not convinced," Idwal confessed. "She reckons I'll have a duty to procreate and well..."

"She can't have kids?" Mona finally worked out Nia's heartache. "Can't you find a way...?"

He shifted uncomfortably. "That's what I want to ask you. Is there any chance I can just have a peek at how the ovaries are supposed to look or work? I'm not a doctor. I don't know what's right. Mostly I can work it out from diagrams, but I don't want to get this wrong. I'll only need a minute."

It was a little awkward, but it was acceptable, and he was definitely more magician than physician as he screwed his eyes shut and placed his hand on her abdomen. Idwal seemed satisfied with his findings once he had opened his eyes again.

"Got it. Thanks, Mo." Another small awkwardness followed. "It's none of my business of course, but you and Cai had better be really careful over the next couple of days. Unless you *want* Tom to have a brother or sister."

"We're always careful." She changed the subject. "I thought Nia would be at the meeting, I wanted to…"

"She's not even contemplating the thought of saying goodbye to you Mona. Nor am I."

Though that wasn't true, he'd said it with his eyes, and she carried on. "Rob knows the ropes. I want him to be a big part of Tom's life: Siân and Sioned too." She stroked her baby's head tenderly. "He needs to be surrounded by love. I've written a letter for Tom, you know… for when he's old enough. It's in his bag."

Idwal nodded. "You still think it will be tomorrow?"

"It won't be long now. They've been lurking for a while. With the way the tides are at the moment, we're guessing at the early hours of the morning. Just waiting for confirmation from the Coastguard now."

"We'll be ready." He kissed them both.

≈

There was a huge amount of activity in and around the training room. The numbers of core fighters had swollen as the women trained and tested last year stepped up again. They were checking weapons and equipment, ahead of tomorrow's attack. Both corridors were full, as each warrior prepared alone or in small units for the battle ahead. Sioned stood with her elite group of fighters, checking and rechecking straps and swords. They had trained for this. They had made their choices, just as she had.

Mona led a path through these men and women, helping them tighten body armour, letting them show or hide their fear to her. She reminded them of their strengths, and suggested patterns to keep them focused. Mona had trained them all, and knew what she could expect from each of them. Finding the face she was looking for, Mona changed direction, but Dafydd intercepted her.

"You should be resting. We'll need you fresh when the time comes."

She nodded, trying to keep tabs on her quarry over his shoulder. "I thought it might help."

"They'll expect you to lead from the front, but it's not time yet. Anyway Cai has just spent the last hour doing the same thing. They're ready, Mo. Go and get that baby to bed." He put his hand on her shoulder. "Cai's waiting for you."

Mona smiled in agreement. "I'm going." But she carried on past him as he wandered off, and grabbed Carmen firmly by the arm. "Follow me *now*," she muttered under her breath. "Don't make it obvious."

Mona was a couple of corridors away by the time Carmen found her. "I need your help and I'm running out of time," Mona answered the woman's curious gaze bluntly.

"Don't tell me *Cernunnos* has done it again."

She had a crooked grin on her face, but it was stiff and false. Carmen was scared.

Mona guessed she was talking about Cai, but didn't have the time to be side-tracked. "I want you to find something for me." Mona passed her a key. "This is a master, it will unlock every room in the place. I want you to search for something in these rooms." She handed over the scribbled list. "It may look something like this."

Mona held up the black plastic curve so Carmen could examine it. "It's some sort of mobile phone. Bring me anything that even slightly resembles it." Mona paused and checked over her shoulder. "We can put them back later if we're wrong."

"You're after the spy?" Carmen studied the list. "Your brother's on here, and Cai. Surely you don't suspect him?" Despite herself she was horrified.

"I suspect everyone. Start at the top."

"Why me?"

"Because you're a thief," Mona said simply. "You're clever, and devious, and I can trust you to come up with a plausible enough excuse in any given situation. You might get caught, but I'm sure you'll brazen it out."

The atmosphere between these women would never be easy, but it altered slightly as Carmen gently touched Tom's fat cheek. "Is he a good baby?" she asked quietly.

Mona was taken aback by the new tone. "I don't know really." She shrugged. "He's my baby."

"Are you going to die for him, Mona?" Her question was so brutally direct.

"I hope not," Mona said. "Maybe," she added softly.

"There's always hope." Carmen's smile was small but real, and Mona touched the woman's shoulder.

"Be careful, and come to me as soon as you find it. No matter what time."

The Galician Druid nodded and swirled away in a haze of perfume.

≈

Arwel had become frantic, and it wasn't helping. Ever since Nia had made the discovery about Tom, the need to uncover the traitor in their midst had become an all-encompassing obsession. Nia had allowed him to work in the privacy of her library, and he was there now, pacing aimlessly back and forth – deliberating over the meagre evidence laid out on the desk before him. There was something. That same splinter throbbed in his brain and he sat down again to sift through it. Starting at the beginning – one more time.

≈

Tom was getting really heavy and his sling bit into Mona's shoulder. Soon he'd be waking up for another feed, and she wanted to bathe him and see him smile again before Rob took him to safety.

Mona wasn't surprised to see Rob waiting for them when she returned to the room. Tom began to chunter as Rob eased him out of the sling, away from his mother's reassuring heartbeat.

"Won't you need this cot?" Mona asked once everything had been packed into the various bags, ready for Tom's departure.

"I thought you two might need it tonight. Anyway I know where it is. I can get it any time."

"Yes, of course." The silence was painful. "And you're sure of the plan?" Mona asked for the umpteenth time and Rob nodded in exasperation. "Then tell me again, just to be sure."

"At the alarm, Cai comes to me with Tom. Idwal will meet us there. Cai joins you in the fight. You win, and then meet us in the bar for a victory drink, ok?"

"That's right." She tried to smile. "That's right... good. Well I suppose..."

"Don't try to say goodbye to me. If Nia's not taking it, then neither am I."

"Fine." But she kissed him goodbye anyway. "Teach him all your music."

≈

Mona knew Cai would reappear, as soon as Rob had gone.

"I'd like to give him a bath," she told him.

"It's all ready," he said calmly.

Tom smiled in the bath, and while flailing around on the bed, and even when she gave him his last bottle. Cai left them alone, and if he noticed the fat tears splashing on the child's head, he didn't make a comment.

Mona must have fallen asleep as she fed Tom, but woke as Cai settled him into the cot by their bed.

"Come and have something to eat," he whispered.

"You've cooked?"

"No, reheated, but it's food. We've missed everything today."

"What time is it?"

"9.30."

Only a few more hours. Dafydd had received word of a large fleet having recently left the Irish coast. The attack would come to them in the early hours.

"Plates, knives and forks. You've pulled out all the stops!"

Cai gave her the satisfaction of a dry chuckle but knew her pathetic joke was the only thing keeping Mona together. He poured them some water and sat down opposite her.

She tried a mouthful of food, and it turned to dust in her mouth.

"I'm not hungry."

"Eat."

He was right. She needed to eat or there would be nothing in the tank for fighting, and Mona took a few more reluctant mouthfuls.

"How many people have you killed, Cai?"

"Not many, five."

"How did you kill them?"

"Sword mostly, broken necks. Why?"

Mona sat still with her knife and fork poised over the meal. "I don't want to kill – or fight and die. I want to live and be happy." She left the meal and the table. "I'm going to check my gear."

Mona walked to the chest of drawers and saw everything laid out meticulously on the top. All her weapons and leathers on one side and Cai's on the other. The swords were honed and deadly; she didn't want to look at them.

Mona could feel Cai standing very close behind her, and it was hard for her to turn and admit it to him. "I'm scared of dying now... since Tom."

"So am I," he murmured, pulling her towards him by the belt and starting to unbutton her shirt.

"We should rest, sleep."

"I need you."

Mona felt him undoing her, flesh and bone, not merely undressing her, and she tried to block him mentally.

"If we make love now, I may never find the strength to leave."

$$\approx$$

Sex had always been a variation on a fight for Mona; power, passion, ecstasy. However, as they lay against each other on their bed tonight, Mona found that each touch and every caress was tainted with a loss that sweetened and lengthened the fabric of time. Mona lay cradled in the arms of someone she loved. Cai had somehow managed to calm a part of the wildness in her soul, and it hadn't weakened her, as she had feared it might. Mona was the equal to anything that lay ahead.

Cai spoke first. "You're more optimistic than you think. If there was no hope, we wouldn't have used a condom."

Mona's mind had become too fluid for sane conversation. "Who's Cernunnos?"

He smoothed her head and kissed where he had smoothed. "He's an antlered Celtic god. Why?"

"Carmen mentioned him... I think she was talking about you. I just wondered what she meant."

Mona felt Cai's tension. "I used Carmen," Cai confessed and Mona was glad she couldn't see his face. "I hurt her... when I was trying to hurt you."

"I know."

"I'm sorry."

Mona grazed her lips across his ribs. "Celtic god?" she prompted.

"Cernunnos," Cai began, as if quoting from a text-book, "is the Celtic antlered god of aggressive male power, genetic vigour and fecundity. Often drawing parallels with the pagan Greenman."His voice lowered awkwardly. "It used to be my nickname."

Mona didn't make any comment.

"As part of their attempt to discredit Paganism," he continued. "The Christians used his image to depict the devil, so…"

"Horny devil, I get it."

When they awoke at the appointed time, Cai and Mona washed away their tenderness and dressed themselves in armour and resolve. Mona strapped Tom to Cai's chest and they parted wordlessly, at the junction of two corridors.

≈

Rhona knocked lightly at the library door and, knowing Arwel wouldn't hear, she crept in almost immediately afterwards. His white hair was spilled over the books he'd fallen asleep on, and she stroked it softly. "Arwel." She pressed her lips up against his ear and kissed it, very lightly.

"What time is it?" he asked, as she put the mug in front of him.

"Two in the morning." Rhona didn't enquire how the work was going. She would already know if there had been any success.

As she cupped his thin hand in hers, Arwel came back from another place, to really look at her. "Where will you be for the battle?"

He'd asked this question so many times, but she was patient in replying. "I'll be with the children. I'll keep them safe."

His pale blue stare wasn't demanding that. "Please keep yourself safe."

Arwel seemed morbidly worried, so she tried to lighten the mood. "We'll all be fine. I've even bought fluorescent stickers – so we can see each other in a blackout. The kids are actually excited."

Rhona made a groan of forgetfulness, which enervated Arwel. "What? What's wrong?"

"It's just that the stickers keep coming off." She smiled, trying to put him at ease. "I meant to get some stronger glue, that's all."

Arwel stood up suddenly, grabbed her shoulders and kissed her. He backed towards the door and pointed randomly. He'd found the splinter. Now he had to pull it out. "I love you, Rhona!"

≈

It may have been the quickest that Arwel had ever run, and very shortly, he arrived at his grandad's rooms, banging on the door. Ifan didn't responding quickly enough, and so he kept up the noise until the old man answered it.

"Invoices, delivery notes, purchase orders. I need them all – right away." Ifan knew enough of his grandson's talents to obey without question.

They were looking for an invoice for an industrial strength adhesive. The solar-powered stickers on the fleet had been extremely difficult to remove – both Cai and Dafydd had mentioned it more than once. There would obviously be no record for the bugs and the back-up stickers, but the glue might have been ordered and invoiced at a later date. Whoever had made that purchase was almost definitely their spy.

It took another hour of searching but when Arwel showed him the single piece of evidence, Ifan knew the lad was right. The knowledge devastated them both... and time had run out. Arwel stood up, not quite knowing what to do next, but Ifan was already arming himself.

"No, I'll go, Taid." The boy performed better in combat than Ifan, though it was marginal.

Ifan shook his head vigorously. "You're too precious, too valuable. I won't lose you as well."

Arwel started to argue. There really wasn't time for this. "We'll go together then."

"No. Stay here."

It was an order that Arwel had no intention of obeying, and he stomped to the door, past his grandfather.

"I said NO!" Ifan bellowed as he brought the butt of his sword down, hard against the boy's head.

≈

Mona had jogged the perimeter twice and there was still no sign of activity on the strait. A tiny skiff pootled a little way off shore and there were a couple of pleasure boats further out, but nothing like the expected hordes. Dafydd stood anxiously in the radio room looking non-plussed.

"We just got Coastguard and RNLI on channel sixteen. They report dozens of vessels coming in fast, from all directions."

"When should we see them?"

"Soon... now even." He shook his head. "I don't... understand."

Suddenly, Mona did – too late, and she gasped at her monumental stupidity.

"They're already here." She swallowed back the oncoming hysteria. "Leave someone to maintain radio contact, but no one is coming. Who's on the entrance by the lower jetty?"

"Peder and Cadan."

"Follow me, Dafydd. Get your sword out."

The smell of sulphur was overpowering as she and Dafydd approached the lower jetty entrance. Peder and Cadan were still warm in death, and she raced forwards past them praying: that there was enough time, that she wouldn't be too late. They both skidded to a halt at the sight of Carmen, who was sitting up against a wall; her breaths were quick and shallow. "Help her," Mona shouted to Dafydd as she ran on by.

Mona's legs seemed too slow, the corridors too long, and Mona willed away the dread of what she would find at their end. She could see bodies on the floor outside the room, and her momentum stuttered as her mind screamed to a halt.

241

Idwal and Cai were sprawled together in a heap, as if blown back by a bomb blast. She forced herself to move forward; to check for another small body, crushed amongst them. Cai lay on his back, two deep gashes on his chest where Tom had been cut from him. She felt for his pulse and sobbed with relief when she discovered the faint beat, but recoiled instantly from the taint of poison in him. She saw the strong pulse in her brother's neck and staggered upright and towards the horror that must wait inside.

Mona scanned for a tiny broken body, the sounds of his cry, but there was nothing – he was gone.

"She took him, Mona." The whisper came from behind her. Ifan was propped against the wall, a pillow wedged at his side.

"Who did?" Mona knelt down beside him to hear his rasping and moved the pillow back to see the dagger still imbedded in his chest cavity.

"A woman. His grandmother, I think. We… we were tricked." Mona shook her head. She knew.

"Technology, Mona." Ifan saw she had already worked it out. "We were too late. Too stupid… they have him now." He pushed her prying hands away from his wound. He didn't want to be healed.

"No, I'm going for him," she vowed and he shut his eyes in pain. "You will need Cai."

There was so much more he needed to tell her. Mona couldn't do this without him. "Ifan, no, please …wait… what else?" But he'd gone and her heart screamed.

Outside, Idwal had struggled to his knees, and was clutching Cai with both arms around his chest. Her brother's eyes were closed, he was muttering and black vomit dribbled over his chin. Mona's heart expanded with love and gratitude and she knelt down beside them, rubbing Idwal's back as he sicked up more black fluid onto the lino. Mona looked around for something to wipe his mouth with, and found herself watching Dafydd as he carried Carmen towards her, limp in his arms.

"She's dead... there was nothing I could do." He whispered as he carried the small body past her and into the room.

"Did she say anything?"

"Yes," Dafydd whispered, tears already in his eyes as he made to lay the small woman on the bed.

Mona couldn't prepare Dafydd for finding his father, but she readied herself for his grief. There came a soft sobbing from the hidden side of the bed and for a wild moment Mona thought Ifan still lived – that she'd been mistaken. But his slim, curled body was still there, cooling on the floor.

Her heart clenched in on itself again, as she inched around the bed. The horror wasn't over. Bryn rocked Rob in his arms, smoothing back his hair and kissing him on the forehead.

"He's not dead, he's not dead, he's not dead."

Rob did appear as if he slept, his beautiful face as graceful in death as in life, his golden locks still shining with health.

Mona's mind broke with grief, but she could hear someone powering down the corridor. She turned in time to see Arwel's arms windmill to stop him as his brain processed the carnage he now faced. It wasn't sorrow but fury that throttled her now, and she used it to clear her head. Leaving Dafydd and Bryn to the dead, she moved to Arwel, and Mona read a clarity she desperately needed in his eyes.

"I know who it is, Mo. Taid wouldn't let me come," he whispered.

Dafydd handed her another thin black device. The one Carmen had found.

"Can you help me with Rob?" she croaked, talking to Arwel but glaring at the curved object. Arwel stared at Ifan, then back to Bryn and she suddenly understood.

"Let go of him," she ground out through bared teeth. Mona's tone and ferocity brought Bryn's gaze to hers, and she saw the guilt in his eyes as he backed away.

Bryn curled his arms around his own body, now they had taken Rob from him. He just watched them wrestle the huge frame onto the bed, next to Carmen.

Mona's face wasn't capable of showing the extremity of the emotion she was experiencing. "Check on Cai please, Dafydd," Mona said, not able to take her eyes from Bryn. "How does it work?" she demanded, passing him the phone.

18

Time

With Dafydd's help, Mona settled Idwal and Cai in their double-room. Her brother nursed him while Mona wept out what was left of her heart over Rob. She found letting go of his body unbearably traumatic. He still smelled of Tom and talcum powder. Rob had never been excessively vain about his appearance but Mona found a brush and his golden hair shone with perfection when the healers finally took his body from her. They laid him alongside the four others, until their Passing rites. Ceremonies Mona would not attend.

Now that she'd said goodbye to Rob, a constant ticking had started in her head. Each second marking her son's absence – all wasted seconds. Mona just wanted to sail, run, swim or crawl to his side but she couldn't. She didn't know where he was, yet.

Dafydd had taken Bryn to the cells beneath the *Conway*. Both he and Mona had instinctively bayed for his blood, but Arwel had kept a cool head. The traitor had vital information about Tom's whereabouts, and would need to be appropriately dealt with and questioned.

≈

Bryn hadn't escaped Dafydd's wrath entirely though, and he lay on the floor of the cell, curled in a foetal position. Mona imagined he was comforting his gut. And he would need to, if it was anywhere near as damaged as his face.

Bryn's injuries were extensive, but Mona had needed to wrap her arms around her legs to stop herself from exacting more pain from his body. Bryn would be made to pay for Rob, for Cai, for Tom. He would pay, of course he would, but not yet.

"I haven't got much time, Bryn." Mona forced herself to speak to him. She'd been advised by Arwel to leave the sword and dagger at the cell door. His counsel had been wise, because intermittent waves of intense hatred and revenge washed over her. It was at those moments that she'd felt for her weapons.

It had been over half an hour, and he still hadn't uttered a word, though he was conscious and staring.

"*Lladda fi* – Just kill me." If she hadn't been sitting so close, Mona would have missed the words, mangled as they were through his swollen lips. "Kill me. Please." A mere whisper.

Hope flared. "Is that what you want?" Mona tried to take the venom out of her voice. He closed his eyes and nodded as vigorously as his injuries would allow. "I can do that for you, Bryn. I want to, so badly… but please, *please* help me first." Mona rocked back and forth on the cell floor, and knew she had failed to keep the mad desperation invisible. "Where has she taken him?" *Tick, tick, tick.*

"It doesn't matter. You won't get him back. He's been planned – for so long." Bryn's cut face and lips were oozing with the effort of speech.

"Tell me where… I'll do anything. What do you want?"

"Just kill me," he repeated.

"You fucking insect," Mona snapped at his self-pity and she grabbed Bryn from the floor by the shoulders, holding his broken features to hers. "I loved Rob too… he was mine as well. How dare you take the easy way out? How dare you lie there whimpering, when it was you who betrayed us… you who killed him? You fucking… fucking coward." She released his shoulders, and Bryn's head hit the concrete. Mona marched over to the bars to suppress an all-out assault, leaning her cheek against the cool steel uprights. *Tick, tick, tick.*

Behind her, she heard Bryn struggle to his knees, then his feet. Finally she sensed his massive bulk, hovering behind her. "I can give you information, but you won't get him back... you need to understand that."

"Can you contact them on the phone?"

"Yes, I can. I will. But you must do it, Mona. Once I've helped you... you must kill me." She agreed, but that wasn't enough for him. "Swear it. No matter what happens." And Mona realised his desperation mirrored her own.

"I will, Bryn, I swear, but I haven't got much time."

≈

Dafydd strapped Bryn roughly to a chair in the centre of the room. The man's treachery had killed both his father and brother. Dafydd drew his sword and stood beside the chair – immoveable.

Nobody healed Bryn. Nobody wanted to touch him. Mona found it best to close her eyes while listening to his questioning. Idwal watched from the bed as he wearily trickled power into Cai, who still lay unconscious beside him. Arwel took notes.

Bryn began speaking in a monotone. He tripped at certain points, but he told them of the Irish clan he came from. He spoke to them of the Archdruid, Seamus and his chemist wife, Caitlín; of their obsession with the power of the *mark*. How they'd known of Mona and Idwal; had tracked and killed their parents and uncle.

All the while, they had waited for Mona to appear in Moelfre, as Seamus knew she would. Colm had been stationed at the college and Bryn at the *Conway*, already lying in wait. It had taken more than five years for them to trust Bryn. He'd changed his accent and his history. Bryn had befriended Emlyn, then kept his head down, his ears open and paved the way for his brother, Fintan, not Gareth. Each appalling truth, layer on layer. It was impossible to comprehend, and Mona was too dumbfounded to even think of a question.

"Why? Even if he makes this super dark, powerful Druid, what then, what does it achieve?" Arwel asked the pertinent questions, and Bryn had lost what little energy he had found.

"I don't know now. I thought it was power – magic, I suppose. That's what they've always said, '*reclaiming the power of the Druid*'. I never knew just how sick and perverted it all was, until…"

"You must be high up in the organisation. They must trust you. How high Bryn?" He finally met Mona's gaze, but she didn't even recognise the emotion in his eyes.

"*Nhw ydi fy rhieni* – They're my parents."

≈

The training room was quiet now. The troops had been stood down and were mourning their comrades in the time-honoured fashion: drinking and singing away the pain till dawn.

Mona locked the door anyway. She'd tried a couple of times, but hadn't been capable of forming her patterns. Eventually, she resorted to kicking and punching a bag until her body was used up and a plan of sorts had formed. Tom's time was running out.

Blundering back into the room, she saw Bryn had gone. "Where is he?" she demanded.

Idwal still sat on the bed with Cai, who had at least moved into a different position.

"Dafydd's put him back in the cells." Mona glanced up with a gasp, stopping abruptly on her way over to Cai. "It's ok, Arwel's with him and Bryn isn't going to kill himself. I hear you've come to an agreement on that." Idwal scrutinised Mona. "Do you really believe you'll be able to kill him – in cold blood?"

"Yes." She had no doubt about that at all.

Mona ignored her brother's reaction and came to sit by Cai. She pushed the wet, black hair from his forehead and kissed him there.

Mona meant to stop but couldn't, and she continued kissing his face and lips over and over again. It was making Idwal uncomfortable, so she stopped and straightened.

"I've got a plan. It will be a straight swap – Tom for me. I'll take Bryn and Cai with me. Cai will bring Tom back and I'll escape later. Bryn's got the mobile phone... to start the negotiations."

Idwal swallowed and nodded, rearranging his grip on Cai. Mona had expected an argument, aware it was quite a fragile strategy, but Idwal kept mute. "How soon will it be before Cai can travel?" She asked him her most pressing question.

"Two to three days," he replied a little too quickly.

"You've got three hours," Mona stated woodenly. "I'm going to get ready and prep the boat."

There wasn't another option. She couldn't hope to do this without Cai, and within minutes she was marching towards the boathouse.

≈

As the door clicked behind Mona, Idwal finally managed to take a full breath, which he then exhaled slowly. "Well that's just about the shittiest plan I've ever heard. What do you reckon, mate?"

Cai's eyes shot open, and they were the colour of rage. "Help me up," he growled. "And get Bryn back up here. I've got some more questions for him before he makes that call. We need Arwel."

It hurt to speak, move and think and Cai wanted to vomit very urgently.

≈

Hywel's boat had been prepped. Mona had turned over the outboard, having checked the two-stroke and oil. There were a couple of VHF radios on board, one baby and three adult life jackets, flares, weapons, bottles, food and water. She'd had the Coastguard track the small skiff, and it had nearly reached its destination in the east coast of

Ireland. Bryn would direct them from there. Dafydd didn't think her plan was very good, but when pressed, hadn't come up with any sort of alternative. The three hours were nearly up and Cai would be waking.

Mona was almost entirely sure that everything was under control, until she walked back into the rooms, and then nothing existed but Cai. Black-blue eyes in a grey face. He looked too fragile to hold, and she fell to her knees at the bedside, folding his cold, rough hands into hers.

"I let her take Tom," he rasped. It seemed a huge effort for Cai to talk and Mona wanted to shake her head to silence him, but he had already read the truth in her eyes. He had failed her. Cai pulled his hands from hers, he covered his eyes with the heel of his palms, not wanting to read her judgement.

"We can get him back," she explained quickly. "I've readied the *Marc'h*." Mona moved her arm around his shoulder and started to exert upward pressure. "We need to go now – right now. I'll help you up."

Cai didn't move or answer, but pressed his eyeballs in further, fingers tugging savagely at his hair.

"Mona, stop it." Idwal was firm as he dragged her from Cai to face him. Her eyes manically searched his for the answer she needed, but he wasn't giving it. "He needs time, Mo."

"But I haven't got time. Tom needs me, *now*. I can't do it on my own," she pleaded, her voice thin and breathless.

"No, you can't. You've just had your son kidnapped." His voice softened. "You've lost Rob, Mona. You're not thinking straight. That was an appalling plan, and none of you would have survived it."

The clock in her mind ticked wildly out of control. She examined her brother's impassive face, and then ran for the door. He was ready and grabbed her, holding her close against him as Dafydd moved in on the other side. They both grappled with her until the struggling slowed. When Mona's head finally dropped, Idwal squashed her, breathing into her ear.

"We've got an idea that might work, Mo. We've got a better plan… just listen, please."

The numbness was broken by the sound of Cai vomiting into a basin and Idwal released her to him.

"Tell me, then," she demanded once the retching had stopped.

≈

Arwel took a good long look at Bryn. It seemed his uncle Dafydd had administered even more punishment on the journey back from the cells.

"Can you untie him please, Dafydd?" Arwel asked the Archdruid with extreme politeness.

"Are you fucking *mad*?"

Dafydd's thunderous stare didn't faze the boy at all. "We need information, and this man needs to breathe if he is to function properly." Dafydd didn't untie the captive, nor did he argue – he merely turned and left. Arwel freed Bryn, bringing him painkillers and water.

The table was strewn with the evidence of the plan. Both Arwel and Idwal referred to it constantly, asking Bryn to confirm and explain as the tactics unfolded. Mona soon became very aware of the flimsiness of her previous scheme, as she listened with horror to the details of his clan's setup.

Arwel remained the most clear-minded, and through his intense questioning, a plan of a completely different type and scale started to take shape.

"I still don't think you understand the importance of the technology," Bryn lisped wearily. "My father is one of the foremost brains in the field, he's a mastermind. Seamus has supplied all those big companies with ideas, but has kept himself ahead of the game." Bryn held up the thin black device. "These phones are light years in front of anything else around. That fake invasion would have taken just a few taps on his computer." Bryn took another sip of water, leaving blood in the glass. "He can create mayhem and make it all totally untraceable. My father…" Bryn grimaced at the title. "Seamus," he amended. "He specialises in viral technology. If Ifan had allowed mobile phones, or anything with a microprocessor here, you would have been finished years ago. Ifan may not have understood it, but he was right to recognise the threat."

Arwel nodded, partly in agreement of Bryn's assessment, and partly to commend his grandfather's wisdom. "And what about defence, fighting, how are you trained?"

Bryn laughed harshly. "My father's arrogant. I suppose it comes with the territory, but in his opinion… and he's probably correct, the system he's built is completely fool-proof." Bryn forced a tablet into his broken mouth and dribbled more water in. "Fighting is too primitive for him, and they lost a fair number in the fight against us last summer. He fancies himself above all that, though…"

"So if there's a way to disable the system, the technology, then there's a chance?" Arwel probed.

"In theory, but…" Bryn was reaching for words, for a concept that would describe his father. "Look, he's been waiting for the *mark* to appear for years. *Since before we were all born.* It's more than an obsession with him… it's a religion. I know he's interested in Tom, but what he really wants is you, Mona." He glanced over at the bed. "And not just to breed from, but to have and use in some way… a way I can't even begin to understand." Arwel's calm faltered as Bryn continued to explain. "He truly believes that someone born with the *mark* has immense power, that they can do anything. He's devoted his life to it. It's a trap." The silence was deafening – overpowering.

"How can we trust you, Bryn?" Cai croaked, wiping his mouth. "If that's your real name."

Bryn returned a level gaze. "Cormac. And you can't, but I'm all you've got."

"How long?" Cai coughed. Vomiting had made his voice hoarse. "Since you last contacted them, your family?"

Bryn raised his head. "I've been reporting in every month, for five years," he confessed in a whisper.

Arwel stopped taking notes and looked straight into Bryn's swollen eyes. "My father trusted you... and you killed him. We've all trusted you with our lives... for years." Bryn's head sunk to his chest again, and he didn't answer Arwel – there wasn't anything to say. "There was supposed to be an attack at Samhain," he mumbled. "But I didn't give the green light signal. I haven't made contact since then." He gave them a shrug. "I don't care if you believe it or not, it doesn't matter now. Nothing matters now."

"I believe you. I'm guessing you made your choice when the *Conway* was invaded." Bryn dipped his head infinitesimally as Cai croaked on. "And it does matter, if Rob's the reason you're helping us." Bryn flinched at Rob's name, but Cai's rough whisper was insistent. "But we need to know everything, Bryn, and I think you're holding something back."

"I'm not stupid," Bryn choked out. "I know you've been working on Mona's problem with the language." He wiped a hand over his forehead, sighing. "And you would think that it would *help*, but it won't. You can't pretend or lie to him."

Mona gasped. "He can read minds?"

"No, he can read bodies. He only has to touch you – and he will." Bryn stared at Mona. "My father will be able to see inside your body. I told him about your weakness early on, and he will expect that it's been healed." Bryn made quite sure everyone in the room understood his warning. "It is the *very first thing* he'll want to know. He's obsessed and mad, but he's clever and careful too."

Arwel and Idwal exchanged a glance and Mona caught it. They were thinking of re-instating her weakness. "No, no, I need to be strong. I need to be able to fight."

Bryn cast a confused eye on Idwal, and he explained. "You're right, Bryn. Cai and Mona have overcome her weakness, but she can block it over again." Her brother gave Mona the most straight and pointed of looks.

"What difference will it make?" she shouted angrily.

Bryn lumbered over to confront her. "If he knows you're strong, then he will have four men hold you down while he rapes you. If he thinks you're still vulnerable, there'll be fewer. He's a monster." Bryn stared through her now to previous horrors. The screaming and the sobbing – the smell of death. "He has a farm. It's full of young women of child-bearing age. Druids captured from all over Ireland."

Nobody wanted him to, but Bryn continued, and Mona's mind leapt back to the botched kidnappings last year.

"There isn't a clan left in Ireland that he hasn't stolen from. He breeds with the women, but only the boys are kept. When the babies are old enough, they're tested. If they pass, there is further testing... throughout their life... until a job is found for them. If they fail the first test... they're destroyed." Bryn's voice was a terrible monologue. "The tests are hard and most die. All the women die eventually... from complications sometimes, but mostly by their own hands. The best breeders and most powerful are well treated, but drugged into compliance. Even they kill themselves... if they get the chance." It was relentless. "Fintan and I were full brothers, and Seamus had him... practising on these women since he was fourteen. He couldn't wait for Fin to fulfil his destiny with you, Mona."

"And your mother?" Mona whispered as Bryn fell back onto the chair again.

"My mother, Caitlín, is a powerful magician. That black gunge Cai's puking up... is her invention." Bryn raised his hands in search of inspiration. "I don't know... she's a biochemist of sorts. At some point she starts injecting it into the most talented of us – a single injection a week. They believe it enhances the inbred talent and I think it works to a certain extent, but of course it's most effective as a weapon. Cai is the only person I know who has survived a direct attack from my mother."

Arwel referred to the notes beside him. "But not all the blades are tainted." He peered up. "Why is that?"

Bryn inclined his head. "It's difficult to make, expensive and time consuming. Only a chosen few are gifted those blades." He waved a hand at the cells beneath him. "Only the assassins."

"That explains their absence in the Irish fleet last year." Arwel turned a page, and then looked over at Bryn again. "Will we encounter any in open combat?"

Bryn shrugged. "I doubt it, but I'm not certain. You may never know – until it's too late."

Even Idwal was stunned. "Is there anything else? Anything else we need to know?" What more could there be to conceal? Surely there was nothing left to horrify them, but there was something… and Bryn was finding it hard to voice. "What is it? What else?" Idwal urged.

Bryn closed his eyes rather than look at anyone with his answer. "Seamus and Fintan. They've never had sex with a woman who really wanted them. Fintan had been ready for anything but desire. It overwhelmed him, Mona. That's how you managed to kill him. It could work with Seamus – it's the only way I can see you beating him. As awful as it is, it's the only plan I can see working."

"How did you know?" Mona's voice had fallen to less than a whisper, and Arwel had stopped writing.

"Who do you think was guarding the door? I heard it all," Bryn admitted in self-disgust.

Idwal prepared himself to protect Bryn from his sister's rage. If they needed anything now, it was to keep Bryn alive. However, she moved past the traitor to stare across the Irish Sea, and it was Arwel who brought his skinny arm back and punched Bryn soundly on the jaw.

"I'm going for a walk," Mona announced weakly. "I'm way past thinking about this. You'll have to work out our best chance of success between you… and just tell me what you've decided. I'll do anything I have to." She touched her lips to Cai's feverish forehead and left quietly.

There was only one person she could turn to, and she found Nia in the library surrounded by books, and taking notes. Nia leapt up as Mona lurched in.

"What? What's happened?"

≈

Cai had taken a turn for the worse, and Idwal joined him on the bed, trickling power into his bloodstream as subtly as possible. It would be unwise to show the strength of their hand to Bryn, despite his seeming redemption.

Arwel opened the door to Nia, but her hard gaze was for Bryn. They had shared a love of music and Rob. They had formed the unbreakable bond of creating art with each other. Nia was someone else whose eye he would never be able to hold again, though she didn't bother trying for long.

Idwal let go of Cai, and walked to meet her in the centre of the room. Her eyes were luminous, cut to ribbons with the knowledge she'd just learned from Mona.

"You know?" Idwal wanted Nia to *unknow* it, to protect her, even from the information. "Where is she?"

"At the range." Nia was stiff. "I wanted to ask you, without her here... she wouldn't want me to ask." Her lips trembled as she spoke. "I'm offering to stand in for her. I want to know if it could work."

Idwal couldn't reply. Imagining Nia in such danger was too painful for him to comprehend.

"No, Nia, it wouldn't work. Seamus can sense power, even from a distance. It wouldn't do any good," Bryn's voice scraped on. "And I have another brother, Diarmuid, who can gauge power through colour. He's a connoisseur and Seamus will make sure he's standing by. He'll be watching your colours."

Idwal moved towards Nia, relief obvious in every cell of his body.

"Don't touch me, Idwal." He stopped dead in his tracks. "How can you choose me to live over her? You don't know how much she's already given. *You weren't here.*" Nia shouted now, apoplectic with rage for the first time in her life. "How much more do you think she can take?"

"I'm not choosing her to die instead of you, Nia. There just isn't a choice."

≈

Mona stood in the old boatshed, staring down at her trembling hands. They were square, rough and ugly. Mona had already killed three men with the awful power that came from them. They were weapons she had absolutely no idea how to use, and perhaps it was time to start trying.

Stretching out her arm towards the battered target, Mona tried to replicate the destructive energy. It wasn't the same sensation as healing or sucking out poison. That was a simple pushing or pulling motion and her mind could grasp and remember those actions.

Every time she'd killed, Mona's entire body had reacted, not merely her mind or hands. The power had come from deep within her loins, and its release had always been an exquisite relief. Mona recalled each of the triggering attacks: Colm, Gareth, Hywel. She urged her body to recall the tipping point, and began to sense some stirrings deep inside her. Mona remembered Emlyn and Nesta, and her anger lit the fuse. She saw Carmen and Ifan lying dead in that awful room and the current started to flow. Mona forced herself to remember Rob's smell as he lay dead in her arms – her mother, her father – and she screamed as her hands heated.

"*Cai*," she screeched. "*Tom*." And ropes of lightning scrawled drunkenly from her fingers. A desire to destroy and burn filled her with its sweet urgings, but she hauled it back, letting her arms drop.

Her attack had left random burnt lashings all over the walls and ceiling of the wooden structure and Mona looked back down at her ugly hands once more.

≈

Mona returned to a silent room. Idwal stood uncomfortably beside Nia, and Mona moved to the space on the bed vacated by her brother. She dragged Cai over towards her and began pulling any lingering poison from him.

"What are you doing?" Idwal asked.

"Following orders. I'm listening, carry on." Mona closed her eyes, as Arwel began to divulge the tactics.

The plan was as bizarre and perverted as Mona had feared, but there was a small chance of it working – so they had no choice but to take it. The nausea had stared to affect her, but she could hold on until Bryn finished talking.

"There's one more thing, well, two really. You'll need to wear something more feminine." Bryn pointed at her combat gear and body armour. "You should appear as vulnerable as you can." He paused at Arwel's withering look. "It's what he's used to: submission."

"And the other thing?" Mona felt calmer now, but she really did need to rid herself of the poison.

"Even though they are all essentially his slaves, Seamus handfasts himself to every one of the women. I thought it was a way of legitimising it in his own twisted mind, but I think now that it has some spiritual power for him. Some link to the women, above and beyond the physical." The room was stunned by the strangeness of the evidence. "I don't know, it's just a guess… I don't know." He shrugged his shoulders slightly. "But I thought it might help if Mona was already handfasted."

Mona ran to the bathroom and Cai sat up, with a little more colour in his cheeks but deep weariness in his eyes.

"*Oedd hi yn dweud na?* – Do you think that was a *no*?" he asked Idwal.

19

Handfasting

Despite the threat of rumbling thunder, Cai and Mona decided the ceremony should take place on the shoreline, under the stars. Idwal, Nia and Arwel had left to prepare for the shortest of handfastings.

The sickness had now stopped for both of them, but Mona relentlessly passed her energy into Cai while they lay up against each other on the bed. He could feel his strength steadily returning as hers diminished.

Dafydd wanted to prepare for his part in the rescue and asked Idwal to perform the ceremony who was appalled at the request. He didn't have the first idea how to perform a pagan handfasting.

"You can speak the language now, I hear," Dafydd said stiffly.

Idwal shook his head. "*Come on.* It's not just reading words out loud, Dafydd, you of all people…"

"I can't do it." He stared over the shoreline. "It's never been my job. I can't do it. I don't want it." He was already striding away. "Nia will help you."

Idwal watched Dafydd go as Nia moved quietly to his side. He frowned at her. "I can't…"

"Yes, you can. You have to. The Archdruid asked you not me." She handed over a book and put the lamp down. "I'll help you through it."

≈

Nia came for Mona and Cai in the early hours. She led them from the building to the shore, asking them to enter from the East into a small circle of hurricane lamps. There were three candles stuck into the sand, but their fragile flames had been snuffed out by the gale the second they'd been lit. Despite her declining vigour, Mona was stunned to see her brother inside the circle where he concentrated on a large book that Nia held for him. Arwel stood behind them illuminating the book with his lamp.

Cai, of course, knew the ceremony, but even through the fatigue, Mona was puzzled by the peculiarity of the questions Idwal asked them.

"How long do you wish this bond to last - a year and a day, seven years, this lifetime or all your future lives?"

Idwal tied their wrists together with a leather cord and passed their joined hands through smoke, fire, earth and water. They made vows, and jumped over a broomstick together. Nia and Arwel sang a short unaccompanied song, which was intended to be joyful, Mona thought, but was far too full of darker emotions to succeed. They kissed and left the circle to the West.

The thunder and lightning seemed somehow apt, but the rain was constant and their cloaks grew sodden. Arwel took them away to dry, happy to have something tangible to do.

≈

Mona and Cai were still attached by the cord. They were leaning up against each other and feeling slightly dazed, when Idwal approached.

"You can undo that now, it's just symbolic." He forced the laugh into his voice and they looked at him and then each other.

"Yes, of course." Cai unravelled the cord and stuffed it into his back pocket.

"Can I have a word, Cai?" Idwal walked a little distance away and Cai followed, reluctant to leave Mona, for even a short time.

"You're stronger." He held Cai's shoulder. "But *please* don't let her go too far. You must stay in control, for both of you." Idwal glanced over at his sister. "You know what she's like. I suggest you let her sleep in between bouts of healing. You'll both need to be strong for... what's ahead."

"She's trying to give her power away. For when the time comes."

Cai could hardly articulate the last few words and Idwal tried, but couldn't find an answer. "We've got a lot to do before the midday tide. You two must rest."

Cai walked back to Mona, but stopped as he saw Nia approach. The women held hands and their foreheads touched.

"So, I'll come up later, to help you dress. How are you?"

"Different... something has changed."

"You're bound to him... in the eyes of the Goddess, Mo. For all your future lives. *Of course* it's different."

"I didn't think I could feel any more for him than I did, but..."

"You sound sad about it."

"Not sad... I would have liked my mum and dad to have met him. I'm pretty sure they would have approved."

≈

The August rain had soaked them through and without the protection of the cloaks, Mona and Cai were both trembling with cold as they fumbled to unfasten their clothes. Mona was so exhausted that she considered giving up with the trousers. She craved only rest. Cai helped her, and they soon formed a naked shivering knot under the covers. As the chattering stopped, sleep arrived. He was relieved Mona had fallen asleep before him. At least the power transfer would stop for a while.

Cai awoke suddenly, gasping and trembling, his heart too big for his chest. Though still in his arms, Mona remained deeply asleep. As he peeled his body from hers, she opened her eyes. They were grey and tired, and she closed them again instantly.

No more. He couldn't take any more of her power. It thumped and fizzed ceaselessly through his veins and Cai was forced to construct a barrier of pillows between them. He missed the touch of Mona's body against his, but was fearful for both of them if the power transfer continued.

He couldn't help but wonder if Mona felt this potent all the time. He had never experienced anything like it before. Cai felt invincible.

≈

When Mona woke, she opened her eyes to the most intense blue-eyed scrutiny. Cai lay on his side, his head propped up on one arm. There was a pillow between them, but he watched her solemnly, and she felt sure his stare had wakened her.

Though she could do with more sleep, Mona realised the time had come to prepare for the journey to Ireland. "Did we get married last night?" she asked, not sure if the ceremony on the beach had just been a bizarre dream.

Cai smiled radiantly at her over the pillow barricade. "*Dyma fy adduned priodasol i ti* – This is my wedding vow to you. *Priodas gydradd yw hon* – This is the marriage of equals." He quoted from the brief ceremony and Mona thought if she could muster up the energy to blush, she might have.

"Then why are you all the way over there? There's bound to be a honeymoon part to this."

"You were healing me in your sleep, Mo. You've got very little left," he warned.

Mona remembered some words and recited them back, though not as accurately as Cai. "*You cannot possess me, for I belong to myself. But while we both wish it... I give you that which is mine to give.*" Her voice was horribly weak but she forced meaning into the last phrase. "*You cannot command me, for I am a free person.*"

"If I move these pillows, will you promise to stop healing me? I'm *healed*, I'm *full*. If you charge me up any more – I'll burn out, woman."

Mona sighed tiredly. "Wimp!" Cai moved the barrier and pulled her tenderly towards him.

She closed her eyes in anticipation as their bodies touched. "I want to remember you, Cai. I'm going to be thinking of this…"

He kissed her to stop the words from being formed. Words that should never have to be said.

"I pledge to you my living and my dying, each equally in your care. I shall be a shield for your back, and you for mine." He spoke into her lips.

≈

Cai was already dressed and armed when Nia tapped lightly on the door.

"She's still asleep," he whispered. "I've got everything ready for her, over here." He touched the fabric of the black dress and sighed. "I chose this for her… because it made her vulnerable." Cai vividly remembered her chucking it against the wall. She had wanted him to give it away but he had kept it. "What does that make me, Nia?"

She cut him no slack. "A man."

"I'll be back up with Idwal," Cai said as he left.

≈

Mona was roused and showered in a trance, and even the smallest tasks seemed too difficult to achieve. She'd been weakened, and perhaps that was for the best. Nia helped her into the dress and shoes. "You've lost weight, Mo."

"Well, Cai didn't say what a rotten cook he was when he tricked me into marrying him, did he?"

Nia's hand tightened around the cosmetics bag.

"I know you crack jokes to make yourself feel better, but I find it hard. I really don't understand it." Nia was close to tears.

"It's just the way I am. Come on; get some of that war paint on me."

They didn't speak again until Nia had finished her ministrations. "Mona, I found this the other day... in your cloak. It's something I still don't understand fully, though you know how I've tried." Nia handed her an object wrapped in leather – her final college piece, the *mark*. Mona stared at it and then at Nia. It must have got wrapped up with the laundry.

"Have you found out *anything* about it?" Mona asked.

Nia shook her head slowly and sadly. "Well, it's a symbol of power, but I only ever found one reference to it – nothing more." She peeled back the leather gingerly. "So I was forced to study it as an object, as a Celtic symbol."

"And?"

"It differs from traditional Celtic knot work, in several ways."

"What ways?" Mona croaked, staring at the shapes within the triangle, before picking it up. This was the physical symbol of her power and it terrified her. The metal was cool to the touch, but she felt the vibrant throb of energy in its core. Nia had once described it as a personal battery pack and she remembered using its energy to heal Cai's leg.

"All Celtic symbols are different from one another, unique. There are many categories and sub categories of design, yet most of them share several characteristics that this does not."

"What's that?"

"Celtic art has an emphasis on symmetry and complexity. There is very rarely a beginning and an end, but see here." Nia pointed to a break in the metal work, which Mona had never taken much notice of. "There's a gap. This piece isn't an endless knot."

Mona stared again at the iron. She'd always assumed it was a continuous run of metal, sure that's what she'd had in mind at its making.

"Does it mean anything?" she asked quietly.

Nia shrugged her shoulders in defeat. "No idea at all, but look at the swirls. They're not even the same size."

"What does Id think? Should I take it?" Mona asked hoarsely.

"I haven't told him… you need to have something up your sleeve… something that they can't factor in. The margins are too small anyway, and I don't think they understand what's at stake." Nia coughed and murmured. "I haven't ever seen Cai happy; not the way he was last night."

Nia held Mona in her arms, and the men walked into the room. Idwal looked like the executioner, Cai the judge and Arwel could hardly bear to look at her at all. As he passed Mona her cloak, she slipped the leather package into a pocket.

"I'm ready," she said as firmly as she could.

"If there was any other way…" Idwal shook his head, knowing there wasn't. "I'm trying to create the thinnest of blocks – it should be easy to break through. If there's a chance, Mona, you *must* take it."

Idwal didn't really want to touch her, but finally, he pressed one hand to her head, and the other to her waist. He pulled back immediately, as if electrocuted, but Mona reassured him, as he glanced madly from her to Cai.

"Don't worry, I know you have to do it," she said sadly.

Idwal paused, and agreed with a stiff nod, before replacing his hands. There was no pain in the reinstatement of the block. It was just like the closing of a window. When it was over, Mona's clock began ticking again.

"*Naeth o weithio?* – Did it work?" Idwal asked, still fairly unconfident in his abilities.

Mona nodded. She presumed her brother was testing to see if the procedure had worked, but Mona could no longer understand the Welsh she'd so recently learned. Assuming the Celtic tongue had once again become a weapon against her, Mona forced down the growing anxiety.

"Let's get Bryn to make that call."

"You two go ahead," Nia said gently. "We'll be down in a minute."

Nia waited until they were alone. She noticed that Idwal had paled enormously, but there were a few things she needed to explain, and there was no time for sensibilities. "I'm coming with you on the boat,

Idwal. There's a part I can play that will give Tom the best chance of survival... a part everyone else has overlooked." She was calm.

"I'm not even discussing it. No." Idwal was far from calm.

"I'm leaving on the boat with Mona, Idwal Jones, and you can find someone else to marry. I'll see you at the dock."

"Wait, Nia. Wait... let me explain, will you?" He didn't try to touch her, sensing her new volatility. "I've lost nearly all the people I love. Please don't make me lose you."

"If we lose Mona or Tom tonight, because of something I could have prevented... then you'll have lost me anyway."

"You're not Mona, *you'll die*," he shouted, desperate to drag her back.

"Nobody is Mona. Not even Mona now!" she screamed. "You have no choice, Idwal." There was a moment of snarling silence.

"What's the plan?" He finally broke the stalemate.

"I'll tell you on the boat," she answered firmly.

20

Journey

Bryn stood at the helm of the *Marc'h*, and Cai pored over the chart. The traitor had made the call and his family knew whom to expect. However, he knew nothing more and could guess even less. Bryn was anxious.

"They've got four VSV's," Cai said, scanning the horizon nervously, but Bryn was already shaking his head.

"He won't risk using those again. The authorities are on the lookout."

"They are?"

"They are now," Bryn grunted. "I tipped them off a long time ago. He can't afford to take that chance."

"Seamus can't trust you anymore. It's a suicide mission," Cai said quietly.

"That's not what's bothering me. I'm sure we're just walking Mona into a trap."

They both searched the churning waters for help.

"We haven't got a choice. She would resort to plan A if we gave up on this one."

≈

Mona was weak and cold, but doing her very best to hide it from Nia.

"I can search for him as soon as Idwal gets us in. I'm all prepared." Nia said, lifting back her cloak to reveal an extremely tatty and soiled dress. She had tied two swathes of equally grubby cloth around her waist.

"I can make this into a sling for him," Nia persisted. "I've studied the layout and I know where to look." Mona felt sick inside and Nia could see she wasn't at all convinced. "I'm his best chance," she added defiantly.

"I know," Mona groaned. "It's only a shame… you never really got to grips with fighting."

"I can do this." Nia's tone was absolute, though she quivered with fear.

Mona huddled under her cloak and stared out into the grey waves. It was one of the few times in her life that she couldn't muster up any humour to help her deal with the pain. Her child had been taken, and Mona was exhausted with fear for him.

Cai slipped his arm around her as soon as Idwal relieved him at the helm. Mona's lips were a little blue, and he rubbed his hands up and down her arms, creating friction and heat. Mona couldn't warm up, even when he curled her into his lap. He felt the fabric of the dress under his fingertips.

"I've never explained about making you wear this dress, Mo." She knew he was trying to apologise but it didn't bring comfort; nothing now mattered but Tom. "We will bring him back." Still she didn't respond. "He's my son too."

Mona stared up at Cai with her washed out eyes, frowning at him.

"He's our child now. I want you to let me love him… I *do* love him." Mona couldn't bear the bald poignancy, and remained silent, but Cai couldn't. "When we met in the doorway at Swnt you remembered me. I remembered you."

"Is that what you believe?" She had just enough energy to lift her eyebrows.

"Yes," he answered emphatically. "I haven't forgotten those memories." He stared into her half-closed eyes, forcing in the memory of their first touch.

Cruel blue eyes smile at her across the stink of battle. He lets fly the whistling stone from its sling, straight, true, and her head slams back as the rock shatters her golden diadem.

"That wasn't a memory, Cai. How could it have been?"

"I'm not sure... a memory of a legend, it seems absurd to even think... but Nia's always saying that myths are our real... "

"*Don't.* It was nothing, just a... "

"And what about Meilyr and Canaid? I know that place, Mona; it's the fourth-century settlement at Llugwy. I think we shared the memory of a past life..."

Mona put a cold finger against his lips. "No, that can't be right..."

"Yes, it can. It's what I've been taught. It's what I know in my bones." Mona was too tired to respond with her usual cynicism. "I'll spend all my lives searching for you," he whispered.

"What if we don't meet?" Mona mouthed.

"I don't want to think about that." Though he did, and Cai saw a lost life. "We've got each other now... in this life." He held her tighter.

"Not without Tom... I don't think I can go on living without him," Mona replied simply, turning her gaze back to the sea.

≈

Nia cast an anxious look at Cai and Mona. He'd cradled her in his arms like a child, and she seemed to have no fight left; it was unnerving. Nia's own sense of resolve had been growing. It had been forced to grow by the decisions she'd made. She was no longer willing or able to sit in the library, reading about the heroes of the past. This was her time to stand up and be counted, and she prayed to the gods that she would succeed. "How long?" she asked.

Idwal had kept his distance but now hovered.

"Twenty minutes. We'll be dropped off first, so you need to jump quickly." He squinted into the horizon as if hoping to catch a glimpse of something. "We haven't got time to moor up, and Bryn's pretty sure we've been tracked for the last couple of hours, at least."

It was an extremely long twenty minutes and, looking at the craggy coastline, there didn't seem to be anywhere safe to land, but at last Bryn called them forwards to the bow of the boat.

"I'm going to put the nose in there." He motioned to a small inlet, a little more denuded of rocks than the rest of the jagged coast. "You first, Nia."

She jumped without a moment's hesitation, staggering and slipping on the wet stone, but keeping upright. Idwal was behind her by the space of a heartbeat.

≈

Cai woke Mona as gently as he could. "Five minutes. I can see them at the jetty."

Mona stood, holding the rail for support. She counted five men. "They've got guns," she said quietly, as Bryn brought the boat about. Cai threw one of the men a line.

"Remember," Bryn offered his final gem of advice. "Never believe anything he says. He will play with your mind – and he will win."

Two of them boarded instantly, and Mona was at a loss as soon as the shouting began.

Cai felt immensely powerful, full as he was with Mona's borrowed energy. All fear had receded into the very back of his mind. These men were thugs, big and rough. He'd met them before and they remembered it.

"Get back, you Welsh fuck!" One of them poked him in the chest with the barrel of his gun before grabbing Mona roughly by the upper arm.

"Don't touch her," he warned. He could take on both these men and win.

Bryn intervened. "Let him help her off the boat lads, they don't want a fight, just to talk."

"*A Chormaic!*" One of the men shouted, speaking the name like an expletive. "*Níl ionat ach conús d'fheallaire!* – You fucking traitor!"

He brought the gun level with Bryn's chest. "You killed your own. I saw you. I was there on the shore that night..."

"I've chosen my side," Bryn replied softly. The man spat in his face and turned away, pushing Mona and Cai ahead of him onto the jetty.

Mona immediately recognised Geraint among the men on land; the nasty little abuser who'd attacked Sioned last year. He must have snuck over here when Ifan had exiled him.

Geraint appeared overjoyed to see her.

"I've waited a long time for this, bitch." He grinned lasciviously.

While his companions patted Bryn and Cai down for weapons, Geraint opened Mona's cloak wide, to conduct his own brutal search. She kept her face impassive as he groped her roughly.

"Save it, Cai," Bryn warned as he watched Cai seethe with rage. "I told you how it would be. They won't hurt her."

Mona only knew that Bryn was trying to placate Cai by his tone. She wouldn't think of him as Cormac, but it was the only word of the conversation she'd understood, so far.

≈

The three captives were led up the twisting cliff path to a large house; an old country estate, with numerous blocks of outbuildings. Everything, though magnificent, seemed a little dilapidated.

They didn't enter through the mansion's ornate front door, but were shown through a side entrance, which was opened by a slight man in his late forties. He wore an impeccably smart suit, had a shock of wiry grey hair and mad, mad eyes. There was just enough similarity between father and son for Mona to understand that the man before her was Gareth's – Fintan's father.

The man's unbalanced gaze took them all in, but finally rested on his son. "Traitor." The man spoke dispassionately, but his voice was clear, melodious and very deep for such a slim man. "Aren't you going to introduce us, Cormac?" he asked with forced civility.

"You know who…"

"Nevertheless," the man interrupted in a terse whisper.

"Mona, Cai, this is Seamus, my father." Bryn introduced them half-heartedly, but neither attempted a reply. Bryn's warnings of mind games were still buzzing in their ears.

"Delighted." Seamus spoke in English, but Mona knew his voice would be lethal to her if he used Irish. He scrutinised them all, but seemed most interested in Mona. "So, I have you here at last. Welcome to my Command Centre." Seamus opened his arms theatrically and they followed him in.

Mona, flanked by Cai and Bryn, was led into a room full of computers and monitors. There were banks of machines and a whole wall dedicated to screens showing a mixture of live camera footage, technical drawings and monitoring graphs. To Mona, it was a wall of random information, but she could see Cai trying to decipher what he saw.

"Don't even bother trying, handsome. You're completely out of your league," Seamus taunted. The guards had receded, but not disappeared.

"Where's the child?" Mona tried to make it sound like an offhand enquiry.

"*Women!*" Seamus barked, trying to elicit mock support from Cai. "Only ever interested in their babies! No time for us, once they've got their little babies. Isn't that right, Cai?"

Seamus slithered behind a central consul, and made himself comfortable in the large office chair. There were a few little men around, constantly tending screens and readouts, who appeared oblivious to the guests.

"Ah, Tom. My little experiment," he deliberated playfully, and Mona stopped breathing; Seamus had started playing the games. "Tom didn't work out as expected, I'm afraid, my dear. But we'll have better luck next time." Seamus sighed whimsically, and then, with the mercurial speed of the insane, he became savage. "Because I'm not going to leave the job to inept offspring this time." He cast his son a poisonous glare. "You know what they say. *If you want a job doing properly...*" Seamus looked at Mona with a glint in his eye. "I bet my brother was all over you like a rash," he giggled.

Mona wasn't really following but kept her face straight. "Colm. *Colm*, my big brother," Seamus explained, seeing through her pretence. "Timid little idiot, but still..."

"So he's not here?" Mona asked again, sounding almost uninterested. She heard the door open behind her and watched Seamus's demeanour alter profoundly. His body stiffened, his eyes hardened.

"*Feicim go bhfuil ár gcuairteoirí tagtha, a Dhaidí* – I see our guests have arrived, Daddy." The voice, like the face, was a near duplicate of the psychopath now standing before her. Two smaller, red-headed men flanked the young Seamus double.

"Where's Diarmuid?" the older man demanded. "I asked you to bring him here... I need his..."

"Oh, you know Diarmuid," Cian teased. "Runs and hides at the first sign of danger." He grinned at his father. "Don't worry, you've always got me."

"So you've abandoned your post, Cian?" Seamus asked with barely disguised anger.

"I've left a replacement," Cian replied affably, and Mona shuddered at the intoxicating timbre in the young man's voice. There was a complete lack of humanity in the sweeping glance that assessed and disregarded her in the same instant. "You weren't wrong, Cormac," he smirked in Bryn's direction. "She's a big woman all right. I bet she's a handful in the sack?" He stretched up a skinny arm to pat Bryn's shoulder – and recoiled. "No!" He spat, all pretence of humour gone. "Get a hold of him, you two."

Cian ordered the weasel-faced twins to restrain Bryn, who did not struggle against them. He grabbed Bryn's head between his bony hands and seemed to squeeze and suck information from it simultaneously. "You're a fucking poofter!" He whirled to his father. "He's a homosexual." Cian uttered the words with such melodramatic abhorrence that Mona almost laughed out loud.

As Cian backed away from Bryn, Seamus took his place, and repeated the head-holding exercise himself. At the end of his assessment, Seamus drew back just far enough to spit a mouthful of phlegm into his son's eyes. "I'm thoroughly ashamed of you, Cormac. You disgust me."

Bryn raised his chin and carefully wiped the insult from his face. "You have no idea how happy that makes me, Seamus."

Cian bayed in delight as the blood drained from Seamus's face. "You're not going to let the cock-sucker talk to you like that? Surely?" His eyes flashed deviously at his father, and Seamus lost control.

"Get out of here!" he screeched maniacally. "Get back to your post."

Cian smiled again, enjoying the slight shift in power. "Calm down, father dear." He stared meaningfully to the ginger twins, who straightened and rearranged the guns strapped across their chests. "Let's not argue in front of our guests."

At the unspoken challenge, the anger slid out of Seamus. It was replaced with a surge of testosterone, the dosage of which increased with every step he took towards his younger rival. "Are you threatening me?" he asked when their chests met. "Do you seriously think you're up to it?"

Cian took a step back, but he had no intention of submitting to his father either. "I just want to help you," he argued rationally.

Seamus tilted his head back and guffawed cruelly. "How much more 'help' from my sons do you think I can survive, Cian? You talked me into buying those VSVs. Look how well that turned out."

Cian allowed his father the amusement but wasn't about to rise to the bait. "The boats were a mistake." He held his hands up in acceptance of his folly. "I know that now. But the guns are an advantage, aren't they?"

Seamus didn't give an opinion, and Cian continued to wheedle. "I take after you. I don't suffer from the same weaknesses as my brothers." Seamus backed off slightly, nodding his head in reluctant agreement, and Cian capitalised on his advantage. "All they had to do was kill him and fuck her." He flourished a hand at Cai and Mona. "Between them they only managed half a job." Cian twisted his head, though not his eyes to Bryn. "Confusing for you, Cormac, I know; he is a bit of a dish."

Cian and Seamus had begun arguing – in Irish. It was clear from their posturing that this was a power struggle, but Mona couldn't work out if the row advantaged them or not; she was too busy closing her mind to the sound. Neither of the men had directed their language at her, but even so, Mona's mind swirled with apprehension. The interplay between both resonant voices had started to enhance the magic and danger of the Irish Gaelic. Eyes shut, Mona clamped both hands over her ears.

Cai found himself as lost as Mona when the Gaelic began. Only Bryn could speak both Irish and Welsh, and he was giving nothing away. Mona had leaned back against the desk with her eyes and ears shut to their conversation. Cai wasn't sure how much danger she was in, but felt an overwhelming urge to protect her from it. He moved towards the desk, but Cian prevented him from reaching her with a pull on his arm.

"Not so fast, boyo." His glance darted between Mona and Cai, before a foul smile blossomed on his gaunt cheeks. Cian's hand slid to Cai's wrist, and he held it there for a couple of seconds before Cai shook him off. "Ooh, you poor man," Cian laughed. "Got it bad for her, haven't you?"

Cai returned his gaze, applying Bryn's mind-game advice to Cian now and keeping his face blank.

"Yes!" Cian enthused. "She's not like all the other sheep you've tupped, is she, Cai?"

Seamus chortled at his son's witticisms but the return to English had freed Mona from any imminent danger. Cian licked his lips and he began to saunter in Mona's direction. "Wouldn't mind seeing how the ewe performs myself."

Cai's fists clenched involuntarily and Bryn threw him a cautionary glare. Mona, however, had straightened and though her arms hung loosely, she began to gently flex the fingers on both her hands. "Come here and say that, you little wanker." Cian stopped, his audacity not quite enough to move any nearer. "How brave are you, really?" she asked slowly, and Cian looked to his father.

"Go ahead," Seamus grinned. "You wanted something to prove. Here's your chance, son."

"Don't do it, Cian," one of the twins muttered. "We know what she can do."

The balance of power had shifted again, and Seamus broke the stalemate with a belly laugh. "Stand back, child," he said pushing Cian behind him and advancing on Mona.

"Be careful, father. We were warned…"

"You're not bad, Cian," Seamus admitted, incongruously ruffling his son's hair in another rapid mood change. "Your powers have definitely improved. Cormac was holding on to his dirty little secret pretty tightly." He took another long look at Bryn before ambling over to Cai. "But you're not good enough. Not yet." Standing mere inches from Cai, Seamus bent at the waist to stare into the young Welshman's eyes. "She puts up a good show, but I haven't got anything to fear from the woman. She isn't the power source here; it's this prick." He pirouetted elegantly and tapped his nose. "I can smell it." Seamus inhaled, closing his eyes.

Cian glared between Cai and Mona. "You mean…?"

"Oh no," he grinned. "She bears the *mark,* my boy."

He glided to Mona, his eyes trained on the branding at her chest. "You've passed him your power, haven't you?"

"Why would she…"

"A ploy, I presume," Seamus leered, moving nearer to Mona all the time. "It won't work, sweetheart," he pouted, revelling in his outlandish performance. But in the time it took him to shift back to Cian, his attitude had altered yet again. "So make sure you're better prepared next time you come sniffing after my job. Now, get back over there!" he scolded, humiliating Cian with his tone. "And take your snivelling monkeys with you." He motioned with a nod of his head towards Cai. "Try to hold back the stud. I can almost taste his potency from here."

With a perfunctory bow to his audience, Seamus retreated to Mona. Focusing his bewildering attention on her, Seamus began to talk.

"You *are* handsome, Mona. Not exquisite like my Molly. I think you've underestimated her attractiveness Cormac, though clearly... she's not your type, eh?" Mona had to block the mention of her mother's name; it wasn't important, only Tom mattered now. "Molly came from the Newgrange clan up the coast. I wooed her for years and she left me for that Welsh half-wit." He pointed around the room. "I would have given her everything." His features screwed up in astonishment. "Your father wasn't even a Druid!" Seamus enunciated each word and Mona blanked the reference to her father. She was intent on the dangerously unstable, little man. "I got them in the end, as you know." Mona's heart clenched in spite of herself. "Don't you want to know about your little Tom?" he wheedled, and Mona felt the combined scrutiny of Bryn and Cai, willing her to keep playing the role. "Or aren't you the maternal type?"

Tom was being held captive here, somewhere in this house, and she wanted to force or beg Seamus to tell her where. But keeping a lid on the desperation, Mona pushed her shoulders into shrug. He seemed to grow bored of the game and, easing back his cuff, Seamus glanced at the face of a heavy gold watch. Its grotesque proportions dwarfed his slender wrist as he gestured to another wing of the house.

"He's with my dear lady wife, being doted and fussed over. She's got her little Fintan – back from the dead." Seamus rolled his eyes, before studying Cai from beneath his lashes. "Though I'm pretty sure she'll stop all that when she gets a glimpse of you." He flung his attention back to Bryn, suddenly spitting fury. "It was your job to stop that happening, you imbecile. You should have called the attack earlier, before he had a chance to impregnate her." Seamus grew weary of that little tirade as well. "Never mind. I've got her now. She's young enough, and at least we know she can breed."

Seamus was talking some rubbish – mind games to trick her – and Mona didn't even register them.

"Perhaps we can sort something out between us, Seamus?" Mona asked casually. "I'm not particularly interested in the brat, but I'm not a monster." She swallowed her anxiety. "Why not let Cai take the boy and leave?"

Seamus's laughter was lunatic, and he bounced to his feet to stand in front of her. "But, Mona... I've already got you." His index finger whispered over her cheek. "No, the child and his father will die... that's a given." After another glance at Cai, Seamus seemed more certain of his decision. "Do you have any idea how much of a disappointment this has been, *boyo?*" he jeered sarcastically. "Years in the making ruined by yet another fucking Welshman." Seamus sucked his teeth and wagged his head. "Why is it they always fall for you? You're such a bloody dour lot."

The plan was skewing horribly out of orbit already. "I could make it worth your while," Mona added quickly, the façade slipping slightly.

"I've heard that about you." He smiled at her radiantly before shouting an order to Cian. "Guard them closely, and remember what I said." He twisted to Bryn and his face turned savage. "Don't kill them yet. They all deserve some truly excruciating treatment."

≈

Diarmuid had deliberately chosen this part of the headland to hide. Cian had revelled in sharing the most intimate parts of their father's plans for the *marked one*, and consequently, Diarmuid wanted to be as far away from the jetty as possible when they brought the woman in. If he couldn't help her, he wouldn't watch her debasement.

Diarmuid lay back against the standing stone, its bulk hiding him from view. If he were a different man, a stronger man, he would have stood up to his father a long time ago, but thirty years of the debilitating sight had disabled him.

The hunger was upon him again; his sole and constant companion. Diarmuid only ever felt really happy when he ate. The addiction had taken a great toll on his body and he was finding it harder to move around than ever before. His thoughts swung to Aislinn then skittered away again. He'd tried to comfort her after each 'visit' she'd been forced to endure from his father and brother. He'd helped her through the appalling pregnancy and birth of her twins, but she wasn't well now, not well at all. It wasn't his fault. He'd done everything he could for the girl. Lying to himself brought the hunger on again and he sat up, attempting to shift it elsewhere.

Diarmuid felt their power before he saw it. A huge great lion of a man bursting with the sharpness of limes: he was acid grape, vibrant green chilli. Each step the man took towards Diarmuid's hiding place was full of new spring growth – asparagus tips, forcing their way to the surface. The woman behind him was a warm yellow: soft buttered bread drenched in honey, plump ripe grapes in the sun.

≈

Nia had found it difficult to scramble up the rock face in the long dress and cloak but Idwal hovered behind her and she knew he'd never let her fall.

"Carry me – if you think it'll be quicker," she said eyeing the terrain of the path ahead over the headland.

Idwal lifted her over his shoulder and set off at a brisk pace, his great long legs eating up the distance. He was grateful that she'd come to this conclusion herself, as Nia was becoming awfully difficult to persuade for such a tiny person.

They had been dropped a couple of miles north of the estate. Bryn had been as specific as he could, considering his five-year absence, and they were ready for the roving sentries.

"Put me down," Nia ordered as two men came into view. "Hide."

There was precious little for Idwal to do but flatten himself into a boulder's recess as Nia made a run for it in the other direction. She made a loud whimpering noise as both men gained on her, pulling their attention from Idwal's hiding place.

"*Don't let them touch her skin; you never know who holds a poison blade.*" Bryn's words of warning screamed in Idwal's brain as he exploded from the ground, knocking the men flat from behind. They were unconscious when he slit their throats.

Idwal was unsurprised to find Nia grimly dry-eyed at his brutality. She searched one man for the phone, while he worked on the other. They carried no blades.

After he'd kicked the bodies and guns from the path, they ran on. The phone had been upgraded from Bryn's model, but it was similar enough for Idwal to manage an Irish-sounding bark into it when it rang.

As the electrical substation loomed, Nia started to understand the enormity of the task ahead for Idwal. Surrounded by chain-link fence, it was liberally daubed with yellow signs warning '*Danger of death*'.

"I've got to short circuit the overhead wires," he explained while taking a rucksack of tools from his back. "As soon as that happens, we run for the estate. I'm going to have to destroy much more down there, so you need to be out of the way. Understand?"

"I know what I have to do," she replied, feeling decidedly less brave than she'd banked on. Nia's heart was in her mouth as he killed the padlock with the butt of his short sword.

Idwal stood motionless for a few seconds, beneath the overhead wires that carried the electricity from the bleak headland to the estate. He pulled open the telescopic tube and prayed Cai knew what he was talking about. He'd been told that the pole had to touch both wires at the same time to effect a full short circuit.

As he made the throw, Idwal thought the pole too short, the angle too shallow. But the immediate noise and conflagration sent him flying back to Nia with a grin. She nodded and melted away from him on a path of her own.

≈

His hunger had made him follow them. Diarmuid had never felt such healthy power before. There was something in the freshness of the man's green that reminded him of Aislinn, but his power was of another magnitude entirely. Diarmuid began to suspect this man was *marked* and that Cormac had misled Seamus. A little blooming of affection for his half-brother fluttered at the thought.

The Green Man had despatched two of his countrymen already and Diarmuid recognised that some greater plan was in the making, so he slunk back into the shadows, to watch and follow.

≈

Cai knew this moment had been coming. It was all part of Arwel's plan, but blood changed to water in his veins as Seamus opened Mona's cloak and trailed his eyes up and down her body.

"Oh, Mona, what a fine figure of a woman you are," he croaked his appreciation.

Both Cian and the ginger twins were restraining Cai, and he could do nothing but watch, as Seamus snaked a hand around her waist and started crooning to her in Irish.

"Let me see how this works now. Speaking is not enough. I have to really mean it, don't I?" Mona remained stiff and unyielding as his hand travelled further down her hips. "*Tá gach rud ceart go leor, a stór. Mise atá ann, Cai* – It's all right, my angel, it's me, Cai. It's just us two here; show me how much you want me – how much you love me."

It was a double assault. Seamus's voice speaking Irish had absorbed music and magic. He tortured her with its irresistible melody, and Mona began to yield to him. She kissed his face and neck, slowly drawing him in to her as he continued inexorably with the experiment. Seamus's breathing became increasingly laboured, as Mona reacted enthusiastically to the kneading of her breasts with a gentle gasp, moving her hips in a circular motion against his groin.

"Stop this," Bryn barked, but his mumbling father was lost in the pleasure of the young woman, and had pushed her back against a wall. "*Seamus!*" Bryn bellowed.

"What?" he panted. "What do you know of real passion? You think *I'm* perverted, Cormac! At least this is natural... at least I stick mine where it should go, son."

As the intensity was directed away from her, Mona snapped back into reality, releasing her grip and edging away.

"Not so fast, you little tart." His eyes lit up with lust again. "I'm going to enjoy making you moan, Mona. Let me see how ready you are." He held her head in his hands. "Such a strange little aberration to have in the brain... so very useful." Seamus licked the length of her face slowly and moved his hands to her abdomen where he pushed and prodded against the fabric of the dress.

His actions were methodical at first but then increased in tempo and violence until he stopped – quite unexpectedly. Seamus whirled to where Cai was being contained and began punching him, repeatedly and savagely, in the gut.

"Not again, not again." He left Cai and moved to Bryn. "Why didn't you kill him when you had the chance? She's pregnant again... you fucking idiot." He was screaming now, hysterical. "Why can't anyone follow simple, fucking orders?" he spat before closing his eyes and covering his ears, almost childishly.

Mona tried to use the time to attract Cai's attention, but he was still doubled over. Without warning, Seamus seemed to recover his poise and take a deep breath in. As he exhaled, he became the effete businessman once more, tugging gently at his cuffs and covering over the obscene timepiece.

"No matter. That's no matter." He smirked. "I have a draught to take care of that little seed." He pointed to one of the twins holding Cai. "*You.* Get us some refreshments. Something a little special for the lady, I think."

≈

282

Despite the intended savagery of the blows, Cai had braced himself, and was more or less unharmed by the older man's physical ministrations. Mona's power had made him strong. However, the mental blow had been more than crippling enough. Cai hadn't understood the mad Irishman's words, but he'd pieced together his actions. Mona was pregnant again – with Cai's child. He had two children now. And they were both going to die.

The lights went out and buzzed back on immediately, a little dimmer, together with the tell-tale hum of back-up power. Cai guessed it was the UPS system – the uninterruptable power supply – maintaining the load, until the generators had a chance to kick in. The vice-like grip of Ginger Two on his right arm loosened minutely in reaction. It was just enough of a distraction for Cai to smack his head back against Cian's nose, while extending a frontal kick, hard into the groin of his minion. Bryn had started administering similar justice to his compatriots.

All Cai wanted to do was get to Mona, but he wouldn't make it across to her before Seamus did, despite his desperate lurching.

≈

Mona could smell the saliva on her face. She'd kissed and held Seamus. She remembered his excitement, his hard little penis jabbing at her through their clothes. Then, after the stomach groping, he'd shouted at Cai, and hit him. Now the power had failed and Cai was attacking – *too early*. It was far too early, and Seamus had a gun pointing at him, but Cai wasn't stopping. Mona summoned all her strength and bellowed.

"*Stop. Cai, stop.*"

He did stop, three metres from her with Seamus between them. Fighting for some composure, she spoke very deliberately. "You must speak in English, Seamus. I cannot understand a fucking word you've just said."

Seamus lowered the gun as Cai and Bryn were brutally

recaptured. "Keep him under control, Cian. If it's not much to ask," he spat.

Cian mumbled something, but his nose had split, and his eyes were watering. The twins secured Cai roughly at Cian's almost unintelligible command. One of the little technicians hovered for an audience with Seamus and was given it.

"There's been a short circuit at the substation."

"Send two to check," Seamus barked without taking his eyes from Cai. "I expect your backup is thrilled with itself." When he lifted the gun again, it was trembling with his rage. "How stupid do you think I am? I have three huge generators here, a UPS system and a full bank of lithium ion batteries. A new addition to my estate."

He sneered at Bryn and Cai's head fell to his chest.

Seamus then spoke directly to Mona – in English. "In short, my dear." He used an aristocratically exaggerated English accent. "Your Welsh mountain pony has recently discovered that Tom is *not* my grandson but *his* child, and that you're already knocked up again with his second."

Seamus seemed barely able to contain his fury and Cai looked over at her now, his eyes full of some sort of apology. She wondered why Cai was even listening; it was obviously a trick – hadn't he heard anything Bryn had said?

Seamus started to lay down the law again. "So, I've got a little drink for you here. It will take all that Welsh nastiness away, and we'll start afresh." Seamus talked to her as if she was a child and he lifted a glass from the tray. "To us." He clinked the glass against hers – his held champagne.

"Why not wait till later, Seamus. I'm sure we'll have a better time… if I'm feeling well." Mona forced desire into her eyes.

"No," Cai whispered and Mona moved closer to him.

"Sorry, Cai. Can't you see it's hopeless?" She traced her thumb across Cai's cheekbone and sighed. "I'm doing what's best for me now. I know it's a shame about Tom, but frankly, Seamus has got so much more to offer." Mona let her hand drop and raised her chin with attitude. "I wouldn't have bothered with the brat at all if I thought it was yours. You've got no *magic,* Cai, no *money.* Why would I stay with you?" Mona looked down at her feet and didn't recognise them in the elegant shoes. "We've had a great time, but I'm afraid you haven't got anything I'm particularly interested in. Sorry."

"My gods, Mona, you heartless witch! It must be the English upbringing," Seamus giggled, brimming with admiration. Mona leaned forwards to kiss him deeply on the mouth, her hand straying to the front of his suit trousers. "Yes, yes, a trial run," he panted. "I've got all the time in the world to fill you up with my babies. I'll keep you constantly pregnant." He rubbed his hands over her backside. "It's a good job you're so strong."

"Don't be a fucking idiot, Seamus," Cian screamed at his father. "Don't touch her! *That's* what you told us. Can't you see what she's doing?"

"Don't talk to me like that, you bloody imbecile! I told you how it was, and I don't expect to be questioned by the likes of you. Just get on with your job." Seamus dismissed his hysterical son with a wave. "And leave the grunt work to me." The older man was almost oblivious to everything, but he spared Cai a glance of mock pity. "Isn't it funny?" he said with no humour at all. "Only women can make you cry like that." He smiled. "Don't worry. I'll put you out of your misery later. Can't keep the lady waiting." Mona bent to pick up her dropped cloak. "You won't need that, my dear, I'll keep you warm," he said in a parody of kindness.

"I'm a little chilly," she replied.

"An ice maiden, I'd say."

They both laughed as he steered her out of the room and down the hall.

21

Seduction

Idwal had seen a couple more Irishmen jog out of the machine room and up towards the substation. He prayed they'd left it unlocked, but his chief concern was accessing the outbuilding without being seen, which would be difficult because of its proximity to the main house.

After considering several approaches, Idwal decided on walking with brazen confidence across the courtyard. The door handle yielded and Idwal walked in, his sword delving deep into the belly of the first man he met. His friend panicked at the sight of the blonde giant, but there was nowhere for him to run. Fist met face, his head slammed back into the metal of the diesel tank, and the man was unconscious before he slid down its side.

Idwal found a large stash of semi-automatic weapons, which he disabled one at a time, before restacking them neatly. There would be more weapons around, but at least he'd evened the odds – marginally.

He found the gasping of the injured man uniquely distressing in the small room; it could take hours for him to die from the stomach wound. So Idwal drew the sword across the man's throat, ending his suffering through more violence. Blood coloured his hands and Idwal cringed. He'd had enough of killing already today.

Forcing the barbarity from his mind, he began to work quickly, turning off the valve from the tank, and then cutting the fuel lines to each of the generators, as he'd been instructed. Cai had estimated that each generator would have five minutes' run time once the fuel line had been disabled, due to the amount of diesel present in the chunky fuel filters. As one generator died, the next would take its place. When the last generator was finally starved of fuel, the UPS would restart, very quickly and very greedily draining the life from the huge battery bank. All the power would cease in twenty minutes. Idwal prayed it would be enough time.

Dusk was falling as he locked the door behind him. Throwing the keys into a hedge, he eased back to the meeting point, aiming to liaise with Nia in less than ten minutes.

≈

Yellow Woman and Green Man had separated, and Diarmuid had been torn about which one of them to follow. Now though, he had weightier issues to ponder. He'd seen two more of his father's guards on their way to the conflagration at the sub-station. Both men lowered their guns when they saw it was only Diarmuid.

"Where have you been, fatty?" One of them screamed at him as they hurried to the fire. "Fucking useless waste of space."

Diarmuid heard the other man's reply, and an unusual mixture of courage and hate finally ignited in his big gut. Grabbing one of his brethren around the neck, Diarmuid began to wring the life from him. By the time the second man realised he meant business, it was too late to run or struggle. Squashing the life out of armed men had been much easier than he thought it would be, and Diarmuid felt euphorically empowered by the split-second decision.

Following the Green Man's lead, he threw their guns out of reach and answered the control room over the phone. "We're on our way." That little bit of play-acting might only buy a few more minutes, but at least it was something.

Diarmuid was trying to decide how next to help the Green Man, when all the air was punched from his body. Though too disorientated to discern the flavours, as he fell to the earth, Diarmuid tasted the red and green of warrior and healer. He expected to die imminently and tears came. They weren't tears of fear, however, just tears of shame. Regret for a wasted life. He'd heard tell of the Welsh savagery, and anticipated the sting of cold metal against his neck.

"*Céard atá ag dul ar aghaidh anseo? – What's going on here?*" It was an Irish, not a Welsh voice, but not one he knew. There was something about the accent. Newgrange, he thought.

"Who are you?" Diarmuid asked, staring up into the faces of two young men.

"Who are you?" The red one asked back bluntly. "We watched you kill those guards."

The more he spoke, the more Diarmuid heard. "You've come for the girls," he choked past his fear. "Aislinn and Kathleen."

"Yes!" the green one answered with a spark of hope. "Where are they?"

Diarmuid covered his face and began to weep again.

≈

Nia found the *farm*. A row of livestock stalls had been converted into individual bedrooms. They all seemed to be abandoned, and the doors stood ajar. Each door had a lock on the outside, and Nia could see that they'd been used to house the women for breeding. Her brain screamed at her reckless stupidity. This wasn't what she'd been designed to do. She wasn't brave or strong.

Nevertheless, Nia entered and tentatively scanned each room for signs of life. In each empty stall she saw filthy sheets, soiled with blood and excrement, small bare cots and the stink of disease. There was a closed door at the end, and her courage nearly failed at the smell of corrupted flesh seeping from underneath it. Nia gathered her fledgling courage and slid back the lock. She walked into a charnel house.

Nia didn't have to lift the sheet on the young girl to know her blood was poisoned with infection. She was skin and bone; green eyes in a grey, wax face. The girl held the bodies of her dead twins against her. "My babies," she whispered.

Nia felt on the verge of fainting at the intensity of the smell but forced herself onwards to comfort the girl.

"They're such pretty babies. Can I hold them?" To talk above a whisper was impossible. The boy had been dead probably less than a day. "I've got something for the pain." The young mother nodded barely. "What's your name?" Nia asked gently, as she prepared the drink.

"Aislinn." The girl looked up at Nia from the bottom of a well of pure tragedy.

"You will sleep." Nia couldn't say the word *die*, but it didn't matter, Aislinn already knew.

"Will it be quick?"

Nia nodded. "Have you got any family? Someone to take care of the babies?" There was no point in breaking the girl's heart before she died.

"My sister, Kathleen." She fluttered a skeletal hand over the dead boy. "And Diarmuid."

Nia nodded blankly and stared down at the deadly poison in her hands. She had made enough for fifteen women. This girl would be able to slip away from the horror in minutes, but it would be murder. She dripped the drug between the girl's parched lips, and held Aislinn's hand while she died, incanting the rites of passing as best she could through the cramping in her throat.

As Aislinn gave up her feeble hold on life, Nia's tears dried to anger and a stony resolve started to stiffen her backbone. Gently, she collected the emaciated bodies of the babies into her sling, having to prise the girl from her mother's side. Nia had to pause in the act though – this baby was still warm.

≈

A cold, sick dread fell over Idwal in waves: five minutes late; eight minutes late. A rustling crunch nearby, and he drew back into the undergrowth, sword out. Nia walked by him and he shot out an arm, dragging her back into the thicket with him. *Thank god*, she had the baby and they could make for the headland to set off the flare. Nia handed him a child, but it wasn't Tom. It was a naked, skinned rabbit of an infant. Not dead yet, but not far off.

Nia knew they couldn't talk. "*Gwna hi yn well* – Heal her," she mouthed.

Idwal shook his head vehemently. *Tom, Dafydd.* Nia had strayed off the path, away from the plan.

She gazed at him for a long moment before revealing the dead boy. "It's too late for her brother, please… just try. I'm going for Tom."

Nia touched the girl tenderly and left in the direction of the main house. Idwal watched her progress in agony. He had no choice but to wait for her now. Shuffling back into the green depths, he clutched the baby girl to his chest and tried to trickle tendrils of life into her flickering soul.

≈

Diarmuid had led the Newgrange men to his hidden spot. He sat with his back against the standing stone, massaging his chest where he'd been punched. The ache was easing quicker than his shame.

"You're from here?" Red asked. "You're one of Seamus's men?" Diarmuid cringed away, readying himself for an attack that never came. "We don't want to hurt you. We just want the girls back. Can you help us?"

Diarmuid nodded slowly. "I can help you, but you should know that Aislinn's not well… at all."

"What's wrong with her? How bad…?" the younger lad spoke urgently; these girls mattered to them.

The warrior interrupted him. "And Kathleen?"

"I can help you find them," Diarmuid said. "How many are you?"

"Just us, I'm afraid. My brother and me." Red put a steadying arm on the younger lad's shoulder and Diarmuid discerned more than just crimson in the man; it was a burnished red – he was an Archdruid in the making. "Our clan is in near collapse. Niall, our leader... the girls are his daughters... and he's rudderless without his family." The young man dropped his head and his voice to an imploring whisper. "We've come to take them home."

"How did you get past the...?" But Diarmuid didn't need to finish his sentence. There were no guards any more.

"We've been skulking outside the perimeter for days. Never thought we'd get in undetected, and then... the power station... just blew up." He motioned up the hill. "It's pandemonium up there. What's going on?"

"That's the Welsh," Diarmuid stated simply. "They've come for one of their own too." He thought of the Green Man and came to a decision. "We need to find the Welsh leader."

"Take us to him." The warrior smiled and Diarmuid could see Aislinn's likeness in him; strawberry hair and soft green eyes. He pushed his hand forwards to help Diarmuid stand. "I'm Conall, and this is my brother, Joseph."

≈

A potent mixture of hate and shame had uncoiled itself in Bryn's belly. It had threatened to come out of his mouth, as he watched Seamus usher Mona to his bedroom. They had just witnessed the most sickeningly vivid display of Mona's vulnerability, and knew that once inside his room, without them, Mona didn't stand a chance.

Cai was supposed to be monitoring the failing power. It was his job to decide when to make a move, but looking across at him now, Bryn could see nothing but a vacant wilderness of pain. The ginger sidekicks were holding him tightly and Cian incited them through his smashed nose.

"For fuck's sake… kill them, kill them now," he barked, holding his face together.

"Not sure that's a good idea." Ginger One sounded torn between his two masters. "I've seen that look before. He wants something special for this one and the baby. Better let him have his fun, don't you think?"

A second generator thrummed into life in the machine room outside. Fifteen minutes, then, Bryn noted.

"Don't you get sick of it all?" Bryn asked loudly, trying to distract them from the sound.

"Shut up, gay boy," Cian snarled back.

"Do you really think he'll job share, Cian? Wasn't that just about enough humiliation for one day?" Bryn mocked. "You're a fool if you think he'll ever change."

"I'm the best he's got. You've always been a fucking fairy." He pointed at Bryn. "And Fin was never up for that job; he didn't even want to go. I should have been sent to nail the bitch."

"How old are you?" Bryn asked, knowing the answer. "Eighteen? Nineteen?" He laughed dryly. "I wouldn't have fancied your chances with Mona. And," Bryn lowered his voice, sparing a glance to Cai, who seemed oblivious, "Fin got the job done, after all."

"He says this Welsh prick's the father." Cian shoved Cai's shoulder, but he didn't react.

"And you believe him?" Bryn asked with clear incredulity.

"He's not?" Cian's confidence wavered.

"I was there, remember?" Bryn shook his head. "I thought you were smart, Cian. Can't you see what he's doing?" Cian didn't respond and Bryn spoke again. "Seamus knows the boy is Fintan's. He's going to pretend to kill it – to put you off the scent. He doesn't want to share the prize." Bryn fed the doubt in Cian's mind further. "If he was Cai's son, the boy would be dead already. Wouldn't he?" The third generator kicked in – ten minutes, then.

Cian was lost in these new machinations and hadn't noticed the

292

change in sound. "She'll produce more." He cocked his head, down towards the corridor and Mona.

Bryn laughed manically in an effort to further disguise the tonal change. "How do you think he'll be able to control her? Haven't you seen what she can do?" His laughter stopped dead and Bryn's voice lowered. "Oh no, you weren't there."

One of the server operators approached. "There's a bigger problem with the electricity, Cian. We're on the third back-up generator. I reckon there's something up in the machine room, probably the fuel filters. Do you think I should...?" The little man peeked down the corridor.

"No. I'll take care of it," Cian said confidently and he called over the biggest man he could see in the room. "Come here and hang on to this fucker. We'll go and check it out." The brute glanced at Cai nervously, but Cian reassured him. "For god's sake look at him. What can he do now?"

Indeed, Cai had sunk to the ground on his knees between the men, both arms pulled up to his back. The third generator died.

≈

Once outside the Command Centre, Cian started to make his plans.

"We should get some reinforcements in there," one of the twins said, hurrying to keep up with Cian's suddenly fast stride. "That sheep shagger's a right handful."

"Aren't we going to the machine room?" the other twin asked as Cian led them in a fast, low creep away from the outbuildings.

"No," he hissed. "Let the Welsh have Seamus." He giggled. "Let them chop each other to bits with their poxy swords." Black eyes glittered as he faced them. "I'll clean up with the guns."

"Where are we going?" Ginger Two asked.

"We'll hide, and wait," Cian muttered. "Follow me. We'll need a few more..."

"Who?"

"Declan and Kieran." He smirked. Find them and bring them to the shed."

≈

Mona's hand crept to the pocket of her cloak. Her fingers probed for the leather package, scraped back the covering and touched cool iron. Her life essence had been transmitted into this object during its making. That power was there for her now and it slowly began to trickle back in through her fingers. Mona forced the stream up to her brain as she meandered slowly down the corridor, arm in arm with the madman.

Seamus had grown excited, not only about his imminent sexual gratification but also with the forthcoming fulfilment of his life's work.

"I believe any male from our union should be capable of incorporating all your skills and maybe even healing as well- given your mother's talents. I have the skill of the bard in my loins, as you will no doubt remember from Fintan." He smiled blandly. "I think we would have to discard any with your particular... handicap." Seamus scrutinised her reaction, but Mona merely answered with a shrug of the shoulders. "It may only exist in the female line, of course," he persisted, almost to himself, getting lost in the idea.

"I can't say I'm that bothered about having 'magic babies'." She quoted with her fingers. "As long as I don't have to look after the little bastards." Mona narrowed her eyes at him. "But what I really want to know, Seamus... is what can you do for me? I want something in return for popping out your brats."

Seamus closed his eyes and then opened them with admiration and lust. "At last! A woman who understands me." They were nearing a door. It was almost certainly his bedroom, but Seamus couldn't wait and Mona tasted his acrid mouth again, his tongue lapping against hers. "You're a hard tart, Mona. Not sweet and loving like my Molly."

Her mother's name was an obscenity in his mouth and she clutched frantically at the symbol in her pocket. *Keep him talking – I need more power.* They'd reached the bedroom door. It didn't have a handle or lock, but some sort of retinal identification system.

"All the mod cons." He was the wolf again. "I don't know if you're still hoping for young Gawain out there to rescue you, but I'm fairly certain this is the end of that little relationship, don't you? And as charming and inviting as you've been, my dear, I'm going to have to play safe, and woo you with my words again."

Mona could feel the thrust of her power, forcing itself against the fragile barrier in her mind, but she needed more time.

"Make me think you're Cai again," she rattled out quickly. "You'll get much more from me that way." Mona ran her free hand inside his jacket. He smelled more of man than aftershave now, but he slapped her hand away irritably.

"What can he give you that I can't? He's a surly puppy. I'm a fucking prodigy."

She moved a hand to his tie, loosening it with a sultry whisper. "He's very good in bed. Why do you think I've stuck around? It certainly wasn't for the conversation."

Seamus pulled away from her to perform the eye scan, but she could see him hardening at the crotch of his trousers. How long had it been since Idwal had cut the supply? Fifteen minutes? Twenty? She'd lost track of time.

They were in the bedroom now, and Seamus had already started to croon in his delicious Irish voice, while starting to undress: first his jacket, and then his watch. Seamus *was* Cai, he *loved* her and they would be handfasted. Wasn't he speaking the words of commitment right now? His hands were all over her body, pawing relentlessly through the material. He tugged at the cloak and with one last squeeze she relinquished the iron as it fell to the ground at her feet. The barrier yielded infinitesimally. She needed a few more seconds – if she spoke now, she could drown out his voice.

"Rip the dress. Rip it up the front," she urged him.

Seamus looked truly shocked at her demand, but she dragged off his jacket and started on the buttons of his shirt, slipping her hand inside to his chest.

"Rip the dress, Cai," she moaned again, before he could speak. The pressure in her mind was heightening as the power pounded relentlessly against the weakening membrane.

Seamus fumbled frantically at a bedside table and eventually produced a small dagger. Mona sat on the edge of the bed, and forced her knees as far apart as the dress would accommodate; stretching the material for a clean cut. Seamus made a tiny nick in the hem and she pushed his hands away, ripping the material to the waist herself – her legs free at last.

The sight of Mona's lacy knickers and stockings was intoxicating. Seamus fumbled at his fly while she eased herself back into the middle of the bed. He became incapable of speech in either English or Irish and was panting as he crawled onto the bed, still trying to rid his lower legs of the suit trousers. Once they were freed, he moved her legs apart and trailed a finger along the fabric covering her sex.

"I'll take them off." Mona spoke, so Seamus couldn't. She raised her hips and wrenched off her knickers, while he moved his penis back and forth in his hand.

"*Scaoil isteach mé* – Let me in," he croaked in Irish.

There was a thudding at the bedroom door, something heavy was being beaten rhythmically against it, and Seamus almost turned towards the distraction. Mona replaced his hand with hers, and his eyes closed in bliss as he rode forwards and back within her grasp a few times.

"No!" she hissed.

Mona shunted the fire in her hand directly into his genitals. The fire spread quickly along his entire body, and the smell of sulphur filled the room. Seamus's body scorched and crumbled, leaving Mona covered in hot black sand.

22

Molly

Idwal had fastened the baby girl against his heart, strapping her inside his vest top. She was alive and her breathing had become slightly more regular, but if he didn't get water into her soon, the child would die and nothing could prevent it. Nia hadn't returned with Tom, and Idwal knew he had no choice but to leave for the headland. Dafydd needed to see the flare *now*. Idwal would have to come back for Nia.

The estate was in blackout and panic. He'd watched the mayhem unfold and estimated that only twenty-five Irish fighters remained, though they were all around him as he eased from his hiding place. Hoping that everyone was too busy to notice him, Idwal crept along, out of the line of vision. Once out of danger, he opened up and sprinted as fast as he could while carrying his fragile load.

Reaching the top of the headland, Idwal squeezed the trigger on the flare gun. It caught, recoiled and shot from the gun, fifty metres into the Irish sky. The fleet from the *Conway* had trickled out in ones and twos on the same tide and had been dallying in Irish waters for a couple of hours. The flare would make sure they landed. *One flare for the attack; two for the abort.*

Idwal estimated he had a twenty-minute wait before being joined on the cliff top by the rest of the Welsh squad. He was desperate now to find some way of getting water into the child. There looked to be plenty of water around, but it was all salty and hope was fading. He closed his eyes against failure, sensing the dehydration in her little body. Idwal reached out with his hands onto the thin soil of the cliffs, sending his root system of power into the earth, and asking for its help, begging it to lead him to clean water.

Slowly, he began to sense the location of the water through his fingertips as the power in him chased along through the shallow dirt. Following its lead, he found the source within five minutes and eased the baby away from his chest.

Idwal dripped the water from his finger into her mouth. It took many attempts to make her respond, but eventually she started sucking on his finger. Trying to speed up the process, he made a cup with his hand, but it was the wrong thing to do. Idwal couldn't control the flow, and he drenched her. The child reacted by opening her eyes in shock at the sting of cold water – a flash of green. Idwal reverted to the slower but safer method, and when he could sense an improvement, he re-wrapped his precious bundle and made for the jetty.

≈

Cai was still kneeling on the floor when the blackout finally came. Despair morphed into a white, hot rage and he head-butted and kicked his way out his of captor's grasp with a frenzy driven strength. Snatching the weapons from his downed victims, Cai could see Bryn struggling with several men in the half-light. He ran them through with a couple of savage blows and pulled Bryn to his feet, bloody but capable of fighting on. "Mona?" he uttered with far too much unstable emotion. One of the computer operators was cowering beneath a bench. Cai picked him up and spat the question into his face. "Where?"

The small man swallowed, shielding as much of his face and body as possible from the wild man. "The door is locked from the inside… there's no other way in or out."

Bryn ran to the main entrance, and locked the doors to the reinforcements trying to gain entry there. Cai had dropped the technician and was in search of a battering ram. He couldn't find anything nearly big and heavy enough; his rationality had never left him so utterly. Bryn shouted at Cai several times before he registered.

"I know another way out of here. I'll hold them for five minutes. Get her out." Cai acknowledged the order and looked about frenetically for some inspiration. He found it attached to the wall in the form of a fire extinguisher and ran with it to the only obvious door in the corridor.

The engineer in him recognised that smacking the scanning device would make no difference at all, but the caveman in him didn't, and he hammered until the scanner hung in bits from the wall. With the same primal sentiment, he started slamming the extinguisher into the metal door itself. But after a minute or so of useless violent effort, his body stopped working and his mind started. He needed a hammer, a chisel and a long lever.

The mayhem in the control room meant nothing to Cai. He just had to get to the tools – which would be kept in an adjacent building. Getting there required cleaning these men out of his way, so he set to with the pair of blades. Bryn worked at the door as they breached it, Cai by the window, but the superior numbers of the enemy queuing up to die were slowly weighing them down.

≈

Bryn was tiring, the weight of the sword getting heavier in his hand. They were still piling through, and he wondered vaguely if what he'd done today would allow Rob to forgive him – when they met again. A flicker of movement from almost behind him yanked Bryn back to reality. It seemed one of the computer operatives was looking to stab him in the back.

That attack never came, because the technician staggered to a halt, falling to the ground and clutching frantically at his neck. As he fell, Bryn saw the man's killer standing at the mouth of the corridor. Mona's hand still hadn't reached the end of its arc after throwing the dagger, but she was already marching towards him barefoot and on fire with energy. She stooped to pick up another two weapons and joined the melee.

The dusk was abruptly lit with an artificial pinkness and the shouts of the enemy ceased, as they began to consider an additional attack from behind. A few already committed fighters continued to battle away among the blood and blades. Cai paused long enough to check on Bryn, and faltered as he witnessed Mona laying waste behind him. She carried twin blades and wore the face of death. Her dress had been ripped from the hem to the waist, and when she moved to strike he saw her stomach and her legs were covered in blood. Cai flailed towards her in slow motion through the carnage.

Mona slashed and kicked the enemy with a gruesome elegance. The numbers of conscious opponents were diminishing, but those who were left were fighting for their lives and two attacked her at once. One of them engaged her with his sword, while his comrade tackled her to the ground. Mona stuck the swordsman through the gut, but Cai watched helpless as the tackler hauled her down into the bodies beneath. With newfound energy, he leapt over the remaining obstacles and brought his dagger down, over and over again. Cai slipped among the screaming and bile, urine and faeces, and he was still stabbing – until a strong arm held his aloft, wrenching the dagger from his hand. "Stop," Cai heard. "They're dead, Cai, all dead." Bryn pulled him up out of the mire and held him back until he stopped thrashing.

Mona crawled to where she could breathe. Her mind screamed for Tom but she needed to rally her strength before she could save him. Laying her filthy body on a cool, clean patch of stone, she forced herself to take a few deep, restorative breaths. But noticing her abandoned cloak, Mona crawled along the ground a few more inches to snag it. She dragged it towards her and reached for the treasure in its folds. She felt Cai land on his side next to her, cut and covered in blood. Mona stretched out to his blackened hand lifting the power from the iron into her body, and out again into his.

Cai inched closer. He wanted to touch her, to make sure she was real. *"Syt nes di gael allan?* – How did you escape?" he asked in whispered Welsh, way beyond translation.

"Dadgloi y drws – I unlocked the door." It was a very sad smile. *"Dwi wedi ladd o* – I killed him." A single tear slid out of one eye streaking a path through the blood.

Bryn was in a far worse state than Cai, and Mona cocooned the traitor against her for as long as they had. After a little while, Cai arrived back at their patch of floor, holding out some stolen clothes to Mona.

"Let's get going. Dafydd's arrived and he's attacking… everywhere. It's our chance to find Tom."

≈

Bryn had explained, in detail, Caitlín's three primary domains. In Bryn's opinion, his mother was far more volatile than Seamus, and he'd urged Nia to take no chances with physical contact. She'd dealt with the *farm*, now there only remained the lab and her private quarters to brave.

Nia had left Idwal's hiding place just as the second generator failed. Realising her timescale had been badly compromised; she'd hurried towards the house. The sound of a stabled horse, neighing in fright, caught Nia's attention, and she strained her ears to pinpoint its location. Bryn had described a subterranean entrance to the lab, and Nia looked but couldn't find it in the failing light. However, she could see movement and panic in what appeared to be a kitchen.

Through the window, Nia saw a young girl of about sixteen rushing around in a quandary and shaking with indecision. It seemed the girl suddenly made up her mind, leaving the kitchen by the back door. On that path, the girl would walk directly past her. Nia jumped out and grabbed the girl as violently as she knew how, forcing the point of the small dagger into her side. "Where are you going?"

Nia's Welsh accent scared her and the girl closed her eyes, mewling and sniffling. "Don't... don't kill me."

"Where are you going?" Nia repeated and dug in savagely.

"Up the coast... I need to get to Newgrange. It's where I'm from. Please let me go. I just... I don't want to die." So, she was a kidnap victim, and Nia's heart softened, but not enough to stop her opening the cloak and showing her the dead baby boy.

The girl's hands flew to her mouth, but she bowed her head in shame. "The babies." Tears were mingling with snot. "They always die." Her tone was squealing piglet.

"You could have saved him, his sister as well..." Nia began to lose her restraint. "*You knew*. You *must* have known. Why didn't you help her?"

The girl sagged and began crying again, repeating over and over, "*Don't want to die... I don't want to die.*"

Nia backed off and pulled back the dagger slightly. "Why weren't you in the... farm?"

"I was," she sobbed. "For a year." She made hard work of the words. "I can't have children, they kept... trying, but I can't have children... I work in the house now." She pointed behind her, and Nia's heart contracted with a pang of camaraderie for the young girl.

"What's your name?" She lowered the dagger.

"Kathleen." She touched the dead boy's hair. "Aislinn's my sister." The girl had calmed a little now, but still gulped her breaths.

Nia couldn't afford to explain about Aislinn, and forced herself to ask the girl another question. "Do you have any keys? For the lab? For her rooms?"

The question startled Kathleen back into babbling anxiety, but she fumbled in the pocket of her skirt. "Only for the lab. I have to clean it sometimes. It's..."

She passed the keys over and Nia's mouth dried as she formulated her next question. Calming the girl's shoulders with her own trembling hands, she asked. "Do you know if there's a baby boy here? He's about fourteen weeks old."

Mention of the little boy brought a smile to even Kathleen's world-weary eyes, and she nodded. "Little Fintan, he's so bonny." She then checked herself with sudden understanding. "He's your baby. You've come for him... all of you?"

"Yes... yes I have." Nia didn't have to feign the sudden hope. "Where is he?"

Kathleen's expression fell and her voice dropped automatically. "With the *bitch*... she's always got him with her. Even when she's in the lab." She paused. "You'll never get him back."

"I will, but please... show me the way and I'll let you go." It was Kathleen's turn for pity, but she did show Nia the way.

≈

Diarmuid, Conall and Joseph had watched the Green Man sprint up to the headland. Yellow Woman was nowhere to be seen, but Diarmuid could just about pick up her sweetness on the air. She was nearing Caitlín's end of the house. A hot dread drenched his back when he realised it was her intention to steal Fintan's child from the hag.

"Shit," he swore, feeling pathetic and useless again. "I don't know where he's going, but the girls are this way." He pointed towards the *farm* and gritted his teeth. "And someone else could use our help."

Diarmuid cursed his lack of weapon, though a gun would be of little use to him – his massive fingers would struggle with the trigger. Anything would do: a cudgel or a shovel. Inspiration struck, and Diarmuid changed direction, heading for the old tool shed. "Stay here and keep your heads down," he advised the Newgrange men in a whisper. "I'll be back in five minutes."

Diarmuid scanned the path ahead of him and broke into a waddling jog. He didn't have much time; the woman could have found her way in by now. He'd need to hurry if he was going to be able to help her. Diarmuid reached the tool shed and pushed at the swollen wooden door, but it wouldn't budge. The door had been

303

locked or seized and Diarmuid tried a second time, using all his momentum to shoulder-barge past the obstruction. The sun hadn't quite set, but it was dark enough inside the shed to need a light and he groped the walls for a switch.

"*Ní dóigh liom é!*" – Oh no you don't!" Cian's slippery voice oozed beside his ear, and he heard the safety catch release from the twins' guns.

Diarmuid saw Declan and Kieran hunched at the back of the shed – cowards like him, hiding from the fight. Cian's proximity began to hurt him and Diarmuid put his hands to his ears to stop the buzzing.

"*A' bhfuil tinneas cinn ort, a Dharma?* – Headache, Darma?" His brother crooned, before pursing his lips against the big man's cheek. "I've watched you do it. You know that, don't you... *fatso.*" Diarmuid cringed in dread, waiting for the pain to pass. "I've watched you kill them all... those poor little girls. Does it make you come when you wring the life out of them? Is it their last gasp that makes you spurt?" Cian laughed softly, right into his brother's ear. "So, at last I find we have something in common."

It wasn't shame but fury that made Diarmuid lurch up and snatch the gun from the skinny arms. "I'm putting them out of their misery, you sadistic piece of shite. They're happy to die after you've finished with them." Cian's face registered a split second of surprise, before he smiled. The twins acted unanimously, jerking the butts of their guns into either side of Diarmuid's head. He was unconscious before he fell.

"Can I shoot him?" a twin asked breathlessly.

"No. I'll need his sight later. Leave him here and lock him in. Let's go and see if my dear old dad is still alive."

≈

The *farm* had prepared Nia for the cruelties of the lab, and she skirted past the jars and cabinets not wanting to see what horrors they held.

She didn't notice any signs of life on her passage through and up the backstairs to the bedroom. Kathleen had been right: Caitlín had left the door between the rooms open. The constant work Tom required had made her tired and a little sloppy about security.

When she reached the landing, Nia saw the large closet that Kathleen had mentioned – where she'd hidden from the woman, on many occasions. Each step Nia took was excruciating, and her heart raced with fear. Every cell in her body told her to run and hide, but she forced herself onwards. She heard talking from the far side of the room, and Nia dared the smallest of peeks around the door. Caitlín's back was turned and Nia darted to the open closet. Hiding among the musty long dresses, she started to organise her breathing and calm her palpitations.

Caitlín talked to Tom who was laid out in the middle of a large bed. Her words were loud and slurred.

"Lovely fat legs, Fintan… you always had the loveliest legs." She poured herself a large whiskey and downed a swallow. "You're eyes are so blue now, just like mine, just like your mummy's. We used to have a happy time… didn't we, Fintan, my love?" Her tone changed abruptly to a keening sob and Tom started to cry. She shrieked at him savagely in reply. "Shut up! Shut up! Why won't you shut up?" Nia lost her breath entirely for a split second. Would Caitlín hit him? But the mood had changed again, just as quickly. "I'm sorry, so sorry, my little man… Mummy didn't mean it. You must be a hungry boy."

Caitlín picked him up and Tom calmed slightly, but Nia could tell he was desperate for a feed. Caitlín staggered to a chair with both baby and bottle. Nia had a good view of the woman from this angle. She was extremely striking – slender to the point of emaciation with bleached hair and a once beautiful, but now ravaged face. Her eyes were very blue.

While she fed Tom, Caitlín lit a cigarette and drank another large whiskey. She blithered constantly to the child. "We'll ignore that man, that bad, bad daddy. He doesn't love us anymore… that's why he says those things. You've got my eyes, Mummy's eyes."

She repeated herself endlessly, tiring and falling asleep just as surely as Tom. Mid-droop, Caitlín rallied abruptly, took the half-full bottle from his lips and plopped the baby into the cot, before falling heavily across her own bed.

Nia waited, breath held. Time was ticking by, and she touched the fingers of the dead boy at her chest. She knew what she had to do and began creeping forwards. The light in the room changed suddenly, a pink glow. It froze her thought and movement, and Nia's courage started to crumble.

23

Tom

Cai held out some clothes to Mona – dirty clothes from a dead man but she took them gratefully. "You'll have to unzip me," she whispered.

Bryn couldn't work out why this simple request brought such distress to them both, but he intervened.

"We have to split up, Cai. Mona and I will search the lab and her rooms. You go and check the *farm*." Bryn could see Cai trying to formulate an excuse, any excuse, to stay with Mona, but he had no choice. "I'm pretty sure that Tom will be with Caitlín in her rooms… but we have to look everywhere."

"But…"

"Mona doesn't need to see the *farm*." Bryn's stare and tone were hard, and Cai finally agreed with a reluctant nod. "It won't take long, but check each stall." Bryn was clear. "Mona and I will approach her rooms through the lab access. You come around from the far end."

Cai had studied the plans – he knew the layout and they watched him stride away, a sword in each hand.

There wasn't much left of the dress, but she was glad to be rid of it, and as Mona pulled on the trousers, she felt a return to herself. "Nice family," she made herself joke to Bryn. He seemed too shocked to formulate a reply, but she'd moved on. "What are we going to do about Cian?"

"Difficult to say with that little weasel." He finally chuckled slightly at Mona's bravado. "What a fucking mess," he sighed. "Dysfunctional doesn't even touch it."

"Tell me about it," Mona muttered, doing up some buttons.

"We're not all bad. Diarmuid's a good one… strange but decent. You'll need to keep him alive – if you can." Bryn had something more to say and now was all he would have. "Those things Seamus said – you mustn't believe them, you know. They're not true, Mona, *any of them*. They were all part of his game. Cai isn't Tom's father."

"I know."

"Does he?"

The question surprised Mona but she looked past Bryn at where Cai had so recently stood. "Yes," she said slowly.

"I want to tell you… you should know that I loved my brother Fintan. When we were young, we used to play together, laugh, make toy boats… you know… we were brothers. He wasn't a bad man, Mo. Fin never wanted any of this… he only ever wanted to play his music." She'd finished dressing, and tried to concentrate on Bryn, understanding his words and trying to believe them. "He didn't have any choice… living here, our parents…" Bryn scraped back his hair and sighed. "He was my brother, Mona. Try to understand that… if only for Tom's sake."

"I will try to remember," she mumbled, hoping she sounded sincere.

They gathered their weapons and left. Bryn didn't have to warn her about the lab, she sensed the need to walk on through, as quickly as possible. Mona was alert to sounds of life but focused on the door and the stairs leading up to where she knew Tom would be incarcerated.

The top of the stairwell afforded a good view of the whole room but Mona registered only two things: the body of a woman on the bed and her son's dark hair, sticking up from the crisp whiteness of the cot blankets.

It was the simplest thing in the world – to move forwards five metres, pick up her son and run away with him. She moved carefully, quietly, not wanting to fail at the final hurdle. Three metres. Now two. The woman remained motionless on the bed and Tom looked bundled up and easy to grab.

Ripping bullets, thudded against the wall, followed by the shotgun crack of fractured glass. The woman sprang from the bed – a striking viper. She stood at its foot, burning her electric blue gaze into the intruders. Both parties were equidistant from the baby and no one moved any closer.

"Cormac?" her voice was deep and croaky.

"It's over Caitlín. Give him up. Tom belongs with his mother." Bryn had reminded her of Mona's presence.

"You killed my son. You killed my boy."

Her tone was both frightening and childlike. Mona didn't know what to say, but it seemed a good idea to keep talking. "It was an accident. I didn't mean to." Her eyes kept dropping down to Tom. "I'm sorry," Mona said, darting ahead fractionally.

"Don't you move!" Caitlín shrieked. "Don't you dare touch him!" Caitlín picked up a blade and brandished it expansively. Recognising the threat, Mona put her hands up and took a deliberate step back – away from the cot.

Bryn adopted the same stance but continued to inch towards her. "Why did you have to kill Rob?" He became a desperate child in that instant.

"He was in the way, love. He wouldn't let me take the baby," Caitlín explained gently.

Bryn batted away her voice. "I loved him."

Caitlín's face contorted with confusion. "But he was a man."

Bryn's tears were falling freely. "Yes, he was the best of men. And I loved him… with all my heart." He wiped away the tears. "Come on, Caitlín… Mother. No one else needs to die. Let me help you." Bryn's voice cracked with emotion, and she looked at him with such a turn of tenderness.

"But we've all waited so long for him, Cormac. I can't let him go now." Her voice was soft and pleading and Bryn moved closer, to disarm her gently. Caitlín's eyes were made even bluer by the gathering tears. They didn't fall, though, as she plunged the dagger straight into her son's heart with a primal screech.

Mona knew Bryn was dead, even before he reached the ground.

"He was a pervert. He had to die." The woman explained her actions extremely rationally to Mona, who was now acutely frightened for her sleeping child.

Caitlín spared a pitying glance at Bryn as she retrieved the blade from his chest cavity. Mona didn't dare risk an attack. Tom was too close, and his grandmother too unpredictable.

"You don't look like her – like Molly." Caitlín became conversational as she wiped the dagger blade on her black silk dress.

"No, I look like my dad." Mona had no idea if it was the right thing to say, but Caitlín huffed in bored agreement, her skinny little shoulders shrugging up and down. "He loved her, you know... she was the only one." Caitlín's cobalt gaze bore into Mona's soul. "Seamus thinks this isn't our grandchild." She waggled the knife in Tom's direction. "Could he be right?"

The woman sounded completely lucid and Mona replied too quickly. "No. Absolutely not. He has your eyes." Maybe she'd been a little too quick. "Anyone can see that."

Both women moved towards the cot at the same time. "But you're not entirely sure, are you?" The situation was sliding out of control as the madwoman's paranoia notched up another level. "Are you? You little slag!"

Caitlín moved closer to Tom with the dagger – too close. "No, no, you *are* his grandmother, please." Mona could only beg now. "We can share him... just let me hold him. Please... I only want to hold him." Mona's hands were snaking out to the cot; she could almost feel his hair. Caitlín held the dagger above Tom now, but it was a feint. She wouldn't kill him now. Not if she had waited this long.

The dagger arced down in an over-powerful thrust, stabbing Tom directly through the centre of his soft little body. "*Ní fhéadfainn dhul sa seans* – I can't take that risk." Caitlín's teeth were coated with a black slime as she smiled.

≈

Cai had left with the intention of a quick, clinical check of converted stalls. After that he aimed to sprint around to Caitlín's rooms by the front door. He knew Tom would be with her; nothing else made sense. However, a hysterical and gun-toting young Irishman barred his way. The boy's comrades lay dead and dying at his feet – Dafydd's work no doubt.

There wasn't time for this and Cai moved out of the shadows for a confrontation. The young man squeezed the trigger inexpertly, and the gun planed out of his hands in an uncontrolled arc, forcing the bullets along the wall and window above him. Glass shattered and fell, giving Cai time to advance and dispatch the youngster. He took the fallen gun and dropped it into a water butt.

The sound of more fighting was coming his way. It was dark now and difficult to gauge friend from foe, but this fight would halt Cai's progress and he intervened.

Cerys and Gwen worked as a double act, each so in tune with the other that they had become one lethal unit. Cai attacked silently from behind as the enemy were too intent on the women to guard their rear. They dropped like stones and he stole towards the *farm*.

Moving inside, Cai gagged at the reek of rotting flesh. The smell of death was so overpowering, he knew it must be an adult body in decay. Yet as he crept further down the corridor, Cai's sense of impending dread grew at what he would find in that far room.

The dead woman was really young – Sioned's age he thought with pitying horror. Cai searched but found no dead child, and moved out of the stench, closing the door behind him. Fighting had stopped in this area and he sucked in the fresh air outside.

Into the night he heard Tom cry – a single short scream. Where had it come from? Above him? Caitlín's rooms? Cai's legs pumped up the stairs and he launched himself at the door. Expecting to find more resistance, he charged through it at speed.

≈

The women were either side of the cot. Mona on her knees clutching the cot bars with her faced pressed against them, and Caitlín withdrawing a dagger blade from Tom's body. Cai's heart lurched to his stomach and then to his legs bringing him to a faltering standstill.

Mona was lost in a jagged sea of bewilderment but his entrance had snapped up Caitlín's attention. She pointed the blade at him and Cai saw it was slicked black, not red. Tom would not survive the poison – even if the wound wasn't fatal.

"*You!*" her voice cracked with accusation. Caitlín appeared at a loss for a second but Cai saw her mind beginning to work again, as she turned both brain and blade to Mona.

Cai wouldn't reach her in time. The blade had already started to come down and Mona had completely lost the ability to defend herself. Cai threw his sword before he could even consider the outcome; an accurate power throw to the throat. Caitlín's blood was a very dark red and she tried, in vain, to stop it gushing from her neck, as she sank down to die beside her son.

Mona dragged herself to standing by using the cot bars. Cai's heart ached at her tenderness as she reached into the crib and scooped up Tom's body before settling him at her neck. She kissed his dark head and held him against her, moving her weight from hip to hip out of habit. She didn't notice Cai until he took them both in his arms – his broken little family. Mona gazed at him with an expression he'd seen in her face before: the pure distilled grief of a parent for a child.

"My power won't go in." She wasn't yet weeping – the enormity not yet processed. "He's so cold, so light. I thought I could warm him up… but I can't."

Light. Cold. "Can I hold him?" Cai asked gently. Mona shook her head, but he asked again. "Just for a minute?" She didn't pass him over, but Cai eased the dead child out of her arms. This baby wasn't a piglet but a bird. Cai pressed his lips to the child's forehead and it was ice cold.

Watching Cai kiss Tom's head seemed to speed up the processing for Mona and she started to choke with violent realisation. Her son was dead – she hadn't been able to save him.

"I'm putting him back in the cot for a minute, Mo." She was coming apart.

After he gently laid the baby down, Cai peeled back the blankets – there was no blood. A deep wound but no blood – this baby had been dead a while. Gingerly and discreetly he lifted a tiny eyelid to reveal a dark brown eye. A weakness spread down his legs and he silently thanked every pagan deity he could think of, before adding Nia to their number.

Mona's body language told him she ached to pick up the baby again. "Mona, look at me." Though he could hardly bear her to, she did and he pulled her to his chest, holding her too tightly. "*Dim Tom ydi o* – That isn't Tom. Can you understand me? It isn't Tom." Mona tried to pull away, but he held her fast. "I heard Tom cry, five minutes ago. This baby has been dead for a while."

Cai showed her the wound and the little boy's brown eyes. Not Tom.

24

Goddess

Idwal's tasks had not been those he'd imagined. Instead of fighting, he had found himself knee-deep in blood and bandages. Since he'd found clean water here, the area had become a makeshift hospital, and he'd spent every moment since Dafydd began the attack healing and worrying.

At first, Idwal had panicked over the bullet wounds, too frightened to try his strange healing energy on the horrifying injuries. But after several excruciating attempts, he was getting the hang of easing out the bullets and healing the holes left behind.

Little Molly had been strapped to him throughout, and she'd started to get a little fractious. The flash of green from the child's eyes had reminded him of his mother and from that moment on he'd used her name for the baby. Idwal thought her grumpiness was a good sign, and that she might need feeding again. He'd found bottles of milk packed alongside the medical supplies on the boat and wanted to attempt another feed before going to find Nia. Idwal didn't dare think about how long she'd been missing, and it was way past the time that Mona and Cai should be returning to the headland. For them, though, the chances of survival had always been slim.

Dafydd was one of the casualties who'd taken a bullet. The new Archdruid was in pain, but healing without infection. "What have you got there?" He'd been watching Idwal fiddling with the bag on his chest for a while now.

"I've been trying to feed her but she can't quite get the hang of it." Idwal had been used to feeding Tom, who sucked down great swallows of milk at every breath but Molly just didn't have the strength. He lifted a fold and showed her to Dafydd.

"She's tiny," he gasped. "My youngest came too early. Give her here... let me have a go." Dafydd rearranged himself to sitting, trying not to wince.

Idwal seized the chance to make her comfortable in Dafydd's arms.

"I've got to go to the others," he said, and Dafydd nodded in reply. He knew this; he'd been thinking the same. "Everyone else will be ok for a while," Idwal reassured him. He'd made sure no one on his ward would die in his absence. It was the missing that concerned him now. He kissed Molly's head, armed himself and took off down the hill without a backward glance.

≈

Loath to touch anything of Caitlín's, Mona had nevertheless washed her face and hands at the woman's sink. Finding it a monumental task to marshal her roller coaster emotions, Mona checked her wounds instead. She was bleeding from several places on her arms, face and head but no more than Cai, and at least none of the blades had been tainted.

"What now?" she asked him, still trying to pull herself together.

Cai gauged the activity in the courtyard outside. He was looking down and out of the shattered windows, trying to keep himself hidden by standing to the side. Cai moved away from the window but kept his voice low. His eyes held bad news.

"There are three, maybe four. We need to get past them, and they've all got guns."

"What about the way back through the lab?" Mona asked, trying to crank herself back into action.

"We can try, but they know we're here now. They'll come in and get us if we don't appear soon. We haven't got long."

She felt for the ironwork; it still throbbed with power. "Come on then," she said, putting it away again.

Cai didn't move. "Come on where?" Cai was incredulous. "Please don't tell me you're considering walking out into the courtyard, armed with two short swords and a dagger."

Mona hated that tone and it made her reply sound sullen. "We haven't got a choice."

"There's *always* a choice. You need to start thinking, Mona. Walking out there isn't bravery. It's stupidity."

Cai always used his brain to find another way. It was his most admirable quality and Mona lowered her weapons and her head. "You're right. I'm sorry. It's only… sometimes I believe I'm invincible. There must be an alternative."

Cai was too busy thinking to acknowledge all her words, but he looked up at her manically at one in particular. "What did you just say?"

She was non-plussed. "Sorry?"

"No, you said invincible." Mona nodded, hoping that wasn't actually part of his plan. "Ok, have you seen anything metallic we can use as shields?" Cai ran his fingers through his hair, as the plan took shape.

"Metal doors in the lab – on the cupboards," Mona barked with sudden inspiration, as her mind began to kick in at last.

He was already half-way down the stairs, and she raced after him. "We'll use these as shields." Cai had found a screwdriver and began to release the doors from their hinges. Mona would have tried to rip them off before resorting to tools, as she acknowledged to her shame.

Cai explained his plan, while working on attaching crude, rope wrist-straps.

"This is thick stainless and should be able to take some punishment." He passed her a door. "We'll both have to throw our

316

daggers straightaway, because we won't get a chance once the shooting starts. As soon as that happens, you need to start your magic." Cai smiled at her with total confidence. The lunacy must be catching.

"Magic? I thought you had a plan?"

Cai took the ironwork from her hand, shocked at the sting of power. "You're going to use this in reverse." He shook it excitedly. "It's just physics," he beamed. "I know you can use your power in a couple of ways: to draw out poison, or to force in, like healing. It's the same power, with a different polarity. Think of it as electricity." Mona nodded, with him so far. "I believe you will be able to push your power into and through the iron, amplifying it in the process."

"What will happen?" She was dazed by the concept.

"I don't know exactly, but I'm certain it will affect either the guns or the bullets or the men, maybe all three. I'm pretty sure that's up to you."

Mona shook her head. "Are you talking about a weapon?" The familiar fear of her power nestled in the pit of her stomach, and Mona's mind lurched back to the violence she'd unleashed in the boatshed.

"If you like," he replied. "But really it's whatever you decide. You're the magician."

"Cai..." He had too much faith. She was just a girl from Kent who was quite good at taekwondo.

He took her by both arms, enclosing her in his faith. "Seamus devoted his life to your *mark*. He believed the bearer could do anything. I've seen you do incredible things, Mona, but I think they're only the beginning."

"I... I need to practise," she stalled.

"No time," he said emphatically. "Get your dagger out ready. We'll use the lab entrance."

≈

There was only one man patrolling the quad and Cai waited for him to make his turn, before easing open the door and launching the dagger. His aim was true. The man fell and Cai tensed to leave. Mona hauled him back.

"It's a trap. They left one there as temptation, but using the quad is suicide. We'll be sitting ducks."

Cai agreed. Seamus's men would use the other entrance to attack from both sides. They made Caitlín's room again in seconds, flattening themselves against the wall just as the enemy breached from the exterior stairwell. Cai gave Mona the nod and she let loose her power through the iron and into the chest of the assailant. She felt the familiar thrill of power and heat, which flared into a bright light as it was amplified through the metal. The man didn't even get a chance to scream and ash filled the room.

Cai picked Mona up from the floor. She'd overestimated the power by several fold and was almost depleted. "I should have poured it out slowly," she sighed, annoyed at her folly. "I threw the whole bloody lot at him. I've hardly got anything left."

They heard a worried call from downstairs. *"Céard atá ag dul ar aghaidh anseo? –* What's happening?" it shouted tentatively.

Cai tried for an Irish accent, pulling Mona with him to the door and keeping his head down. "It's ok. I've got her."

Mona continued to take strength from the iron as they fumbled their way down the steel stairwell, but it had less to give now. She could see one man at the bottom and he didn't look convinced by Cai's accent. He cocked the gun, and Mona tried to visualise pouring the power just into its muzzle – leave the man, kill the gun.

There were fewer fireworks this time, but all she left was a melted gun and charred human remains. There was still one man left, and he came into view as they stumbled to the bottom of the staircase. Mona only saw the feet approaching. "There's nothing left in the iron," she whispered. "I'm almost out."

Cai had fallen on top of her, poised to absorb the bullets with his own body, once the firing started. "Take mine," he hissed. "Take my life force," he said, fumbling for a solution. She tried to suck some energy from Cai, but it wouldn't come, he was a sealed unit, and Mona gave up.

Geraint sauntered over; he walked with a limp. "Well isn't *this* nice, Mona?" She had managed to move her head clear of Cai, so she could at least aim the iron in Geraint's general direction. "I'd love it if you begged for mercy."

Mona concentrated on a trickle, *only a trickle* and raised her eyes and iron to the barrel of his gun, just the gun – and then let it go. All power drained, Mona let her face fall against the damp earth, reaching to touch Cai as her eyes closed. There was a trembling in the ground, a great vibration in the soil, and then the darkness.

≈

Idwal was still cannoning down the bank to the manor house as he saw Cai pull Mona down the steel spiral staircase. He watched a moonlit stage and was helpless in the audience as a great light reared from Mona – burning a man alive. There wasn't enough time to prevent them falling and he was still too far away... he wouldn't be able to stop the last man from shooting them at point blank range. Idwal blundered onwards as the gun faltered and failed. He watched the man throw it aside and pull out a sword to finish the job. Only ten metres away now and Idwal fumbled for a dagger. Could he be accurate at this speed?

The ground lurched and rumbled, there was a rhythmic pounding, and it increased in tempo and proximity to his right. A huge white horse cut in front of him and bore down on the gunman with murderous intent. Idwal fell to his knees in homage as his momentum ceased. He stared up at a goddess. She was *Epona,* the Great Mare. She was *Macha.* She was *Rhiannon.*

≈

Nia jumped from the horse to make sure Geraint had been incapacitated. She couldn't find a pulse in his neck and guessed that the impact had broken it. An adrenaline rush wobbled in her legs and Nia sank down next to Cai and Mona, who were both breathing, but unconscious.

The horse was distressed and had bolted, but Nia hoped the mare would calm now, as she slowed and headed for a patch of green grass. Nia didn't notice Idwal until he loomed above her and then he was all she could see. He wrapped her in his big arms and lifted her off the ground.

"They're ok," she breathed into his shoulder.

"A horse?" Idwal squeaked, awed by the tiny woman.

"I know! She's Seamus's," Nia almost giggled.

Idwal put her down but kept hold of her hand while he checked the pair on the ground. "I can't believe…" Idwal had to let go of Nia's hand to untangle them and dispense a hurried healing. "The trauma in their bodies is enormous."

"Did she survive?" Nia asked and Idwal knew by her tone that she meant the baby girl.

"*Molly*," Idwal breathed with pride. "I called her Molly after… she'll be fine, she's *so* strong."

"We could love her, Idwal. She could be our daughter."

Idwal's eyes filled with sudden tears. "Yes," he said as they fell down his cheeks. Nia's face was dirty, her hair dishevelled, and Idwal marvelled at her. "Tom?"

Nia nodded but his name seemed to bring on urgency in her. "I've got to get his milk from the boat."

"They're up there with Dafydd." He pointed. "On the cliffs… I should stay here with these two."

Nia eased his head down to her, so she could kiss him. "I'll be back soon. Please be careful."

"I'm not worried, Nia. I've got the Goddess on my side." Nia had already started to smile, when the sound of fighting snatched his face from hers. Torn between his duties, Idwal looked to Nia for help.

"Give them another blast of power and go. They've made it this far, and I won't be long if I ride up there and back."

Once Nia had caught and heaved herself atop the huge mare, she turned to watch Idwal dragging the unconscious bodies towards some cover, before setting off again in the direction of battle.

≈

Someone was touching his face, slapping it and talking, but it wasn't Cian. Diarmuid still lay on the dirt floor of the shed.

"Wake up, Diarmuid." Relief washed over him at Conall's reassuring voice and he inched his bulk to sitting. "The Welsh have overrun Seamus. The fighting sounds like it's died down to the west... but there'll be skirmishes."

Diarmuid rubbed the bumps on his head. "How long have I been out?"

"Only twenty minutes, but a lot has happened." He squatted down to look into Diarmuid's eyes. "Let Joe have a feel of your head a minute."

Joseph left his post by the shed door and bent down to tend the lumps and bruises."

"You're a healer!" Diarmuid whispered with shock.

"Not a very good one." Joseph smiled apologetically.

"I don't know." Diarmuid smiled back. "I'm a bit better already." Just being this close to the boy's calming green settled his soul. "Aislinn is a healer. Are you related?"

"Cousins," Conall replied as he braced himself to pull Diarmuid from the floor. "And we need to find them both."

It took a while for Diarmuid to catch his breath again after the exertion of standing. "We're still best to find the big Welshman."

"Do you think they'll treat us fairly enough if we go out there with our hands up?"

Diarmuid thought about what he knew of Green Man and answered immediately. "Yes, I do."

It was a long, slow walk towards the sound of activity. Diarmuid bunched against the Newgrange men as he passed the split and broken bodies of men he'd known all their lives. Beside him, Conall held a white feed sack above his head, but it was Diarmuid who led them to the lawn area behind Caitlín's lair.

Streams of colour bombarded Diarmuid's sight as they mingled at the confluence ahead. At its very centre, four blood red warriors were lapping at the last of the enemy defence. They were raw meat, red chillies and sweet pepper.

Colour was everywhere: fresh greens, and bitter lemons, caramelised peaches and burnt ochre oranges. The great Green Man ran into the wheel and all the other colours swirled around his power, breathing in the healing energy.

≈

Idwal ran blindly to the sound of fighting, and found the last few notes of battle being played out on a lawn. Cerys, Gwen, Alun and Glyn had engaged with what had to be the last of the resistance. Despite their fatigue and injuries, the superiority of their training was winning out and Idwal wasn't surprised or upset to see the remaining enemy fighters submit. Glyn glanced over to Idwal, as if asking him to accept the surrender.

There was movement from behind him, as another three men appeared from the undergrowth. Their arms were held aloft, and they bore a white flag. Idwal beckoned them over slowly. They were unarmed, unscathed and were led by a large bald man whose face was bloated and asymmetrical. On hearing more movement to his right, Idwal halted their progress, palm outwards.

"It's ok, Id," Glyn wheezed, leaning over his sword. "That's Dafydd and the rest of the squad."

Idwal breathed a sigh of relief that the Archdruid had come to officiate over proceedings, and he beckoned the prisoners over once more.

≈

Tom was crying. He was screaming in a way Mona had never heard before and it dragged her from the depths of unconsciousness. She couldn't clearly remember how they'd ended up in this ditch, but reaching Tom was now her sole aim, and she wasn't able to zone in on his direction. Cai clambered to his knees beside her and pointed to a wooden stable block about forty metres away. Tom's tortured screams grew louder, and they both began to pick up speed, releasing daggers and swords from sheaths and belts as they approached the stable doors.

Their silent agreement meant that both Mona and Cai kicked against the door in unison and launched themselves into the middle of the building – landing fully braced to attack. A young girl was holding Tom as he screamed in fury, his head purple with rage.

"Give him to me," Mona bellowed as she stalked the short distance. She would have thrown the sword if the girl hadn't been holding Tom so closely. Cai instantly realised that Mona was on the point of murder to reclaim her child and he sprinted between them. Ripping the boy from the teenager, he handed the baby to Mona with energy he didn't know he had.

"He's just really hungry. Nia's gone for milk," the girl blurted to Cai, still trembling from the confrontation.

Mona took Tom to the nearest bale of hay and stripped the howling infant, checking and rechecking every part of his naked body. When she was fully satisfied of his wellbeing, Mona sank down among the hay and rested her face on his squirming chest. Tom kicked his legs and banged against her with his fists. Eventually, she laughed at his temper and then dressed him again.

Before Cai could ask any questions, Nia burst through the doors, clutching the lead of a giant horse and holding a bundle that looked and sounded like a baby. She advanced on Mona, brandishing a bottle from somewhere.

Tom finally exchanged screaming for sucking, but Mona didn't let go of her son as she hauled Nia towards her in amazed gratitude. "You saved him," she mumbled into long wet hair.

"Kathleen helped. I couldn't have completed the switch without her. See here…" Nia pulled back the corner of her bundle to show Mona the strawberry-haired baby. The little girl was tiny, perfect and strangely familiar. "I found her in the farm… her mam…" Nia couldn't say anything more about Aislinn. "Idwal saved her." In the now relative quiet, Nia scanned the barn. "Where is he? Where's Idwal?" The note of worry caught Cai's attention. "There was fighting," she explained warily. "And he went."

"Which way?" Cai asked, rearranging his knife belt and moving towards the stable doors. "Come on," he urged Mona, but she didn't move to give Tom to Kathleen as he expected her to.

"I can't leave him… I've only just found him." She clutched the baby against her and backed away slightly.

"Tom will be safe here with Nia and Kathleen." He understood her dilemma but Mona's help out there would be vital. "Idwal needs you, Mo."

"Please, help him," Nia begged softly, tears beginning to fall onto the bundle at her own chest. "We'll protect Tom."

Mona closed her eyes, gritted her teeth and kissed Tom's forehead, leaving a bloody smudge there. She deposited both Tom and bottle in Kathleen's arms and gave Nia a dagger.

"No one in or out. Bolt and bar the door after we leave."

≈

Initially, Cai and Mona jogged from the shed, trying to pick up the sound of any skirmishing. Cai changed direction when he saw a congregation on the grassed area behind the house.

It was quite dark now, and it seemed that the fighting had slowed or even stopped. He could see Idwal and Dafydd talking. Cai recognised Cerys and her comrades as he neared, and she waved over at him.

Cerys's hand was still in the air when the bullets ripped through her upper chest. Cai heard someone scream as the sound of the machine gun bore on and on, cutting down the four resting Welsh soldiers together with the Irishmen they'd been fighting. He stumbled forward through glue as he watched Idwal and Dafydd fall to their knees in shock. Mona sprinted past him into the arena, screaming her fury.

Into the gloom, a blinding sodium light clunked on, followed by its mate on the adjacent wall.

"You see, boys, the gun is mightier than the sword." Seamus stood at the top of the staircase, holding the machine gun, his voice filled with universal loathing.

Cai shaded his eyes against the glare and realised that though the voice was identical to its sire's, it wasn't Seamus standing in the spotlight but the younger, swarthier version. Looking at him now, Cai could see Cian was just past adolescence and so slightly built that the gun in his arms appeared burdensome. The cruelness of the white light added an extra pallor to his skin, and his shark's eyes were trained on Mona.

"I have four armed men here, bitch. How do you fancy your chances now?"

≈

Black buzzing screams filled the air and Cian's breaths were wasp stings in Diarmuid's mind. The Green Man had fallen up to his knees in red, but there was nothing left for him to heal. Cian had slaughtered not only the Welsh warriors but also his remaining kinsmen. Diarmuid watched in horror as more of Cian's sickly yellow hardened into black. The colour wheel around him had now been infected with Indian ink and he heard Conall beside him swear in hatred. Diarmuid's last salient thought was for the Yellow Woman. Then came a hurricane from the left.

Forked lightning stabbed the air, sucking oxygen and sanity away in its wake. There was no smell but ozone. No taste but fear. Brute force flattened the fields of colour in her path, leaving them paler in her wake. A storm surge of Prussian blue powered into the void she left behind. Blue changed as it crashed on, shifting between slate and violet, its taste left the tang of raw sea salt on Diarmuid's lips, as he struggled to the surface and air. The sound of surf receded from his ears and then Cian's oil slick slipped against them once more.

"What did Daddy say?" Cian adopted a nursery tone. "Just don't let her touch you." Before instantly becoming cynical. "Pity the arrogant arsehole didn't take his own advice."

Diarmuid had fallen to the ground but was now able to move his head and open his eyes. He found it physically painful to look at the *marked one* but found if he concentrated on a point past her, he could make out the shape of a woman at the edge of his vision.

Even stationary, her body writhed and spiked with random electrostatic discharge. The power surged as she raised both arms to the balcony, a current formed at her core sending out ropes of high voltage destruction into Cian and the twins. Hot sulphur and sand rained down, but the woman's appetite had only been aroused – it was far from satisfied.

The *marked one* turned towards Diarmuid and the young men at his side. She raised her arms again, and Diarmuid felt a sucking down of his gizzards into the ground. Power was being sapped from him, through the earth and up into her being. She extracted from every power source simultaneously. All colours dimmed and sagged towards the grass at her calling – all but blue. The blue warrior enveloped her in a wave, and his colour changed from slate to turquoise as she lit him from within.

"Mo!" Cai caught hold of her arms. "*Dyna ddiogon* – That's enough, they've surrendered. It's over."

Mona released the euphoria of power and found herself in Cai's arms, being restrained in his arms. He stared at her for a moment, worried.

"I just… I don't really know…" But she couldn't finish the lie. Mona knew exactly what she'd wanted to do, and how she'd felt. The promise of power had been delicious and she now craved it hungrily. Yet admitting that to Cai, even after everything that had happened today, was abhorrent.

One of the prisoners, a bald, fat man, stared up at her from the grass. He looked at Mona as if he knew her secret – as if he had witnessed her temptation.

25

Dilemma

Idwal was numb. He'd fought, and killed and healed. Now they were asking him to take charge and he wasn't sure he was up to the job. Images from the past twenty-four hours played in a loop through his frazzled mind. It had all been horrible, but Mona's gruesome explosives had thoroughly sickened him. He still remembered that awful sucking from his core and the memory frightened him.

He and Cai sat around a large wooden table in some sort of drawing room, both still caked in muck and blood. Dafydd had asked him to question the prisoners, and Idwal didn't know if it had been the pain of his wounds or the loss of his soldiers that had sent the Archdruid back across the Irish Sea so quickly.

There were only three prisoners in front of him, and Idwal began by asking them about the others. "How certain are you that you're the only one's left?" He felt too weary for cleverness and too sick of violence for intimidation.

"They're all dead bar two." Diarmuid was a huge blob of a man with lopsided and bulging features, but he was softly spoken and cooperative. "I've checked the bodies, as you asked. Only Declan and Kieran are missing."

"Have you any idea where they've gone?"

Diarmuid shook his head slowly. "They'll have crawled under the nearest stone to hide." Loathing was clear in his tone.

"And what about you?" Idwal turned to the sandy-haired brothers beside Diarmuid. There was a familiarity about them that he couldn't place.

"We're from the Newgrange clan." The older lad, Conall, pointed north. "A little ways up the coast. We came to find our cousins…" He stopped talking and stood as Nia and Kathleen edged into the room.

Kathleen, red-eyed with grief, held something in her arms – a child. *"Tá sí básaithe, a Choin … tá Aislinn básaithe. She's* dead, Con… Aislinn's dead."

Nia placed her hand in Idwal's at the heart-breaking reunion, as yet unable to translate their Irish through her own tears. Conall swept Kathleen and the baby into his arms, soothing and rocking her gently. Joseph started to sob and Idwal was stunned to see Diarmuid draw the lad towards him, crushing him against his chest.

Idwal squeezed Nia's fingers. "What are they saying?" he asked. The small family group had relocated to the far end of the table, and they were talking in Irish.

Nia squeezed back and smiled sadly. "Kathleen's telling them how you saved Molly." She kissed him lightly at his temple. "Thank you." He leaned into her without replying. It had been an honour to save the child's life.

"Molly?" Conall approached with a quizzical look on his face.

"Yes." Idwal smiled, a little abashed. "Spur of the moment thing… after my mum… you know."

Conall leaned in further, and there was that tug of familiarity again, deep in the Irishman's green eyes. "And you're a healer, I hear?" Idwal shrugged and Conall sat down on the nearest chair with a bump. "It may be that we're related." Idwal frowned sceptically, but Conall explained his theory. "Irish Druid healer called Molly. Sounds like my second cousin. It could be a coincidence but…" Conall ran a hand over his sandy head. "We've even got the same hair dye," he joked gently.

Idwal couldn't seem to process the idea – too much had happened today. "Tell me," he pleaded. "Tell me why all this has happened?"

Conall's face fell and he tried to hide it by glancing over at Kathleen and his brother. "Maybe another time… we need to talk about Molly's future."

Idwal felt Nia squashing the life out of his hand and they followed Conall to end of the table.

≈

Cai watched the drama ebb and flow. He was shattered, filthy and desperate to return to his own little family. He felt uncomfortable under the stare of the big Irishman opposite. "Are you ok?" he asked to break the awkwardness. "Do you need anything? Water…"

"You love her? The *marked* one?"

"Yes," Cai replied slowly, not quite sure where this conversation was headed. "We were handfasted… just yesterday." Despite everything, Cai couldn't help the tiny jolt of joy.

"And the child?" Diarmuid asked quietly.

"Of course." Cai frowned. "He's my son now. We'll…"

"How much do you love her? Enough to…?" Diarmuid winced slightly and stopped talking. "We've got a visitor… red," he cringed. "Very red."

Sioned burst into the room followed by an out of breath Arwel. Cai leapt up and pulled his sister towards him, finding it hard to let her go, even when she struggled.

"Tom?" she asked. "Mo?" Cai nodded and hugged her again. "Are they? Are they…?"

"Sleeping. We're here to…"

Sioned didn't let him finish. "There's Garda all over the place. Al phoned the Ovate lawyer, and he says he's coming over, but he can't get here until…"

"How come? It's so remote. How did they hear?"

"You blew up a substation, Cai." She rolled her eyes as Arwel and Idwal approached to discuss the problem at hand.

"And there was a lot of gunfire heard, apparently. I've no idea how to placate the police here, and we don't really have time to…" Arwel began hurriedly.

"Can I help?" Conall drew near to the huddle. "It would be better coming from an Irishman." He spoke to Arwel, but seemed unable to stop staring at Sioned.

"Come on, then," Sioned said, tugging at his sleeve, "or they'll be down here like a swarm of locust."

As the room emptied and people drifted away, Cai looked for Diarmuid, but he had gone. He was too tired to be alarmed. Though the man was technically a prisoner, Cai didn't think he'd go far.

≈

Tom didn't seem to mind that he was lying on a bale of hay. Or that his mother stank of dead men's clothes and blood. He was happy to lie back, kicking his legs and chuntering to himself. Mona's hands were filthy from battle, so she only touched him with her lips from time to time, content just to watch him breathe in and out.

"It's Fintan's child, then?"

Despite the filth, Mona snatched Tom up against her. The fat Irishman stood a couple of metres away, staring again, at both of them now.

"What are you doing here? Aren't you a prisoner? What do you want?"

He backed up and lowered his mass onto a far bale, putting his hands over his eyes. "It hurts me to look at you." Mona searched the barn for friends. "They're preparing to burn the dead," he sighed. "Your husband didn't want to wake you."

"Who are you?" They both knew he posed no threat, and it was discomfort she felt near him. That and curiosity.

"I'm Diarmuid, Seamus's eldest son. Sired when he was fourteen with a woman that everyone has forgotten. I think I must have been one of the first experiments." He waved a chubby hand down his face and body. "No wonder he went back to the drawing board." The sad smile improved his features slightly. "I've had my uses though. I'm a Seer, I *see* power in colours." Mona sat back down again and started to rock Tom on her lap while she listened. "Healers are green, bards yellow, and warriors are red," Diarmuid explained. "Your brother is bursting with green, I thought he bore the *mark*. Until I saw you." Mona remained silent: she wanted him to go and leave her alone, but she knew what he'd come to say. "You would have sucked them dry. All of them; not only your enemies."

"Cai stopped me," she answered quickly and Diarmuid agreed.

"This time. He may not always be there."

"He will," she whispered through gritted teeth.

"Your power is immense, uncontrollable and growing. Even sitting there with your little baby." He shook his head. "I've watched your family – all day. They are good people, with a wealth of vibrant healthy magic." Diarmuid's eyes were very sad. "If you can't find a way to control your power, it will destroy them. It's only a matter of time." With his head still cradled, Diarmuid eased himself up and turned to leave.

"Can you help me?" Mona's whisper told him she knew it all to be true.

"I don't know," he replied.

≈

Diarmuid stood a little apart from the mourners as they congregated before the fire at dawn. Conall had eased the way with the Garda and the funeral pyre was part of the cover story – a stag party getting carried away with their clay-pigeon shooting and barbecue. The Ovate lawyer would smooth out any unwanted questions when he arrived, and for now the Druids were still safe, still hidden.

Idwal had asked Diarmuid to speak for the Irish dead, but he would only speak for his brother, Cormac. Conall would speak for Aislinn and her dead son.

Mona's salty lover spoke for some of the fallen Welsh warriors and Diarmuid watched the man's unusual essence seep through the blue spectrum as he talked and sang his grief in Welsh. As he listened to the music of the language, Diarmuid revelled in the feast of colour. Red mixed with gold, enveloping green and falling into yellow. But Cai was blue. Diarmuid had never encountered the colour before, never encountered a power he couldn't evaluate and this man fascinated him.

Cai seemed a quiet and self-contained sort of person and his swirling eddies had eased to a dark but gentle swell as they all processed back together. But Diarmuid watched him transform as he caught sight of Mona at the top of the hill. He stopped in his tracks and breathed in her smile. Her presence caused a blooming of phosphorescence in the violet, and then she opened her arms. At the simple invitation, Cai was gone, sprinting up the cliff path, his blues lightening and surging until he was wrapped around her. Mona's light ached to drown in his depths, and Cai's vast blue emptiness craved her effervescence.

Diarmuid forced himself to look away as the kisses deepened and their bodies interlocked.

≈

Mona was still sleeping on the hay bales. People had taken to various beds in the house after the ceremony but she had fallen asleep here. The wake would be starting in about half an hour and everyone had been asked to attend.

Sioned had come to thes stable an hour ago with more supplies for Tom, and Cai was armed with everything the baby could throw at him. Yet when the time came to wake, Tom didn't cry. He merely stretched his little body in a delicious yawn and opened his eyes to look at Cai with a calm blue stare – sizing him up.

Cai stared back as he fed Tom and each time Cai smiled at him, the baby returned it with such gusto, that milk oozed from the side of his mouth, dribbling into the fat folds at his neck.

They were both quite wet by the time the bottle had been emptied. Cai realised, belatedly, the purpose of the small squares of cloth, which had been packed with the provisions. The bag sat on the floor, just within reach of his free hand, but Tom had grabbed his thumb, and had no intention of letting it go. Cai laughed at his tenacity and strength, and Tom laughed a deep, throaty chuckle in reply – shocking himself quiet. Cai chuckled at the new sombreness of his little face, and the cycle began again.

≈

Mona awoke to the sound of Tom and Cai giggling. She watched them for a couple of minutes without moving – not wanting to break the spell. Cai would be a wonderful father: strong, calm, and kind. Mona's love for him choked her.

"I've never heard him laugh like that before," she said, propping herself up on an arm.

"He thinks I'm funny," Cai replied as he wiped more goo from Tom's face.

"Well he's the only one." The little quip reeled Mona back to normality.

"Are you ready for this?" Cai asked.

"No," she said massaging Tom's foot.

"Tough. We've all got to go." Cai was positive but Mona groaned loudly. "What is it?"

"I'm in for a real bollocking from my brother."

"Archdruid, you mean."

"What?"

"It's all been arranged, Siân and Dafydd will share the management, but Idwal has been appointed Archdruid." He smiled at Mona. "Idwal and Nia will handfast straightaway."

"But what about the baby thing?" Mona asked, taking in the new information slowly.

"A lot has happened while you've been sleeping it off." Cai lifted Tom to his shoulder. "You've got family in Newgrange."

"What family?"

"Aislinn and Kathleen are your cousins. Conall and Joseph are some sort of second cousins. Which means…"

"Molly is family," Mona finished for him, and lay back on the hay to stare at the ceiling. Idwal, Nia and Molly – another little family in danger from her unstable power.

Cai stroked her arm with his index finger. "You should smile, Mo. This is our happy ending."

"I am. It's only that…"

"What?" He frowned.

"I'm out of control. *It* is out of control… that energy sucking…" She recalled the sweet, stolen drug of power in her veins and shuddered.

"What sucking? What do you mean?"

"I started to draw power from the others… Idwal, that fat man." She looked Cai square on. "But you stopped me… before I could hurt them."

Cai shook his head. "I stopped you from hurting *yourself*… draining *yourself*."

"So you didn't feel me pulling…"

"No. I didn't feel anything." He touched her face. "You're afraid of your power, and you should be." He closed his eyes in wonder as he recalled her pyrotechnics. "But all you need is time and practice. Nia will help you, and Diarmuid seems to know something about it. Talk to them if you're worried, but be happy – it's over."

"Yeah." Mona smiled shakily, reassured by his words. "Let's get drunk!" she grinned.

≈

335

Kathleen held Molly tightly against her. She hadn't known if her sister had ever even named this baby, but thought Aislinn would have liked the name.

Nia's arms ached to take Molly back, but she sat patiently with hands in lap while the adoption process took place. Arwel had taken charge, and sat now at the head of the small table. He'd crammed everyone into this alcove off the drawing room while preparations for the wake were underway out there.

"So, are we all here?" He peered up from his journal.

"Everyone who's coming," Idwal answered. "I asked Diarmuid, but…"

"That's ok. He's not an interested party."

"He helped us," Kathleen murmured. "He was kind, especially to Ais… especially after…" She broke down and Nia soothed her softly.

"But he isn't a relative, that's all I meant," Arwel said less officiously, before carrying on with business and turning to Conall and Joseph. "How positive are you that you're related to the Joneses?"

"I can double check the records when I get back, but I'm sure your mother, Molly" – Conall glanced at Idwal – "was my second cousin. She had a twin called Brendan, a brother called Niall, red hair and a gift for healing… I can…"

"No." Arwel finished writing. "If that's enough for you, then we'll go from here." He coughed and looked calmly at Kathleen, then Conall, then Joseph. "You are Molly's next of kin, and under Brehon Law you have the right to bring up this child." He pointed at the sleeping bundle in Kathleen's arms. "This is your opportunity to do so."

Nia held her breath as Conall searched his family's faces. "Kathleen has been… through a lot, and though she owes a debt of honour to her sister…" Kathleen sobbed quietly but nodded. "Joseph's a half-wit," Conall continued, trying to lighten the mood and ruffling his younger brother's head. "I'm going to be too busy getting the Newgrange clan back on its feet." He smiled at Nia. "And I'm not sure I'd be able to give Molly everything she needs or deserves."

There was a long, full silence while Arwel finished transcribing Conall's words. "And are you all happy that Idwal and Nia become her adopted parents?" Nia let out her long-held breath as each of Molly's family members agreed. "Then it's done," Arwel said, turning his journal around. "I just need signatures, unless there are any questions."

"Not a question as such." Nia cleared her throat. "But I wondered if Kathleen would consider coming back with us to the *Conway*." The young girl glanced up at the mention of her name. "I know we could do with the help."

"Yes. I'd like that." Kathleen peeked over at Conall. "I can't face going back... yet..."

"Don't worry, Kath, I'll be talking to your da. We've a lot to get through." He looked at Idwal and asked, "I'd be able to come and visit...?"

"Just to get a glimpse of Sioned..." Joseph interrupted cheekily before Conall jabbed his brother in the ribs.

Idwal laughed. "You're all welcome to come and stay... as often as you want to. We've got a lot of wounds to heal, and we're going to have to do it together."

When Molly started to creak and stir, both Kathleen and Nia left the room to tend her. Conall and Joseph also took it as their cue to leave.

"If that's all, then?" Conall said softly.

"Yes." Arwel stood to shake Conall's hand. "What sort of problems do you have to sort out at Newgrange?"

"Niall, our Archdruid."

"My uncle!" Idwal said as the idea struck him.

"Yes. Your uncle has had a bad few years. When his wife died... well... he's had some problems..."

"Drunkard!" Joseph muttered, and Conall gave him a hard stare. "What? *He* asked," Joseph explained, pointing at Arwel.

Conall closed his eyes, frustrated with his brother. "There's a time and a place, Joe..."

"Sorry I mentioned it," Arwel apologised, diffusing the tension between the brothers. "See you at the wake."

"We were thinking of sitting it out in our room," Conall said warily. "Getting an early night. We don't want to cause any trouble with your lads."

"No," Idwal insisted. "It's vital you come. All of you... Diarmuid included. The healing between us starts tonight."

"If you're sure?"

"Absolutely," Idwal said before breaking into a grin. "Anyway, I'm sure Sioned will protect you."

Joseph giggled infectiously as Conall dragged him towards the door, his cheeks glowing.

≈

Both Idwal and Arwel started to snigger as soon as the young Irish lads were through the door. "Sioned?" Arwel mouthed. "He hasn't got a chance."

"No," Idwal agreed. "Still, if it means he'll come to the wake, there's no harm in giving him a little hope."

Idwal took the journal and signed his name. "Thanks for doing that, Arwel. It means a lot."

"Congratulations on becoming a father," Arwel grinned. "You know that means no sleep – at all – for months, maybe even years. Ask Mo."

Idwal frowned at the mention of his sister's name. "Have you spoken to her yet?" he asked, suddenly serious.

"Not yet. Why?"

"There was a moment." Idwal sifted through the memories he'd try to bury of the last forty-eight hours. "After she'd burned Cian and the twins."

"Go on," Arwel was intrigued.

"It was as if she got a kick out of it."

"The killing?"

"No." Idwal shook his head slowly trying to decide what he meant. "Not the killing, but the power. It was like… she didn't want the power to stop… like she wanted more."

"And?"

"And… I don't know… she began sucking it up… from everyone around her."

"Did anyone else…"

"No. Look, Arwel. I don't really know what happened… it's just…" He dragged both hands down his face. "It's just late."

"Yes, and it's time to party."

≈

Mona hadn't wanted to sleep in the house. She hadn't even wanted to walk back inside it, but Cai had coaxed her in and managed to find them this space to use as their base. It was a tiny spare room, too crammed full with boxes of books to be used as a bedroom. It smelled damp and old-fashioned, but it contained a bed and small sink, which was attached to the wall with a mirror stuck above it.

Mona was shocked by what she saw in the mottled glass. Her left eye was black, swollen and half-closed. She ran her finger along the pink jagged line that ran from her right jaw all the way to her hairline. The rest of her face was peppered with fading bruises and puncture marks. It felt like a lump of her chin was missing. Mona's jaw and teeth ached, even though she'd been extensively healed.

"How come I look like this and you get away with… dashing?" Mona asked dismally.

"I can't think!" Cai rolled his eyes at her. "Sioned brought you up a change of clothes." He pointed to a carrier bag by the door.

Mona began pulling garments from the bag and onto her body while Cai unpeeled Tom from his baby grow. She'd already stuffed her feet into the boots and was buckling the belt when she felt Cai's gaze. "What?" she asked at his quizzical, then amused look.

339

"Nothing," he replied. "Why don't you check to see if there's an eye patch in there?"

Mona had actually started searching before she got the joke. "Ha! Very funny, Prince Charming!" she said, fastening a cloak around her neck.

"Even better!" Cai giggled.

Mona picked up her only possessions from the side: the mp3 and the *mark*. Putting one in each pocket, she hoisted Tom's heavy bag and took the weight across her chest. "What have you packed in here?" she asked, following Cai from the room.

"Everything I thought he might need."

"Everything you thought he might need – for a month!"

"Sorry!" He smiled. "I'm just a beginner."

Cai carried Tom high, his head resting against Cai's shoulder as he led her through the corridor and down the stairs. Mona didn't have any real recollection of the mansion's layout and was oblivious to where they were going. The clean-up had been speedy and reasonably thorough, but there were still grisly reminders of the fight and the tang of blood through disinfectant. Mona blanked her gaze to any of the evidence, focusing her eyes on the back of Cai's head and her son's sleepy face on his shoulder.

Mona was expecting to hear the wake before they reached the drawing room. She'd expected music, but there was none, and the room looked too big for the skulking Welsh warriors, who bunched around the walls like teenagers at a party. For a split second, Mona hunted for Cerys and Gwen among them before her throat cramped and the grief began to rise.

A decent fire glowed in the hearth against the back wall and the table groaned with untouched food and drink. A small stage had been set with chairs and instruments in the corner, but no musicians sat among them. There had been too much loss and horror for a wake, and Mona felt an urge to turn around and leave. As if sensing her intention, Cai shifted Tom a little higher and drew her further into the room.

"Why are you dressed like a sixteenth-century pirate?" Arwel asked as he loped up to her, glass in hand.

Mona looked down at her clothes. "Don't know," Mona answered but spied the perpetrator approaching. "Ask Sioned."

"I always said you reminded me of Gráinne Ní Mháille," Sioned chuckled.

"Who?"

"Don't you remember anything? Gráinne Ní Mháille – Grace O'Malley, the Irish pirate."

"Why on earth would I remember that?" Mona said squeezing her tight.

"Anyway, that's what you get for leaving me behind," she growled. But Mona didn't try to defend herself or explain, she merely squashed the girl closer.

"It's not fancy dress, Mo." Idwal appeared in good spirits but Mona could see a desperate tiredness behind his façade.

"So do I have to bow or kneel, Archdruid?" Mona teased.

"Neither," he grinned. "But you do have to call me sir, and definitely do what I tell you."

"Take no notice," Nia said as she bustled in beside him, with Molly in her arms. "I want to introduce you two properly."

The baby was awake and content, her green gaze calm and intelligent. "Hello, Molly." Mona caressed the baby's strawberry-blonde halo. "Come and give your aunty Mo a cuddle," she said as she eased the baby from Nia.

"Isn't she amazing!" Sioned said, touching Molly's button nose. "Now I'll have to spoil both of them."

Mona was too engrossed in her new niece to notice the change of atmosphere when the Irish contingent walked into the drawing room. But the hostility became all too apparent as the conversations around her stalled and body language stiffened. Her brother was the first to react. After taking Nia's arm and walking over to the new arrivals, Idwal outstretched his hand in warm welcome.

Mona recognised Kathleen and Diarmuid, and guessed that the two lads were the second cousins Cai had talked about. "Which one's Conall?" Mona asked Sioned under her breath.

"The gorgeous hunk shaking Id's hand," Sioned answered in a daze. "Joe's the little brother." It was difficult to estimate their ages in the dimmed light, but Mona guessed Conall to be nineteen and Joseph about seventeen. "And you should hear him talk... that Irish accent!" Sioned made a swooning gesture. "He's bloody lush."

Sioned's candour and enthusiasm made Mona chuckle. "Just you be careful," she said, prodding the young woman in the shoulder, but Sioned merely rolled her eyes. Mona scrutinised young Conall for a few seconds. "Nah. Not my type." She dismissed him with a wave. "Looks too much like Id."

Sioned did a double-take and scrunched her nose. "Ew! Are you trying to put me off or something?"

"Come here," Mona said hauling Sioned in for a one-armed squeeze. "I love you, you know."

"I know," Sioned said returning the cuddle.

"What are you two whispering about?" Cai surprised them both.

"Nothing," they answered in unison.

"What does a woman need to do to get a drink around here?" Mona asked and Sioned took it as her cue to leave them.

"I know where I'm not wanted," she said blithely as she wandered towards the refreshments.

"One each!" Cai said, rearranging Tom and nodding towards Molly.

"Mine's wet," Mona replied feeling Molly's damp bottom.

"And mine's smelly," he laughed, screwing up his nose. "Want to swap?"

Nia came hurrying over. "Give her to me," she said, holding out her arms to Mona.

"Take Tom," Cai said, quickly depositing Tom in Mona's now empty arms. "I've been summoned to the Archdruid!"

"What for?"

"I'll tell you later." He kissed her cheek and backed away, an excited glint in his eyes, though it may have been alcohol.

≈

Cai found Idwal, Arwel and Diarmuid in Seamus's Command Centre. All three men shared the same expression of revulsion and incomprehension as they studied the wealth of computer hardware surrounding them. Cai, though, felt differently about this technology. Yes, Seamus had abused his power and knowledge, but it needn't be that way. Even before he sat down at the controls, Cai could visualise all the beautiful things he could achieve with this gift. The equipment was blank and lifeless at the moment, but Cai could virtually taste the potential that would be unleashed once power had been properly reinstated to the site.

"Doesn't even have any buttons." Idwal eyed the main consul warily.

"Oh yes she does," Cai said, running his hand over the solid curved structure. "She's just hiding them away."

"So?" Arwel asked slowly. "Do you know how to find them?"

"I'm not entirely sure," Cai answered, peering more closely at the shapely monitor on the desk.

"But..."

"Biometrics!" he said suddenly. "Seamus used a biometric device on the bedroom..."

"Bio what?" Idwal asked, completely out of his depth.

Cai was too engrossed to answer, so Arwel gave it a go. "I believe it's the marrying of biology with technology. An eye scanner, a fingerprint activated..."

"Exactly," Cai agreed. He was impressed with his little brother's knowledge, but turned to Diarmuid. "Have you ever seen your... Seamus... using a specific finger or putting his eye...?"

Diarmuid had chosen to stand as far from the hardware as possible, and he shook his head. "He was always very secretive. I

343

don't believe even Cian knew for sure – but he did talk about retinal scanning."

"What!" Idwal exclaimed. "You mean we need Seamus's eyeball to... open it up?" He jumped to the nearest conclusion. "We're totally buggered, then!" He flopped his arms to his sides with an air of futility.

"Not necessarily." Cai grinned at him from underneath a bench. "There's always another way."

Idwal smirked and pointed at Cai as he backed from the room. "Keep up the good work. I'll be right back with the drinks."

Diarmuid watched in fascination as Cai's essence lit up, pulsing a cornflower blue as his investigations progressed. That done, the three men had settled in a corner of the room with their drinks. They'd asked him to join them and he'd moved a little closer, but didn't feel like getting too near. The golden youngster, Arwel, was clearly a novice drinker and had already begun slurring his words after the second glass. The two bottles of wine, however, had merely fuelled Idwal and Cai, and the ideas were coming thick and fast.

"The potential is..." Cai searched for a word while gesticulating wildly and sloshing wine from his glass.

"So... when you say potential... do you mean financial...?" Alcohol had slowed Idwal's speech.

"Financial, ecological, academic." Cai leaned over and seized the Archdruid's shoulders. "We can do *anything* with this technology."

"Not bad things though..." Arwel shook his head and finger in drunken unison. "Seamus did bad things... very bad." It took him a while to remember where Diarmuid sat, but gazed at him when he did. "Do you know anything about..." he flailed a hand at the screens, "this business? Who did he sell things to?"

Diarmuid didn't know much, but he told them all he knew. "Cian found out a few things... names mostly... made it his business to." He felt nothing for his dead half-brother, but saying his name was painful. "Some legitimate, some not. Governments, probably some terrorist organisations..."

The list of clients sobered the men a good deal, and they fell silent while digesting his news. They'd begun talking again by the time he'd backed out of the repulsive room. He left to look for Mona.

≈

"Let's change them in there." Nia pointed to a little room off the main area.

Mona followed on with Tom and his bag. "Funny old wake," she said as both women knelt down to tend their children. Mona had taken off her cloak and the babies were lying on it.

"The lads will come round," Nia said as she unpacked Molly's nappy bag. "I've asked Sioned to make the introductions."

"Not a bad idea," Mona replied as she began unbuttoning Tom's baby grow. "You're getting the hang of this Mrs. Archdruid stuff already."

Nia's face fell. "I don't know if I'm up to it... not with Molly now and..."

"Oh come on! You'll be brilliant... both of you," Mona encouraged, but Nia still seemed unconvinced and Mona changed topic. "When are you getting married... handfasted?"

"Lughnasadh. It's a traditional time for handfasting. Many couples..."

"You could have just said August!" Mona interrupted Nia's studious reply with a large slice of humour and Nia chuckled at herself, and then giggled.

Nia's trilling laugh was infectious and Mona joined in for a few seconds, enjoying the release. But the tone of the laughter changed, and Nia put both hands against her mouth as hysteria morphed into great sobs of grief. Mona could see the struggle behind her friend's eyes, as Nia's mind, normally so cogent and ordered, grappled in vain to make sense of the emotional overload. Relief and happiness vied with grief and horror.

"It's ok... Nia," Mona soothed. "It's ok... it's over."

Nia's lips wobbled as the trauma of the past few days assaulted her again and again. "Cerys," she gulped. "Gwen."

Mona eased Nia's shaking body against hers. "Don't think about it... try not to think about it."

After a few more dragging sobs, Nia's breathing settled into a more regular pattern. "I'm all right... I'll be all right." She patted Mona on the back, and dried her eyes on a sleeve. Tom started to grumble and Nia pushed the heels of her hands against both eyes. "I need music," she stated simply. "We all need some music. Don't we, Molly?" She pulled the baby into her arms, and kissed her tenderly.

"Tom's hungry," Mona said, rooting around for a bottle in the bag that Cai had packed. "I'll feed him and be straight out." She was amazed to find a full bottle, and two clean empties neatly stowed among his entire wardrobe of clothes. Mona smiled at Cai's proficient handiwork.

Curling them both into the comfortable-looking armchair, Mona relaxed as Tom began to feed, the sound of his rhythmic sucking drawing her eyes closed. Mona's mind craved the oblivion balm of sleep. She needed it to numb the memories: the sword slamming into Bryn's heart; the steel in the dead baby's body; Cerys, Gwen, Ifan, Rob...

"Can I come in?" A tentative knock drew her attention to Diarmuid, who waited with irritating deference by the door.

"How long have you been there?" she bristled.

"I was waiting until you were alone. I heard your friend crying..."

"She'll be fine. Nia's not used to... the brutality."

Mona heard a few toe-tapping chords from a fiddle, and wondered who could be playing it. Diarmuid still hovered but Mona refused to make eye contact or risk any conversation.

"I've never heard a full conversation in Welsh before," Diarmuid said gently. "It's different from Irish, I can't understand it at all, but there's a similarity..."

"What do you want?" Mona said under her breath.

"Nothing really... I'm leaving, as soon as it's light enough."

She looked at him then. "But Cai said you might be able to help me."

He seemed puzzled. "I can't help you Mona. I'm only a Seer."

"I thought you were going to help us out...?"

But Diarmuid was already shaking his head. "I've told your brother and the blonde lad as much as I know. I want to leave. I have to... I've been here too long."

"Where will you go?"

"There's a place," he said very slowly.

"What sort of place?" Mona heard the words Diarmuid hadn't said. "A place that could help me?"

Diarmuid shrugged. "I'm not sure if anyone can help you, Mona. You could burn us all in an instant – and enjoy it."

"How do you know?"

"Because I can *See*." His expression grew sombre as he stared at the baby in her arms. "And I'm not sticking around to watch any more tragedy." His next smile was almost happy. "There's so much potential in that room." He indicated with a backwards nod of the head.

"Tell me about this place," Mona asked, dragging Diarmuid from his reverie.

He shook his head, back again in the present. "No. If you want to come, meet me by the cliff path at dawn. I'll wait for five minutes."

"And Cai could come?"

Diarmuid took a long time deciding before he answered. "Yes. He could come, but he may not be able to."

"What do you mean?"

"Just that he may have his hands full here."

Mona opened her mouth to reply, but forgot what she wanted to say as the music started again. The fiddle was plaintive this time; slow and rich and sad. A second fiddle joined the first, answering melancholy with grief. Mona didn't recognise the third instrument at first, but after a few more bars, she realised that it was singing. A young woman's voice, singing in Irish. Kathleen.

Her voice haunted the melody that the violins knitted. Diarmuid leaned his bodyweight back against the doorjamb, tilted back his head and closed his eyes, letting the poignancy wash over him in waves.

"Her voice." Mona couldn't say any more than that.

"Everyone has their own magic, Mona. Even if nobody else can see it." Tears were beginning to slide from his eyes and down over his chins. "They used to sing together... she used to sing this... with Aislinn..." He swallowed lumpily. "I could have stopped it... should have done something... more."

Kathleen crooned on relentlessly, wearing away Mona's flimsy defences until she remembered Rob; finally understanding that she would never see him again. The grief welled up and formed in her eyes, but she stared at Tom's peaceful face, doggedly recalling Rob's tenderness.

"*Dyna ti cariad* – There you are, my love." Cai had blundered inelegantly past Diarmuid, and Mona dragged a sleeve over her face and smiled; '*cariad*' was so much more intimate than its English translation.

"Issera problem?" Cai slurred as he wavered towards the armchair.

"No." Mona smiled up at him. "It's the music."

"Ah." Cai closed his eyes and slumped to his knees. "*Llais fel angel* – The voice of an angel." He lay his head on Mona's right knee and put his hand on Tom, who was splayed out on her left. "*Fy mabi bach* – my little baby."

Cai felt for Tom's hand and wiggled a calloused finger into the baby's fist. Tom reacted by squeezing Cai's finger and Mona felt his grin against her leg. "Look at his fingers... his fingernails, they're just like real fingernails... but little... so small." He pondered the concept as if it was a philosophical revelation. Mona kept a straight face and nodded solemnly until Cai started to chuckle at his own nonsense. Twisting his whole head into her thighs, he let out a huge happy sigh that reverberated through Mona's pelvis. "I've got so much to tell you, Mona Jones."

"Snap!" she said, using the opportunity to broach the possibility of a journey as quickly as possible. "Diarmuid said that…"

"Idwal's got this plan… we've got this plan…"

"Hang on… I only wanted to say that Diarmuid and I have been talking… about my power." She looked up to find the Irishman, but he had gone, and in his place stood her brother, leaning on Nia and waving around a bottle of wine.

"Whadyouthink, Mo?" Idwal boomed, grinning inanely. "It's gonna be a piece of piss."

"That's such a strange phrase," Cai stated in drunken bewilderment to no in particular.

The Archdruid was also too far gone to listen or care, and Mona saw she would be wasting her time tonight, and changed tactics. She would find Diarmuid later and convince him to stay until tomorrow. With any luck everyone would have sobered up by lunchtime, and they could discuss the matter rationally.

"Come out here with us – this is s'posed to be a party!" Idwal turned to Nia, kissed her and Molly, then launched back into the drawing room, bottle aloft. Nia rolled her eyes at Mona and hurried after him.

"What were you saying… before?" Cai asked muzzily.

"Nothing." She ruffled his hair. "I really need that drink."

≈

Sioned and Conall were deep in conversation, and Cai seemed puzzled rather than concerned at their cosiness. He swayed and frowned as Mona settled Tom into Sioned's arms.

"She'll be all right? Won't she, Mo?" he asked, taking her by the hand and stumbling onto the dance floor.

"Yes," Mona chuckled. "But will Conall?" The music had slowed again and Mona's face fell; she'd really wanted to shake out her aches to the pounding jigs and reels.

"Ah. This is better," Cai said, drawing her near and letting his hands wander.

Mona winked. "Bet you've never danced with a pirate before."

"That would be telling," Cai whispered against her cheek.

Her bruises were still tender and Mona pulled away to look at him. "What did Id want, then?"

Cai squashed her to him as his excitement returned. "Seamus ran a computer company from here." He appeared to sober-up as new ideas hit his brain. "It's big, successful and possibly the answer to all our problems."

"You mean...?"

"We'll take over the running of the company. Thin out the worst of his clients and work from there."

Mona remembered snatches of Bryn's synopsis; his father had been a computer mastermind. "But how can you... it's not as if..."

"I'd need help, for sure, but I know my way around technology." Both Cai's hands squeezed Mona's buttocks tightly.

"So," she said carefully as reality began to dawn. "We'd have to live here... in this house?" She repressed the shudder.

"No," Cai said adamantly. "No, not in the house, and not in the outbuildings either." He shivered himself at the memory of the squalid stalls. "I've talked to Arwel and the estate runs on for miles. I can build something for us, in the grounds." He stopped and grinned. "We can build something together."

Mona didn't know what to say. There was too much to take in. "How will it be the answer to all our problems?"

They had stopped all pretence of moving to the music, and Cai kissed her tenderly before he explained. "The profit from the business will not only shore up the *Conway's* finances, but possibly even run to helping out the other Celtic nations. Idwal wants to tie the Sea Kingdoms closer together. Arwel wants to build a school on Ynys Môn; to reinstate the old ways of Druid apprenticeship. Nia has found books..."

"In the room we were in..." Mona remembered the crates of fustiness.

"That's just the tip of the iceberg. Nia thinks she can find a way back to the magic..."

"And what do you want?" Mona asked.

"I want to use the technology." His smile was so wide. "I want to break down the boundaries on renewables. Really get stuck in."

"Is this what you want, Cai?"

"Yes." He nodded, closing his eyes and breathing against her neck. "More than anything. And I can make it all happen, Mo. I'm the only one here who can."

"Then that's what we'll do," she said, enfolding him and knowing she couldn't leave now. If Nia had found all those books, there was a good chance she'd find a cure for her problem.

"Sorry, Mo." Idwal stuck a large arm between them. "Gotta speak to my Technical Chief." He was at least a bottle of wine drunker. "Had an idea."

Separating them, the Archdruid draped an arm around Cai and led him back into the alcove room holding another full bottle in the other hand.

≈

Sioned handed Tom back eagerly and gave Mona an extravagant wink as she pulled Conall out the drawing room. Mona grinned back and then started to actively plan her next move. Arwel sat alone at a table, the only one not dancing, and Mona joined him, confident that he'd have a sensible solution to her dilemma.

"How's it going, Al?" She asked, squeezing in next to him. Tom's dead weight was straining her back and arms.

Arwel turned to her slowly, a definite green to his pallor. He held up a palm to her face and covered his mouth with the other hand. "I've got…" He retched, panic in his eyes. "I'm going to be…" Arwel fled across the room, one hand holding his gut, the other tight across his mouth.

"That'll teach him." Nia tutted as she plonked herself down next to Mona, looking as sober and tired as Mona felt. "Your brother's a bad influence on young Arwel."

"Have you seen Diarmuid anywhere?" Mona asked, conscious now that all her options were closing down fast.

"Not for a few hours," she sighed as Molly started to crank up her grumbling. "I'm out of bottles! Have you got any left?"

Mona felt around in the bag but found only three empty containers. "Sorry." She grimaced.

"Here, take Molly and I'll make up a batch for both of them." Nia collected the empties and marched off.

It took a huge amount of effort to care for the two small babies – even for the short time that Nia was gone. Molly's unhappiness eventually pulled Tom from sleep and Mona found it impossible to calm them both.

"How on earth do people cope with twins?" Nia asked in a reverent hush.

"Nia?" Mona began, picking her words carefully, so as not to panic her friend. "I've got a bit of a problem." Nia looked up, immediately concerned. "It's to do with my…"

"Oh no!" Nia cried as a familiar smell wafted between them. "Molly's filled her nappy again!" She put the bottle back down. "I'm going to take her up. It's nearly dawn." She smiled weakly at Mona. "We'll talk in the morning. Can you let Idwal know?"

Nia fled from Mona almost as quickly as Arwel had – leaving all six bottles of milk on the table. Mona scooped them up and stuffed them into the already bulging bag.

Idwal was her last hope, and she heaved the bag on to her shoulder again and hoisted Tom a little higher. Mona found both men in the alcove room. Cai had passed out on the floor, and her brother was sprawled and snoring on the armchair. Mona nudged him. "Id… Idwal," she hissed, getting more aggressive with each failed attempt to rouse him. Mona needed her brother now. Diarmuid didn't have to listen to Mona, but if the Archdruid demanded it, Diarmuid would have to stay.

There was a lightening of the gloom in the drawing room, and Mona grunted angrily as she grabbed up her cloak from the floor between the drunken men. There wouldn't now be enough time to wake Idwal *and* catch Diarmuid before he left. Her aggravation ramped up as Mona was obliged to put down both baby and bag to pull on the cloak; the summer dawn looked decidedly chilly, and she'd have to wrap Tom in its folds.

Tiredness and pain were snapping at the heels of her irritation, and by the time she'd reached the foot of the cliff path, Mona was livid. It accelerated to rage when she saw that Diarmuid had already started the climb.

"Oi!" Mona gave him both barrels with her finest estuary English. "You said you'd wait!" she hollered. Tom woke up noisily at her outburst. "Get back here!" she screamed at him, even though she could see he was already doing his best to pick his way back down the slope. Tom needed changing but Mona had run out of patience and jiggled him frantically as the big man approached. Diarmuid stopped about ten metres from her, seeming to cringe away. "What?" she bellowed.

"Calm down, Mona," he murmured backing away even further. "You're... too unstable for this." He covered his face. "You're hurting my eyes."

"You said you'd wait!" His cringing demeanour had the reverse effect on her temper, and Mona started to sense a familiar energy warm her body.

"The baby!" Diarmuid pointed at the red-faced boy in her arms. "Calm down... if only for Tom's sake." He took a shaky step nearer. "Come on now... try to get some control back... breathe," he soothed.

Diarmuid's words slapped Mona in the face and she hugged Tom gratefully as the heat flowed away from her body, leaving remorse behind. "You said you'd wait," Mona repeated woodenly.

"I did... I've been here for fifteen minutes." He looked at her luggage. "Are you coming with me then?"

"No. I can't. I've come to ask you to stay, just for a while. Speak to the Archdruid about ... my problem... and maybe ..."

"No." He gazed longingly towards the west. "I have to go."

"Please," Mona said, stroking Tom's head. "I can't leave Cai... he's got a job to do..."

"I'm not able to help you, Mona... and I'm not staying to watch you burn them all." He glanced back up towards the house. "So much green and gold – so nearly ripe, so nearly ready."

"There are books!" Mona remembered Nia's find. "Nia will help me..."

"Books won't help you. And even if there were a solution in a book, how long would it take her to find it? She has Molly now." Diarmuid slumped against the base of an old standing stone, rubbing his oversized fingers over some carved marks on the surface. "Have you any idea how close you are to meltdown?"

Mona sank down beside him, but didn't answer his question – she couldn't bear to. Instead, she kept her hands and brain busy with changing Tom on her knee. "What shall I do?" she asked, once Tom was comfortable.

Her voice shook Diarmuid from a trance. "Can't you sense her power?" Mona narrowed her eyes in confusion. "Tara." He touched the ground at his feet with a reverent tenderness, holding his hand there and closing his eyes. "I can feel her heartbeat here." A smile touched his lips.

"And she can help me?"

"*Tara*, Mona." Diarmuid's mouth twisted into a smile. "The birthplace of magic. Where the Goddess lives."

"The Hill of Tara?" Mona remembered one of Nia's Celtic history lessons. "Where the High Kings of Ireland..."

"Yes." Diarmuid shook his head in wonder, caressing the ground again. "But there's so much more to her than that... so much more."

"You think I can find help there?"

Diarmuid began the lengthy process of rocking himself forwards onto his knees before attempting to stand. It gave Mona time to consider her options. She couldn't rely on Idwal or Nia. Molly and the *Conway* would have to become their priority. Arwel and Cai would be up to their armpits in this computer business. And if what

Diarmuid said was true… Mona herself would be their biggest threat now.

"No one can help you. You have to do this by yourself. But if it was me…" He inhaled the dawn air. "I'd start at Tara."

Mona made her decision and considered the practicalities. How long would it take? A week maybe two? She'd learned Welsh – she could learn anything. Mona looked over at the bag. Tom had more than enough supplies.

"Have you got a pen and paper?"

"No." Diarmuid seemed perplexed.

"I want to leave a note… for Cai." Diarmuid had finally made it to his feet. He dusted himself off. He was ready to leave. "Hold him for a minute." Mona passed over Tom. She felt around in the bag, and then patted herself down. She didn't find a pen, but her left hand pocket held the mp3 player and the right, her *mark*. Stuffing her hands into both pockets, Mona squeezed her possessions hard. One was a weapon, and one was her life.

Giving the mp3 player a final caress, Mona wound the earphone cord around the scruffy little machine and stuffed it into a crevice of the standing stone. She knew Cai would find it there. He would be angry with her. He would be furious to find her gone, but Mona knew that Cai would find the token of her love and understand it was meant for him. A promise to him that she would return.

Taking up both bag and baby, Mona prepared to climb the cliff path, thinking only of Cai. She hadn't even kissed him goodbye

Notes

The Mabinogion

The collective name given to eleven medieval Welsh tales, found mainly in two manuscripts, the White Book of Rhydderch (c. 1350) and the Red Book of Hergest (c. 1382–1410).

The Táin Bó Cúailnge

Known in English as the 'The Cattle Raid of Cooley' the story is the central epic of the Ulster Cycle in Irish Mythology. Queen Medb (Maeve or Maebh) of Connaught gathers an army in order to gain possession of the most famous bull in Ireland, the Brown Bull of Cooley which is the property of Daire, a chieftain of Ulster – the chief warrior of which is the hero Cúchulainn.

Ancient Irish Sites

Brú na Bóinne (Brew na boynya)
A complex of megalithic remains dating back to the Neolithic period. The complex is sited in the Boyne Valley in County Meath, Ireland, and is best known for the impressive passage graves of Newgrange, Knowth and Dowth.

Tara

An area of megalithic earthworks in County Meath, Ireland. It comprises several parts: **The Hill of Tara**, a seat of ancient power on top of which stands the **Lia Fáil**, or the Stone of Destiny. Among the ancient constructions is the **Mound of Hostages**, a Neolithic passage tomb. Tara has long been regarded as the epicentre of Pagan spirituality in Ireland, but has sadly been desecrated by the Irish government with the building of the M3 motorway extension through the Tara valley, destroying numerous prehistoric sites.

Slíghe Roads

There were five ancient Celtic roads that stretched out from Tara to all points across Ireland. **The Slíghe Roads: Slíghe Chualann** went south-eastwards, crossing the Liffey near Dublin. It then ran close to the coast by Booterstown, Blackrock and down into what is now Co. Wicklow. **Slíghe Asail** ran westwards to Loch Owel in Westmeath dividing the kingdom of Meath into two parts, north and south. **Slíghe Mudlúachra** ran to the north Antrim coast. **Slíghe Mór** went southwards to Clonard and on to Galway. **Slíghe Dála** led to Kilkenny.

Ancient Welsh Sites

Bryn Celli Ddu

An important Neolithic passage tomb near Llanddaniel Fab, Ynys Môn. Aligned to celebrate the Summer solstice.

Din Llugwy

Site of an ancient village near Moelfre, Ynys Môn. Comprising three eras: a third millennium BC burial chamber, a fourth century hut circle, and a twelfth century stone chapel.

Celtic Tribes in Modern day Wales

Cantiaci
A Celtic people living in Britain before the Roman conquest. They lived in the area now called Kent, in south-eastern England. Their capital was Durovernum Cantiacorum, now Canterbury.

Demetae
A Celtic people of Iron Age Britain. They inhabited modern Pembrokeshire and Carmarthenshire.

Silures
A powerful and warlike tribe of ancient Britain, occupying approximately the former counties of Monmouthshire, Breconshire and Glamorganshire in present-day South Wales.

Gangani
Celtic people of Iron Age Britain. They lived on the Llŷn Peninsula.

Ordovices
One of the Celtic tribes living in Britain before the Roman invasion. Their tribal lands were located in present-day Wales and England between the Silures to the south and the Deceangli to the north-east.

Acknowledgements

Anon., *The Mabinogion*, tr. Siôned Davies (2007)
Anon., *The Táin*, tr. Ciaran Carson (2008)
Ellis, Peter Berresford, *Celtic Women* (1996)
Ellis, Peter Berresford, *The Druids* (2006)
Ellis, Peter Berresford, *The Celts* (2003)
Hutton, Ronald, *Blood and Mistletoe* (2011)
Moffat, Alistair, *The Sea Kingdoms* (2001)
Sykes, Bryan, *Blood of the Isles* (2006)

www.hiraeth.me
www.facebook.com/Hiraeth.a.story